NO QUARTER
ASKED
NO QUARTER GIVEN

BY

STEPHEN TAYLOR

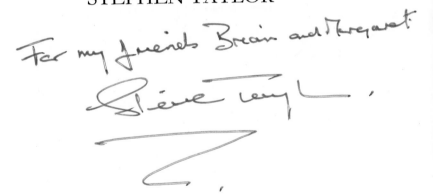

For my friends Brian and Margaret

Steve Taylor,

First printing April 2008

Copyright © Stephen Taylor 2008

NO QUARTER ASKED
NO QUARTER GIVEN

ISBN-10: 0-9552315-3-1
ISBN-13: 978-0-9552315-3-7

Bound by
Tudor Bookbinding, 3 Lyon Close, Wigston, Leicester

NEW WRITERS UK BOOKS
An Imprint of DSC Publications

**Published and Distributed by DSC Publications
PO Box 8753, Leicester, LE7 4WU, England**

DEDICATION

This book is dedicated to my late wife Jean. She was my soul
mate and I miss her dearly.
Also for my teenage daughter Helen, who I'd like to say took
over the household chores so that I could steal some time to
write it. I'd like to say that but she was absolutely no help at
all. Nevertheless I thank her for her love, which has kept me
going.

CHAPTER 1

London, 1805

'Sammy, is that you Sammy?'

Samuel Medina started, looked around. The light was beginning to fail, but he perceived the merest presence of a figure in a doorway. He hesitated for a moment, but this was no place to linger. He had a powerful physique and was afraid of no man, but the London streets were dangerous places. He was not going to be lured into some desperate, dark corner where he might find himself heavily outnumbered by this stranger's companions. Samuel knew his power would be irrelevant if someone drew a pistol. He turned and strode briskly away.

'Sammy. Don't go Sammy, it's me,' the voice called urgently.

Samuel stopped abruptly. Puzzled, he swung round. There was something about that voice. 'Who's there? Come out and show yourself, Sir.'

The shadowy figure resting its frame limply against the doorway stood upright in response to Samuel's stern command.

'Show yourself, Sir,' Samuel said again, agitated now.

'It's me. Don't you know me Sammy?' the figure shuffled out the shadows.

Samuel peered into the half-light. The street-lighter had done his duty: the recently constructed city oil lights were burning, shining into the night. Erected on iron posts, each one bearing two large, glowing glass globes atop great iron branches, they had been installed to bring some safety to the streets after nightfall. Despite the city's pride in their installation, the lamps were inefficient and the overhanging buildings created shadows. Samuel had to wait while his eyes adjusted to the gloom, but there was just enough illumination to see the man who stepped forward. He was wearing a pair of green velvet breeches, which must have cost a pretty penny when new, but were now old and worn, shiny and grubby. The coat did not match, being a dirtied maroon, nor did it fit, but equally it must have been fine in its day. The man's hair was greying and thinned; his face unshaven, his eyes sunken.

'Don't you know me Sammy?' he asked again.

Samuel Medina paused, exclaimed, 'My God!' Realisation of who it was pierced his consciousness. 'It's *John Campbell-John!*'

'You remember me then?'

'Oh yes.' Samuel took a step backwards. 'I remember *you* alright: you don't forget a liar and a cheat. You don't forget embezzlement - you don't forget betrayal,' he worked his mouth and spat a gob of spittle onto the cobbles.

'Betrayal is an ugly word, Sammy boy. Was I that bad then?'

Samuel's hands curled into fists. 'What would you call it then?'

'It was just self-preservation that's all. I had to... well; go to ground for the sake of my health, so too speak,' Campbell-John shuffled his feet, grinned nervously.

'*Your* health!' exclaimed Samuel, his anger barely contained, the words sticking in his throat, 'I have no time for this. It's the Sabbath, I need to get home.' He turned abruptly and walked hurriedly away. It was his gut reaction to seeing John Campbell-John again. He wanted nothing to do with the man.

As Samuel walked, his footsteps kept him company, echoing back to him from the cobbled stones and the wooden overhang of the buildings in the narrow street. The night was drawing in but the moon had not yet risen and he shuddered suddenly, but not from the cold night air. Clip-clop went his feet on the cobbles, and in the distance a muted clip-clop sounded as the stranger walked after him. Samuel's mind toiled as it wandered back, self-absorbed, obsessing on earlier times, with recollections, some good, but some far from good.

Approaching his home he saw the welcoming glow of the candles his wife had lit at dusk, for it was the Sabbath – she always kept two candles burning in the window from sunset on Friday evening to sunset on Saturday evening. It was a mellow light, but a reassuring one and he gave out a small heartening sigh at the sight of it. He turned and looked backwards down the road, but there was no sign of John Campbell-John – his footsteps had faded away. Samuel shook his head, unable to believe what had just taken place. He was comfortable with his life now, but that comfort had been shaken by the reappearance of a figure from his past; one he had tried to erase from his memory. He looked again at his enticing window. There would be a festival meal attended by the whole of his family to consecrate the start of the Sabbath day. They would start the meal as they always did, drinking wine whilst singing the Kiddush – the sanctification. He took the Sabbath meal with his family and said his

Jewish prayers as its head. The bread was blessed, and after the meal he sang songs with his children.

Later that evening, his wife and children long gone to their beds, Samuel sat by his fire and reflected. He took a tankard of ale and mused some more until he determined he too would go to bed. He rose, but then paused and hardly aware of what he did, went to a bureau and took out an old box. Placing it on the table he removed the lid. An odour of must and dry dust filled his nostrils. The box contained papers, letters and keepsakes. Reading some of the letters, his gaze was caught by two silhouette miniatures – one of himself and the other, not of his wife but of John Campbell-John. He remembered the night they had been made: a night of elation when he'd had not a care in the world. Looking at the image, the features of his youthful companion crystallising in his thoughts, he was prompted to rummage in the box for other keepsakes, souvenirs of happy times that were now springing like leaping salmon into his mind. Despite himself he wanted to reminisce on old times again, to cast aside all those negative emotions that had been so dominant for so many years.

A knocking at his door broke his concentration. He knew instinctively who it was. The fire crackled; he stared into the dancing flames ignoring the knock. But it persisted, growing in volume and determination until he could ignore it no longer. Jumping up in alarm, he angrily pulled the door open, recognised John Campbell-John. 'Be gone with you before you wake the neighbourhood!' he exclaimed, slamming the door shut and returning to his chair in front of the fire. For a few moments all was quiet. But then the knocking started again, this time accompanied by a muffled voice; a voice he did not want to hear, a voice that had fuelled anger within him for fourteen long years; anger that had demanded revenge and retribution and taken many years to subside Now it was back again, burning passionately within his breast; dominating those brief moments of pleasurable reminiscence. It was a vindictive and destructive spirit.

'Be gone I tell you,' he yelled, the words tapering away when he realised he would awaken his family.

'Sammy boy, let me in I need to talk to you.'

'But why should I want to talk to you?' said Samuel through the door.

'Because,' said John Campbell-John, but then he paused, as though he could not find a creditable reason. 'Because...' he paused again, 'because you were the best friend I ever had, and I treated you grievously. I need to …to…make amends I suppose.'

Samuel was in turmoil, but slowly he opened the door. He could not have explained why. 'You had better come in and sit down.'

'Thank you Sammy boy, I will.'

Gazing intently at his visitor, Samuel thought how pathetic the man looked - considerably older than his five and forty years. Despite himself, Samuel found much of his anger had drained away. Confused, he indicated a chair, fetched two tankards of ale and gave one to Campbell-John. They drank slowly, sitting in silence by the fire, staring into the flames. 'Have you come to pay me back then?' Samuel asked at length.

'If only I could Sammy boy,' said John, 'but the money was all gone a long time ago.'

'Now why doesn't that surprise me?'

A smile crossed John's lips and Samuel, noticing it, for some reason smiled too, though he knew not why. It was a shared memory, a joint recollection that had been triggered by that phrase. They knew each other so well; had shared so much together. When John betrayed him it had been all the more painful because of that: the betrayal so much more acute; a double-edged sword of friendship and rivalry; friendship and enmity; of heightened emotions and disproportionate reactions. But suddenly, despite it all, friendship reasserted itself. It was irrational, but powerful for all that.

'Why now?' asked Samuel. 'You haven't come looking for money have you? Because if you have you'll get none here.'

'No Sammy, I haven't come to take money from you. I could tell you lies and say I'm rich, that I am doing well, but I think it's obvious from the way I look that the last few years have not been kind to me. In fact I didn't come to seek you out at all. I come to London occasionally to - shall we say - do some business.'

'And can I assume we are not talking about honest business?'

'You know me too well Sammy – yes a bit of counterfeiting - coining and all that.'

'A grubby business,' Samuel said, looking down his nose, 'affecting all good men of commerce.'

'That's as may be, but a poor man can scrape a living at it.'

'A poor man can make a living by honest commerce,' Samuel paused, listening. He gestured to the door, 'Or by his labour. Do you hear that?'

John listened intently for a few seconds. 'What? It's only the night-soil collectors, isn't it?'

'Exactly! Out labouring when good citizens are in bed; emptying the cesspits, carrying great tubs of shit on their shoulders. The work is hard an unpleasant but they earn a good living – they can charge a pound for emptying a cesspit, and that's good money. A good living, do you hear,' he repeated passionately, 'but they earn it with their *honest* toil.'

'But that's not work for the likes of me Sammy, and you know it.' Campbell John glowered, 'And dare I say that passing counterfeit coins is also a business of the Irish and the *Jews*?'

Samuel frowned, shook his head, 'It's a business of the *immigrants*; the Polish and German Jews of East London: Whitechapel and Mile End. They are poor and uneducated; have to live by their wits. I was born and raised in Bethnal Green,' he added as if that explained the difference.

'You defend them because they are Jewish.'

'I defend them not; they bring shame on my people. They are of a different Jewish culture to me, they are Ashkenazim – German - from Central and Eastern Europe.' Seeing the look of puzzlement on John's face, Samuel explained: 'My people are Sephardim – Spanish - they are the Jews of the Mediterranean. I must have told you before that my family came from Portugal in the 1730's to escape the Portuguese inquisition? What's more I am from the middling class – I have nothing in common with Ashkenazim Jews; I am educated and can turn an honest living. The life of my people is better because of *my* honest toil. These Jewish immigrants undo all the good work of us honest Jews.'

The words poured out of him as if he needed somehow to defend himself, but seeing the knowing smile on John's face - a smile that said, *there you go again – you've not changed at all have you* - Samuel felt suddenly foolish and was surprised when John resisted the temptation to tease him.

'Aye, that's true Sammy - you *are* a credit to your people. All I ask is that you do not judge me too harshly; I must also live by my wits.'

'But you are educated; you have an alternative to petty crime.'

'Maybe,' said John.

Samuel leaned forward, 'So why now, I ask again?'

'Like I said, I saw you merely by chance and I slipped into a doorway so I could observe you. But then I just couldn't resist speaking to you, I thought you looked well – that you looked prosperous. I was pleased for you. I found myself happy to see you.'

'And what do you come to offer me by way of reparation?'

'I can offer you nothing – except to build some bridges - if you'll let me.'

'And how do you propose to do that?'

'I don't know, Sammy.'

'I haven't been called that for fifteen years,' Samuel mumbled quietly, adding in a fierce whisper, 'I ought to thrash you.' He looked intently at John who met his eye and smiled back affectionately.

'Aye, that was always your first instinct, wasn't it?' John smiled knowingly, 'and the thought did cross my mind before I spoke to you.'

'But you spoke to me anyway?'

'Aye, I thought it worth a good thrashing—to speak to you again.'

Samuel reflected on those words for a time, staring into the fire. Somewhere in the distance a dog howled breaking into his thoughts. He looked up, asked quietly, 'So what now then?

'Perhaps we can reminisce,' John shrugged. 'We had so many good times, didn't we?'

'Yes we did, didn't we?' Samuel's face lit up as he broke into a laugh. 'Yes we did that right enough,' he chortled again.

'We did more than that Sammy boy,' said John excitedly, 'we *changed the world Sammy!* Didn't we? You were the most famous man in England. You couldn't go anywhere without being required to present yourself to the public. Three huzzas - all the time three huzzas they gave you - from the lowest to the highest in the land. Even the Prince of Wales himself commanded an audience.'

'More than that, John; I met his father the King too,' Samuel asserted, smiling proudly. 'I had an audience with King George after you left, but yes - I also had the honour of an interview with the Prince of Wales. He thought I was wonderful.'

'And you filled his purse many times for him, Sammy; 'cause our future King would gamble on anything in them days. He liked long odds did Prinny, and you always gave him that. I still don't know how you managed to keep winning – you were by rights much too small, you know. How did you do it, Sammy boy?'

'I mastered my art, John. You fight on your own terms not your opponent's.'

'Aye, and you were never short on confidence were you Sammy. In fact you could be an arrogant so and so.'

Samuel emptied his tankard, slapped it down with a grin, 'Yes I was - it's true. I thought I could beat the world; that nothing could stop me.' Suddenly he frowned, the smile on his lips vanishing as quickly as it had come. 'And yet I finished up a prisoner within the rules of the Kings Bench.'

'What? Debtors' prison?'

'Yes,' said Samuel, 'Debtors' prison. Thanks to you John Campbell-John, you bastard! You left me to pick up your debts didn't you.'

John looked down, picked at his fingernails, 'I'm sorry, I didn't know. Or perhaps I didn't want to know. Besides, all you had to do was fight to pay them off. Why did you not just do that?'

A log shifted on the fire. There was a crackle of sparks and the smell of singed matting. Samuel peered into the embers introspectively, 'They wouldn't let me.'

'Why not?'

'Sir Oliver Ruddle – that's why not!'

'That bastard – what had it got to do with him?'

'He was the main creditor; he bought up my debts and swore out a charge against me. It was revenge you see – he couldn't get you so he was intent on getting me. He had lost to us so many times in the past, so many lost bets, that he wanted me in prison more than he wanted his money back. So I was in debt but wasn't allowed to fight to get the money to pay off those debts.'

'How long?' asked John.

'A year and a half.'

'*A year and a half!* You must really have hated me.'

'Oh yes, I hated you.' He grimaced, face bleak. 'My family were starving whilst I was in prison. My hatred helped me to endure the ordeal. We'd spent so much money when we had it, and then suddenly I couldn't raise a farthing.'

John gave a dry chuckle, 'But we did spend money *didn't* we Sammy – we lived liked princes though, didn't we?'

'Oh yes, we did that right enough, but perhaps, if *you'd* paid your dues along the way...' Samuel turned his mouth down, 'If you had, then things may have turned out differently.'

'Yes, so many regrets Sammy boy, so many regrets. But so many great memories as well.'

'Yes, I suppose so.'

The two men fell silent for a while. Suddenly Samuel smiled, 'Do you remember when we first met? I'm not so sure that *I* do.'

'Oh I do Sammy boy – how could I forget. I remember it well Sammy boy - I remember it well. A spring morning in 1785 and a brash young Jewish boy wanting to fight the world...'

CHAPTER 2

London 1785

Captain John Campbell-John cut a fine figure of a man. He wore the uniform of an infantry captain, which complemented his fine physique and good looks. He strode with full military style; his shoulders square accentuating every inch of his tall, 5 foot 11 inches frame. His blonde hair escaped and flowed from the back of his shako, and he was the epitome of what he was – the quintessential military second son of an English country gentleman.

Except that he was none of these. John Campbell-John was not his real name and he was not a captain; nor was he the son of a country gentleman – that is to say, not the *legitimate* son. He was born to an intelligent, pretty but naïve governess who had been employed to educate the Squire's children, a task she was rather good at. So much so, that when she became pregnant by him, rather than lose her he arranged for her to marry his bailiff. The situation was frowned upon, particularly by the local minister, and was the subject of gossip and disapproval in polite circles, but in terms of suitability the match was considered appropriate and far better, given her status, than marrying her off to his gardener. For many years afterwards, the Squire continued to enjoy the best of all worlds: he had a first class governess, well educated children, and a mistress at his beck and call whenever his fancy turned to thoughts of an ardent nature, or to be more precise, whenever his consumption of wine left him feeling randy. Added to this, the lady of the house, turned a blind eye to the whole affair. It seemed that everyone was happy - with the possible exception of the bailiff, one Campbell John. But he was only too well aware of his place as a servant and knew better than to complain, so he kept his feelings to himself and got on with his job. In return the governess made him a good wife and as the years passed and her youth faded so did the Squire's interest in her, and eventually Campbell John had her to himself.

Into this unorthodox - but by no means unique - world, was born to the governess a son. The child was accepted by Campbell John as his own and somewhat perversely the boy was christened 'Edward John'. Perversely because by coincidence, the master of the house had also fathered two legitimate sons: the first, similarly called Edward, was five years old when the younger Edward entered this world, and the second son, George, preceded him by only a matter of four months.

As the boys grew up they were allowed to play together, and it was acknowledged that the younger Edward was an acceptable playmate for his half-brothers, especially George, so long as the boundaries and conventions were not infringed. The problem was that the boy was unaware of these boundaries and as he grew up, showed no inclination to learn them. There was also the problem of his name: as the mistress of the house was heard to remark: 'You cannot have three boys playing together with two of them answering to the name of Edward; it is all too confusing." So whenever the younger Edward was at the big house he was called 'John', and only on Sundays was he known by his given name - and even then, only by his mother.

The growing John was accepted about the big house despite his obvious disregard for conventions. This was because the Squire took a shine to him and indulged him, much to the annoyance of his wife. John was everything George was not. He was outgoing where George was timid. He was entertaining where George was a bit dour. He was rugged where George was scrawny – it wasn't that George was frail, he was just undersized. They both did well at their studies, but John was quick-witted where George was a bit of a swot. The problem for the Squire was that John was everything he wanted in a son, whereas poor George was a bit of a disappointment. The Squire saw in young John a chip off the old block. Every day, watching the boys play, he was reminded of this fact – John even looked like him, whereas George - well, poor old George did not - nor did he resemble his mother. In a cruel twist of fate it was the Squire's legitimate son who looked like a cuckoo in the nest.

As the boys grew they got into more and more mischief and it was John who was the main perpetrator, but always with enough nouse to taint George with his roguery. And like many children of that ilk, he had the natural ability to get away with his mischief purely by the force of his personality. He would look at his natural father with a twinkle in his eye and the Squire's stern face would switch uncontrollably to a smile, and after dismissing the boys, he could be heard roaring with laughter. If he could do no wrong in the Squire's eyes, however, his wife grew to hate him, as did the elder Edward, who grew jealous of his father's affections for his half-brother. George, on the other hand, loved him like a puppy dog.

When John was nineteen, the Squire died. He had promised to look after John in his will, but it was claimed that no will existed. The estate was entailed, the first son Edward inherited, and John's continued residence was at the will of the new young master of the house, who soon had the excuse he needed to rid himself of his young half-brother. Typically, John had failed to mend his ways; he had been bedding the daughter of the local coal merchant and when her father came round to the big house, enraged and armed with pistol with the purpose of emasculating the man who had defiled his daughter, John was banished. He was sent on his way with five guineas, a horse and a change of clothes, and was expected to be thankful for that. He had no trade and only his wits to sustain him, but he had been sheltered from any sense of responsibility in his youth. Within days he was penniless and forced to sell his horse. Within days of that he was again penniless. And so he turned to soldiery – he took the King's shilling and joined an infantry regiment. If his father had lived perhaps he could have purchased John a commission, but his lot was now as a common foot soldier.

To his amazement, he loved it. There were many hours of boredom in the soldier's life – time that needed to be filled. Into this vacuum there was endless scope for his roguery – for gambling; for wenching; for pranks. John was just the man to fill this vacuum. He was forever on a charge, promoted to corporal and then busted again. This time in his life, however, added guile and worldliness to his array of talents: it was a secondary education. These talents may not have been admired by the honest citizen, who had to rely on honest toil, but John was learning how to con his way through life – honest toil was not to be the route for him.

And then, on one drunken evening a plot was hatched and a bet was proposed. The officers of his company had been invited to a country ball, along with officers from the rest of the regiment and the bet was that John should go and pass himself off as an officer. Impersonating an officer was a very serious offence, but even after sobering up, the notion took hold of him. He had the education, the accent, the knowledge of the *big house* – he would do it. A bribe was made to a laundry wench and an officer's uniform purloined. The success of the venture astounded even him. He was accepted totally – even officers from his own company, who had many times put him on a charge, failed to recognise him. Officers never really looked enlisted men in the eye – but it was much more that that. John learned that evening that people see what is in front of them – image is all-important. If he looked and sounded like an officer, then to all intents and purposes he was an officer. A life lesson had been learned.

Some time afterwards, on a fine spring morning he strode purposefully down a London street. It was his first time in the capital. Buoyed by his successes at impersonating an officer he had deserted his regiment and invented the persona of 'John Campbell-John'. His intention was to use this to con his way through the city - to make his fortune. He had thought little further than that; no detailed plan had evolved in his mind. He would find lodgings and use his bogus status to get credit. If he were not in funds when payment became due then he would merely disappear and start the process all over again somewhere else. Today, however, John Campbell-John was to hit the jackpot at his first attempt.

He had started his reconnoitre of the city in the affluent West End, which was inhabited by the rich, the gentry, merchants of great fortune. The streets were clean and well-tended, but all was quiet with little scope for opportunity, so now John's perambulations took him towards Smithfield Market. For hundreds of years Smithfield had been the chief livestock market for London. Known as Ruffians Hall it was always teeming and crowded with people. This was a chaotic and brutal place, where animals herded through the streets of London were slaughtered; it was a place of death. But it was also a place of entertainment: jugglers, street theatre, Punch and Judy. The more lewd the entertainment the better the lower classes liked it. As John walked, the stench of the city suddenly hit him. It was an offence to leave rubbish about in front of your own or your neighbour's house, but despite this, it was the practice of the lower sort to throw into the street, ashes, rubbish, broken glass, offal, dead animals and the contents of their chamber pots that had missed the night soil collectors – not to mention their overflowing cess pits. This, together with the volume of faeces and urine excreted by the thousands of horses in the capital, and the herds of cattle and flocks of sheep being driven through the streets to market, made a rich, glutinous mixture. John wrinkled his nose at the disgusting odour of 18th Century living. He was a country boy; the smells of livestock and their effluent were well known to his nostrils, but they were nothing compared to this. And on top of it all was the very special odour of Smithfield Market itself - of blood, flesh and faeces - and then, incongruously, the sweeter smell of roasting meat. A pig was roasting on a spit, a great dripping pan beneath catching the fat as it dropped. The smell of the roasting flesh somehow transcended the stench of the market. John nevertheless put his handkerchief to his nose and for a moment the smell had his full attention, but then he turned and looked up an adjacent street, becoming aware of a fracas. Moving towards it, he stared over his handkerchief, drawn somehow to what was happening.

An impromptu ring was being formed outside a greengrocer's establishment; a fight was about to take place but the two adversaries seemed to be totally mismatched. The first was a stout athletic man in the prime of his life, standing nearly six feet tall, but his adversary was a youth of eighteen or nineteen years of age, standing no more than five feet eight inches. He had removed his shirt and stood ready to fight wearing only his breeches and a pair of yarn stockings. His thighs were powerful and his upper body lean, but even so John could see only a mismatch. An eager and enthusiastic crowd was, nevertheless, being formed and odds were being given as to the outcome. Three to one against the youth seemed to John very poor odds as at first sight he had neither the strength nor the size to best his competitor – surely, he thought, ten to one would be more realistic? And yet there were some takers. John could not have passed this opportunity by even had he wanted to; the temptation was irresistible. As though some Archimedean revelation had just been bestowed upon him, a design registered in his mind: here was the prospect of funds, an opportunity for advancement – it was an irrational thought. This was no more than a street fight and they happened all the time. And yet his instincts told him he was right.

With an engaging smile, he moved over to address the underdog. 'What occasion brings you to this fight, youth?'

'I am apprenticed to these greengrocer's premises, sir, and this fellow has insulted my mistress on account of her being of the Jewish religion,' said the youth.

'And is this *your* fight, lad?'

'It is, sir. When my master remonstrated with the fellow for his impropriety, he became more abusive and challenged him to a fight.'

'So it's not really *your* fight, is it?' said John, taken aback by the youth's educated speech.

'My master is not a young and athletic man, sir. The man is a bully and I intend to punish him for his insolence.'

'You have an eloquent tongue to match your bravery, young man, but I fear your resolve is foolhardy. You have neither the size nor the strength for this fight. Let me broker a truce on your behalf.'

'Thank you sir for your benevolence, but I beg leave to embrace this challenge. I may not have the size nor the strength, but I have the science to best this man,' the youth asserted.

'You have an education, that is clear, and if your fighting is as fancy as your words then we may yet all be surprised. Do you have a second for this set-to, and if not then may I offer my services?'

'No sir I do not have a second, and I will gladly accept your services.'

'Then let us get to it,' said John.

What followed was a revelation to the crowd and especially to John Campbell John. He had witnessed several set-tos in the army; they were usually brutal affairs, the conqueror being the biggest and strongest fellow. But this lad had an athleticism that counteracted and nullified the strength of his opponent. At the beginning of the contest he took a posture so that both knees were bent with the left leg advanced, his arms held directly before his throat, his chin and body inclined diagonally towards his opponent. For the first five minutes of the contest the youth advanced and retreated so that his opponent's punches fell short, or were parried. As the other man tired his shots became increasingly wild and easier to evade, all the time draining his stamina and strength. After twelve minutes the youth changed his tactics and began to attack, advancing and landing clean shots and then retreating before the ponderous blows of his antagonist could connect. After seventeen minutes his challenger was bloodied and exhausted, while the youth had not a mark on him. A solid blow to the ribs sent his opponent to the ground gasping for air, and he had to be revived by his second before being sent out to fight again. This happened four more times until his opponent was no longer able to stand and cried 'Bested!'

The crowd had swelled enormously during the fight, many having been drawn from Ruffians Hall, including some sporting looking gentleman who had taken immense pleasure in the performance of the youth. John donned his shako and went for the opportunity.

'Nubbins, sirs,' he cried and thrust his cap before them, 'let us all show our appreciation.' With that he produced his last sovereign from his tunic tossed it into his cap and thrust the cap before the gentleman. It had the desired effect: a bright golden guinea was plucked from a silk waistcoat.

'Bravo to the lad,' cried the sporting gentleman. Other coins followed, as John cajoled the assembled crowd who were now keen to pat the youth on his shoulders. '*Bravo!*' now cried the throng in unison enthralled by the lad's display. One gentleman suggested that he was good enough to fight professional fighters, and the cry of *bravo* went up again. The coins began to flow more rapidly and John needed both hands to support the weight as he carried it over to the victor, 'There's a tidy collection here for you lad. Where shall we go to count it?'

'The Boar tavern sir,' said the youth, 'but give my opponent a guinea for his sport today.'

'Well said, lad,' one of the sporting gentlemen remarked, 'we've all had good sport here today.'

'Two tankards of ale landlord,' said John, 'and do you have somewhere where my good friend and I can discuss a little business?'

'Been fighting again, young Samuel?' said the landlord.

'Aye sir, but it was not to be avoided.'

'It never is with you lad, is it?' The landlord winked pointedly at Samuel and showed the pair to a cubicle.

As they sat down, John thrust out his hand. 'John Campbell-John and to whom do I have the honour this fine day?'

'Samuel Medina, your servant sir.'

'You have fine manners for a working lad, Samuel Medina.'

'Thank you sir; I was educated at a Jewish school and have some learning.'

'And you have some fighting ability too lad,' said John.

'Yes sir – I was never bested at school.'

'But that was no child you have just beaten, Samuel lad, where did you learn to fight like that?'

John Campbell-John saw something in this young man – something special;—something he could exploit. John was not motivated by anything noble, merely his instinct to make the most of this situation.

Supping his ale, Samuel surreptitiously eyed the young gentleman across the table and wondered why he was being so kind. It had been good of him to collect a purse for the fight, but Samuel, naturally suspicious of strangers, was not sure how much to trust him. He was indeed born to Jewish parents, who were by no means affluent - they were of the middling class of society, but they nevertheless sent their children to a Jewish school. As a boy, Samuel had been tutored in English grammar, writing and arithmetic, as well as his Jewish studies and he was instructed also in Hebrew. He was a bright and willing student and prospered at his school. But there was another side to him – he was an extrovert. He loved the limelight and he had one special talent that gave him the attention he craved. He could fight – it wasn't that he was quarrelsome, he had in fact quite a sunny and genuine nature, it was that he liked to show off. He was also taken with stories of heroic deeds, especially legends of King Arthur and his knights. He justified the need to fight by convincing himself that these were chivalrous actions in the true sprit of the Arthurian legends. He would come to the rescue of anybody whether they needed it or not. Whenever he was involved in a fight his father would reprimand him sternly, but if he could show that he fought in self-defence or for an honourable motive then he was freely forgiven.

At the age of thirteen he had been apprenticed to a tea dealer and went to live with the family, but he got involved in a fight with his employer's son and was dismissed. There followed a string of occupations, much to the displeasure of his father, most ending with his dismissal and usually because of his fighting. The purchase of an apprenticeship gave a young man a good start in life and allowed a lad of enterprise to tap into the prosperity that London offered, but it was costly to his father who had eight other children for whom to provide.

Samuel's latest employment, with the greengrocer, had lasted longer than usual; not only because his employer was himself a Jew, but also – and perhaps even more importantly - because he saw in his apprentice a measure of protection. It was a sad fact of life that Jew-baiting was a popular sport in the poorer areas of London. Any Jew was liable to be kicked, cuffed, pulled by the beard, spat upon, or otherwise assailed in the street. Passers by did not interfere any more than did the law: Jews were excluded from holding any office under the crown or appointment in civil government, nor were they employed in the justice or education systems. And yet, paradoxically, however bad this was, Jews still enjoyed a greater degree of social and religious freedom here in England than they did on the Continent, which was why so many of them came here. But the young Jews of Samuel's generation were no longer prepared to stand for this baiting and had begun to fight back. Most fought out of necessity, in self-defence, but Samuel did it out of – well, not so much the pleasure of the *fight*, but of being in the limelight. He knew he was an attention seeker – his friends were always telling him so. At the first signs of an insult to himself or someone else, he would challenge the perpetrator to withdraw his words – to apologise or be thrashed for their insolence. The result was that in his post-school life he was fighting increasingly frequently, but now his opponents were usually bigger and stronger than he. Samuel had a natural athleticism, a grace of movement; a natural ability to move well and evade his opponent. These talents he put to good use in this period of his life, and as he learned how to fight bigger men, his skills increased. He knew he was, after all, still a boy, but with a boy's ability to learn and learn quickly. He had developed a science of the pugilistic art that was all his own, to the point were none in the locality could stand against him – and he just a boy of nineteen.

Now, looking at Campbell-John's inquisitive face, Samuel felt a thrill of excitement coursing through him, though he could not have said exactly why. Perhaps because his instincts told him the man across the table recognised him for what he was: an untapped resource – a master craftsman masquerading as an apprenticed greengrocer.

'So come on lad, tell me where you are from and where you learned to fight like that,' John repeated.

'I am from Bethnal Green and I am self taught, sir. I am a Jew, and that means I have to be able to protect myself.'

'And how much have you earned from your fighting, lad?'

Samuel looked down at a stain on the table, a slight flush suffusing his cheeks. 'Why I have never earned anything before, sir.'

'Nothing?' John was amazed. 'So how much do you think we have here?'

'I don't know.'

'Well let's count it shall we?' John emptied his shako onto the table.

'Five pounds twelve shillings and seven pence,' he pronounced, counting the coins into neat piles.

'And a sovereign, sir.' Samuel looked wide-eyed across the table.

John looked down, shook his head. 'I think not. We have counted together – there is no mistake.'

'But you took out a sovereign as we crossed the road to this tavern, sir,' said Samuel.

'You have a suspicious nature, young Samuel,'

'That's as may be, but I will not be cheated.' Samuel frowned.

'Cheated! I'm not here to cheat you lad.'

'Then put back the sovereign you took.' Samuel stood up, and fixed John with a stern gaze. 'If not, sir, I fear we have to go outside to settle this.'

Discomfited, John shifted his position on the bench, looked up, met Samuel's gaze. The lad had large brown eyes that were warm and compassionate. He wore his hair in a pigtail and his face was unshaven in the style of an Englishman rather than wearing side ringlets and a beard in the style of his father. His general countenance reflected his kind-heartedness, his olive skin and aquiline nose being softened by those two great soulful eyes. He had one of those faces which, while not handsome, was warm and encouraging; the kind of face that attracted the fairer sex, John thought with a grin. Now, however, all trace of compassion had left Samuel's features.

Hiding a qualm of disquiet, John Campbell-John sat back and looked at him intently. He had thought the lad would be easy to manipulate, but now saw that Samuel was no fool. Those large brown eyes penetrated back into his consciousness. He perceived that the lad's challenge was serious and that he had the resolve to back it up, and with that, John also perceived within himself a scintilla of fear. Fear was not something he was familiar with – he had lived a life virtually without restraint. He had always done whatever he wanted and to hell with the cost, but now, suddenly, he was faced with consequences: immediate consequences. He knew he could not best the lad in a fistfight; he had his sword, but to use it would undoubtedly separate him from this seemingly God sent opportunity. With that thought, his cunning took over.

'Aye lad, you're right I did remove a sovereign,' said John, deciding that discretion was called for, 'but I was not trying to cheat you. It was merely the float. To take up a collection you have to get it started, to get those sporting gentlemen to dip into their pockets. I am not in the best of funds at the moment and I haven't got a sovereign to spare.'

'Nevertheless, sir your sovereign was put in my collection and by my reckoning that makes it mine.'

'Very well Samuel Medina, your point is well made.' From his tunic, John plucked the errant sovereign and threw it on the pile of money before them. Samuel's features softened and a smile crossed his lips as he resumed his seat. John returned his smile, but it was more forced than natural.

'I am a generous man though, John Campbell-John,' said Samuel to John's surprise, 'I am obliged to you for taking up a collection for me. You can take a guinea from the collection for your trouble.'

'You are a strange man Samuel Medina,' said John, 'You would fight me for a sovereign and now you give me a guinea.'

'Aye, maybe I am, but you should know that I am *not* to be cheated,' said Samuel, 'and neither am I a fool.'

'No, you're not that, Sammy lad.' John rolled the coin in his fingers. 'In fact, I see prosperity for both of us; I envisage a great partnership if you are interested. How say you?'

'I am interested in bettering myself, sir,' said Samuel, 'but I take it you want me to fight and I'm not sure that is the route I want for myself.'

'I promise you Sammy lad that money is the quickest way of bettering yourself. If you can become a man of property then many doors will open for you,' said John.

'And what will be your part in this partnership,' said Samuel.

'I'll be your second, I'll be your manager, I'll arrange the fights and negotiate the purse. I'll find you a patron to back you and we'll have great adventures along the way.'

'And what will your cut be for these services?' asked Samuel.

'Fifty – fifty, Sammy lad; what do you say?'

Samuel grimaced. 'Seventy five – twenty five is more equitable.'

'Sixty – Forty,' said John.

'Seventy five – twenty five,' repeated Samuel.

John thought for a moment. 'Very well, then we have a deal.'

Samuel shook his head. 'No sir, we do not, I don't yet know whether you are trustworthy.'

'Then we must spend some time together Sammy lad, get to know each other. And let us start with tonight – let us spend a half sovereign each on revelry.'

Samuel's jaw dropped, 'A half sovereign in one night, sir! That is wild extravagance is it not?'

'Oh yes Sammy boy, it is that. Tonight we will be young men with money to spend and tomfoolery on our minds. Are you with me lad, shall we dine and sup and see where the night takes us?' Finishing his ale, John smacked his lips and grinned at his young friend.

Samuel looked intently at this stranger who was offering a glimpse of a lifestyle that was hitherto unknown to him. His background and education had taught him to be cautious, but he was an extrovert. He sensed that for all he and Campbell-John were from different backgrounds, they had at least that one thing in common: they were both extroverts – extreme extroverts. Samuel felt some invisible bond between them and this temptation overruled his caution.

'Aye sir, let us make a night of it. Let us see where fate takes us.'

'Well said Sammy boy,' said John, 'and that must be the last time you call me sir. From now on it's John and Sammy. I see a great friendship between us.'

CHAPTER 3

The Royal Oak was not a tavern Samuel had visited before. As he entered, the potent smell of stale beer accosted his senses. The window frames were small and the glass in need of cleaning, so that his eyes needed a moment to adjust to the muted ambient light. As his vision emerged, so did the noise - the noise of men engaged in raucous conversation, laughing, and singing and eating. Then the smell of cooking hit his nostrils, the aroma of meat juices driving away the unpleasantness of stale beer that contaminated every item of furniture in the tavern, and which the sprinkling of sawdust on the stone floor did little to eliminate.

'Why here?' he asked John.

'One of my fellow officers in the regiment recommended it to me,' said John. It was only partly true. 'There's a drinking club that meets here.'

'I wouldn't have thought this was a place for officers,' said Samuel.

John ignored the comment but leant across the bar and whispered something to the landlord who nodded in the direction of the staircase. 'Come on Sammy lad,' said John, 'let's go upstairs to the private room. We shall eat and sup well tonight.'

The private room was spacious, but equally dimly lit, with a large dining table taking pride of place. There were about twenty young gentlemen present, most of whom looked to be in their twenties and from their appearance, Samuel thought they were from the middling classes. John shook the hand of a middle-aged gentleman and engaged him in conversation. 'Ahh, new members, capital,' Samuel heard the man say. They were shown around, handshakes were exchanged vigorously and his Jewish name did not appear to trouble any of the assembled members. And then the older man called for a collection of the club subscription.

'It'll be four shillings Sammy lad, said John.

'But I can get dinner in a steakhouse for one shilling and sixpence,' said Samuel, 'beef, bread *and* ale.'

'Ah but this will be better Sammy, and there'll be entertainment later,' said John.

'What sort of entertainment?' Samuel looked pensively at the coins he had taken from his pocket.

'You'll see,' said John, picking the necessary coins from Samuel's cupped hand and ushering him to a seat at the dining table.

Several large steak pies soon arrived followed by numerous bowls of vegetables and large jugs of gravy. The serving girls then returned with pitchers of ale and the assembled members took the opportunity to gorge themselves. Large portions of pie were cut and allocated and plates piled high with potatoes and vegetables then copiously doused with gravy. The conversation was raucous and surrounded the pursuits of these young men – gambling, wenching, and cock fighting, but it turned also to other entertainments: the theatre, executions and animal baiting being obvious favourites, but grumbles were also expressed, particularly concerning their positions and the wages they could command - or not as the case may be. As the beer flowed Samuel and John felt more at ease, eating and drinking their fill, partaking of the revelry and contributing to the conversation.

'I have a wizard yarn,' said John loudly so that other diners could hear. A number leaned forward at the prospect of a good tale. John's intention was to integrate them into his and Samuel's company, and he felt a good joke would be the perfect way of doing so. 'It's a real snorter - I heard it in the officer's mess,' he continued which of course was a lie. He had heard it in the ranks. 'A corporal goes into a tavern and orders a tankard of ale from the landlord. He takes a gulp but as he does so he sees another soldier who looks just like him at the other end of the bar. Hey soldier, he says, I couldn't help but notice that we look alike. You're right says the other soldier, what town do you come from? Doncaster says the corporal. *Doncaster*, says the other soldier – so do I. What street do you come from? West Street, says the corporal. *West Street?* Me too, says the other. What number? Number 54 says the corporal. That's incredible, says the other soldier – so do I. What are your parents called? Harold and Kitty says the corporal. *Harold and Kitty*, says the other soldier – I don't believe it.'

John looked up and saw from their faces that he had the full attention of the other diners. They were all leaning forward in anticipation, and the interest in the yarn had spread down the table. Judging the pause to a nicety - he had them like the best music hall performers - it was time for the tag line.

'Oh bloody hell, says the landlord,' continued John, 'send for the Sergeant at Arms. *The Johnson twins are pissed again.*'

Laughter erupted and John was patted firmly on his back in appreciation. 'Capital story,' said one of the young gentlemen. They had been accepted into the fold.

As the evening wore on Samuel noticed there were other young ladies joining them and that they were not serving girls. 'Who are *they?*' he asked John.

'You'll see,' John said enigmatically, winking at a young gentleman seated on the other side of Samuel.

'No, come on,' said Samuel, 'who are they?'

'*They* are the entertainment, Sammy lad,' he answered.

'Entertainment – have they come to sing and dance for us?' asked Samuel naively.

The young gentleman seated at the other side of Samuel sniggered and John laughed aloud in response. He then looked at Samuel and too late, saw the resentment in his face.

Samuel felt he was being made to look a fool and he did not like that at all. His response to such situations was always the same. He stood and in one fluid movement threw his knife violently onto the table. The conversation was brought to an abrupt halt and the assembled company looked at him in surprise. He became aware that everyone's gaze was suddenly fixed on him.

'You mistake me greatly sir if you think that I can be the butt of your humour,' he said forcefully. 'Perhaps we need to settle this outside.'

For a moment an uncomfortable mood purveyed the room. Silence fell, punctuated only by nervous coughing. John saw that Samuel was serious, and as he looked around the room he realised it was incumbent upon him to resolve the situation. He forced a broad smile to mask his uneasy countenance. 'Oh come on Sammy lad,' he said, 'sit down and stop being such a stuffed shirt. I'll tell you exactly what's going on. This is more than just a drinking club – it's – well, it's a cock and hen club, if you know what I mean.'

'A cock and hen club - what's a cock and hen club?' asked Samuel.

'Well can't you guess, Sammy lad,' said John, 'what do cocks and hens usually do together - think about it?'

Samuel sat down as realisation took hold of him. Flushing hotly with embarrassment he looked around at the assembled faces, but they gradually began turning their gazes away, more interested in their eating and drinking and the ladies who were now arriving. Samuel leaned forward and whispered to John. 'You mean they're – *prostitutes* – they're *Mabels?*'

'Well that sort of thing – they don't all work the streets. It's safer this way,' said John.

'But where? I mean, how does it work?' asked Samuel.

'Don't worry, it's not compulsory. Just spend some time with them; eat and drink and talk, but if you like one of them and - you know – and you want to – well, do the dirty deed, then agree a price and there are cubicles for you to go to. It's all very gentlemanly, I promise you.'

'But I'm a Jewish boy, I've had a Jewish education - I've studied my Torah. We don't do this sort of thing – I'm a...' Samuel then paused in mid sentence and just looked back at John for a moment.

'Oh,' said John absorbedly, grasping the situation, 'you mean you're a...'

'Well yes,' said Samuel interrupting him before he could say the word 'virgin'.

'Oh,' said John again, 'well as I said it's not compulsory. Just enjoy yourself Sammy lad and do whatever you want to. But this might be a good time for you to progress from colt to stallion if you know what I mean.'

John wandered off and Samuel observed him doing exactly what he had advised: he engaged a woman in conversation and she quickly put her arm around his neck, draping her body against his seductively. Laughter soon followed and all this was fuelled by more drink. Samuel noticed John's hand glide upwards from the woman's waist to cup her breast from below. As was the fashion, the woman's dress was cut low to display her bosom to its full advantage, and this particular bosom was ample, pushed upwards by her stays so that the fleshy masses overflowed and rose and fell in concert with her breathing. She smacked John's hand playfully away, but there was no hint of real protestation in her manner.

Samuel soon found he was sitting by himself. He felt isolated and uncomfortable. He did not fear any man, but he was intimidated by these women. He sat by himself for twenty minutes, observing the others and taking refuge in his ale, which he continued to consume in the hope that it would give him the courage to join in the revelry. And then John returned with his new lady friend. The woman was older than John, probably in her mid-thirties. Her dress was loud - a swirling pattern in red and emerald - but it was grubby and had seen better days. Her hair was worn ridiculously high to match the fashion of the day, and towered above John although she was in fact several inches shorter. Her hair was jet black, but to Samuel it looked artificial: most likely the result of a chemical dye purchased from the apothecary, and clearly her hair had been starched, the front curled by curl papers and the whole ensemble vigorously scented, as had her body, Samuel thought, his nostrils twitching. The woman's musky aroma preceded her as she approached. It was not unpleasant.

'This is my friend Sammy,' said John, 'I know he looks older but he's only eighteen. Sammy this is Moll, my new friend.'

'Delighted to make your acquaintance, Moll,' said Samuel.

'Oo-er don't 'e talk nice Johnny,' said Moll, her accent thick with the sounds of London's East End. 'Sounds like a proper young gentleman so he does. That's why I like to come 'ere - young gentleman like him know 'ow to treat a girl right.'

'Yes Moll my girl,' said John, 'we're both young gentlemen, but Sammy here is looking for something a little different.'

'I *don't* think I am John,' said Samuel huffily, 'and anyway I'm *nineteen.*'

'*Trust* me Sammy lad,' said John, turning then to Moll, 'you see, Sammy here is - well shall we say he's inexperienced in the ways of liaison – an initiate if you know what I mean.'

'Oh I *do* understand, deary,' said Moll, who then whispered 'you haven't been a victim of cupid's little sting yet have you, young sir. We need to find you someone who'll take your fancy. Someone you can be sweet on - leave it to me.'

She leant forward and pinched Samuel's cheeks between her thumb and first finger and repeated, 'Leave it to me deary,' and then breezed away leaving her potent scent behind her. John sat down and thumped his tankard on the table so that ale spilt out of it, but neither man took any notice. Once again, John noticed annoyance in Samuel's eyes.

'Come on then, out with it, what's the matter now. You're a touchy so and so Samuel Medina aren't you?'

'I'm *alright* – I don't need you to – well get a woman for me. Just leave me alone, there's plenty of ale to sup. Just leave me be.'

'Well alright then, if that's what you want,' said John. 'But Moll's gone now to see what she can find for you. Let's just see who she brings back to the tavern - if you're not interested then – well, that's fine. But I did say I would take you on an adventure tonight, and I'm trying to do just that.'

'Yes you did, John, and I'm grateful for that, it just that…'

'I know Sammy lad, you feel like an apprentice on his first day at work. We've all been there you know,' said John, 'but from now on you can trust in me for your education. You're book learning has been fine but you now need a teacher in the ways of life - and I think a good start would be for you to learn the difference between a tart's fucker and her farter,' he laughed coarsely.

John leaned forward and held his tankard aloft inviting Samuel to acknowledge it. Samuel's scowl dissipated and he took his tankard and thrust into John's, the dull clink of pewter against pewter establishing their alliance, as if some imaginary treaty had just been signed. Some twenty minutes later Moll was back, interrupting their conversation, awareness of her scent arriving before she did so that they looked up several moments before she reached their table. She was leading someone by the hand, but was obscuring whoever it was behind her. Then she turned, placed her hands on the shoulder of a young woman and manoeuvred the girl forward.

'This is Ginny,' she said.

A young, slender, reticent figure presented itself, her head held slightly to one side. Her cheeks were suffused with pink and her eyes slightly staring as if she was overwhelmed by the circumstances in which she found herself. She reminded Samuel of a rabbit confronted by a stoat. She was wearing a blue-green lustring dress, the silky material lined with white. Her stays pushed up her breasts, but their fullness was illusory as in truth she had little bosom to display. Her eyebrows had been plucked and replaced by black painted ones. The fashion of the day was for black eyebrows–and like all fashions they were seized upon whether they were flattering or not. Her lips were painted vivid red, but mercifully her face had not been adorned with powder or rouge. Even so, what had been done to her face distracted from her youthful beauty and contradicted her blue eyes, flaxen hair and pale complexion. Samuel concluded that someone had attempted to make her look older than she really was – worldlier; more desirable. The process had succeeded on the first two counts, but it certainly had not on the third since it masked what was most desirable about her: her youthfulness.

Too embarrassed to speak, Samuel did not initially acknowledge her. When their eyes met they both flushed and looked away. Moll laughed. 'We 'ave got two little bashful love birds 'ere ain't we deary.'

'I think the best thing is to leave them alone together,' said John.

'You're right Johnny,' said Moll, 'let's leave 'em to get to know each other.'

Moll pulled John by the arm, leading him away. Looking back, he caught a glimpse of Samuel's face; the youth's expression of uneasiness said clearly that the last thing he wanted was to be left alone. Ginny's face mirrored Samuel's, except that her unease was overlaid with trepidation.

'Come on Johnny, they'll be all right – let nature take its course,' Moll tugged his arm.

Samuel watched as John gestured to him with a shrug of his shoulders before retreating with Moll on his arm. For a few moments Samuel stared after them, hotly aware that Ginny had sat in John's vacated chair and trying to stem the panic that was making his pulse race as her skirt brushed against his leg. The two sat in silence and embarrassment, both unsure and neither confident enough to talk to the other. And then Samuel took a deep breath, said. 'My name is Samuel, Samuel Medina.'

'And I am Ginny Farmer, sir.' She spoke in a West Country accent.

After another pause, Samuel cleared his throat, said, 'You're not from London then?'

'No sir, I've only been here a few days. I've come to London looking for work, but.., well it's not been easy to find, sir.'

'What sort of work?' Feeling hot and uncomfortable, Samuel looked everywhere but at Ginny's face.

'Well I was a lady's maid, sir – before I came to London.'

'And the gentry bring there own servants with them when they come to London for the season, don't they,' said Samuel.

'It seems so, sir.

There was another pause while Samuel tried to think of something else to say.

'I like your dress,' he said eventually.

'Thank you sir,' she looked down, blushing. 'But it's not really mine, my cousin borrowed it for me - I couldn't afford this. And then she and her friend did my face – I only had a few minutes to get ready after Moll arrived. They weren't going to bring me here until next week.'

They looked at each other, both feeling some relief that they were in similar circumstances and were to some extent kindred spirits – and then they both realised that they were staring at each other and looked hastily away.

'You know what goes on here?' Samuel mumbled into his tankard.

'Oh yes sir, my cousin has explained it all – I have to be - to be *considerate* to the young gentlemen.'

There was another pause when embarrassment suddenly returned to both of them. 'Would you like a drink, Ginny,' said Samuel, 'what would you like?'

'I've been told to ask for gin sir, but to be honest I don't really like it.'

'Do you like ale,' said Samuel, 'would that be better?'

'Oh yes please sir, ale would be fine.' Reaching for a spare glass, Samuel poured ale from the pitcher. Ginny took a deep gulp before putting the glass down, her fingers, Samuel noticed, were trembling. He picked up his tankard, held it in her direction; she picked up her glass again and the two vessels were clunked together and they both said cheers as they drank further from the depths of them. They continued to drink for some time beginning to feel more comfortable with each other.

'So why London?' Samuel asked eventually.

'Well I have a cousin here, sir. I thought she was in service and could help me find a job. But it turns out that she is not in service at all – actually she's a - well she entertains gentlemen.'

'Oh I see,' said Samuel. 'So, will you go back?'

'Oh I can't do that, sir.' There was trepidation in her voice.

'Why not?' asked Samuel. She hesitated and then finally averted her eyes before replying.

'You don't want to know my troubles, sir.'

'Now come on lass, tell me why you can't go back.'

'I was told not to talk about such things sir, I was told to talk about you, not me.'

'Well, were you also told to do what you were told lass?' Samuel smiled at her.

'Aye sir,' Ginny looked away from his kindly stare, suddenly self-conscious again.

'Well I'm telling you that I want to know why you can't go back.'

She was still unsure but she looked at him with her large puppy dog eyes. 'Well sir – it was the Master, sir,' she said hesitantly.

'And who was your master?'

'The Squire sir, but I don't think I should tell you his name.'

'And what did he do to you – or is that obvious?'

'He took a shine to me, if you knows what I mean.'

Samuel smiled, finding her soft West Country burr charming. 'I think I do – so you've run away then, have you?'

'Well yes I have sir.'

'But is this any better – would they take you back if you returned?'

'No - no I don't think so sir.' There was suddenly alarm in her voice.

'Are you so sure lass?' said Samuel.

'It's complicated sir – the Master threw me out,'

'Why lass?'

'Well sir,' she hesitated again, 'you see I had a baby – his baby. The Master had the Minister find a couple to adopt her, but the Mistress found out who the father was and I was told to go...' She stopped speaking, looked down, a tear glistening on her cheek.

'But what about your family? Samuel prompted softly. 'Come on lass, you've gone this far.'

'I was brought up in the Foundlings Hospital in Bristol, sir. I was abandoned as a baby and brought up as a strict Christian and then put into service. They would disapprove of me getting pregnant if *they* knew, and I couldn't get a job locally because *everybody* knew. So I thought, I'd come to London where nobody knows me.'

'I thought you said you had a cousin here?'

'I don't tell lies sir,' she said alarmed, 'it's just easier to say she's my cousin. We were both at the Foundlings Hospital together. *She* was put into service in London.'

'And how old were you?' said Samuel.

'Sixteen when I got pregnant sir, seventeen when the baby was born,' she said dolefully, but then she forced herself to sound more cheerful and continued, 'so you see sir, I know what to do – if we...'

'And how much were you told to ask for?' said Samuel.

'Oh dear,' she said, 'Moll'll be annoyed with me. I was supposed to ask for half a sovereign because I'm a virgin. And now I've gone and told you I'm not.'

Samuel smiled unexpectedly and that smile pierced through the embarrassment like a hot knife through butter. They both relaxed slightly. She returned his smile and they both drank again.

'I'm happy just talking if that's all right,' said Samuel.

'That'll be fine with me, sir.'

'Will you call me Samuel?'

'Yes sir,' she replied and then giggled when she saw his face and realised what she had said. 'Yes Samuel,' she repeated.

'Do you know what you are getting yourself into, Ginny?' asked Samuel.

'Oh yes,' she hesitated, 'prostitute is not a nice word is it. The Foundlings Hospital brought me up a good Christian girl, and I was conscientious with my studies. I'm a bright girl sir, but I have little choice do I, if I don't want to starve. I'll use my looks because that's all I have at this time. My cousin says we can keep off the streets if we can find a room and attract gentlemen of means – we can make a future for ourselves.'

'I hope you can Ginny,' said Samuel.

'I'm resigned to it Samuel, you mustn't think I'm unhappy with the prospect, I'm not – it's just that I'm – well London is such a very big place. I really don't know what to expect. It's a little frightening.

They talked together for another two hours, but as they talked the topics became lighter and more inconsequential. They giggled together and reminisced about their childhoods and how different they had been. She was a country girl and he was a city boy. She had never met a Jew before and knew nothing of Jewish ways, and he endeavoured to enlighten her. But then as time wore on she became agitated again.

'What is it?' said Samuel.

'Moll expects things of me – she'll expect me to - you know.'

'But I thought you were happy just to talk,' said Samuel.

'I am,' she replied, 'but I'm expected to earn some money.'

'Don't worry,' said Samuel, 'I've recently come into some funds. I have enough for that half a sovereign for you.'

'You are a good man Samuel,' she said, 'but I've got to learn to do this, and - well,' she paused and looked at him intently. Here was a man who was being considerate. It was unexpected, but she was so very pleased to receive it. 'Well I'd like the first time to be with you,' she said, 'it'll be easier if you know what I mean.'

'I'd like that as well,' said Samuel.

They smiled at each other and then that smile turned to a grin and then into a beam, as if they were some mischievous children about to do something naughty. They both shrugged their shoulders to gesture that feeling to each other, and then Samuel stood up, but quickly sat down when he realised he didn't know where to go. Then he stood again and sought out John Campbell-John, who smirked, hurried over and slapped Samuel fiercely on the back in the way men do to gesture approval, yet still retaining their manliness. He teased him by calling him '*stallion*' but then directed him to a door leading to several cubicles. Samuel returned to Ginny and put out his hand and she took it willingly, but they didn't speak until they entered a cubicle.

It was dimly lit, and furnished only with a small table and a well worn, leather-bound lounger that was open at one end and had long since lost its attractive aroma of freshly tanned leather. In fact it was rather shabby and frayed, but Samuel and Ginny had other things on their minds than the state of its upholstery.

They sat down together and both breathed deeply in unison, and then giggled when again they realise what they had done. She leaned across and kissed him gently on the lips and closed her eyes instinctively as she did so. Observing her, he thought he should do the same. The kiss was long, but tender rather than passionate. Nevertheless, it was invigorating and he felt a stirring in his loins. When the kiss ended he put his forehead against hers. 'How are we going to do this – should we lie down?' he gasped.

'No,' she said, 'let me sit on your lap.'

He nodded and she rose and then straddled his legs and sat down facing him, but almost immediately got up again and looked down at his thighs. She tentatively put her right hand on his left thigh and surprise showed in her face. She had only really seen him from the waist upwards whilst he had been sitting at the table.

'Your thighs,' she said incredulously, 'they're huge.'

His thighs were indeed huge – he was a natural athlete, but years of practising his unique style of boxing had also had the effect of accelerating his muscular development. His thighs rippled with sinews but, in addition, he was now nervous and his thigh muscles had tightened.

'I wouldn't say huge,' said Samuel, 'but, yes, I'm very athletic. I'm a Jew and that means that I have had to learn to protect myself. It has helped develop my physique.'

'Are all Jews like you then, Samuel?'

'Well no – not exactly. Does my body upset you?'

'Oh no, Samuel,' she returned to her sitting position straddling his legs and undid the buttons on the front of his shirt. It was loose fitting in the style of the day, with large baggy sleeves, and it had hidden his physique from her. She pulled it backwards over his shoulders to reveal his arms. She looked at him, a slight frown of concentration creasing her brow, and then looked up into his eyes. 'Look at you - your muscles, your biceps; your chest! You're like the strong man at the fair.'

'Am I? Does that not please you?'

'Oh no – I mean *yes*, it does please me. It's just that I – well, I hadn't realised you were so powerful.' She ran her hand over his chest and felt the firmness of his torso. She found it pleasurable and so did he.

'I'm not really like the strong man; he has bulk to make him strong. I am an athletic man – I would be exhausted after a few minutes if I had to carry all that weight whilst I am fighting.'

'Do you fight a lot Samuel? You don't seem like a bully or a quarrelsome man.'

'No I'm not, but I've had to fight all my life, it goes with being Jewish.'

She continued to run her hand over his chest and then over his shoulder and down his arm. She then looked at him and took his hand and put it on her bosom. He looked back and smiled pleasurably at her. He cupped her breast gently through the material of her dress but then didn't seem to know where to go from there. She slipped her own hand down her cleavage and exposed her right breast to his gaze. It was small and milk white in contrast to his olive skin and her nipple was hard and erect, but he did not understand the significance of that. He did not appreciate that she was becoming as aroused as he was. He fondled her gently and she continued to caress his chest. She took *his* nipple between her thumb and first finger and he quickly learned to do the same to her, which was the reaction she had wanted. They began to writhe together as their passion grew and she was pleased by his natural gentleness. Then she remembered what her cousin and Moll had told her. Prostitution was a living - sex was to be her profession and not to be enjoyed. She must not believe anything a gentleman told her, especially overtures of love, claims that she would be looked after, or even married. Even in the unlikely event that the man was serious when he said them, in the cold light of day he would only let her down.

But she *was* aroused – she could not deny that, even if she had been told not to give in to such feelings. She had expected the evening to be an ordeal, but now she was encountering feelings of sexual gratification. She did not know how to cope with this situation and her common sense wrestled with her emotions. But in the end it was no contest; they were just two young people in the midst of desire responding mutually to each other. She threw her head back and a small yelp slipped out at the delight entering her body through her nipple.

She took her weight on her legs so that she could raise her dress. She did it slowly revealing her slender, milk white legs, and then her taut, milk white thighs until her pubic hair and woman's secret parts were revealed to him. Physically she was in sharp contrast to him. He was powerful with olive coloured skin, very dark hair and large brown eyes, and she was a slight, pale skinned girl, flaxen-haired with eyes of powder blue. Moreover, he was Jewish and she was a Christian but, nevertheless, at that moment they were connected, coupled in their desire for one another.

'You can touch me, Samuel, if you want, that is.'

She guided his hand and he stroked her gently and although his fingers did not penetrate, he felt the moisture and smelled the musky scent of her. She liked it anyway and closed her eyes for some seconds in bliss. When she opened them she looked down at his loins and saw the stirring within his breeches. She cupped the protruding bulge that was now visible and then looked into his eyes and nodded. He undid the front of his breeches to release himself from their shackles. She gasped at what she saw, quickly masking her surprise with a smile. Neither her cousin nor Moll had warned her about the appearance of a circumcised male member. She attempted to sit down upon him, but such was Samuel's inexperience and ardour that penetration was not achieved. He took hold of his member and tried urgently to direct it, but ignorant of the female anatomy, he failed. He was now in a state of extreme excitement, grasping and fumbling, struggling to hold back his climax.

Ginny reached down and their fingers met. She looked into his eyes and gestured, almost imperceptibly, that it was alright. 'Let me,' she whispered.

He released his grip on himself, exhaling the breath that he seemed to have been holding indefinitely. She took him in her hand, running her fingers up and down the rigid shaft, making Samuel gasp in exquisite anguish. Satisfied, she rose gently and guided him inside her. She began to rise and fall upon him, slowly at first, and he raised his hips to meet her on the downward movements. As their passion grew and control diminished, their movements became increasingly frantic. But their love making was over almost before it had begun, the explosion of his orgasm sending Samuel into paroxysms of ecstasy. For a moment he remained motionless within her, and then he put his strong arms around her and held tight for several minutes, not wanting to leave the encompassing warmth of her body.

Much of the apprehension Ginny had felt since arriving in London temporarily drained from her and she felt safe for the first time in many weeks, his arms seemingly protecting her from the world. They sat quietly holding each other for a long time, until there was a call from outside the cubicle – another couple wanted it. They tidied their garments, gathered themselves together and pulled the curtain back. It was John Campbell-John and Moll.

'Do we have a stallion here?' asked John as the couples passed each other.

'Aye,' said Samuel, without boasting.

Moll grinned. 'And I'd lay odds a very fine stallion what's more.' She laughed out loud when she saw the effect of her words. Flushing with embarrassment, Samuel and Ginny had both looked down at the floor. 'But they're still two little bashful lovebirds, ain't they,' Moll winked at John.

Samuel and Ginny returned to the dining room and sat down together, talking intermittently, their silences no longer from embarrassment; there was no awkwardness between them now.

'Will you come again – here – to this club?' Ginny asked reticently.

'I'd like to come and see you again,' he replied, 'but it depends on whether I am in funds. I'm only apprenticed to a greengrocer and my remuneration from that will not permit me to come here.'

'Oh, I thought you were a young gentleman of means. Did your officer friend give you the funds for tonight?'

'No – I have given *him* the funds.'

'But I don't understand,' Ginny's brow creased in puzzlement.

'I had a set-to earlier today in the street,' said Samuel, 'and he took up a collection for me. I've only met him today.'

'Have you any of that money left,' she said.

'Oh - sorry Ginny.' Samuel took money from his breeches and gave her a shiny coin, 'I owe you half a sovereign don't I.'

'I didn't mean that,' she said, 'I just wondered if I'd see you again.'

'Maybe,' said Samuel, 'John wants me to fight for money.'

'And will you,' she said, 'I don't *want* you to fight but – then again I do want to see you again.'

He smiled at her – that comment gave him a nice warm feeling. 'Fight - I really don't know – I don't know whether I can trust him,' he said. 'I've had so many jobs in the last few years, and this is the first one I've held down. I have to think this through – I have to be sure.'

Moll and John returned. He looked flushed from his own exertions and she was rearranging her bosom back into her stays.

'Come on Ginny,' Moll pulled her to her feet. 'You have to circulate. There's still a few gentlemen left for you to meet.'

Ginny was led away. She looked back at Samuel with a sad little smile and mouthed 'Goodbye.'

'Its getting late Sammy boy,' John drained the last mouthful of ale from his tankard. 'We need to make plans – have you thought any more about my proposal; our partnership?'

'Yes, and I think I'm going to decline.'

'Why Sammy?' John was disconcerted, 'I could go to eighty - twenty if you think the split isn't fair.'

'Thank you John, eighty – twenty is a sound basis for a partnership, but I am settled in my employment. I have been a disappointment to my father so far in my life. I have been unable to hold down a job because of my fighting, and remember, I'm a Jew. It is the obligation of all Jewish children to honour their father and mother for they are the representatives of God.'

'Of course you do Sammy, but can't you do *both*? We can arrange the fights on a Sunday and I'm sure your Master wouldn't object.'

'You tempt me John Campbell-John, but the answer is still no.'

John Campbell-John was a cunning man and he recognised in the situation that this was not the time to press his prospective partner. He was far from beaten however, and he would wait until another time before pressing Samuel further.

'Very well Sammy lad, you know your own mind.'

'Aye I do John.'

'But I hope we can pursue another kind of partnership,' said John, 'a partnership in friendship. I feel that we have forged such a relationship tonight. Don't you agree Sammy?'

'Aye, that I do John,' he replied, 'and I hope a long friendship.'

They clunked the tankards together and Samuel emptied his. John attempted to do the same, but then looked into it puzzled, having forgotten he had already drained it dry.

'Now Samuel, my friend, I think I need a friend this Sunday – will you be my second in this endeavour?'

'Aye I will, and what is the nature of this endeavour.'

'I need to go to Northampton to collect a debt.'

'Do you envisage trouble?'

'Not really, but it would be reassuring to have you at my side. What say you?'

'Aye,' said Samuel robustly, 'then you shall have me with you. We go to Northampton on Sunday.'

CHAPTER 4

Northampton was at its unwelcoming best as the stagecoach approached the town. The rain had been drizzling intermittently throughout the whole journey, but there was virtually no wind and a pall of smoke hung in the air. It was Sunday so that the business of the town was not contributing to it, but there was an unseasonable chill and many of the town's inhabitants had lit fires. It was a dreary sight and a dreary day as the two men stepped down from the coach and looked to the ground to shield their faces from the spray - it gave them a shifty appearance; as if they were intruders come to spy on their fellows, but they had little intention of doing so. All they wanted was to get out of the rain.

The stagecoach had cost them a shilling each for the journey, and they considered it money well spent in view of the weather conditions. John Campbell-John had paid the fair for Samuel Medina because he had asked him to be his companion for the day in his quest to recover a debt. What had at first seemed a good day out was beginning to lose its appeal. It was mid-morning on a spring day, but it seemed more like mid-afternoon on a winter's day, with dusk fast approaching to put the sun out of its misery, having failed this day to assert its superiority. John took off at a pace and Samuel followed him unconsciously without thought, and neither man spoke until John stopped abruptly and looked around him. The puddled streets were drab to match the flat murky light. This was not an affluent part of the town, the houses small and ramshackle. The desolate scene reflected the gloomy day.

'Do you know where you are going?' asked Samuel.

'Sort of,' said John who seemed perplexed and all at sea. He paused and then looked around again. 'I think a tankard of ale would be welcome and perhaps some victuals before we do anything else,' he turned to Samuel.

'Capital,' said Samuel, adding, 'where to?'

John took off again as if he had suddenly gained his bearings, and after about a fifteen-minute walk, they rounded a corner and came upon an alehouse. They both stopped and looked and the swinging sign, John in confirmation and Samuel by way of information. It read '*The Turks Head*', above a representation of a dark-skinned man in a turban. John turned to Samuel his brow furrowed reflecting the uncertainty he felt.

'It may be best if we go in separately – you know as if we don't know each other. We can talk inside as if we are just casual acquaintances.'

Samuel gave a shrug but then a nod of concurrence. John set of again quickly spurred by the need to get out of the drizzle, and Samuel followed after a couple of minutes.

The streets had been quiet and chilly but Samuel's senses were met in contrast by warmth and noise. There were the intermingled smells of ale, stale beer, burning wood and cooking, and a near overwhelming sense of people. It was teeming, not only with the regular Sunday lunchtime clientele, but also those who had abandoned their normal activities because of the rain, so that they seemed to swarm like bees in a hive. They were all men, and they yelled and shouted and sang in a cacophony of noise. Samuel loved it at once. As he entered he saw John taking off his cape at the bar, to reveal his military uniform, and he heard him ask the innkeeper what victuals were available.

'I can do you beef and ale, young Captain,' replied the innkeeper.'

'That's sounds good fare to me, Innkeeper,' said John and gestured his further approval with a nod.

'That sounds fine for me also,' said Samuel as he too approached the bar. He stood a distance from John to maintain the illusion that they were strangers. The ale was served immediately and the beef followed shortly afterwards, and it was as welcoming as it was plentiful; both men were hungry. The innkeeper made conversation with John as they ate, and the whole atmosphere was one of conviviality. But all that changed in an instance. A loud and vulgar voice bellowed out behind them.

'I smell a Jew boy, if I ain't mistaken,' said the voice. A hush fell like a cold morning frost. They both turned to see a large man staring aggressively, with belligerence in his eyes. He was young, not more than about twenty-two, standing about six feet and athletically built, but he was unkempt and scruffy with several days' growth of beard on his face. His stance was confrontational, his legs being wide apart, his two thumbs tucked into the front of his breeches. 'Hey you, *Jew boy*,' he repeated, 'the last *Jew boy* that came in here had to be taught a lesson.'

Samuel looked him up and down without a hint of fear in his eyes. He would make no attempt to placate the man, or to find a way out of the situation. The extrovert in him would take over his responses – and more than that he would enjoy it. It was a situation he had found himself in many times before, the only difference now being that he was a long way from home, and badly outnumbered.

'Now Judd, let's have none of this,' said the innkeeper.

'You stay out of this,' replied Judd, a vindictive smile erupting across his face as he spoke,' this is between me and the Jew boy.'

'Do not take liberties with my faith, my man.'said Samuel the condescension evident in his voice.

John tried to hide a smile; the comment was exactly what he expected of Samuel. Judd looked round at the assembly, who were watching with apprehension in their eyes; *they* knew what kind of man this Judd was. He was the local bully and he liked nothing better than to humiliate a stranger, and a Jew added spice to his malice. They did not themselves like Jews, but this was overridden by a perverse compassion – they felt sorry for Samuel for they knew what was about to happen. But Judd had his audience and he played to them.

'*Whoa!* A la-di-da Jew boy - do you here that fellas?' he said, 'I think he definitely needs that lesson.'

'The lesson shall be yours, you rude, uncouth fellow,' said Samuel.

'Be careful young sir,' whispered the innkeeper leaning over the bar, 'this is Judd Dobbs. Don't mess with him – he's cock around these parts.'

Ignoring the warning, Samuel continued to address Judd. 'You mistake me greatly, fellow, if you think I fear to stand against you.'

It was not the response Judd Dobbs expected and for a moment he was lost for words. But then a voice from behind shouted, '*Go on Judd – get the Jew boy,*' and the excitement pumped through his veins at the thought of a fight. He took a step forward raising both fists, and Samuel took his fighting stance with his legs bent, one fist extended in front of the other. It was time for John Campbell-John to intervene. He drew his sword and stepped between the two men. 'Whoa!' he shouted. 'Let's just hold on for a minute.'

'You stay out of this soldier,' said Judd, 'this is not your fight.'

'Aye, you're right,' said John, 'but I'm a sporting gentleman and it seems to me that this is an opportunity for some sport and a wager. If there's to be a fight then let us have a proper fight. Are you willing stranger?'

'Aye,' said Samuel.

'Innkeeper, can I set up a ring in your yard?'

'Aye Captain,' replied the innkeeper.

'And the stranger here needs a second to act for him – *Who will stand as his second?*' he shouted to the inn's regulars. There was of course no response to this enquiry. 'Then I will offer my services,' shouted John to the crowd. He then turned and spoke to Samuel. 'Will you accept my offer stranger?'

'Gladly soldier,' said Samuel playing his part instinctively.'

'Gentlemen, it is now coming up to noon - shall we say the set-to will be at three of the clock in the yard,' shouted John. There was a cheer from the crowd. 'What is your trade fellow?' John asked the antagonist.

Judd, looking bemused by the way things were going, shuffled his feet. 'Er – I'm a Coal Heaver,' he said.

'And you sir?' John turned to Samuel.

'I shall fight under the name of Samuel the Jew,' he proclaimed.

'So it will be Judd the Coal Heaver against Samuel the Jew,' shouted John to the stunned crowd. 'And for those of us who want a wager, we need someone to run a book. Innkeeper! Will you run the book?'

But the innkeeper was disinclined to do so; everyone in the alehouse would be certain to bet on Judd and as far as he could see the Coal Heaver was the only possible winner. Seeing only losses from the venture, the innkeeper shook his head gesturing his rejection of the offer.

John shrugged, looking around at the blank, curious faces. 'Will anyone else run a book for the sporting gentlemen among us?' Again there was no response. 'Well then - *I* shall offer my services to run the book. Will that be agreeable with you, Innkeeper?'

'Aye Captain – I be agreeable,' shouted the innkeeper with some relief.

'Well then,' proclaimed John, 'we now need to establish odds. I would estimate that Judd the Coal Heaver stands at least four inches taller than Samuel the Jew, and more than two stones heavier. He must be naturally stronger and therefore a worthy favourite. I will offer five to one *on* Judd the Coal Heaver and five to one *against* Samuel the Jew.'

Uproar broke out as the assembly realised they were not going to be offered even-money against the two men. They thought they had smelled an opportunity for some easy winnings; a naïve stranger in their midst, but it was all part of John's plan to establish credibility. '*Gentlemen, gentlemen,*' he shouted above the noise, clapping his hands to quieten them. 'I am here by good fortune, and I have offered my services as an honest broker. I must offer odds that will encourage some of you sporting men to bet on the underdog. Come gentlemen, you can have your sport without emptying my purse as well,' he gave a wry grin.

The response, however, was rejection and the uproar recommenced. They were intent on profiting from the stranger's ignorance and cared little for the financial well-being of the man running the book. 'Very well gentleman,' declared John again, *two to one* is the best I can do. Those who want to take those odds can place their bets with me at the bar. The set-to will be at three of the clock, and the innkeeper will be referee. I will stand as second for Samuel the Jew – who will stand as second for Judd the Coal Heaver?'

Judd looked around him, but nobody came forward. The bully was unused to such formalities and so were the alehouse regulars, but he now realised he would lose face if nobody was willing to second him. It was the second's job to agree the terms of the fight and to look out for his man's interests. But Judd was no more than the local bully and like all bullies he had no real friends; most of his acquaintances paid him lip service in their efforts to keep on the right side of him. In desperation, he gestured to one of his drinking companions and the large man reluctantly came forward.

John hid a smile of satisfaction. This was exactly what he wanted - an uneducated and unsophisticated man who could be manipulated should the need arise. John spent the next hour taking money, chalking the bets on a slate and getting the gamblers to sign against it or at least to make their mark. Everything was to make the venture seem above board, to seem respectable. John was masquerading as a man of position, but he needed also to reinforce that illusion.

He knew that by offering odds of two to one, the bets would be higher than they would have been at evens; he was provoking people's greed, making the gamblers among them speculate more for the same possible return. He knew that in the speculators' minds this was no gamble, merely the evident beating of a Jew and the fleecing of a soldier. When the book was closed, absolutely no bets had been placed upon Sammy; John had taken £28.15s, but would have to pay out £43. 2s. 6d should Judd the Coal Heaver win. Not that John had a chance of doing this for he had only £4. 10s. to cover any such situation; Samuel Medina just *had* to win for the plan to succeed. John was, in fact, the biggest gambler of them all.

'Can you take him, Sammy lad?' he asked in hushed tones, having taken Samuel to the far end of the bar where they would not be overheard.

Samuel nodded. 'He will out-strength me and he is young and athletic, but I have been in that position before. I believe I would normally best him in about half an hour.'

'I don't like that word *normally*,' John grimaced.

'You need have no fear, John,' said Sammy. 'He has been drinking heavily the whole while you have been taking bets. That will give him courage but it will also slow him down and affect his stamina. He will be out on his feet within fifteen minutes without me having to hit him. The man's all hammer and no nail.'

'Capital – capital, Sammy lad,' whispered John, 'so what rules do you want me arrange.'

'It matters nought to me,' said Samuel arrogantly, 'his only chance is to hold me and hit me, but I am confident I can also out-wrestle him. Just make sure he cannot hold me by the hair and hit me; other than that I am happy.'

The alehouse kitchen was hardly an adequate venue for the meeting of the seconds, but that was all that seemed to be available to them. John, the innkeeper and Judd's second crammed into a corner much to the displeasure of the innkeeper's wife and the two serving girls who were trying to cook and serve meals whilst the meeting took place. The men were forced to move more than once during their discussions.

'Are you familiar with Broughton's Rules, gentlemen? John asked. Judd's second shook his head; the innkeeper nodded, although without any conviction. 'Have you refereed before, Innkeeper?' John continued.

'No, but I know what to do,' the innkeeper replied boldly.

'Good,' said John, 'then I suggest that the rules are based on Broughton – agreed gentlemen?' Both men nodded, but after a moment the innkeeper said apologetically.

'Can you just remind me what exactly they are – for Judd's sake, if you know what I mean?'

'Certainly, said John with bravado. 'A square of 3 feet shall be scratched in the centre your back yard. Each second is to bring his man to the side of the square, and place him opposite to the other. It shall *not* be lawful for one to strike at the other until they are fairly set-to. If, when the set-to has started, a man has fallen, then his second has half a minute to bring his man *up to scratch;* to the side of the square. If he does not within that time, then he shall be deemed a beaten man. Only the two principals, the two seconds and the referee shall be allowed near the square. Neither man is to hit his adversary when he is down or seize him by the hair, the breeches or any part below the waist, for that shall be deemed a foul. The referee will also act as umpire in the event of a dispute.'

'That sounds perfectly fair and clear to me,' said the innkeeper feigning a knowledge and experience that he didn't possess, 'but how big will the ring be?'

'This will be defined by the lookers-on, who will be pushed back against the perimeters of the yard, with the scratched square at its centre. We would look for an area of about twelve feet square for the ring, and a further gap of a foot round the edge to separate the crowd. Perhaps you could find me some posts and a rope to keep them back, Innkeeper?' John said as an aside.

The innkeeper nodded as he and John turned to Judd's second looking for his response, but none came; his countenance displayed only bewilderment.

'Well sir?' said John.

'What?' said the second.

'Do we have your agreement to these rules?' prompted John.

'Can't they just fight, like?' he said.

'So they shall, my man,' said John, 'but the wagers are dependant on the result. We must be clear when we have a winner so that the winnings can be paid out. You see that don't you, sir?'

'Aye – *aye!*' said the second with misplaced authority, for he did not really understand what John was talking about. For him a fight was just a fight, and bets were made with your drinking companions across an ale-strewn table.

'Capital – capital,' said John, 'then let us enjoy our sport today.'

Word of the proposed set-to had spread like a forest fire around the neighbourhood, so that when John and Samuel emerged into the yard a cheering crowd of spectators met them. The clientele of the alehouse had swelled to around 150 people and the yard could not really accommodate them properly: people sat on walls and neighbouring roofs, and hung out of windows. The fighting ring was reduced to no more that nine feet square. Seeing the throng, John's immediate thoughts were of a missed opportunity in that an admission charge of a shilling could have brought him at least another £7. 10s. Aside from this, he also now worried that the sheer number of people would block his escape route, which he needed in the event of Samuel losing. With no means of paying off the wagers he had only his silver tongue to extricate him from such a predicament. He was suddenly gripped with alarm: in such circumstances passions would be running high and no amount of soft soap would succeed; people would simply not be prepared to listen.

Samuel, on the other hand, seemed to be fearless. Further, the roar of the crowd released all the showmanship in him. His natural exhibitionism was suddenly freed, spurred by the sight of this expectant throng. He was stripped to the waist wearing only his breeches, stockings and shoes, and the crowd got their first view of his physique. His barrel chest and powerful arms were accentuated by the drizzle that continued to fall, so that his olive skin glistened like the patina on a bronze statue, and a number of the spectators began to turn to each other, nodding their heads in recognition that the Jew was after all a man of strength and athleticism. On reaching the ring, Samuel took up his fighting stance and shadow boxed for a few moments bringing a mocking roar from the crowd. Turning to the audience, he bowed acknowledging their roar with a wave of his fist, which he had thrust high into the air, saluting as if he were already the victor.

Judd arrived moments later and again was met by a cheer from the expectant crowd. He had removed his topcoat but retained his shirt. He was a back yard brawler and that was all he knew, but he was good at it. He knew that even a formal set-to was normally a brutal affair, won by the most powerful man. He was bemused by all the rigmarole, but he was confident nonetheless.

The innkeeper announced the rules under which the set-to was to be fought; emphasising in particular that if the crowd invaded the square he would declare the match *no contest* and all bets would be void. The crowd booed loudly at this, but it was no more than enthusiasm and they were enjoying the unexpected spectacle that was now unfolding before them. They had come to see a beating but it now seemed they were to see a contest after all.

John then introduced '*Judd the Coal Heaver*' and the crowd cheered the man on whom their wagers rested, or in some cases just because he was the local man. Judd came forward instinctively, gesturing his acknowledgement with a nod before returning to his second. When '*Samuel the Jew*' was introduced the crowd jeered, but surprisingly, amongst those jeers were some cheers as well. Samuel came forward brazenly and then raised his hands before performing a revolution so that everyone could see him. The crowd responded and the mixture of cheers and jeers for the showman posturing before them increased in volume.

The innkeeper summoned the seconds to bring Judd and Samuel to the side of the square and asked each one in turn if his man was ready. Both replied '*Aye*', whereupon the innkeeper signalled to a man who was sitting at the front holding an impromptu bell. The bell was rung - the fight was on.

Samuel had developed his own unique boxing stance from his scientific study of pugilism and immediately took it up. His posture was inclined; both legs bent, the left leg advanced, arms directly before his chin. Judd came forward standing upright and this exaggerated the difference in size between them. To any uncommitted spectator it looked like an appalling mismatch. Straight away Judd aimed round blows at Samuel's upper body.

Samuel smiled to himself, dismissing his opponent as a man who was ignorant of boxing. He retreated skilfully so that the first few shots missed their target, and the crowd booed their displeasure, but then he parried a left and then a right. It had been his intention to box defensively until his adversary's superior strength was lessened by fatigue, but the round blows Judd was throwing left the Coal Heaver exposed. Samuel instinctively realised that a forward strike would reach its object before a circular one, and aimed a straight left through his opponent's non-existent guard. It landed forcefully on Judd's nose, which began immediately to run red with blood.

It was Samuel's first blow, but it staggered Judd nonetheless and a look of incomprehension overtook him as his senses returned. He wiped his nose and looked down at the blood on his hand and sleeve, his chest swelling with anger. He now ventured forward wildly, trying to grab his opponent, but Samuel was a master at keeping his balance, easily able to evade Judd's grasp by changing position either right or left.

This was the pattern of the fight for about eight minutes, by which time Judd was already showing signs of fatigue, and Samuel, having read the signs, deemed it time to go on the offensive. He evaded a round, right-hand strike by moving fleetingly to his left, and was just preparing to strike a downward blow to his opponent's head when he lost his footing on the slippery, drizzle-soaked cobblestones. He put both hands down on the ground to break his fall and came to rest on one knee. The bell rang out to signify that a man was down, but Judd was not to be stopped by any such rule. He turned and grabbed Samuel by the head with his left arm and then pummelled him with his right hand.

John shouted out *'Foul!'* prompting the innkeeper to try to stop Judd, but with little success. The bell began to ring continuously and pandemonium broke out. The crowd stood and bellowed their discontent, for surprisingly some of them had now changed their allegiance to Samuel. Many had been on the wrong end of Judd's belligerence and the thought that he might possibly be beaten was beginning to dawn on them.

John now entered the square and together with the innkeeper managed to loosen Judd's grip so that Samuel was able to free himself. Judd's second then followed, complaining bitterly to the innkeeper, but his protestations were waved away because he had agreed to the rules. *'He has just a half-minute then,'* yelled the second at the innkeeper, who nodded his approval.

All eyes turned to Samuel who was helped away by John. 'Are you all right Sammy lad,' said John throwing water over his charge and then slapping his face fiercely when no immediate reply came. 'Sammy lad,' he continued, 'talk to me Sammy.'

'Get me to the side of the square,' Samuel mumbled barely comprehensively, his eyes still betraying the fact that his senses had not yet cleared. More water was thrown over him and he shook his head in a renewed effort to cast away the shackles that had clamped his wits. He leaned heavily on John as he was taken back to the side of the square to signify his willingness to continue.

Wielding a towel, John gave his charge a rough rubbing down, murmuring in his ear, 'Stay away from him until your senses clear.' Blearily, Samuel nodded to indicate that some of his faculties had returned as the innkeeper yelled, *'Fight on!'*

Samuel walked gingerly forward and then veered to his left. Judd raced across the square to get at him. Samuel now changed body position subtly to the right to evade the lunge, but at the same time grabbed Judd by the shirt and using his opponent's momentum, swung him around so that the Coal Heaver lost his footing and he was thrown heavily to the ground. The bell rang again, but Judd's hurts were not severe, although he had been badly grazed on the arm, shoulder, and face - and like his nose, these wounds sprang with blood. More importantly, however, it had given Samuel crucial seconds in which to regain his wits. Both men eagerly re-approached the side of the square, Judd throwing off his shirt in the direction of his second as he did so; he did not mean to be vulnerable to a throw again.

'*Fight on!*' yelled the innkeeper again. Judd rushed forward. Samuel had expected it and skilfully sidestepped him, aiming a powerful downward right to the side of Judd's head. Though dazed the Coal Heaver did not go down, but the pattern of the fight was now set, with Samuel continuing to evade his antagonist's lunges while connecting with powerful blows to Judd's head and torso.

As fatigue set in, Judd's swings grew increasingly wild and he began to sway. After eighteen minutes he was out on his feet.

The set-to was now a forgone conclusion. Samuel could have ended it at any time he wanted, but the showman in him surfaced and he began to demonstrate all his skills to the baying crowd, eventually standing back, his arms raised as if victory was already his. Half the crowd cheered, followed by jeering from those who had wagered heavily on Judd. Teasingly, Samuel had left himself in an exposed position, his hands not in any position to defend himself, but Judd was unable to take advantage of it.

Unable to pursue his tormentor, the Coal Heaver stood swaying in the centre of the ring, his features bloodied, his legs wobbling. He bent over and vomited profusely. Samuel stood back and waited while Judd, taking great gasps of air, straightened himself, wiping the excess vomit and blood from his mouth as he did so. He again brought his hands up to defend himself, but he continued to sway.

'You have taken liberties with my faith you vulgar fellow,' barked Samuel addressing his remark to the crowd as much as to his opponent. 'If you will offer me your apology then I will cease this thrashing and we can take a tankard of ale together.'

The crowd roared again – they had never seen such a display. Samuel had a natural ability to work an audience and this seemed every bit as skilful as his pugilistic talents. He now put his hands on his hips and pranced backwards and forwards like a matador before a defeated bull, delaying the kill so that the crowd could share his delight in the victory. But unlike the bull Judd was being offered a stay of execution, although whether he understood that after the beating he had been given was uncertain.

John yelled at Samuel to finish Judd off; he wanted certainty about the result for him to collect his winnings. The crowd similarly yelled for the victor to carry on, although in most cases for the less noble reason of sheer bloodlust. Nevertheless Samuel repeated his offer.

'Come my good fellow, will you offer me your apologies?'

Judd's second and some of the gamblers implored the Coal Heaver to fight on, and with his last ounces of strength he dragged his weary legs forward in an ungainly shuffle and lunged a wild round arm punch at Samuel. It was easily evaded, but as Judd's body recoiled to a square-on position, a devastating blow from Samuel connected and he dropped like a stone to his knees, falling forward onto his face. His second tried hard to revive him within the half-minute available, but there was no fight left in him and the innkeeper raised Samuel's arm in triumph.

Many of the crowd now began to drift away, some clearly disgruntled at losing their wagers, but to John's surprise some of the crowd that remained continued to cheer. There appeared to be no suspicion from them that there had been a set-up. They milled around Samuel eager to pat him on the back and congratulate him, and the throng ushered him back into the alehouse to start festivities. Drinks were bought and lined up on the bar for him and a night of unexpected revelry commenced. The atmosphere was one of elation that appeared to be shared as much by the crowd as by Samuel and John. This was borne out of basic human nature – the need for a day of reckoning. They were revelling in the fact that Judd the Coal Heaver had got his comeuppance at last. As the evening wore on Samuel was assailed with stories of Judd's violence, his loutish, brutish behaviour.

John Campbell-John announced that he would repair to the innkeeper's kitchen to pay out the winners who had wagered on Samuel the Jew. He knew very well that nobody had actually placed such a wager, but it was all part of the confidence trick, and he duly went through to the kitchen and idled for ten minutes or so, making himself unpopular with the innkeeper's wife. On his return he stood a round of ales to cement his popularity with those who were still present It had the desired effect, but he need not have bothered; Judd the Coal Heaver was not a popular man. The innkeeper advised that he expected a good house for the evening when word got around.

The innkeeper was proved to be correct and the *Turks Head* began to fill up again. The fight over, gambling and wenching were now on John's mind. He looked around and decided that a half crown would probably procure him one of the finer looking lasses that were beginning to arrive. But gambling was his first priority.

'Who will join me in a round of cards,' he proclaimed and three willing takers came forward. He shouted in the direction of Samuel. 'Will you join us also Samuel the Jew?'

'I fear I'm unskilled at cards, sir,' replied Samuel, 'and have little funds with me anyway.'

'Well it is time you learned such skills young fellow,' said John still addressing the crowd as much as Samuel. 'And for your sport today I will stand for your ale all evening and what is more, purchase you lodgings for the night.' He turned to the innkeeper and enquired, 'do you have two rooms available?'

'Aye sir,' replied the innkeeper responding in the same manner as the question, with loud joviality. A cheer went up from the crowd.

Samuel took a seat at the table, his natural reluctance overruled by the excitement coursing through his veins from his victory, now spiced by the ale he was drinking.

'What shall we play gentleman?' asked John. 'What takes your fancy: ombre; quadrille; quintile; picquet; basset; faro; whist; cribbage; put; loo?' He rattled off the names as if he was indeed a gentleman soldier who customarily whiled away the hours playing cards in the officer's mess.

'Brag is played here mostly,' said one of the competitors, 'not your fancy London games.'

'Then brag it shall be gentlemen,' said John, with all the bravado he could muster. 'And Samuel the Jew,' he continued, 'I shall also stand you thirty shillings for your stake in this game.' A groan went up from his dismayed fellow competitors; such a sizeable stake was far too rich for their pockets.

'I'm obliged to you sir.' Playing his part, Samuel took a seat opposite John at the gaming table.

The game continued for a couple of hours and to his surprise Samuel had some success, but as he soon discovered, it is in the nature of the game of brag that winnings can be lost as quickly as they are won, disappearing like water escaping from a leaky canteen. Nevertheless, Samuel found the game exhilarating and enjoyable. John had won most of Samuel's money back, but his winnings overall were only a few pounds. Such a sum a week ago would have been affluence to him, but he now had over £40 in his pocket, more than a year's wages to a soldier, and enough to finance a game with much higher stakes than was to be found in this provincial inn.

The game itself had taken on some celebrity in the inn. There was, of course, the presence of the young Jew boy who had thrashed the town bully, and the handsome dashing army captain who had run the book. This was an unfamiliar and exotic mix for the *Turks Head* and a crowd soon gathered around the table, interested in every hand and applauding what they saw as good play. Both John and Samuel initially revelled in this status as it nurtured the one thing that they had in common – their extroversion. So much so that John in particular began to play to the viewing crowd. His natural wit went into overdrive as he began to ridicule Judd the Coal Heaver and his second.

'That Judd fellow; not the sharpest knife in the box is he?' John noticed the grins among the crowd and felt confident that they were with him. He was right; they liked nothing better than hearing someone putting down the local bully. 'He's about as quick witted as a corpse, is he not?' John continued. The crowd laughed at the comment.

'Aye,' said Samuel joining in, 'he's all candle and no wick.'

'Aye he is that,' said John, 'I bet he thinks a myth is a female moth.' The crowd bayed and the other players slapped the table in agreement. John was now on a roll. 'And that second of his – he probably thinks Noah's wife was called "Joan of Ark!"' The crowd cheered, and emboldened, one of the card players joined in the mockery.

'The pair on 'em likely thinks the four seasons be salt, pepper, mustard and vinegar.' The crowd howled their approval.

The scene for the evening was set: Samuel and John were celebrities – and were to be treated as such. This was a situation John knew he could exploit, and as a consequence he began to tire of gaming. His thoughts turned to other sins. There had appeared amongst the crowd several young ladies attracted by this celebrity, and John in particular began to notice. It was as though some powerful magnetic force came into play and after a time both he and Samuel found they had a woman seated on either side of them.

Wenching rather than gaming was soon uppermost in John's mind. 'Shall we make this our last hand gentlemen?' he asked, to the displeasure of the assembled crowd, adding, 'perhaps we can resume later?' The showman in him knew instinctively that it was always best to leave his audience wanting more.

Samuel picked up his three cards one by one and each time spied a deuce. Three twos! It was the best hand he had pulled all evening and he had learned enough to know that it was worth a substantial wager. At which point he felt a hand on his right thigh. He looked round into the eyes of a young lady seated beside him, who had also spied the three deuces. She eased forward as their eyes met so that there was an intimacy to their closeness. She smiled seductively: a smile that was both an acknowledgement of the strength of his hand and an expression of her interest in him personally.

John was a fine card player and he too had noticed that smile. He tried to decide if it meant Samuel had been dealt an exceptional hand or whether it simply reflected the young lady's interest in his friend - or both.

The woman was not dressed in any finery; Samuel recognised her as one of he serving girls – in fact she was the innkeeper's daughter. She was about eighteen or so and had that chubby beauty that youth presents and age quickly takes away, but ageing had not yet begun and her cheeks were full and naturally rosy. They were replicated in her bosom, only barely restrained by her stays. Above those cheeks were two very large and very round brown eyes, not unlike his own, and they matched the rest of her appearance to perfection. She was big-boned and bonny in the best traditions of an alehouse girl. Samuel looked down at his cards and then back to her eyes. She did not avert her gaze in any display of coyness, whether real or mimicked. It was merely a look of confirmation to remove any sense of doubt – to verify her interest in him. The player to his right nudged his attention back to the game and Samuel wagered cautiously not wanting to give away the strength of his hand. By the time the round came to him again, three players had folded leaving him with just two opponents. He raised the stakes and only John matched him. They continued to raise each other round after round until Samuel was out of funds. 'What will it take to *see you?*' he asked.

'A half-crown,' said John.

'Will you stand me a half-crown?'

John puffed out his cheeks. 'Now here is a lesson for you, Samuel the Jew. On any ordinary day you will not get credit from a *stranger* at the card table. If you can't mach the bet - then you lose.'

'Then sir, I fear I must learn my lesson and lose,' said Samuel as the attentive crowd heaved a collective sigh.

'Hush!' said John, to nobody in particular. 'Well said young sir. But then, this is no ordinary day is it? We have all had good sport today because of you, Samuel the Jew. Yes sir, I *will* stand you that half crown. Come let's play our hands.'

John placed on the table a flushed run: ace-two-three of diamonds, and the crowd applauded. 'Now let that be another lesson for you,' John laughed. 'You can still lose money on a good hand when your opponent has an even better one!'

Samuel kept a straight face, 'Thank you for your good advice, soldier, for it is amply demonstrated by *this* hand.' Slowly, he laid down his three deuces, 'You see; I have an even better hand than you.' The girl at his side leant forward and kissed him on the cheek and the crowd applauded even more enthusiastically.

'The pot is yours Samuel the Jew,' said John, 'and I it looks to me as if you have won the wench as well.

CHAPTER 5

Samuel had revelled in the day. He was at heart a showman and had been able to satisfy that need within him. The day had been about so much more than the street fights he had engineered previously: instead of the usual handful of people he'd had an audience of more than a hundred. Indeed, he reflected, in just a couple of days he had lost his virginity, earned money from two fights, learned how to play games of chance, learned how to wager and on top of it all, had been well fed and drunk his fill. And as if that were not enough, he had been able to do all these things as a showman. In John he had found a friend who shared that showmanship, a commonality of character - if an isolated one; they were not at all alike in other respects.

He climbed the stairs with his spirits high and his arm around the serving girl following John and the Mabel he had procured for himself. Samuel felt no coyness as he had with Ginny and had nothing more than simple lust on his mind at this time. He had entered a world that was new to him: its vices were tempting him and he was intent on drinking from its fountain.

The serving girl showed John to his room and with his wench clinging to him he staggered to the door. They fell through it, laughing as they did so. Grinning as they both attempted to reach the bed before they fell down again, the serving girl closed the door behind them. Turning back to Samuel, she indicated another room. He opened the door expecting her to follow, but she hesitated. He started to speak and then realised he had not even asked her name.

'Nell,' she said, realising instinctively what was his problem, 'I'm called Nell.'

'Are you not coming in with me, Miss Nell?'

'I'm in that room over there,' she said, pointing to the room at the end of the corridor. 'My dad's room is next to yours. He'll hear us if I come in here.'

'I'll come to your room, then,' said Samuel.

'Yes, but you'll have to wait. My dad will be up to bed in a few minutes, and he'll check to see that I'm alone. Give it half an hour and then come to me, lover,' she said with a smile.

Samuel nodded and went into his room. He lay on the bed and waited, fighting to stay awake, but failed; the sleep intent on taking him soon engulfed his inebriated state. He came to with a start when he heard the innkeeper dragging his weary bones to bed, the sound of his leather heels clopping against the wooden floor. Samuel resolved now to stay awake, but again failed miserably.

He awoke to find Nell shaking him back to consciousness. He sat up with a start and was met by the girl's face looming over him. She held her finger to her lips and whispered a pronounced '*Sushhhhhhhh!* Take your boots off and carry them.'

He did as he was bid and she led him by the hand along the corridor to her room. She closed the door, gently removed his boots from his hand to lay them on the floor, then putting her arms around his neck, she kissed him forcefully. She had removed her own boots along with her stays and outer skirt, so that she wore only her undergarment: a thin, linen nightshift. She had reached up on tiptoes to kiss him and as she returned her heels to the ground Samuel was acutely aware of the feeling of her breasts trailing downwards against his chest. He found it arousing, but he also felt suddenly nervous. The girl seemed to posses an experience in these matters that he did not. She sat on the bed and the nightshift fell off her left shoulder, the drawstring around the neckline having already been loosened, to reveal most of her breast. She then leaned back and taking hold of the bottom of her shift began to raise it slowly and sensually, at the same time looking up at him provocatively. She was teasing him – it was tease without any subtlety in that it lacked refinement, but it was successful nonetheless. Samuel was captivated.

Nell was still wearing her stockings, but as the shift edged upwards he saw that they extended to only just above her knees. The shift was calf-length when she started, but in her hands it continued to rise slowly, inch by provocative inch, as if she were Salome herself teasing King Herod. There was no hint of reserve in her performance and she studied his reactions intently. He in turn looked down at her plump white thighs and his expectations were not the only things to rise.

'You haven't had your prize yet, have you?' Nell said shamelessly.

'Prize?' He was clearly confused.

'For winning the fight, silly,' she giggled.

'Oh!' he stuttered, 'I see – yes the fight. And what is to be my prize then?'

'This is to be your prize.' Artlessly, she raised her nightshift further and further until she was fully revealed to him. He looked down at her exposed loins and then back to her eyes.

'Is it not a beautiful prize lover?' she said.

'Aye, it is as fine a quim as I have seen,' he said forcefully, intent on being as gallant as he could, but in fact overwhelmed by the situation.

'Your hand is shaking lover,' Nell looked at it and then back at him, a mischievous smile taking over her features. She paused, impishly moistening her lips with the tip of her tongue. 'It would be a shame to waste it, would it not?'

'Aye it would,' he replied, but the vulgar implication passed him by as he did not know what she meant.

'Come on then lover,' she raised her arm and gestured for him to join her on the bed. She lay back in expectation as he sat down beside her, but it appeared he still did not know what he was supposed to do. He leaned over to kiss her gently on the lips and she kept her eyes open in surprise. It was a tenderness she had not expected, and Nell, surprised to find that she liked it, allowed him to continue.

Samuel exposed her breast with his hand and caressed her nipples with his fingers in the way Ginny had shown him, nuzzling her neck and moving his lips to her mouth as he did so.

Again, his gentleness appealed to Nell. Though young she was sexually experienced, but this was not something she had encountered before. Her previous liaisons had been influenced heavily by alcohol and had reflected athleticism, eagerness and zeal, but certainly not tenderness. Nell allowed herself some time to enjoy it, but all too soon her ardour mounted. She became impatient with him and taking his hand placed it up between her legs. It was soon clear to her that he had little knowledge of a woman's anatomy and did not know how to pleasure her, so grasping his fumbling fingers she manipulated them, her body arching in response to his touch.

Samuel's feelings of naivety escalated, but he resolved to learn all he could from Nell. She directed his movements as if she was conducting some erotic symphony, and he was content to be merely an ensemble player.

Nell began to utter little cries, her fat cheeks glowing red as her sensations mounted and then she arched her back and let out a high, gasping scream.

Startled, Samuel pulled his hand away. Her reactions alarmed him, not only because he did not know what was happening to her and thought he must have hurt her, but also because he was afraid her father would hear the noise she was making. His ardour rapidly diminishing, he raised himself on his elbow and looked down at her flushed face. 'I must offer you my apologies if I have hurt you, Miss Nell.'

She did not respond immediately, but grasped his hand, pulled it back against her and gripped it tightly. She held her breath for what seemed to Samuel like an eternity, and then released it slowly, at the same time relaxing her muscles like a punctured carnival balloon slowly deflating. For a moment she lay limp and then languorously giggled.

Samuel was perplexed. 'Are you alright, Miss Nell?'

'Aye, I'm alright, lover - you haven't hurt me. It was just Cupid's desire that took hold of me.'

'I'm pleased to hear that, Miss Nell.' He breathed a sign of relief.

Amused, she lifted a finger to touch the end of his nose. 'You're a strange fellow, Samuel Medina. Are you always this polite?'

'I hope so. Is it not good manners to be polite?'

'Why yes, but there's a time and place you know and when a young man feels lusty, a girl don't expect such fancy words.'

'Do I not please you? I'm sorry if I don't come up to expectations.'

'There you go again, lover,' she said with a smile. 'You're doing just fine. Come on now, take your clothes off and we'll see what I can do for *you*.'

'I'm sure that I can manage without removing my garments, Miss Nell.'

'Of course you can, but why would you want to?'

'I... that is, I would not...' overtaken with shyness, Samuel hesitated, 'erm... feel comfortable to be naked in the presence of a lady.'

Once more Nell giggled, 'That's all right then for *I* am no lady.'

Samuel did not know how to respond to this. His embarrassment was mounting in tandem with his sense of naivety and all he really wanted was to get the whole thing over with so that he could return to his room. He sat up on the edge of the bed and looked back at her, speechless.

Reading the reluctance stamped on his face, Nell endeavoured to take control of the situation. 'Just relax,' she said kindly, 'and let me take over from here.' She got up and knelt before him, her shift loose and clinging precariously to her shoulders, her luxurious breasts exposed. Making no attempt to conceal them, Nell slowly undid Samuel's neck-cloth and removed it. His shirt was made of heavy linen, cut full with wide, billowing sleeves gathered into a band at the neck and also at the cuffs, where they were fastened with buttons at the wrist. She undid these, pulled the shirt up and away from his breeches and then over his head. She then pushed herself higher on her knees so that she could caress his torso, running her hands over his rippling muscles, her fingers rising and falling in response to his undulating form. She felt his arms; his shoulders, his biceps, his chest, and marvelled in his physique.

'You really are quite a surprise underneath, aren't you?'

'Aye, I'm an athletic fellow all right,' he gasped.

'Now lie back and we'll get rid of those stockings and breeches,' she said.

His breeches were fastened at the back with a waist buckle and reached to just below the knee. She undid the buckle with some dexterity, releasing the breeches so that she could pull them down. He lay there in his draws and stockings, but was too shy to be aroused by her attentions. Next she removed his stockings leaving him reclining in only his draws, which were the next objective in her manoeuvres.

Made of cotton flannelling, knee-length and tied at the waist and knees, men's draws were not the most attractive of items. Samuel, doubly uncomfortable now that his erection had disappeared along with his confidence, was resolved to keep them on for the duration of the coupling, but Nell was having none of it.

Brushing aside his feeble attempt to resist, she undid the fastenings and removed the offending draws. 'The house has fallen down,' she said, looking down at his flaccid state. She then looked into his eyes and smiled playfully.

Her intention had been only to tease him, but he misunderstood. 'I must apologise, Miss Nell, if I am failing to give satisfaction,' he said stiffly.

'Silly boy,' she wagged her finger at him, 'you underestimate my powers of building. I'll rebuild this house back up even higher than it was before.'

She was as good as her word. She took his member and deftly manipulated it, and with that manipulation he began to relax and enjoy the pleasures that she was introducing him to. She straddled his torso and guided him into her, and then allowed him to take a lead. He rolled her over and she allowed him that dominance and was content to enjoy his athleticism as he mounted her. His appetite was returned to him, but there was now no tenderness in his activities, just lusty gusto as if he were some rutting stag in a frenzy of springtime mating. But this was exactly what Nell's previous experience of sex had been: the thrill of the romp and the naughtiness of the nakedness, but without the complex pleasures and genuine excitement of mutually responsive lovemaking. In this respect she too betrayed her inexperience.

When their ardour was spent they collapsed together still entwined on the sweat-stained bed their own adding to the vintage. His strong arms held her tightly; she was restricted and uncomfortable, but there was a pleasure in that nonetheless. The pleasure of merely being held in the arms of a powerful man can itself be a delight, she learned.

They stayed like that for a half hour or so until he released his grip and made to get up and re-robe, so that he could return to his room. She pulled him back and put her arm across his chest.

'No lover, you'll sleep here with me tonight,' she said.

'But your father?' he replied.

'Oh I have to be up before him, you can go back to your room then,' she said.

But this was a lie. She wanted him to stay with her for an altogether different reason. Her bedroom was at the back of the inn, and to the side of her window was a hoist with a small landing on the outside that was used for deliveries. It meant there was easy access to her room without the need to go through the inn. This route had been used many times by Nell's lover - and Nell's lover was Judd the Coal Heaver. Her mission all along had been one of entrapment. Judd was not a man to play the humble role of the honourably vanquished. As one of life's bullies he had no natural friends, but he did have partners in crime, and the winnings from the book that John had run was enough enticement for them to be seconded into his service. Hearing that the two men would be staying at the inn overnight, he had sent word to Nell to make sure Samuel was in her room and if possible without his clothes. This task she had now completed more than satisfactorily.

Relaxing at her explanation, Samuel allowed sleep to take him, and he slept with an unexpected tranquillity, his arm around Nell. But sleep did not come to *her*. Expectancy kept it away, but as she lay listening intently for the sounds that would foretell the coming of her lover, she became increasingly troubled. Conscience can be a powerful emotion and it was challenging her sense of right and wrong. She had thought it the right thing to do to support her man, but that was before she knew Samuel. He would now surely get hurt if not killed and all because of her, yet he had shown her nothing but politeness and respect; he had been a sensitive lover and a considerate companion. Judd was none of these things and she wondered why she went with him, but could not come up with an answer. He never brought her presents; he never took her anywhere; they had fun romping together, that was true, but he was always gone by the morning and he was only ever back when his ruttishness returned. In reality she went with him because, quite simply, he was the dominant male in the town, and a prized catch. Deep down she believed that they would marry; that he would become her mate and provide her with strong children the image of himself.

She lay looking at the ceiling by the dim light of the oil lamp and these thoughts troubled her mind, until she heard a faint sound on the cobblestones outside.

It was the sound of footsteps – someone trying to tread quietly, but failing. The cobblestones were wet in the evening rain and the intruders were wearing heavy boots, their progress hindered by the tendency to slip. She heard low voices and murmurs, and held her breath as she tried to hear what was being said, but the whispers were lost in the sounds of the rain. The pulley creaked as it took the weight of somebody climbing up the rope. She heard the clop of a boot against the landing to the side of her window, and then moments later the sound of the pulley creaking once more, a second man was now climbing up the rope. She eased herself gently out of bed to avoid waking Samuel, and gently looked through the curtains to the cobbles below. She saw four men on the ground looking up at the hoist, which was not in her vision. The trap had been sprung and the quarry ensnared and she knew her part had been played to perfection.

But instead of satisfaction, a different emotion gripped her – that of apprehension. It was instinctive as was her reaction to it. Without any rationalisation in her own mind, she was taken with fear for Samuel's safety, and without a moment's thought, she acted on that fear. She turned and roused him violently, speaking in a heavy whisper so as not to alert Judd and his followers outside.

'Quick! Quick!' She shook Samuel's shoulders, her face only inches from his. 'There are men outside who have come to get you. Go! Go! – you're in danger!'

For a split second the reality of what was happening failed to enter his sleepy mind. He looked at her heavy-eyed with bewilderment. She repeated her warning, 'Go! Go! – you're in danger!' And then Samuel heard the sounds outside the window and suddenly all was clear to him. He sprang from the bed, threw on his breeches and with one arm through his shirtsleeve, he bolted for the door. He scurried into the corridor shouting the alarm for John, but came to an abrupt halt unable to remember which room John was in. He glanced back down the corridor at Nell's room to see her framed anxiously in the doorway, gesturing frantically at another door. *It's that one! That one!'*

Samuel burst into the room Nell indicated, making no attempt to knock. John and his Mabel were still clothed, John having removed only the tunic of his uniform before passing out. The commotion roused him from his drunken slumber, but he was in no condition to respond sensibly and looked up with incomprehension as Samuel pulled him up roughly by his shirt and before he could defend himself, slapped him heavily around the face. About to retaliate, John was sufficiently jolted into making sense of what Samuel was saying.

'John; wake up! Quick! There are men after us – and our money. We have to take flight or fight for our lives.'

Comprehension now hit John like a blacksmith's hammer, immediately followed by rush of fear that cast away the remnants of his drunkenness. He leapt to his feet and looked around, first for his sword and then his money. He buckled on his scabbard, tossed a few coins on the bed for his Mabel and stashed the rest in his ever-bulging pockets. The woman sleepily raised herself onto her elbows, coming awake enough to sense the alarm, but she cared more for the money than her own safety and quickly thrusting the meagre coins into her bodice, she dived under the bed.

'Leave it!' Samuel shouted as his impatience and anxiety mounted. 'You can't run with all those coins weighing you down.'

'I'm not leaving it,' John snapped back at him. And then more reasonably, 'How many are there?'

'Don't know,' said Samuel, 'but it would be wise to assume they know we can fight and will have enough men to best us it should come to that.'

'Agreed,' said John, 'so what do you suggest we do?'

'I suggest that we take flight – and if you can manage it, sooner rather than later,' Samuel added, unable to contain his sarcasm.

'I agree.' A naturally cunning man, John thought for a brief moment, said, 'But a diversion is also called for, I think, to give us time to get away.'

Samuel, one hand on the door, looked back at him. 'Got anything in mind?

'Maybe. Where are they now – have they gained entry yet?'

'I don't know,' said Samuel, 'but they're likely to come in through Nell's bedroom window.'

'Then that's the place to stop them, Sammy lad, if we're not too late.'

The two men charged down the corridor and burst into Nell's room. She looked up at them with a mixture of disbelief and horror on her face at the sight of them re-entering the danger scene. She then looked back at the window, where a large, burly man had just put a leg over the sill; his arm and torso quickly following. Samuel recognised the man who had acted as Judd's second.

'Oh no you don't!' yelled John, who charged at the man hitting him forcefully against the shoulder, his momentum pushing the man back through the window frame. The intruder grabbed the sill to stop himself from falling, but his leg remained through the window. He hung on frantically, but his trapped leg had become a hindrance to him affecting his grip so that he was unable to get enough purchase to right himself. Samuel now joined in, slamming the window down as far as it would go and then lifting the man's leg off the ground meaning to push it back through the window. This proved much easier than expected for once the man's foot had left the ground he had even less purchase than before and his instinctive reaction was to retract his leg in order to strengthen his grip.

'Move away Sammy lad,' shouted John pulling his sword out of its scabbard.

'No!' shouted Samuel, 'I'll not be a party to a killing.'

'I'm not going to kill him,' said John, 'I'm going to hack at his fingers.'

'I'll not be a party to that either,' repeated Samuel. 'The man has a right to earn his living. If you take his fingers he won't be able to do that.'

'Jesus! You're a strange cove, Samuel Medina.' John grimaced in irritation. 'This man and his accomplices wish you nothing but harm. They'll show *you* no Christian charity you fool - c'mon, let me at him.'

Samuel blocked his path, 'Nevertheless, I will show them Jewish charity – the man's fingers remain intact.'

'Is it alright if I just cut them?' John mocked, the tip of his sword wavering before him.

Samuel thought for the briefest moment before moving aside. 'Aye – aye, so long as that is all you do.'

As John ran the full length of the blade along the intruder's fingers, biting into the flesh, the man let out a scream of pain. He didn't loosen his grip, but his hand pumped blood.

'He won't be able to hold on much longer,' said John, 'his friends will have to get him down or he'll fall, and that will give us time to get away. Come on Sammy lad he shouted.'

They ran down the hall past the bemused landlord and his wife who had been roused by the commotion. Samuel stopped, meaning to give them his word that he would return to settle his account, but John, shaking his head in disbelief, grabbed Samuel by the billowing sleeve of his shirt and tugged him onward. They rushed down to the ground floor and then to the heavy front door, pulled frantically at the weighty bolts until they were all released with a carillon of deep thuds, but the door would not budge.

'We must get this open Sammy lad,' said John, 'we need the key to release the lock.'

'I'll go.' Samuel turned and ran back up the stairs, meeting Nell on the landing at the top.

'You'll need these Samuel.' She jangled a large bunch of keys at him having anticipated they would be needed. 'It's this one,' she singled out a large key.

Samuel took them from her, and started to rush away, but turning back to her, said, 'thank you,' and kissed her briefly but vigorously on the lips.

To her surprise she reciprocated and then to her further surprise she said, 'I'm sorry.' Samuel looked at her perplexed, then assuming she was sorry he was leaving, he gave her a broad smile, turned and ran down the stairs, but she shouted after him. 'You stay alive now, Samuel Medina.'

'Aye – aye I will lass,' he called over his shoulder, running to the door and holding up the selected key. John took it from him, but hearing the cries of men in the distance he looked briefly back upstairs. 'Dammit! They must have got the injured man down.' He jabbed the key into the lock, turned it and swung open the heavy door.

Samuel darted through, but stopped in his tracks as John shouted *Whoa!*

'What is it?'

'Where do you think you're going Sammy?'

Samuel gazed at John in astonishment, 'As far away from here and as quickly as possible! They're after us. Move!'

'It's their town remember. We can't get a stagecoach until morning and it's still several hours to daybreak. They have the advantage.'

'So what's your plan?' asked Samuel frantically.

'Simple,' said John, 'we leave this front door open, but then hide in here – inside the inn. They'll assume we've gone and they'll be searching the empty streets all night looking for us.'

They raced back up the stairs, but this time trying to be as quiet as they could. Samuel whispered their plan to Nell, enquiring of a place to hide. Gesturing for them to wait she crept back down the corridor and peered cautiously round the half-open door of her room, edging it open inch by inch until she could see inside. Satisfied, she scurried back to tell Samuel that the coast was clear; Judd and his followers were still outside.

'Where can we hide?' John asked.

'On the roof,' she gasped. 'You can get up there from the room Samuel was in.'

The three of them scampered back, tip-toeing past the room where the landlord and his wife, believing everyone had gone, had retired back to bed. Nell led them quietly to Samuel's room, which overlooked the side of the inn and was not visible from the back yard. She opened the sash window, leant out, looked above her to survey the possible escape route, and returning whispered. 'I think you two agile gentleman should be able to negotiate that climb.'

Samuel, eager as ever, was first to try it. He sat on the ledge facing inwards, eased his head and torso out through the gap and then stood up holding onto the window frame with the tips of his fingers. There was a gap in the rain clouds and the moon peeped through giving just enough light for him to see the task ahead of him. He said a little prayer of thank you under his breath and calling down for the other two to hold his legs, reached across for the cast-iron downpipe and then up to the guttering, which was fixed on spiked brackets driven into the wall just below the eaves. Fearing the structure would not take his weight he held his breath for a moment, exhaled then launched himself out of the window. Using his athletic abilities he swung across, balancing his weight between the downpipe and the guttering, and relieving the strain by standing on a gargoyle fixed high on the wall. To his relief the gutter, downpipe and gargoyle remained fixed and he scrambled onto the roof much more easily that he had feared.

He called down for John, who attempted to follow, but didn't get very far. Having edged his torso through the window, he was sitting facing the room unable to stand because his sword and tunic, pockets bulging with money, got in the way. He removed both and handed them up to Samuel. Now unencumbered, he was able to follow Samuel with little trouble, reaching across to the downpipe with one hand while Samuel grasped the other and hauled him onto the roof. Samuel now slithered down on his belly so that his head overlapped the eave and in a heavy whisper called out for Nell. She appeared at the open window and smiled up at him.

'You must tell Judd and his friends we have fled,' he said.

She nodded her understanding and blew him a kiss.

He blew one back at her and then disappeared from her view.

The shock of what she was doing suddenly dawned on Nell and she stood transfixed for a few moments mulling over her betrayal of Judd, her lover. But then a feeling of destiny came over her: she felt comfortable with what she was doing, as if fate itself was leading her in this venture. She recognised in Samuel a goodness that she had rarely encountered before and her maternal instincts had been stimulated to protect and safeguard his wellbeing.

A few minutes later, six burly men entered her room. A bloodied Judd asked her where Samuel and John were and she did as she had promised, feigning alarm and sending them running out into the black night and the empty streets.

Meanwhile, on the roof Samuel and John stood, leaning angled against the slope of the tiled roof, holding their breath until the footsteps disappeared into the distance - and then John started to laugh. The tension was suddenly broken and their fear dissipated with it.

'Is this not a fine adventure,' Sammy lad?' said John.

At first Samuel just looked around at him in disbelief. His heart was pounding and the excitement still coursing through his veins. His breathing was heavy but as it began to ease he saw the truth in John's words: danger can be an adventure in its own right. A feeling of elation now followed for both of them. John's laughter was contagious and it infected Samuel so that he too began to laugh. They laughed together and fuelled by the mutual bonding that was taking place, the intensity of their laughter increased.

'A riddle for you Sammy boy,' said John, 'what did Sir Francis Drake say before the battle with the Spanish.'

'*A riddle*: at a time like this!' said Samuel.

'Come on Sammy boy, answer the riddle now.'

'Oh I don't know – what did Sir Francis Drake say before the battle with the Spanish?' said Samuel playing his part.

'He said, "Let the Armada wait, for my *bowels* can't",' chuckled John.

Samuel paused, but he couldn't stop himself from laughing; it sniggered out of him like a snorting pig, which made John laugh all the more. Spluttering, the men clutched each other, both shushing themselves for they were getting too loud.

'Here's to more bowel churning adventures,' Sammy,' John gasped, raising an imaginary glass, and then quickly returning his hand to the roof to keep his balance. This set Samuel off again, laughing almost uncontrollably until John quieted him down with another voluble: '*Shhhhhh.*'

'Aye,' said Samuel, 'to more adventures.'

'And to partnership,' said John.

'Aye - and to partnership,' agreed Samuel.

'So are you now happy to accept my offer?' said John.

'Offer?'

'Aye,' said John, 'a working partnership. You as the pugilist and me as your second, your agent, your promoter, and I promise you, Sammy lad, I will make us both rich.'

It was a good time for John to press his case. Samuel was in a euphoric state and the day and now the night had been thrilling for him. He shivered involuntarily; he was wearing only his shirt and breeches, but was too exhilarated to feel the chill and any question asked of him at this time would probably have been met with a positive response. He grinned at John. 'Yes let's give it a go, John Campbell-John, but I will also keep my job as long as I am able. I will complete my apprenticeship if at all possible, for my father's sake.'

'Then we should shake hands on our contract,' said John. The two men held out their hands and firmly grasped each other, completing their handshake in an exaggerated way, and then, as their stability wavered, letting go hastily to grab the moss-covered roof for support.

Samuel shivered again, ducking his head to avoid a bat that was flitting and darting in the night sky. He looked up: they had some hours to wait before daylight. The streets were silent; the town still sleeping. Judd and his henchmen long since disappeared.

John studied his companion in a contented way – he had got what he wanted, and now his thoughts turned to other things. 'The ladies seem to like you, Sammy, and I know about ladies – I can promise you that.'

'I don't know about that,' Samuel shrugged. 'The ladies intimidate me. I never know what to say to them.'

'Well, replied John, 'whatever you're saying seems to work. You seem to fashion something in them I've rarely seen before.'

'If I do then I know not why,' replied Samuel, 'but I am determined to overcome my inexperience. I have endeavoured to master Cupid's arts. I shall not remain an apprentice in this enterprise.'

'Aye that's right - if you are to fight like a man then you should learn to wench like a man. I shall make it one of my first tasks as your partner,' said John.

'We have to get home first,' said Samuel, 'how are we to do that safely?'

'No problem, Sammy; we'll stay up here until the dawn breaks and the streets are busy. It will be easy then just to slip away and mingle with the crowd till we get to the coaching inn. We'll be on that stage coach by ten.'

'But what about your debt John – are you to forgo it?'

John stared at Samuel for a few moments. He had forgotten about his deception and was now faced with a judgement. Should he continue with this ruse or should he come clean. He feared that Samuel would not take kindly to being duped, and at another time he would probably have been right, but he resolved to ride on the waves of elation that were carrying them both. He adopted a sheepish expression, but didn't immediately say anything.

'What!' said Samuel.

'Well, you see - there isn't really any debt,' John confessed a little guiltily, attempting to mould his expression into one of ashamed apology.

'I don't understand,' said Samuel.

'I was here some months ago, and that Judd fellow - well he bullied somebody else, an Irishman.'

Samuel frowned, 'I see. So you thought he'd do the same to me and you'd be able to make some money for yourself.'

'For *us* Sammy lad,' said John, 'for us.'

'But how could you be sure I'd fight?'

'Oh come *on*! I thought it likely that Judd fellow would goad you into it, but even *I* couldn't have predicted the strength of your reaction, Sammy lad. You were like a trout leaping at the fly. What was it you said? *"Do not take liberties with my faith, my man",*' John mimicked. 'You really do talk above your station you know,' he looked at Samuel and allowed himself to smile: that naughty little boy look that he had perfected as a child and which had worked so often in the past – and was to work again.

Samuel returned his smile, 'I have learned that when you talk down to ruffians they never know how to respond. It makes them angry, you know, and angry men are easier to fight.'

'You really *are* a strange cove, Samuel Medina,' said John.

'Aye and you are a trickster, John Campbell-John.'

John gave a shout of laughter. 'So then, we know about each other.'

'Aye we do,' responded Samuel, thrusting out his hand. They shook again and as before, nearly lost their balance, which made them laugh again, but this time as partners.

'And always remember,' said John, a twinkle gleaming in his eye picked out by the shimmering moonlight, 'when you think things are starting to go wrong – it's turning out to be a good day.'

CHAPTER 6

The wealthy and stylish Londoners took their Sunday leisure at the fashionable resorts of Pall Mall, and the Mall by St.James, but such places were not for the likes of the common people. Instead, on this hot summer's day, a large crowd had been lured by the attractions of Marylebone Fields and Gardens, intent on an afternoon's entertainment in the sun.

That was not to say that Marylebone Fields was any less beautiful than the other parks, indeed, its 450 or so acres ranked as one of the most beautiful spots in London, but it was less fashionable and so more used by the common folk. The crowd this day was a strange mix of Georgian society, ranging from meanly clad vagabonds, through working tradesman, to merchants and even sporting gentlemen of rank, for there was entertainment to suit the widest of tastes. Ball games and animal baiting were popular and 'throwing at cocks' was a particular favourite. A cock was tethered to a stake, and for a penny anyone could throw a short wooded club at it. The winner was the man who killed it and took the dead bird as his prize.

The traditional cries of the vendors rang out and enticing aromas filled the air. '*Fresh hot*', cried the tea vendor. '*Hot spiced ginger,*' answered the vendor of another hot beverage. '*Ring bell,*' cried the muffins man, and '*Penny a lot,*' answered the fishwife selling oysters. The day was a heady mix of smells and action and carnival and bustle and alcohol, but lawlessness and rioting was never far from the surface on such days much to the displeasure of the local magistrates, who would on occasion attempt to ban some of the activities. The action today, however, was boxing: two staged battles were to be fought.

The main attraction was a fight between the people's favourite, Big Charles Sweep, and Norbert Openshaw, the Lancashire Soldier. The supporting battle was a match between Irish Michael the Carrier and Samuel the Jew. It was six weeks since Samuel's victory over Judd the Coal Heaver. His wounds had healed well and he was again in the best of health. Today was a Sunday; *his* Sunday, the day of his first professional fight - this time at Marylebone Fields against a seasoned professional fighter. Word of his victory in Northampton had not spread back to London, and John, who wanted it to remain an affair local to the Northampton area, had counselled Samuel not to talk about it. Samuel had reluctantly agreed. He was a strange mixture of sensitive human being and extrovert showman and had found it difficult to hold his tongue when what he wanted was to satisfy the latter trait and boast of his victory. He had walked alone to Marylebone Fields, mostly unrecognised since leaving his own neighbourhood, and as he walked, the heat of the day made him sweat, but there was more to his sweating than the summer sun. Tension was mounting within him and his stomach had begun to knot in apprehension. It was not a sensation he had felt before any other fight – he was not by nature a nervous man and his total belief in his own invincibility had sustained him through all his encounters. But this was somehow different; it was a step into the unknown for him and was adding to his perspiration. Approaching the venue, he walked along Queen Anne Street and a gentle breeze unexpectedly emerged and swirled around him, bringing with it the sounds and smells of the park, and caressing his features like a mother's hand stroking the cheek of her child. He noticed one of the many posters that had been pinned up around the city, and stopped at the sight of his own name. He could not resist reading again the words of the challenge:

AT MARYLEBONE FIELDS THIS PREFENT SUNDAY, BEING THE 15ᵗʰ. DAY OF JULY, THERE WILL BE PERFORMED A TRYAL OF SKILL BY THE FOLLOWING MAFTERS.

Whereas I Michael O'Connor from Ireland, mafter of the Noble Science of Defence having heard the bragging that the young upstart Samuel Medina has been making, am fully perfwaded that if my proper method be executed against him he will not be able to stand against me. For a tryal of which I now invite him to meet me and fight upon the stage.

I Samuel Medina, from Bethnall Green London. Mafter of the said Noble Science of Defence, to give the said Michael O'Connor an opportunity of putting his proper method into execution, will not fail to meet him at the place and time appointed. Hoping the spectators may from thence receive entire satisfaction, affuring them beforehand that the method I shall make use of, will be the way of my new style of fighting.

Samuel read the notice with intense pride, and was particularly pleased with the final sentence. He resolved to give the spectators a show of his skills the like of which they would not have seen before. Reading the notice had the effect of buoying him up, casting away any lingering doubts. Then he entered the fields of Marylebone and the sights, the sounds, and the smells of the occasion greeted his senses, and from that moment the adrenalin that was pumping through his body was hijacked by the showman within him. From now on only his performance occupied his thoughts. He had, many times whilst growing up, come to watch the great fighters and learned of their strategies. He had added to this by reading books on fencing and the duel, and incorporated much of that stratagem into his unique style of fighting. He knew his opponent would be bigger and stronger than he was, but then, they mostly were and he would have to use his athletic abilities to avoid a contest of mere strength. It would be his speed against his opponent's strength. What he did not know was how much Irish Michael had retained of his fighting skills, and how much they had been diminished by age. And so he resolved to do little at the commencement of the contest other than to wait and see, to size up his opponent, to move and see how much the man was still capable of doing. Samuel wandered around the fields taking in the experience, remaining mostly unrecognised. The cry of '*Fresh hot*,' rang out and he turned and looked at the pieman's fare. He purchased, maybe unwisely, an eel pie, but it was still two hours until he fought, and he considered that enough time in which to digest it. The pie was hot in his hands, but he ate it as he wandered, breathing out the hot vapours, until he spied where the stage had been erected. It was atop a mound in the distance and Samuel made his way towards it through the crowds, striding confidently as he went.

John Campbell-John had been true to his word and had worked hard promoting Samuel's first paid fight. He needed a name to attract the crowds, and he had reasoned that he needed an ageing pugilist who was well past his best. This was not so much out of his concern for Samuel's wellbeing as that he was already looking forward to the odds in his next fight. Samuel would go into this fight as a heavy underdog, but John knew that a convincing win would bring the future odds tumbling. He also knew that Samuel would put on a show for the crowd, for his personality would not let him do otherwise, and if he won, he would win well, so John reasoned there must be a ready made excuse available to keep the subsequent odds from tumbling. This was to be the principle of all his future fights – Samuel must appear to have been overmatched, even if in reality he was not.

Irish Michael the Carrier seemed the ideal choice – a man of thirty-eight and a veteran of many pitched battles, he bore the scars of his trade with pride. Like many of his countrymen he had fought in the British army but had been demobbed without any means of support and then made his way to London to earn a living. His face could have been chiselled in marble by Michelangelo himself, his skin riddled with scar tissue stretched tight over his angular bone structure, with cauliflower ears protruding like a pair of wing nuts. He was by profession a sedan chair carrier and that had contributed to his immense strength, but he was also a tall man, standing five feet eleven and with a long reach in proportion to his size. He had retained that strength, but his weight had now risen to sixteen and a half stone, much of which was being carried around his ample middle. He would have a height advantage of three inches, and a weight advantage of five stones over Samuel - it would look to the crowd like a mismatch. The odds would be long and this would give John a chance to make a killing from the bookmakers. But if Samuel were to win then the bookmakers would assess that he had beaten only a fighter who had had one too many fights.

So Irish Michael looked an ideal and inspired choice, but unfortunately he would not at first agree to fight Samuel. He was a past champion and he saw a fight with an unknown as contemptible and beneath him. The answer, as ever, lay in money. It was the tradition under the Broughton Rules that the purse was to be split two-thirds to the winner and one-third to the loser, and this gave John a bargaining stance. He offered to forgo the loser's third so that if Michael won he would take the entire purse. Michael now saw it as no more than - quite literally - a walk in the park, and had agreed to the battle.

But John had been much shrewder even than that. He had canvassed Samuel's neighbourhood so that all the locals had come to see the lad take on a real pugilist. In addition, he had befriended the Editor of a morning newspaper and given him stories of the new lad who had the impertinence to take on one of the masters of the Prize Ring. The brashness of the quotes, supposedly emanating from Samuel, had turned many people against him and a mix of people – those wanting to see the young braggart beaten and those wanting their local man to triumph against the much bigger man - had swelled the crowd to capacity. Whatever one's allegiance, it was to be a David and Goliath encounter.

But John had not stopped there. Under the Broughton Rules two umpires were nominated, one by each of the Principals, and John had donned his captain's uniform and approached Sir Thomas Kettall, the youngest son of the Duke of Howden and a well known sporting gentleman, to act as Samuel's nominee. John had put on a masterful performance of Shakespearian proportions in his role of gentleman army officer, completely convincing Sir Thomas of his bona fides, but unable at first to persuade him to accept the umpireship. John had the long-term aim of getting Sir Thomas to sponsor Samuel's career, but as the gentleman was far from convinced that he even wanted to act as an umpire, John had conceived a further act of deception. He told Sir Thomas a *whopper;* a lie of such proportions that the gentleman was indeed impressed. He told him that Big Charles Sweep was so impressed with the lad that he had agreed to be his second. This was a testimonial indeed. Charles Sweep was the most widely known pugilist in England – the unofficial champion. Now if the lad had impressed *him* then he must be worth seeing. Sir Thomas, intrigued and intent on seeing if the lad matched up in any way to this glowing testimonial, had now accepted the offer.

Unfortunately, of course, there was no such undertaking from Big Charles Sweep, but John was not to be put off by such a minor consideration. He took Samuel down to Sweep's academy and offered his services as a sparring partner and Samuel did the rest. Sweep was mightily impressed with Samuel's agility, his ring craft, and agreed to act as his second before he himself fought the Lancashire Soldier.

As Samuel approached the ring, John was the first to greet him, and Big Charles Sweep a close second. A large hand was thrust in his direction and Samuel responded by shaking it determinedly, but this giant's fist dwarfed his own hand. Sweep was a Cornishman and there was still something left of his Cornish brogue, but his notoriety had brought him into society circles and he had learned how to survive even there. The etiquette of the day displayed by persons of rank had been quickly assimilated by this former village blacksmith so that his manners were now refined and of the politest, with little remaining to give away his Cornish heritage. He was an intelligent man who had earned a fortune from his fighting and had invested it well. Samuel saw much of himself in Charles Sweep and was inspired to follow in his footsteps.

Sweep was immaculately turned out. He was wearing a knee-length frock coat in a blue-grey colour with a high stand-fall collar, the skirts of the coat cut away at the front. The sleeve opening was buttoned perpendicularly to reveal the frill of his shirtsleeve. The coat was worn over black breeches with white stockings and shiny black, buckled shoes. It was the outfit of a gentleman of means, which, to all intents and purposes was now how Sweep saw himself.

'Your humble servant, sir,' said Samuel sincerely, nodding his head politely as he spoke.

'Your servant,' replied Sweep equally politely. 'And how be it with you young fellow?' He then laughed heartily to Samuel's confusion. 'You look nobbut a lad with your shirt on,' he continued. 'The book'll run against you today will it not?'

'Aye it will,' said John before Samuel could respond, 'and that's exactly what we want. We hope to make more from the bookmakers today than we will get from the purse.'

'The book may run against me today,' said Samuel, 'but after today my name will become famous. I can promise you that.'

John shook his head in disbelief.

It was five p.m. when Samuel climbed onto the stage and into the ring. It was the first time he had fought in a formal ring, and this elevated position played to his showmanship. He looked down on the expectant crowd, his chest swelling with pride and anticipation. The summer sun was well past its zenith in the azure sky, and he needed to shield his eyes as he looked westwards at a section of the crowd. Big Charles Sweep followed him and the two stood side by side in the corner of the stage. Sweep put his massive hands on Samuel's shoulders and massaged the defined muscles there. The crowd were unusually quiet and many were impatient as they had come to see Big Charles Sweep fight, not this unknown Jew. The crowd had also picked up on Samuel's apparent lack of stature, in that the Cornishman dwarfed him. There was no doubting Samuel's muscular development, his barrel chest and powerful arms and legs, but the hum of subdued voices began to run round the audience, commenting on his lack of size and the consequences on his betting odds. John had been right in his betting strategy and when Michael the Carrier entered the stage it did indeed look like a mismatch.

Samuel had done no more than remove his shirt and put on a pair of lightweight shoes and his body *did* look well developed and strong, even if he was so much smaller than his opponent. Samuel was introduced to the crowd first and he responded in the same way as he had against Judd the Coal Heaver raising his arms and dancing around the ring, but this time adding some shadow boxing to his repertoire. The audience were not used to seeing such fancy footwork; pugilists were in the main large, savage men not renowned for their lightness of step. Samuel's performance brought forth a mixed reaction of humour and derision and the crowd began to jeer in response, completely overwhelming the cheers from the locals who had turned out to support Samuel. The more they jeered, the more Samuel responded and the more exaggerated his performance became, until Charles Sweep himself led him back to his corner, which provoked more derision from the crowd.

'That's enough lad,' Sweep said, 'you're nobbut a Johnny Raw you know.'

'Inexperienced I may be sir,' replied Samuel, 'but I promise you I'm no novice,' he said with genuine bravado.

'We'll soon find out lad whether you're made of bluster or courage.'

Irish Michael was then introduced to resounding cheers. He had been a crowd favourite for many years and even in defeat he had stood his ground well, taking his punishment like the good fighter he was supposed to be. He had famously fought for one hour and twenty minutes against Big Charles Sweep himself, before succumbing to the big man's skills and then taking a terrible beating. He stepped forward doing nothing more than nod his head with total disdain for today's antagonist. It was clear where the crowd's sympathies lay and cheering rang out long after he had returned to his corner. Samuel's supporters were not in general fighting fans and were not used to showing their support so vocally, but nevertheless he had support amongst the crowd.

The two men were called to the centre of the ring by the referee and the true disparity of size became apparent. It was at this point that John placed his bet with a bookmaker. He was given five to one, and wagered thirty guineas for himself and five guineas for Samuel. They would leave with money or nothing at all.

The bell sounded and Irish Michael came forward, his stance upright and with his left fist extended and his right fist tucked under his chin. Samuel noticed immediately that his solar plexus was exposed by the high carriage of his arms, and as a consequence he was vulnerable to a punch to the midriff, but Samuel would need to counter the man's superior reach to take advantage of that vulnerability.

Samuel took up his crouched stance to protect his own midriff, but circled his opponent rather than meeting him head on. Unlike Judd, however, Irish Michael did not attempt to throw wild punches at his elusive opponent; instead he tried to cut off Samuel's movement and trap him in a corner where he could make his own strength pay. This continued for some time as if they were two mating birds performing a ritual courting dance. After two minutes neither man had thrown a punch and the crowd began to bay their disapproval.

'Tell the lad what to do Charlie,' shouted some wag from the crowd, but Charles Sweep ignored the comment.

Irish Michael, however, was stung by the crowd's derision; it wasn't something to which he had been subjected before. His tactics had been correct. His intention was to save his energy until his antagonist was slowed by his own strenuous exertions and would be available to hit. He now abandoned this tactic and attempted to throw a long left jab at his opponent's head. Samuel saw it coming and side-stepped to his right so that the punched missed him easily. At the same time, he aimed a powerful right blow to the left side of the Irishman's stomach. Samuel heard his opponent gasp as the air in his lungs was forced out between his clenched teeth and knew he had landed the first telling blow of the fight.

But the Irishman was used to pain and his bravery was not in doubt. He now came after Samuel with much more endeavour, throwing straight left jabs followed by round right blows as he came. Samuel was able to retreat from these blows so that they fell short. He then attempted to counter with his own forward strike, but this was parried on his opponents' arms, who then attempted to counter punch, using his reach advantage to good effect. Samuel only just managed to evade these punches by retreating backwards along a diagonal.

The Irishman was showing off his skills; he was indeed a master of the art of self defence, but what he lacked was speed, both of hand and foot. His blows were powerful but cumbersome and his movement around the stage was slow and ponderous. He was unused to chasing after his opponents because they were usually standing right in front of him, trading punches. This change in tactics was to prove disastrous for the Irishman, and he began to blow visibly, his movement beginning to slow even more.

His vulnerability was there for all to see, and Samuel saw it as his opportunity to step up his performance. He had begun the fight by circling anti-clockwise away from his adversary's right hand, but now he changed and circled clockwise, flicking out potent jabs into the Irishman's face, which started to cut up badly. At intervals Samuel planted his feet and delivered powerful blows to both the head and midriff, and after only fifteen minutes, his opponent's bruised and bloodied features stared back at Samuel, but with defiance still ingrained in those bulbous, swollen eyes. The blows rained back from the Irishman as he attempted to turn his rebellious nature into a victory plan, but Samuel parried them, or side stepped or they fell short because Samuel had retreated out of range.

The performance was a spectacle of athleticism and skill, but was one that was a stranger to the crowd, who now began to quieten as the Irishman's supporters realised the predicament he unexpectedly found himself in. At the same time, Samuel's support became more vocal and this was picked up by Samuel. He continued to circle like a wolf waiting for its prey to lose the will to fight, before moving in for the kill. The full repertoire of Samuel's skills was now unleashed and the Irishman was forced to adopt a defensive posture in an attempt to parry the numerous blows raining down on him. After twenty minutes Irish Michael looked a broken man, but he was to stand for a further thirty minutes before he was declared beaten.

The same wag called out to Charles Sweep from the crowd, shrieking: 'You told him good Charlie!'

'Nay.' Sweep's broad features split in a slow grin. 'I told the lad nothing. He already knows more than all of us.'

Samuel now put on a bullfighter posture, hands on hips walking back and forth in front of his opponent - arrogant, provoking, but unprotected.

Lunging forward, his strength already drained from him, the Irishman threw punch after weary punch, but they connected only with fresh air. Samuel moved easily aside, repeating the manoeuvre time and again as he worked the crowd up into a frenzy so that they cheered his every movement, every action. He had achieved what he had declared in the poster. It was his unique style of fighting, unseen before but now idolised by the energized and hysterical crowd who continued to shout and cheer.

Eventually he stopped taunting his opponent, turned to face the crowd and gestured to them. Their blood was up; knew exactly what he meant – it was time for the *coup de grâce*. They screamed out their approval. The crowd was having a good day; they liked nothing better than to enjoy the spectacle of a savage battle between two men intent on slugging each other's lights out – and the more blood, the better they liked it. It was almost as entertaining as watching a hanging, especially when the drop was bungled and the victim lingered, dancing on the rope. But what made this particular sunny afternoon in the park so enjoyable was the totally unexpected result.

Samuel now stood in front of his man and took his guard, and the crowd rang out a cry in support. He jabbed out a straight left into his opponents face, and followed this with two more while cocking his right in readiness. The courage of the Irishman manifested itself in one more attack, but this was exactly what Samuel was waiting for. His opponent charged him one last time, as the dying bull charges the matador, and Samuel, like the matador, delivered the killing blow. He sidestepped and hit the Irishman with a powerful downward blow to the side of his head as he passed, and the exhausted man collapsed.

His seconds ran forward and dragged him away to his corner where they threw water in his face and then wiped away the mash that was blood and sweat and mucus and saliva and then heaved him to his feet. The two seconds dragged their man back to the square at the centre of the ring in the regulation thirty seconds, supporting him beneath his armpits so that his shoulders hunched grotesquely, but as soon as they let him go, he started to sway and his knees to buckle. The fighting reflex was still in him, however, and he attempted to move forward, but his legs would not respond and he did no more than fall forward heavily onto the stage canvas, unable to fight on.

The referee raised Samuel's hand in a victory salute and Samuel accepted it with all the aplomb of the showman that he was. He danced and circled around the stage with his arms raised, working the crowd like a seasoned barker. This was what was important to him, his main reason for fighting; anything else was a justification, a fiction in his own mind. He adored the crowd's adoration. He enticed their cheers and then responded to those cheers with more gestures of victory, which in turn brought even more cheers.

The newspaperman could be seen scribbling away and it was clear to John, watching from the sidelines, that fame would not be far away and would be calling shortly like a celebrated guest. John smiled to himself, his thoughts increasingly fanciful: they would walk together in the future, each supporting the other, each needing the other. From now on there would be a partnership of three and not two – himself, Samuel and fame. He looked across at Samuel, who was still in the ring, responding to the crowd. With a wide grin, John totted up their winnings in his head, and his grin turned into a shout of laughter.

Samuel was still being carried away by his need for adulation. He now took to the centre of the ring and gestured the crowd to quieten. His ability to work a crowd was such that they did so, listening intently, expectant on his every word.

'We have had good sport today, have we not?' he bellowed, and the crowd cheered their approval. 'And we shall have more, for we shall all have the honour of seeing Big Charles Sweep fight, shall we not?' Again the crowd cheered their approval. Samuel turned to Sweep and held his arm out towards him and Sweep responded by bowing to the crowd in acknowledgement. 'And let us not forget Irish Michael the Carrier, he too has given us great sport, has he not?' Samuel shouted to the crowd, who continued to roar. 'The loser today, however, has no purse! That cannot be right, can it? The crowd responded, but John, his laughter stilled, buried his head in his hands for he knew what was coming.

'Then I shall donate one third of my purse to Irish Michael the Carrier for his good sport today,' Samuel shouted. The crowd went wild and their ovation was like sweet music to Samuel. 'And one last thing,' he said, 'the next time I fight I shall fight under the name of 'Samuel the Jew – the Light of Israel.' So great was his ability, that the crowd cheered *even* that, temporarily forgetting the anti-Semitic feelings that were more usually exhibited by Londoners.

Two hours later, John and Samuel sat in the fighters' tent sharing out their winnings. Big Charles Sweep sat with them, his face red and blue from his victory over the Lancashire Soldier. Norbert Openshaw had been a surprisingly difficult opponent and it had taken Sweep one hour and twenty minutes to best him.

Samuel's purse had been reduced to twenty guineas after he had given ten to Irish Michael. His partnership deal with John was an eighty–twenty split; John took four guineas for himself and pushed sixteen guineas across the table to Samuel. From a larger pile he counted out twenty-five more guineas and again pushed this across the table to Samuel, saying, 'I held out for five to one, Sammy lad – that's swelled your purse to forty one guineas.'

Big Charles Sweep bellowed a laugh, 'But you, sir, have a hundred and fifty four guineas, and you have not even fought. You take home more than I do! That is fine work is it not?

'Aye - that it is Charlie,' said John. 'I am a gambling man - but if I had lost I would have had nothing.'

Big Charles Sweep squinted at John. 'Charlie Sweep is another man, and he lives in Cornwall,' he said testily.

'Charles Sweep, your humble servant.' John hurriedly attempted to diffuse an awkward situation. He had forgotten Sweep preferred the more formal address. He bowed as well as he could from his chair, not wanting to stand in case it was taken as a challenge. 'My apologies, sir, for I meant you no offence.'

The big man gave him a stern look, but then a smile returned to his features. 'Then none shall be taken, sir,' he replied.

'But you see, sir,' John tried to change the subject, 'to a gambler, Samuel is something that comes along only once in a lifetime. I have stumbled upon a winner that is as yet unrecognised. The world sees him as only a little Jew-boy and it behoves me to take on the book with as much gusto as I can before the world opens its eyes to him.'

'Aye I see that,' said Charles Sweep.

'Is he not a future champion, sir?'

'The lad has talent alright, but his size will eventually be his downfall I fear. At some point a big man is going to hit him and hit him hard. Then we shall see what he is made of.'

'Aye we shall, sir,' interrupted Samuel with bravado. 'Aye, we shall see that alright.'

CHAPTER 7

Sir Thomas Kettall was entertaining tonight. His London town house in the West-End was bristling with his guests, and he had put on a fine show for them. The London season, however, was a great strain on the finances of even a rich man such as Sir Thomas, but he was also a sporting gentleman, and that too was expensive. It was not so much his string of horses or his hand-made guns, or even his hounds that were injurious to his finances, but that phrase, *sporting gentleman,* was synonymous with gambling: he liked to play cards and he liked to wager on sporting events. Debts followed, inevitably, and at various times of his life he had been forced to go cap in hand to his father, the Duke of Howden, and ask to be bailed out - much to the displeasure of the Duke, who had already endowed a healthy income on his son. Sir Thomas was by no means alone in his profligacy; such wealthy, but debt-ridden young gentlemen were not uncommon around London during the season, but he was luckier than most in that he had an income of his own rather than an allowance from his father. Even this, it seemed, was insufficient when set against his need to gamble.

Young gentlemen were considered much too irresponsible to host their own house parties. With their reputation for drunkenness and debauchery they were also considered a danger to any young woman who attended. They were simply not to be trusted: it was taken as a given that they would observe no restraint, notwithstanding the premium their society placed on breeding and manners. Indeed, it was that very need for certain etiquettes to be observed that had engendered the custom for a mature woman to act as a young gentleman's hostess when he entertained. This could be a source of income for a woman of status, and was especially useful for those who had become financially embarrassed in their later years.

Strictly speaking, Sir Thomas should have by now left the label of *young* gentlemen behind him, but he held onto the lifestyle as a faithful dog clings to its master. Sir Thomas's mother would normally have fulfilled the duty of hostess for him, but his profligacy had estranged him from her and he was obliged to offer an income and accommodation for the season to an alternative, one Lady Juliana Lacy. He had chosen this woman with great care - she was too timid to impose any restraints on him and failed hopelessly in her duty to keep the party respectable.

Today, Sir Thomas was in excellent spirits. Gamblers will always talk about their winnings if rarely their losses, but for once it was the truth, he was ahead of the book. He had placed a sizeable wager at odds of five to one on an unknown pugilist who was having his first fight. Sir Thomas had placed another sizeable wager on the second fight and obtained four to one, and for the first time in many years he was out of debt. He had even been able to pay off the £359 he owed his wine merchant and the £257 he owed for stabling his horses. He was 29 years old and recorded his occupation as 'Gentleman', but in reality he did nothing: he did not labour, he did not study, he did not run an estate as did his father - and as his elder brother would in his turn. He belonged to that privileged group of young men who spent their time simply being gentlemen, for *nothing* is exactly what they did - and Sir Thomas did it exceedingly well. He rode, he fenced, he studied the noble science of defence at Big Charles Sweep's academy, he wagered, he wenched and he drank. He was well educated, but knew little of use. Indeed, he knew more about the classical Greeks and Romans than he did about the vast majority of his own countrymen. He lived in a little cocoon, as did most gentlemen of rank in London society, and yet, unlike many of his peers, he had a strange fascination with the lower classes, mingling with them at the sporting events he attended. Their plight, however, did not really enter his consciousness – they were invisible to his eyes; no more to him than a source of perverse delights that were there to be sampled. And yet Sir Thomas was a personable young man, witty and well-liked in his own set. He was good company and was placed high on the guest lists of others, and his own entertaining was seen as a *must* in the London season.

Sir Thomas had the knack of mixing the ladies and gentlemen of rank with those of the lower sort who would bring entertainment value to the evening, just so long as they adopted the manners becoming to their humble status and neither offended the ladies nor frightened the horses. Not that it was easy to say what might offend ladies from the upper echelons of society, who customarily visited lunatic asylums, public executions and other such delights for their sheer entertainment. But so long as coarse language was kept to a minimum and outward appearances maintained, then virtually anything was acceptable at Sir Thomas's house parties. The dining and drinking started in mid-afternoon and went on late into the evening. Gluttony and over-indulgence was the order of the day, for by providing a cornucopia of luxurious fare, the host was able to display his wealth and rank. There were few if any restraints. Obesity among gentlemen was a badge of status. Not so for the ladies, whose waists – when they were not breeding – were expected to remain sylph-like even without the confines of their corsetry.

One evening, a week after Samuel Medina had won his second professional fight, he and John Campbell-John were invited to a gathering at Sir Thomas's. Samuel was envious of John – he seemed to fit in beautifully, and with his very unusual upbringing, he had the education and manners of a country gentleman. Indeed, Samuel's own childhood had also imbued him with impeccable manners, but he looked apprehensively at the raised eyebrows that greeted him, for his features clearly proclaimed his Jewishness. His anxiety waned when it seemed he was to be tolerated, no doubt as a token of Sir Thomas's audacity, and realising this, he gradually began to feel more at ease.

Both men were extremely well turned out. Samuel had purchased his outfit from a pawnbroker, but was nevertheless elegant in his black suit and ruffled shirt, but his jealousy mounted when he looked at John, who had visited a fashionable tailor and, for the princely sum of £69.19s, purchased several outfits to match his new wealth. Tonight he was wearing a fine dress uniform to complement his guise as *Captain* John Campbell-John. To add a touch of style he had visited Mr Jeffries's shop on the Strand, sword cutter to His Majesty, and for seven guineas, had also purchased a very handsome sword indeed.

The two young men mingled effortlessly, with John taking the lead for he also possessed that most valued of accomplishments - that of wit. He drew many of the guests to him like a magnet, especially the ladies, for although wit was much prized there were few who had it so sharply and in such abundance as did John. In fact both he and Samuel were hits with the ladies, but for very different reasons. John was, of course, dashing and it was easy to see why the ladies flocked to his side, but Samuel's appeal was a little more indefinable. All that bravado he displayed when fighting was nowhere to be seen when in the company of ladies. Despite being a powerful man, he exuded integrity and vulnerability in equal measure and this proved to be a heady and alluring mix. But while both men were attractive to women, the women they attracted were not the same type - except, that is, for one Lady Adele Fitzsymons.

Lady Adele was notoriously flirtatious – well, that was the word used in polite society. In reality she was much more than that. She had a sexual appetite that would not have been out of place in the more corrupt days of ancient Rome. However; while John knew what to do with all the female attention, Samuel, his naivety clinging to him like a ball and chain, did not and although he found it gratifying, he was unsure how to handle it. If he was unsure with these young women, he was positively petrified by the attention of Lady Adele!

During dinner he became aware of a delicate and provocative foot, touching and caressing his calf - moving up and down his leg slowly, stopping and then lingering for a moment before resuming its tempting and bewitching attentions. Startled, he looked around the table. He was seated next to John, who was sitting opposite Lady Adele, whilst facing Samuel was a Miss Alice Ainscough.

Miss Ainscough, though not beautiful, was a handsome young lady with all the attractiveness that only youth can bring. Samuel looked at her blond hair, dressed high with ringlets at the front and sides, and decorated with pearls. Her gown bared her shoulders but her appearance was one of modesty, with only the merest hint of cleavage. She did not seem the sort to be so bold. He looked at her intently for some sign that he may be mistaken, but she was deep in conversation with the gentleman to her right. She sensed Samuel looking at her and glanced at him for confirmation, but when her blue eyes met his, her pale cheeks reddened modestly and her gaze shot back to other gentlemen. The only other possible owner of this alluring foot must therefore be Lady Adele - he hoped he was mistaken. She too was deep in conversation, but with the gentlemen on her left. By Samuel's reckoning, she would need to be a contortionist to be the owner of the miscreant foot. And then—she glanced sideways at him briefly. That was all it was – a sideways glance, yet it contained an abundance of sexual invitation. The woman's eyes sparkled and her mouth pursed almost imperceptibly but it was enough to leave little doubt in his mind.

Samuel froze in his chair, his mood changing instantly from bordering on comfortable and a feeling of ease that he was not out of place, to intense discomfort and a feeling that he was way out of his depth.

Lady Adele's attraction to him was not because of his personality, nor the indefinable vulnerability that he pervaded, but because of his physical prowess. In her eyes he was just a piece of meat, if a very fine piece of meat indeed, but still a piece of meat. He was the perfect specimen of the male gender and she wanted him in the same way an old letch lusts after a beautiful young woman; what is more, she determined that she was going to have him. Which was when the caress changed; it felt suddenly sharp, as her foot stroked his calf – something was sticking into his flesh.

Samuel leant back in his chair as casually as he could, so that he could look discretely under the table. He coughed self-consciously and then glanced down. There, just below his knee, he glimpsed a petite, white-stockinged foot, and pressed down in the silk between the big and second toes was a small envelope. The woman's dexterity was immense; she had somehow transferred the envelope from hand to toe without anybody noticing. He took it as circumspectly as he could, and when he looked up he caught another sideways glance from Lady Adele, satisfaction etched boldly on her features. Later, he read the note; it had neither address heading nor a signature – it read merely: *Call on me on Thursday afternoon at 3.00 p.m.*

Integrity was not normally a problem for John because he did not have any. Samuel on the other hand had enough for the two of them, and herein lay the heart of the problem for John this evening. He had a goal – he wanted access to the card table for it would be a high stakes game and he now had the stake to join it. But he wanted more than that – he wanted to eliminate much of the element of chance. To this end, he had coached Samuel, who would be one of the onlookers, in a number of subtle signals so that he could communicate to John what cards his opponent held in his hand. As far as John was concerned, this was to be a long term strategy and tonight was to be its unveiling. The trouble was that Samuel's integrity was getting in the way. He had reluctantly agreed to do it, despite his protestations, but John was doubtful, when push came to shove, whether he would actually go through with it. This possibility was beginning to irritate John unbearably.

Samuel's second professional fight had been against Peter the Butcher, a young and relatively inexperienced fighter, but with power and stamina. Again the book had run against Samuel, for – as John had so cleverly foreseen – opinions had soon been voiced that Irish Michael was, after all, an old man and Samuel's victory was hardly surprising when all was said and done. John, who had been banking on this outcome, was able to get odds of four to one and had wagered 15 guineas for Samuel and 75 for himself. Samuel had bested his opponent in just over an hour, for what the Butcher made up for in youth and stamina he lacked in technique and was unable to parry any of Samuel's shots. Samuel had winnings from his two fights of 85 guineas, plus his purse money of 36 guineas. It was a relative fortune by anyone's standards, but it paled into insignificance beside the amount John had pocketed: 450 guineas, which, together with his portion of Samuel's purse, exceeded the annual income of all but those of the highest of rank. John had already begun to live the life he felt he had been cheated out of by an accident of birth. Fate had double-crossed him and he fully intended to make up for lost time. This he was doing with all the gusto he could muster. But now fate raised an eyebrow: the high life did not come cheaply and already his funds were down to under 300 guineas.

John believed himself to be an excellent card player and this was supplemented by the innate cunning that life, to date, had required of him. He was drawn to the card table as the moth is drawn to the candle flame, with all its attendant dangers. He also saw the card table as a means to replenish, if not to extend his funds.

At ten o'clock, the dancing was interrupted and two small tables were erected in the coffee room, each table having four lace-edged napkins, one placed on each corner. The napkins had little purpose, merely an expression of style and a statement of wealth. The gentlemen commonly gambled on credit and would issue a credit note for their losses, but this was of course John's first problem: he was not a gentleman known to the London season. However, he had circumvented the problem by lodging 100 guineas with Sir Thomas, who stood surety for him.

Samuel watched as John was introduced by Sir Thomas to his fellow card players: an ageing, military gent by the name of Colonel Fittal; Sir Oliver Riddell, a sour-faced man, and finally, a stout, fidgety man by the name of Ainscough, who, it appeared, was Alice Ainscough's father.

John bowed graciously. 'Your servant, sirs.' Eager to ensure that his cover wasn't blown, he then turned to the Colonel and asked the obvious question: 'May I enquire what regiment you are with, Sir?'

'*Cavalry*, Campbell-John, *cavalry*,' the Colonel's dangling moustache billowed as he spoke. His bushy eyebrows rose as he nodded civilly. 'The Strawboots, Sir.'

John was now on the horns of a dilemma. The Strawboots was obviously a regimental nickname, but as an infantry officer was he expected to know that? Fortunately, Ainscough came unwittingly to his aid, asking, 'The *Strawboots*, Sir?'

Fittal turned amiably to Ainscough. 'The 7th Queen's Own Regiment of Light Dragoons, Sir,' he explained, 'but everybody knows us as the Strawboots. Retired now, of course.' He turned back to John, 'And what's your regiment, Sir?'

'Oh nothing so grand, Colonel,' said John with his well-rehearsed story, 'Infantry, Sir – the Third Buckinghamshire Foot.'

'Don't apologise for being infantry, Campbell-John. I know it's the infantry that wins the battles, and we cavalrymen just take the glory. A good army needs infantry,' Fittal trumpeted, eyebrows wagging.

'You're very gracious, Sir,' said John.

'Nonsense man,' said the Colonel. 'Who's your commanding officer?'

'Tubby Moreton, Colonel,' said John, knowing his facts were correct because it was his old regiment - even if he had been only a common soldier.

The Colonel looked up to the ceiling for inspiration and down again, slowly shook his head, 'No – afraid I don't know him.'

John coughed to mask his elation. He had been prepared to blag his way through, but now there was no need the relief coursed through his veins like an elixir.

The game was to be whist, and the gentlemen took their places at the two tables. John looked around the table at his three competitors, and tried to identify their likely abilities and characters. After a few hands, his initial judgements were, he thought, confirmed. Sir Oliver was a wealthy snob and had the countenance to match. He seemed to be permanently looking down his thin, broken-veined nose at the world and was full of his own importance, to the point where he believed himself to be an accomplished card player, whereas in reality he was nothing of the sort. A life of debt and losses had not shaken him from this belief. John considered that this man could be the source of some big losses tonight and he intended to be the recipient of that good fortune.

Colonel Fittal was a more accomplished card-man but age, and daughters who would soon require dowries had made him a cautious player. The devil-may-care years of large gambling losses were now behind him, although it did not keep him from the green table – he was a gentlemen after all, and that's what gentlemen did. John considered that the Colonel would end the night either slightly up or slightly down but would not be a big loser.

This left Ainscough: he was a rotund man, flushed of face with plump jowls and a ruddy complexion and still wearing a wig, although they were, by this year, well out of fashion. The man had gout, which made him uncomfortable and he constantly wriggled in his chair in an effort to get himself restful and this affected his concentration. He was a wealthy wine merchant, sharp-witted and a man of commerce: surprisingly, despite his distracting gout, he was a very good card player. He was an unlikely houseguest of Sir Thomas, but when you are in debt to your wine merchant then needs must, though Sir Thomas had found, to his chagrin, that he could not win back his losses from this fat man. In society circles, it was expected that gambling debts were to be settled honourably, whereas debts to tradesmen held little stigma and delay in payment held no social dishonour. John *was* a good card player and he knew it, but he resolved to be cautious with Ainscough and to target the obnoxious Sir Oliver.

The card table at such gatherings was as much an occasion for the other guests as it was for the players themselves. It was a spectator sport and the guests gathered around the tables. Well-played hands were politely applauded. The ladies were not excluded from this, and occasionally some very bold lady would actually take a seat at the green table. Samuel looked at John and smiled through his own apprehension at the sight of the dashing army captain who had set the female hearts a-flutter all evening; there was much interest in him now that he was playing. After about an hour's play, his winnings mounting, he was even more the centre of attention.

'Well played, Sir,' said another young military man who stepped forward and patted John on the shoulder after he had played a winning hand.

But now a critical point was reached: Sir Oliver looked at the new hand he had been dealt for what seemed like a time without end. His normal facial expression was that of a man who had been weaned on a pickle, but a smile then congealed on his face. John read the change in his body language immediately. He was one of those men who smiled only with his mouth, while his eyes said something different. What those eyes now said was: *I have here a good hand, and I believe that I have your measure, Sir.* His hesitation was because he could not be sure what sort of a hand John would be playing.

In fact, John had been playing fairly to this point; he hadn't needed to do otherwise. He now looked up at Sir Oliver and then casually over the man's shoulder to Samuel, who had positioned himself there in his direct line of view.

Samuel met his gaze, tensed and looked back at him sheepishly. John's heart sank at the sight of Samuel's shamefaced expression and inwardly despaired at his lack of guile. The man was transparently honourable and he cursed him for it.

Nevertheless, he had anticipated the situation so that Samuel had the minimal of deceit to undertake. If he was to run his right thumb over the top of his cards, this was a signal to ask if the opponent was strong in hearts. Similarly, if he was to use his right forefinger in the same way, it was to ask about spades. His left thumb signified diamonds and his left forefinger signified clubs. John had invested some of his recent winnings in a diamond ring that he wore on his left little finger and if he was to fondle with this, then this was the signal to ask whether his opponent was strong in trumps.

John now fondled his ring, and casually looked up at Sir Oliver's deliberations, but past him to Samuel's troubled countenance. He had been tutored in only two signals to make things as easy as possibly for his conscience. He was to touch his right cuff to signal an affirmative response and his left for a negative.

Samuel did neither. He stood there uncomfortably surrounded by some of the younger ladies, and with Alice Ainscough on his arm, but he was impervious to them. *This is worse than trying to negotiate London's mazy alleyways*, he thought to himself. There didn't seem to him to be an exit from this labyrinth of dilemma.

John cursed inwardly again, and willed Samuel to change his body language, to at least look impassive, and hoped that his troubled countenance would be interpreted as concentration and not subterfuge.

Samuel swallowed, shot a look at John as if to signal mental resignation and touched his right cuff. Having done so, he turned to Alice. 'I have to go – excuse me.' Puzzled, she looked at him, started to follow, but then let go of his arm for she was too interested in watching her father play.

'Gentlemen,' said Sir Oliver snidely, 'I am behind on the evening. I'm sure that you will see it as good sport to give me a chance to win back some of my winnings.'

'Of course sir,' said Colonel Fittal, 'we are all sporting gentlemen here are we not. What do you have in mind?'

'A little spice that's all, sir, shall we say that a doubling of the stakes would achieve that?'

'Capital,' said Ainscough, 'capital.'

'And you sir,' Sir Oliver gestured to John.

John's eyes flashed to his hand – he was light on trumps. Thanks to Samuel, he now knew Sir Oliver's ploy was a crude attempt to buy the hand and capitalise on his strong holding of trumps, but he didn't have the hand to stop him. *Oh no you don't*, he thought to himself.

'Why certainly, Sir,' John said with all the charm he could muster, his eyes sparkling, 'let us raise the stakes as you suggest – from the next hand.'

The pretence of a smile vanished from Sir Oliver's face for a moment, but then he forced it to return. At the same time his eyes narrowed, betraying his true feelings.

'Surely sir,' he said, 'there can be no objection to raising the stakes from *this* hand. That would make for good sport, would it not?'

'Too true, Sir Oliver,' John was all charm, 'but you have to give the fox a head start, for surely that makes for even better sport. There's no sport in just setting the dogs on the brute, is there?' There was a round of polite applause from the onlookers to his wit and he nodded almost imperceptivity. He also knew that he would have to bring the other two on board.

'Well-said Campbell-John,' interrupted the Colonel, with Ainscough nodding his agreement. 'Yes, let's let the brute run for this hand and then we can chase after him in the next.'

Sir Oliver squinted at John, and for a moment that society of exquisite manners held its breath at the thought of what Sir Oliver would do next. What most of the guests knew, but John didn't, was that Sir Oliver collected arguments and feuds like other people collected butterflies. But then the unwritten rule surfaced in time – the rule that said outward appearances must be maintained. Sir Oliver swallowed hard, and then merely nodded politely, wrinkling his nose at the other players, adding, 'as you wish gentlemen, as you wish.'

Having returned from the privy, Samuel stayed out of John's eye line and watched the play. Unobserved, he stared intently at Sir Oliver's face and read the emotions there. He knew the man had lost heavily wagering against him in the fight; it now seemed he was failing to win back his losses at the card table. When Sir Oliver thought nobody was looking, he shot a look of pure venom at John. It seemed he had added another name to his long list of *get-evens*. If revenge was a dish best served cold then he looked as though he intended to eat his fill from the cold platter when the time came. Samuel made a mental note to warn John when the game was over. Sir Oliver was a man who would bear watching.

This should have been the springboard for a killing at the gaming table, and as the evening wore on Sir Oliver continued to lose, but John didn't continue to win. His claret glass was regularly filled and he continued to empty it and after a couple of hours' play his senses were so pickled that his skills at the card table had become blighted. An Achilles heel had been exposed and Ainscough took full advantage of it. John's early assessment of the evening had been found wanting: the Colonel *had* finished the evening without breaking even, but with few losses. Sir Oliver *had* finished with big losses, but *so* had John. Ainscough had kept his wits about him, and exploited John's weakness and consequently he had prevailed. At the close, the assembly applauded politely, and all the players bowed with equal graciousness, and pent up chattering broke out among the onlookers, who analysed the game: the players' tactics; who had played well and who had not. The noise in the room grew louder as people relaxed, imbibed, laughed and conversed.

Miss Ainscough, moved to stand by her father, for she was his companion for the evening. Ainscough was obviously proud of her. He had earlier confessed to Samuel that she had been exceedingly well educated and was more at home in polite society even than his wife – or himself for that matter. The two of them joined John in conversation, as did Samuel, who had managed to squeeze his way through the throng.

'Ah, Mr Medina,' said Miss Ainscough, 'I was quite worried when you left so suddenly. All's well with you, I hope?'

Before Samuel could reply, John, fearful of what his friend's honesty might cause him to say, cut across them. 'I fear Sammy boy is more at home as a player than as a spectator.'

'Me too,' said Ainscough, 'I'm much happier playing than watching. I understand old fellow, I really do.'

Samuel bowed politely to Ainscough and his daughter and they reciprocated with practiced courtesy 'You have had a successful evening at the table Mr. Ainscough, I hear,' said Samuel, trying to move the conversation away from himself.

'Capital, capital, but I fear Captain Campbell-John here wouldn't agree. How much are you down on the evening Campbell-John – 80 guineas?'

'Oh a gentleman never talks about money,' John feigned charm whilst being aware of disapproving looks from Samuel. Irritated, he set out to embarrass Samuel by way of reprisal.

'But I am a mere merchant, Sir,' said Ainscough, 'and I don't find the subject of money disagreeable in *any* way.' The four of them laughed at this witty remark, and John waited a moment before continuing to bait Samuel.

'You have a beautiful daughter Mr. Ainscough, and I know that Sammy here is most smitten with her.'

Samuel's flashed John a look that should have turned him to stone, conscious at the same time that three pairs of eyes were now gazing at him in amusement. If embarrassment is what John had intended, then he had worked it like the most expertly played hand of cards. Samuel was caught between his overwhelming need to be polite and a need to dispel this suggestion. But most confusing of all – he *was* smitten by her. His face reddened - if there had been a battle for blushing then he would have been the English general.

John, observing that Miss Ainscough had noticed Samuel's blushes and judging by her expression, thought them charming, John hid a smile. He was not done yet. 'I know Samuel is much too shy to ask you himself, Sir,' he addressed Ainscough, 'so will you permit me to ask for him. Would it be acceptable if he was to call upon your daughter?'

This now threw Ainscough into a confusion that matched Samuel's. He was a merchant, albeit a wealthy and successful one. He dealt with similarly wealthy and successful Jewish merchants in his day-to-day business and saw nothing wrong in that. Unusually, he counted one of them a friend and had visited his house, where, to his surprise, he had felt more at home than with many people of society and rank. However, there was immense stigma attached to Judaism. It was one thing to trade with Jews, it was quite another to mix with them socially, and an even greater step to allow your daughter to be *called upon* by a *Jew*. Where would it lead? It was not for this that he had had his daughter expensively educated. He had hoped for a match with a gentleman, and a healthy dowry was to be his means of achieving this. It was his intention to pay a titled lady of rank to introduce his daughter into society. He knew this was an acceptable means by which the rich but socially inferior could advance themselves by a match of money to title. For a moment he was dumbstruck and he searched for the words to say. Then he looked at his daughter, for she was the love of his life, and he reasoned that she could have what she wanted. To his surprise her eyes said exactly what she wanted, and what she wanted was for Samuel to call on her.

'You may call upon her Mr Samuel Medina,' he sighed finally. 'And may I remind you that I expect you to behave honourably.'

'Father!' reprimanded Miss Ainscough, 'I'm sure Mr. Medina will behave like a true gentleman,' she nodded faintly at Samuel.

Her father thought - but did not say - that the last thing he wanted was for Medina to behave like a true gentleman, for he knew that gentlemen treated lesser members of society with disdain. True gentlemen were total bastards in his eyes.

'You do not need to worry, Sir.' John addressed Ainscough, then turned his gaze to Samuel, 'For I believe this man to be the most honourable in London.'

'Very well, Sir,' said Mr. Ainscough, 'as I said, you may indeed call upon my daughter, but for now the hour is late and we must be going.'

They all bowed politely to each other and the couple left, but John and Samuel waited until they were out of earshot before speaking.

'I really ought to thrash you, John,' said Samuel angrily.

'That's not like you,' answered John ironically, which only had the effect of boosting Samuel's anger.

'Just stay out of my life will you?'

John smiled, 'And you would have asked to call on the lass yourself, would you?'

'Maybe – maybe I would have, Sir.'

'Oh cut out the civility with me,' said a grinning John.

His lack of response to his confrontational manner angered Samuel even more. 'Just because you were born into a position of rank, Sir, is no reason to belittle my manners. I may not be a gentleman but...'

'Look Sammy boy,' John tried to put an arm around his shoulders, but Samuel shrugged him off. Ignoring the rebuff, John continued, his grin disappearing to be replaced by a look of legitimate concern. 'Look Sammy. Look around you. Look at all these people in their finery and tell me what you see?'

'What do I see – I see people of gentile society, and I am honoured to have been invited here tonight.'

'Well that's not what I see Sammy boy. Do you know what I see – I see dim-witted, greedy people who hide behind masks - people who would not shed a tear if you or I were killed tomorrow. Behind that polite society is a putrid festering dung heap that they try to hide with gallons of the finest perfume. But I can still smell it Sammy boy – I can still smell it.'

'You are drunk, Sir,' Samuel retorted. 'You talk gibberish.'

'My name is John to you, Sammy boy; not Sir – not between us – it is John; and yes, I am drunk, but that doesn't make me wrong.'

'But if you despise them so much, why do you want to improve your position in society? I am in no doubt that *I* am no more than a pawn to you – I am merely your means of achieving that.'

'I don't want to be part of this society Sammy lad; I just want what it can bring me – don't you see that?'

Samuel narrowed his eyes, but did not reply.

'Save all that civility for them,' continued John, 'they may have the rank of gentlemen but you are twice the man of any of them.'

The alcohol was now fuelling John's confessions. He was like a husband who cannot bring himself to say romantic things to his wife when sober, but pours them out to her when drunk, only for her to disregard them just because he *is* drunk.

Samuel stepped away from him. 'You are a user John Campbell-John, I can see that clearly. You will use me until I am no longer any use to you, and then you will abandon me.'

Through his alcoholic haze, John realised suddenly that his attitude to Samuel had changed radically. He had not admitted it to himself before, but it seemed that he did genuinely care about Samuel. He resolved inwardly to fight such a feeling, but for now he had to continue to manipulate him. He grasped Samuel's arm to prevent him from moving further away.

'Sammy – Sammy, you injure me deeply. You accuse me of showing the cloven hoof, even when my motives are not base at all.'

'I fear you feign innocence, Sir.'

'You're doing it again – my name is John. But, yes I admit that when we first met I saw an opportunity to make some money. But I believe we have moved on from there. Have I not schooled you in the ways of society, and have I not enabled you to make vast sums of money?'

'And even more for yourself - but I fear that that won't last long if you continue to gamble with your wits addled by John Barleycorn.' Samuel's voice was raised and suddenly realising it he looked around him, noticed several looks of disapproval, as if he had committed some terrible social *faux pas*.

'Fuck them,' said John, but he lowered his voice nonetheless. He moved closer to Samuel, said conspiratorially, 'Have I not made it possible for you to call on Miss Ainscough, for I know you wouldn't have asked yourself, despite what you say?'

'Well, yes, I suppose so.'

'Suppose so nothing, Sammy boy. I am your friend and benefactor.'

Samuel was thoughtful for a while and then a sense of contrition confused him further. 'I may have been unjust to you John and if I have then I would offer you my most sincere apologies.'

'There you go again, but I suppose your manners are no bad thing if we are to journey further. What do you say Sammy – does our adventure go further?'

'Aye – aye it does John,' said Samuel with unexpected bravado.

'And you have to realise that being a friend of John Campbell-John is like a fairground ride. My life is a constant search for that lucky throw of the dice that Lady Fate has so far denied me.'

'And my life is one long fight to stop Lady Fate skewering me,' said Samuel, 'she clearly wants me to be a warrior.'

'Aye we are strange bedfellows indeed.' John put his arm around Samuel, but now the embrace was not rejected, 'and I will school you on how to behave when you call upon the lovely Miss Alice.'

'It's not Miss Alice that I need schooling for.' Samuel took the small note from his tunic, 'it's Lady Adele.'

John scanned the scant note and a smile erupted across his features, to Samuel's irritation. 'Don't patronise me John,' he said angrily, 'I know I'm a novice in the matters of Venus, but you don't need to ridicule me.'

'There you go again Sammy; I'm not ridiculing you. It's just that you are *Thursday.*'

'*What?*' Samuel's brow furrowed, but then John took a similar note from inside his own tunic, matched them together and handed them back to Samuel. There was only one difference. 'You see I'm *Friday*! It seems that we must do everything in partnership, Sammy.'

Samuel shook his head. 'But I'm not sure that I can do this, John.'

'Aye, I think Lady Adele may be out of your league, at the present, but she'll certainly educate you in the ways of cupid, that's for sure. Let's not give up on this right now for I have something in mind for you Sammy, my boy.'

CHAPTER 8.

The Shakespeare's Head tavern in Covent Garden was not the sort of establishment that Samuel had visited before. It was certainly not for the likes of the common person, and catered in general for gentlemen of rank. It was renowned for the sumptuousness of its fare and, in particular, the richness of its pies that came in Viking proportions. It was a popular meeting place also for gentlemen of letters, who preferred to partake of alcohol rather than visit the new coffee houses that were all the rage. The tavern offered comfort and convenience where a gentleman could relax, play cards, gossip or talk politics, or simply read the newspapers. Samuel was surprised to find himself at ease within its walls and was comfortable with these gentlemen who displayed good manners to each other, and to Samuel's eyes they represented the impeccable behaviour that good breeding had bestowed on them, and to which he aspired.

He ate heartily with John and they both partook of wine instead of ale, as Samuel was intent on training his palate to appreciate this beverage of which gentlemen of rank were appreciative. After dinner they both relaxed with brandy and Samuel mused to himself that he approved of John's choice of venue. What Samuel did not know, however, was that the choice of venue was made with more than the prospect of victuals in mind. John drained his brandy, smacked his lips, then raised his hand arrogantly and snapped his fingers in a gesture to the waiter. The waiter responded quickly and on attending the table merely bowed respectfully, saying the single word *'Gentlemen?'*

'Two more brandies,' said John but added, 'we need to consult with Jack Morris – is the fellow available?'

'Jack Morris is serving at the other tables, gentlemen,' said the waiter. 'I'll tell him that you need a consultation. His shift will finish in about a half hour, sirs, and may I suggest that you take your brandies in the vault, so that he can attend you there. It will be more discreet. I will gladly bring your drinks through to you.'

'You will need to acquaint him with the nature of my business,' said John to Samuel's puzzlement.

'Oh I don't think that will be necessary,' said the waiter, 'it will be obvious to him, if you know what I mean, gentlemen.' He then nodded obsequiously and left.

'Why do you need a *consultation* with a waiter?' said Samuel.

'You'll see,' said John.

'Rum sort of waiter if you ask me,' said Samuel, but John only smiled knowingly.

In the vault John and Samuel savoured their brandies and reclined in the maroon-leather, high-backed chairs, and another waiter came and offered them a newspaper each, which they both accepted. Neither man looked out of place in this elevated situation, and for a few minutes they were both content to read and be quiet, hiding their faces from each other behind their respective papers, until Samuel spoke nonchalantly.

'What are you up to?'

'Oh, just fulfilling that promise I made you,' said John.

'What promise was that?'

'You'll see,' said John from behind his paper.

Samuel put down his own and stared in John's direction, but all he could see was John's newspaper. Newspapers cannot, of course, look smug; nevertheless John's did so. Samuel released an exasperated sigh. 'You can never tell me in advance what you're up to, can you? It always has to be the big surprise doesn't it – the big production?'

'Aye, it does Sammy lad,' said John boldly making no attempt to deny the accusation. 'If you stick with me it will always be the proverbial fairground ride – I've told you that before.'

Samuel smiled at the newspaper, which hid John's face and which now appeared to be smirking back at him despite having no face with which to smirk, and then he returned to his own paper.

Soon afterwards a waiter, smartly turned out in black livery, wearing a large white towel around his waist and carrying a small notebook in his left hand, interrupted them. He was in his mid-thirties, clean-shaven and with his hair well-groomed and tied in a tail at the back. He nodded his head very slightly to acknowledge their higher status, and introduced himself. 'Gentlemen; I'm Jack Morris, I hope that I can be of service to you.'

'Sit down Morris,' putting down his newspaper, John indicated a chair.

The waiter again gave a very slight nod and took his seat. 'Are my services required for both of you gentlemen, or just one in particular?'

'We are looking for something in particular for the young gentleman here,' John gestured in Samuel's direction. Samuel looked back in surprise, still unaware of the nature of the services on offer.

'Ah – I see,' said Morris, 'is it something in the way of - shall we say an initiation?'

'Well, not quite,' said John, 'but that is the sort of area we are interested in.'

Samuel still looked on, the bewilderment mounting in his expression like a schoolboy struggling with mathematics.

'I think I have the very thing here, gentlemen,' said Morris, opening his notebook: 'Miss Betsey – of No 44 Union Street. She is not much more than a beginner herself, a mere eighteen years of age, and is of a fair complexion, blue eyes and good teeth, but nevertheless she has shown that she is prepared to swallow up whosoever may have courage enough to approach her. A guinea will happily procure her services.'

'Yes – I see,' said John but it's not quite what I had in mind. I think someone with a little more experience to impart, if you know what I mean.'

'I'm sure that I can accommodate,' said Morris, flicking through the pages. 'Now what about this for the young gentleman? Miss Polly – of 45 Stevens Street: a sprightly Amazonian girl, who has learned to perform all her manoeuvres in a masterly manner, in particular bush fighting under cover, which she will do in any position in which the musket can be placed. Nor does she recoil if ever so deeply loaded, and she never unloads a piece without the balls ready for another charge. A little more expensive: two guineas will secure her services, but I am sure that she is well worth it.'

Muskets and balls? What the devil were they talking about? Samuel's eyes widened as at last it dawned on him the nature of the services being discussed, although he still failed to understand the detail being considered. 'Hey! You are talking about Mabels, aren't you?'

'And behold, then there was light,' joked John irreverently.

'But *two guineas* - you can get a Mabel in the Strand for a few pence.'

'Aye you can young sir,' said Morris, 'but I promise you that they aren't for the likes of a discerning young gentleman such as yourself. The services my girls offer, apart from being discreet, are far more, shall we say comprehensive. My girls are graduates from the University of Cupid and your satisfaction will be guaranteed.'

'It's still not what we were looking for though,' pondered John, 'what else can you offer - I was hoping for someone with a little more, shall we say... maturity?'

Morris again flicked through his notebook - he stopped for a moment and considered a page, but then licked his fingers and flicked again after rejecting it. This happened several more times until he seemed to be happier with his selection. 'What about this, gentlemen: Miss Lydia – of 22 Rathbone Place. She is a handsome girl, blue of eye with light brown hair and is of one and twenty years. So violent is she in her passions, and so amorous in her constitution, however, that I should therefore advise none but those replete with health, vigour, youth and money to engage with this lecherous girl. The young gentleman here would seem to have the physical requisites, and would it be out of place for me to enquire if he has the wealth, for the girl will cost him three guineas?'

'Mmm,' mused John. 'The young gentleman here has the funds all right, I can promise you that, for in this matter I am to be his benefactor and I will stand the costs. It will be his reward for the good fortune he has recently brought me.'

'Why thank you John,' said Samuel with some surprise, face flushed.

John nodded back politely but then winked as if to taunt him again. The wink signified he was still intent on controlling their relationship. John then re-engaged Morris.

'Now look here Morris, this Miss Lydia, sounds top drawer and I may even avail myself of her services, but it's still not quite what I have in mind for young Sammy boy here. Now do I have your assurance that I have your full discretion?'

'Aye, you do, Sir,' said Morris boldly, 'full confidentiality is assured at all times.'

'Good - good,' John nodded. 'You see, the young gentleman here has an assignation with a lady: a lady of very high rank but also a lady of reputation in the amorous pursuits, if you get my meaning.'

'Aye –I think I do, Sir.'

'Well, it seems to me that your ladies are in the trade of – well shall we say pleasure. Which of course is to be accepted – but they offer the services as the *pleasurer*. The client will be the *pleasuree* in the transaction. Would this be a fair summary of the position, Morris?'

'Aye Sir; that is the nature of the business,' Morris responded hesitantly, unsure where this conversation was now going.

'Well, the young gentleman here, at his assignation will have to be the *pleasurer* and not the *pleasuree*, if you get my meaning. So we are looking for a lady who can act as – well shall we say a tutor in the passionate arts.'

'Oh - I see, Sir,' said Morris mulling over the request, 'a very specific commission indeed and I thank you for taking me into your confidence.'

'And is it a commission that you are able to fulfil, Sir?' asked John.

'It is true it is a difficult one, Sir, but I think I have a very special client for this very special commission.' Morris's body language changed perceptively and he leant forward in his chair, looking about himself furtively as he did so. Samuel and John reacted instinctively and they too leant forward in their chairs. 'I have a client, gentlemen,' said Morris in hushed tones, 'whose details are not to be found in my notebook. She is of high birth, but has fallen on difficult times. She herself has always had the virtue of thrift, but regrettably her husband has not. Gambling – *gambling,* Sir, is the source of this man's profligacy, and the good lady has had her circumstances reduced because of it. I have the honour to introduce very special clients to her, and she may be exactly what you are looking for here – but I must warn you, this lady is very special and the favours she offers cannot be obtained for less than ten guineas.'

Samuel let out a long whistle at the amount. 'Ten *guineas*! I fear she is too rich for my taste, Morris.'

'But not for mine,' said John.

'You can't be serious,' said Samuel, 'I can't let you defray such a large amount on my behalf.'

'I'll hear no more about it. It is a gift – and besides it is no more than I would wager on the turn of a card,' said John.

'Aye, you would that, John Campbell-John,' said Samuel, 'and I fear that it will be your downfall. Your fortune will drain away if you continue in this way.'

'Is this ingratitude I sense?' said John.

'Nay, and I apologise if it sounded that way,' said Samuel, 'but it's just…'

'It's just nothing, Sir,' exclaimed John feigning hurt sensibilities. 'Will you accept my gift or will you not?'

Morris stiffened in his seat anticipating a dispute, but Samuel knew it was simply a performance. He did not always recognise John's performances; in fact, he was unaware that the character of

John Campbell-John was itself a total performance; a fabrication aimed at the whole world. But in this instance he read the clues clearly enough, for John, who had become a master of the nuances of deception, had scattered the clues unsubtly in Samuel's path.

Samuel duly played his part as John intended. 'Aye – *aye* I will John, for you are generous friend.'

'Then that shall be the end of it,' said John, 'it is decided.'

'Well not quite,' said Morris tentatively. 'You see; the nature of my agreement with this certain lady means that I cannot refer just any gentleman to her without her prior approval. In fact, I'm not even at liberty to give out her name before she has approved the liaison.'

'That's a rum sort of way to go about whoring,' said John, 'even if she is a lady of rank.'

'Well that's right, if she was only offering the services of a whore, but this lady is offering much more than that.'

'I'm not sure that I follow,' said John, 'what exactly is she offering?'

'Well, she's offering the services of – well it's quite difficult to explain. The whoring will be only part of it, if you see what I mean.'

'No, not really,' said John as Samuel looked on in bewildered silence.

'Well, I suppose you might say she is offering a fantasy,' said Morris.

'What sort of fantasy?' said John, his interest spiced by the word.

'Well *if* she accepts you, you will visit her home and then she will entertain you.'

'Entertain me?' said John. 'That doesn't seem much for ten guineas. I'm sure that I am acquainted with many a lady on whom I could call. I'm sure that if I presented my card to them, they would likewise entertain me.'

'I'm sure you are correct in this, Sir,' said Morris, 'but in this scenario, so to speak – the lady will entertain you, as, well... as her lover. You will visit her at her splendid residence and spend the whole afternoon there, playing the part of the cuckolder while she plays the part of the mistress.'

'Ah... I see. I like the sound of that,' said John sitting upright in his chair, 'that sounds wonderfully impish, doesn't it? What do you think, Sammy lad?'

'I think it's your fantasy, John.'

'Maybe, Sammy, maybe – yes, but it's open to adaptation isn't. If Morris here explains to the lady that you are a young gentleman whose social standing has recently been vastly improved, and that you are in need of direction in the ways of society as well as in the ways of cupid. Have you read any Greek, Morris?' John turned to the waiter, his mind running ahead of him.

'I'm afraid my reading has not run to such elevated matter, Sir,' said Morris apologetically.

'Never mind,' said John, 'just mention to her the word *Pygmalion,* and she will understand.'

Morris nodded his agreement, scribbling the name down in his notebook to remind himself. 'I'll consult the lady this very afternoon, Sirs, and send word to you of her response. Or it might be better if you stay here, for I am fearful of sending out notes in this matter. The lady might see it as being indiscreet.'

'Very well,' said John, 'we'll stay here until you have consulted, 'I'm sure that I can find a four for a game of cards to keep me company in the meantime.'

'Pygmalion?' Samuel queried, after Morris had gone.

'In Greek myth he was the King of Cyprus,' John smiled.

'I don't quite follow...' Samuel was puzzled.

'He sculpted a statue of a beautiful woman, fell in love with it and it came to life.'

'Well I'm no statue,' Samuel's brow creased with indignation.

John laughed. 'No Sammy boy, but under the hands of a sculptress you are going to come alive!'

CHAPTER 9

It was not a fine day for an afternoon constitutional, but nevertheless three unlikely caped figures strolled through the wide streets that were part of the city of London's affluent West End. In an act of circumspection, they had disembarked from their hired carriage two streets away from their destination, in that prudence had, by command, been bestowed upon them. Their heads were bowed to avoid, as far as possible, the downpour that had, it seemed, saved itself just for them and now came crashing down like a military ambush on an unsuspecting army. The three men approached the two great and imposing wrought-iron gates of a London residence; its splendour proclaiming to the world the status of its owner. They stood for a moment, their heads and eyes raised, as they looked through the railings to the lavish property within, and each one felt insignificant before it.

Two of them need not have been there, only the third had an invitation to call, but the first two were intent on ensuring that the third complete his mission satisfactorily. The third man stood a few paces back from the first two and anxiety was written all across his features as the immensity of the property cut into his consciousness and overwhelmed him. He backed uncomfortably away from the other two, speaking apologetically as he did so.

'I beg your pardon, sirs, but I fear that I cannot go through with this,' said Samuel Medina.

'Oh yes you can,' said John Campbell-John, 'Morris here has arranged everything and the lady is expecting you. And talking of the lady,' he continued to Morris, 'I think it's time you told us her identity.'

'Aye, you are right, sirs, but this information comes with an encumbrance,' said Morris, 'this information must remain confidential.'

Aye, that is understood already,' said John looking also at Samuel. 'Isn't that right Sammy lad?'

'Aye, that is understood already,' repeated Samuel in a mumbled response.

'Well gentlemen, the lady in question is…' Morris paused for effect, 'none other than the Marchioness of Thame.'

John let out a long whistle to signify his astonishment. 'Do you hear that Sammy lad, you're going to cuckold the Marquis of Thame.'

'I'd really rather not if you don't mind gentlemen.' Samuel turned and began to walk away.

The other two ran after him, took him by the arms and tried to march him back to the gates, but he remained steadfast and immobile, not because he was too strong for them, but because he had been rendered paralysed with fear.

'You can do this Sammy lad,' said John, 'I have invested ten guineas in saying that you can.'

'You'll be fine, young sir,' said Morris, 'this will be a privilege. You will be the envy of all the sporting gentlemen in town – that is if you could tell them – which, of course, you can't,' he added hurriedly.

Samuel found himself in a situation that was new to him and that he did not know how to handle. In such circumstances he always returned to his *injured, honest fellow* persona. 'Unhand me gentlemen, for you wrong me,' he blustered, 'I will thrash you both if you do not unhand me.'

'No you won't,' said John matter of factly, which surprisingly had the required effect, as Samuel quietened down immediately. His tense muscles suddenly relaxed to the point where they felt almost non-existent and his legs turned to jelly. Protesting to no avail, he allowed his two companions to drag him back to the gates.

'I thought you were afraid of no man, *Samuel Medina*, and look at you now,' said John, 'cowering like a beaten puppy.'

'I *am* afraid of no *man*,' said Samuel boldly, his pride suddenly wounded. The bravado fell away as he looked up at the mansion before them, 'but this isn't a *man* is it,' he croaked.

'So then where is your problem, Sammy lad?' said John.

'Well it wouldn't be a problem if I were here to thrash her,' Samuel said, 'but I doubt whether that is an option open to me is it gentlemen?'

'Well no,' said John, 'unless of course that is what the lady has in mind for you anyway.'

The two men laughed at this quip, but Samuel did not understand the joke. In fact, their humour had the effect of increasing his anxiety and his voice rose to little more than a squeak, 'What do you mean gentlemen?'

'Nothing Sammy lad,' John patted him soundly on the back. 'We are just having sport at your expense.'

'Then I will thrash you both for your insolence,' said Samuel, trying to force his voice down a couple of octaves.

'It's much too wet to fight, Sammy lad,' said John, 'this day is made for wenching not fighting. Now let's be having you.'

Samuel struggled for the words that would enable him to manage the situation. In the past he been adept in the use of words, but always in the knowledge that, if all else failed, he could fight his way out of trouble. In fact, he had often used words to manipulate a situation so that fighting was the only recourse; used them as a spider uses its web to ensnare its victim. But now it seemed to him that he was the prey, caught up in some other spider's web, and the more he struggled the more tied up he became.

'Ten guineas! – TEN GUINEAS - Sammy lad, that's what I have spent today, and it will not be forfeited I promise you. How much were you earning as an apprentice eh?'

'As well you know, John, I was earning nothing at all aside from my room and board. I know the value of ten guineas I promise you, and don't think I'm not grateful to you, but...' he swallowed, his voice tailing away.

'It doesn't seem so to me,' said John crossly, but then his voice mellowed, and it seemed he was about to give Samuel a way out of his dilemma. 'Would you like me take your place this time then, Sammy?'

Samuel breathed a sigh of relief, his apprehension suddenly eased like a popped balloon. He turned and looked at John, gratitude standing in his eyes. 'Oh, would you John?'

'No I bloody wouldn't,' barked John. 'I've come here to undertake a commission and I intend to see it through, dammit!'

As Samuel's hopes sank, John produced a hip flask from his tunic and undid the top, thrusting it towards Samuel's face. He took it instinctively. 'The stallion needs to be schooled in his duties and that's what is going to happen,' John said. 'A little Dutch courage is all you need. Morris!' he yelled. 'The gates Sir, if you please!'

Morris leapt to do as he was bid. The gates swung open and the two men ushered Samuel through while he tried to take as large a gulp of brandy as he could swallow. The flask cup was still at his lips as it was snatched away and the gates slammed closed behind him. He looked back at the two men grinning at him through the railings. Samuel made one last appeal with his large, puppy-dog eyes, but saw no escape in their expressions.

'Remember my motto, Sammy lad,' said John, 'when things start to go wrong – it's turning out to be a good day!'

Samuel breathed in deeply, turned and walking up to the door, rapping the wood soundly with the ornate knocker. After a few moments a footman opened the door. He was dressed in livery of navy blue velvet, a long frock coat edged all around the cuffs and pockets with silver braid and with epaulettes at the shoulders. He wore a white wig tied in a queue with a navy blue bow; the wig matching his spotless, white-gloved hands.

Samuel stared at this grand figure before him, at which point he realised he had forgotten to breathe out. 'I have a letter of introduction to see the Marchioness,' he gasped, the words escaping in a rush like water from a hosepipe. The footman gestured for him to enter and wait, and sheepishly he did so. Samuel felt that brief moment of Dutch courage ebbing away from him as the footman disappeared upstairs carrying the letter of introduction before him on a silver tray. As he waited, Samuel looked around the large entrance hall and was surprised to see that although it was undoubtedly grand, it was somehow lessened by the sparseness of furniture, so that his initial impression was not of grandeur but of bareness.

When the footman returned, Samuel was shown upstairs to the mistress's private apartment. He climbed the stairs, fearing his legs might give way at any moment, and swallowed hard as he was ushered into her Ladyship's rooms.

The Marchioness was standing with her back to him, peering out of the window and made no attempt to greet him as he entered.

'Mr Samuel Medina,' proclaimed the footman, who then bowed and retreated backwards, closing the two large doors as he did so. The room fell silent as the Marchioness continued to gaze out of the window and Samuel felt increasingly uncomfortable. He tried to see what she looked like, but he had only a rear view of her. He could see, however, that she had been riding. She was wearing a rust-red riding coat over a pale cream gown. On her head was perched a black hat with rust and black ribbons. She was tallish, standing about five feet four, but her raised hair and riding hat accentuated her height. He could gauge enough to see that she had none of the corpulence he had encountered among the mature women at Sir Thomas's house party. In fact, she appeared to him to be a fine figure of a woman. Nervously, he cleared his throat.

Lady Theodora Fulworth, the Marchioness of Thame was a very unusual woman; not at all a woman of her time. She had been born into an aristocratic family, which had not denied her a fine education simply because she was female. An extremely intelligent child, she had relished her studies for they had alleviated much of the everyday boredom that she faced. Much of what was expected of a young girl of her rank she had found tedious and although she found her musical studies stimulating, the skills of embroidery held no such rewards for her. In fact, she was much brighter than her brothers and outshone them academically, which made her the favourite of the family tutor. She also outshone them athletically in that she became a very fine horsewoman, to the endless despair of her mother, who felt her daughter's boyish behaviour singularly unladylike. As Theodora grew into young womanhood, she developed into a tall, handsome woman, and bestowed of a handsome dowry, she was regarded by her family as a very *good catch* indeed.

Into her life had come James Fulworth, the Marquis of Thame. He had a reputation for being something of a wastrel, a profligate, but that was not uncommon in titled gentlemen, and it did not distract in any way from his own eligibility in the marriage stakes. He too was regarded as a fine catch. So at the age of twenty, the young Theodora married the thirty-eight year old James and became - to the gratification of her mother - the Marchioness of Thame.

At first she found him amusing as he certainly had wit, but after a time her appreciation of this aptitude began to fade; partly because she found his lack of other abilities overrode that appreciation, and partly because her waning interest was reciprocated and he stopped trying to be witty towards her. Their relationship had quickly declined. James was a prodigious gambler. His immense need to gamble was matched only by his immense talent for losing. James was unskilled in the very thing that he coveted most. The dowry that his wife had brought to the marriage had been a financial lifesaver to him, but he then proceeded to gamble away that dowry in the same way he had gambled away his own inheritance. His debts to traders were years overdue, but as a gentleman of title his creditworthiness was not in any way diminished, no more than was his position in society – at least not initially. But the Marquis went well past what was considered redeemable, and eventually the avenues of credit on which such persons of rank depended, began to dry up. This, of course, impinged greatly on the Marchioness's own situation because in law all *her* assets belonged to her husband, and consequentially the denial of credit applied to her as well as to her husband.

The gravity of the situation came to head when she was denied credit at her dressmakers. This was indeed serious; to a woman of her standing in society, appearances were all important. She was now thirty-five years of age with a fifty-three year old husband, whose health and looks were ravaged by years of overindulgence, and who was now facing financial ruin. Theodora resolved that something had to be done, for she saw that even such a high-ranking nobleman as her husband would eventually end up in the debtor's prison. She needed a secret income to prepare herself for that eventuality, and for her clothing and riding needs in the meantime. Theodora was an intelligent and resourceful woman and she started by selling off the furniture and other household fittings, but she found that this did little more than cover her clothing needs, notwithstanding that the house was becoming increasingly bare. She needed another source of income.

Her solution was bold in the extreme. She examined her own skills and abilities, determined that she rode well, conversed well, entertained well, and bedded well. She considered becoming a mistress: finding herself a rich and high born gentleman to finance the lifestyle she was so loath to give up. This would have been a solution to her problems, but her profligate husband had made her wary of becoming beholden to any man again. This being so, she had resolved to find some other way to turn her social skills into an income and whoring seemed to be the answer. 'Whore' was not, however, a word she would have recognised, for she was not in the market of offering merely sexual favours. Nor did she see herself as a courtesan, for it was *she* who was of high birth in the relationships she proposed, not the gentlemen.

Samuel Medina was only one in a long line of her clientele, who had come to value her services and who had, miraculously, maintained discretion. She had watched him with his companions at her gates and her interest had been piqued as much by his reluctance as his physique, but she deliberately kept him waiting.

Samuel gazed at her back for what seemed like an eternity - and then suddenly she turned and walked briskly towards him, holding out her hand.

'Mr Medina how is it with you, Sir?' She spoke surprisingly brightly, but as if she were holding something back; masking her true feelings.

'I rejoice that you have allowed me to come to see you, Ma'am.' Samuel took her hand gently as he spoke and was surprised that his own eloquence was still functioning.

She pursed her lips and looked at him steadily. 'It doesn't seem so to me, Sir, for I have been watching you and your companions at the gate. Your reluctance to enter was all too plain to see.'

'My apologies, My Lady, if I have in any way offended you,' said Samuel, feeling now even worse, 'but a lady of your standing is a star so bright that I believed you to be out of reach for so humble a man as myself.'

She smiled at him recognising the compliment. 'You have an eloquent tongue on you, Mr Medina, and I suspect that you will be a good pupil, for I understand that that is to be the somewhat unusual nature of our liaison. Is that not right?'

'If such an arrangement is acceptable to you, My Lady?'

'It is acceptable, Mr Medina, and I will be pleased to…' She stopped in mid sentence. Her forehead furrowed slightly and she peered intently back at Samuel for a moment. 'Oh my,' she said at length, 'there was no mention of this in your introduction, Mr Medina.'

'You have the advantage of me, My Lady.' Samuel was baffled. 'What was not mentioned?'

'Am I to understand, Sir, that you are a – you are of the Jewish faith?'

Samuel felt a mixture of emotions spring into his mind like an avenging knight on the rampage, and at a stroke all his feelings of anxiety were banished from him to be replaced by anger, but he strove to conceal it as much as he could. 'Aye, Ma'am Judaism is my faith,' he said, 'and I am proud to proclaim that to anyone.'

'But the letter says that your position in society has been recently raised, but Sir; a Jew *has no* position in society. That is the way of it.'

'Then society is all the poorer for that, My Lady,' said Samuel, still attempting to be gracious, though his emotions were willing him to abandon such niceties.

She paused for what seemed like a time without end, but in reality was only a few seconds. She appeared to squint at him as her thought processes evaluated the man before her. And then she opened her mouth to speak, but thought better of it, closed it again and wandered back to the window, turning her back to him.

The silence deafened Samuel as if the great bell of Bow itself was pounding inside his temples. He wanted to lash out and antagonistic words formed in his mind in readiness, as if he were loading shells into a magazine ready to be fired.

She turned suddenly, her long skirts swishing as she walked briskly back to him. 'Well said, Mr Medina.'

He stood for a moment, speechless with surprise, as if the shell had misfired in the breech. He could think of nothing better to do than bow slightly in gratitude.

'I have no problems with your faith, Sir,' she continued, 'but let us understand each other from the beginning. Our business together may be intimate in nature, but it is business nevertheless. Do you understand that?'

'I do Ma'am,' he responded.

'Your manners do you well, Sir,' she said, 'society will not shun you because of them and I will tutor you further. But if we *were* to meet socially, I *will* shun you, Mr Medina: firstly, since society may require it of me because of your faith, and secondly, because we are simply not to be acquainted outside these meetings. Do I make myself clear?'

'Very clear, Ma'am,' he now replied firmly, all hint of intimidation having been dispelled, 'and perhaps I should make *myself* clear. If I feel the need at any time to defend my faith then I will do so.'

She squinted at him again. She found his words impertinent and made no effort to hide the fact. She was used only to deference before her, and now this young Jewish man - well he…. but what was he? She realised that she didn't know. Her mood mellowed slightly as her intellect took over from her emotions. She further realised that she was curious. What had been proposed to her was as novel to her as it was to Samuel and John. 'I'll pass over your impertinence for the moment Mr Medina,' she said, 'if this interview is to continue then I think I need to find out more about you. Come, sit with me.' She gestured to him, indicating a sofa.

Surprised by her politeness, Samuel reciprocated with similar courtesy; nodding slightly to signify his gracious acceptance of the offer, he duly sat down. She too perched herself on the sofa, removing her riding hat as she did so, but far enough away to be both open and noncommittal at the same time.

'You say that your circumstances have been raised in recent times, Mr Medina. How so – please tell. What exactly is it that you do?'

'I am a pugilist, Ma'am,' he said, 'I have recently been earning quite considerable sums from the noble science.'

'*Noble Science*,' she said disparagingly, 'yes they do call it that do they not? I have to say, though, that I prefer my men with the blood on the inside.'

Samuel paused for a moment; the comment was not intended to be kind, but it had wit, if a cruel wit. He found himself responding with a small, but audible laugh for the comment had cut through their barbed conversation like a paring knife to the core of an apple He found himself smiling, though it was the last thing on his mind. And she noticed that and responded.

'You have a sense of humour, Mr Medina,' she said.

'I hope so Ma'am.'

'That is good, for I was under the impression that you were a very dour young man indeed.'

'I hope I will surprise you further, Ma'am.'

'I hope so too, and you can start surprising me by addressing me by another name. You can save Ma'am for the Queen, should you ever get to meet Her Majesty.'

'But you have me at a disadvantage,' said Samuel after a brief thought, 'for I simply don't know how I should address you.'

'There is no correct etiquette for meetings such as these, Mr Medina, for they are outside society. We shall be playing roles in our encounters, and they must, by their very nature, assume some intimacy. You may therefore call me "Dora". And I will call you "Samuel" – unless you wish to fantasise that you are someone else?'

'No, Samuel will be fine.'

'Good; then we are moving towards an understanding, are we not?'

'I hope so... Dora,' said Samuel, awkwardly.

'You aren't comfortable with this arrangement are you Samuel?'

'No,' said Samuel, 'but I'm sure that you will find me a willing apprentice.'

'That's not really what I mean. You are not much more than a youth and there is no shame in admitting to inexperience. You should find yourself a young girl of your own age and learn the lessons of cupid together. Do you really need me?'

'But both the girls of my own age that I've ...' just in time he stopped himself from using the word '*fucked*', '...well, they were both well-schooled in the ways of cupid and I felt – well... quite inadequate; and besides neither was a lady of position. I find myself suddenly in a place where I need to move from apprentice to master -

and move quickly, so I've made a commitment to myself that I will now do so.'

'Mmm, I see,' she said. 'You are an unusual young man, Samuel, but I applaud you for your resolve.'

The liaison had not started well. Their conversation had been prickly. There had been a clash of culture, of class and of religion. But now the atmosphere lightened and they took tea together, Theodora schooling her pupil all the while as to the etiquette that would be required of him. She was impressed at how well read he was, far more than many a young gentleman. She counselled him on the way in which women of position lived their lives, explaining how they filled the long, boring days with uninteresting pastimes. Some filled the empty hours by reading poetry or romantic fiction, which in many cases gave them a glimpse of a life that was denied to them by their indifferent, and in many cases absent, husbands who were more interested in gaming, riding and shooting than in making love to their wives - whom in general they had wed merely to feather their own nests. And even when they did enter their wives' beds, they did so alcohol-fuelled with bloated bellies and all the finesse of rutting stags.

Samuel's eyes widened as he listened. It was clear that Dora's low opinion of men was motivated by her own experiences of marriage. He surmised that she had been a virgin when she wed, and knew she had quickly produced two children. With a shard of compassion lodging in his throat, he no longer wondered why her marriage had so visibly soured.

Indeed, Theodora had shared her husband's bed for only the first few of their married years. Having given her husband two daughters, if not a son, she had believed her wifely duties in that area had been fulfilled and she had then taken lovers, but these too, in the main, had been a great disappointment to her. She had met briefly an Italian nobleman, Giacomo Casanova, who was visiting London. He had beguiled her with love notes and poems and had come to her bed as much a grantor as a beneficiary. His aim was to give pleasure; he saw the woman as an equal partner in the act of lovemaking, and a whole new world opened to her. After this experience, she had fallen for the one great love of her life, a love that had been reciprocated, and for a time she had known the wonderful pleasures it afforded of giving and receiving. But fate had proved what a spiteful fellow he is, and her lover had succumbed to a bout of influenza. It was after his death that she had forged a life for herself; surrounded by entertaining and riding and the taking of occasional lovers, until she had succumbed to her pressing need for an income.

However, she imparted very little of this to Samuel, instead, educating him in the need to excite a woman not just in her bed, but also in her everyday life. A tryst had layer upon layer of delights that transcended the mere rendezvous itself. It would give her joyous thoughts that would brighten her monotonous days. A simple note would make her heart miss a beat, and she would take hours of bliss in the endless re-reading of it. Words of love, particularly if truly meant, would gain access to even the coldest of hearts and would be more appreciated than the most expensive of gifts. Dora, at pains to point out that sensitivity in these matters would be rewarded tenfold with affection, continued to shower Samuel with gems of wisdom that were in reality so obvious to women, but somehow unknown to the vast majority of men who commonly invested more time in their horses that their wives. However, it was wisdom from a woman's point of view; it was not advanced mathematics; nor was it a labyrinthine journey. It was in reality a statement of the blindingly obvious, thought Samuel, and like most commonsense, it was not at all common! He recognised it as a statement that would give him an edge, an insight into women that other men could not comprehend, any more than he had himself – until now.

Samuel was a good listener and he was content to sit, metaphorically, at the foot of the master, or in this case at the foot of the mistress. He hung on her every word and she responded to his interest. She found him unusual, this strange man: a man of bravado; a man who could be brutal; an extrovert, but one who could also be a gentle and considerate man. She saw within him that side of his character. A side that he kept locked away; dominated by the Samuel Medina who thought the world was intent on skewering him and therefore had to be fought at every turn.

They talked for hours and a bond grew between them, but in no way did he feel a sexual response to her. There was no arousal, no stirrings, she had not elicited any emotional response from him at all, and therefore, her next suggestion took him completely by surprise.

'You must learn how to undress a woman, Samuel,' she said, 'come now you must practise on me.'

He looked at her with incomprehension. He opened his mouth to speak but nothing came out. He started to say *but I hardly know you*, but managed to hold those words back, realising the folly of them before they left his lips. She noticed his reticence and was at first puzzled for it was fundamental to their arrangement that sex would be involved. But then she found herself pleased by this reticence in much the same way as women respond to men who blush.

'Come,' she repeated, 'this is a lesson that will serve you well. It is common practice for a lady to retire to her boudoir and disrobe in readiness for her liaison. This is partly because of the complexities of women's fashion, and partly because gentlemen do not have the finesse to conquer these intricacies. If you have this ability, however, it will be much appreciated. It will also mean that the passion of the moment will not be lost, and that can be so important. Come – my boots, and remember that it is acceptable to be strong and powerful, but you must never be rough. There is many a gentleman who will tell you that a lady's clothes can be removed quickly and forcefully in the passion of the moment, but I can promise you that in most instances, a lady would not thank you for taking that advice. You must always follow the lady's lead, and you do not remove anything without her approval. She will never, however, actually tell you that. You must look at what she does and be attuned to her behaviour. There will be only little nuances for you to follow. If she moves her body slightly to assist you, then that is a signal to proceed. She may not want to reveal all of her body to you if she perceives there is some blemish that she does not want you to see. You must never press her to disrobe in such circumstances. If she is of mature years she may want to reveal very little to you aside, perhaps, from her breasts. If that is so, you must respect her wishes. Above all you must move slowly. Treat her body as an expensive gift, with the wrapping to be taken away slowly to savour the contents, rather than to be torn away like an expectant child. Come,' she prompted him again, 'my boots, Samuel.'

He stood and positioned himself by her feet. She reclined further back onto the sofa and raised her leg for him to take it. 'Now it is time to be strong,' she said.

He took her heel in his left hand and with his right gripped the boot around her calf. He pulled strongly without tugging and the boot slid easily down her leg. He repeated the operation with the other boot, and again the boot slid away. She smiled her approval to him, but his body language betrayed that he did not know what to remove next.

'My ruff,' she said, anticipating him. He sat beside her clumsily, not sure where to position himself. He leant forward and undid the ruff and then pulled it slowly away from the neck of her bodice, and she breathed a long *'Goood'* to him. Emboldened, he undid a button of her riding coat, but she put her hand on his to stop him.

'Tarry a while, Samuel,' she said, 'undressing a woman isn't a checklist. Cup her breast with your hand gently and see how she reacts.

He slid his hand inside her bodice and cupped her bosom as she had suggested and she purred her response. It felt good to him too and he sensed her nipple hardening in his palm. At last he began to respond to her sexually and he writhed slightly as his arousal began; it was just enough for her to notice. She looked deeply at him and a knowing, gentle smile flickered across her features.

'If you can feel the nipple hardening, you will know that she is awakening to you. It is another of those signs that you need to look for. Now you can move to –yes I think the tunic. Look into her eyes as you do so because you can't do this without her help.'

He undid the rest of the buttons, and then looked into Dora's eyes as he put both his hands under her riding coat and pushed it backwards off her shoulders. She leant forward to help him, and then pulled her arms out and clear. All the time she looked back at him mischievously.

'A kiss would be good now,' she said.

He leant forward and she met him half way. Their lips met gently but then she opened her mouth to complete the kiss with a sucking action, holding his bottom lip between her teeth as she did so. His arousal now gathered apace - this was good, this was *very* good.

'Gown – my gown must be next,' she said, 'but this requires the skills of an expert suitor. Such a suitor will know that he cannot achieve this manoeuvre alone. You will need help, and you must wait for the lady to offer it. If you force matters then the romance of the moment will be lost.'

She took his hand and held it gently to her bosom and then to her mouth, allowing his hand to pass through her fingers as she swivelled and turned her back to him, looking back over her shoulder. 'Undo the buttons at the back,' she added.

The buttons were undone and then she turned back and with the merest of gestures told him to continue. She put his hands on her shoulders and slowly, inch by inch he pulled the gown down until her breasts were exposed to him. He continued, but she put her hand up to stop him.

'This would be another good time to tarry,' she said, 'fondle a breast gently and compliment the lady on it.'

He did as he was bid and fondled her breast. He didn't have to lie to her about it, for he found it a wonder to behold. 'It's as fine as a peach, Dora.' He was a little discomfited when she giggled at his naivety, unaware that she found his inexperience utterly charming.

He returned to pulling down the gown and she raised her bottom and then her knees so that they it passed easily over her until it could be removed and cast aside. She lay back provocatively. She was now wearing only white stockings and her chemise top with the drawstring now ungathered so that her breasts were exposed. He looked down at her. She wasn't fully naked, but it was difficult to image that she could have been any more enticing. Despite her maturity, her breasts were full, having escaped the ravages of breast-feeding, and her athletic nature and lifestyle had left her body toned. Her nipples were large and dark and erect in passion and her dark, tightly-curled pubic hair, shone in contrast to her pale-skinned belly. Her body was enticing to him, as if it was an invitation from cupid himself, but again he was unsure how to proceed.

Theodora read the anxiety in his eyes. 'It is acceptable for a gentleman to only partially disrobe or not to disrobe at all,' she said. 'It is an etiquette of which I disapprove since it deprives the lady of her opportunity for arousal. If the gentleman is bloated by his acquaintance with John Barleycorn, then that is no great loss. But in your case, Samuel, I would advise you to disrobe and follow the lady as to how far you should go.'

He sat upright and removed his black frockcoat. She too sat upright and ran her hands across his torso over his shirt. Her surprise was evident in her body language, as her fingers probed ever more inquisitively and expressively like a general assessing a battlefield before an encounter. She tugged at the bottom of his shirt, inch by inch lifting it free of his breeches, and helped him to pull it over his head. She then leant back to survey his powerful arms; his muscle-rippling shoulders and his deep chest.

'Samuel!' she exclaimed. 'Samuel, Samuel,' she repeated more softly. 'You have no need to feel inadequate - you will take the ladies of society by storm I promise you. By my word; you will!' Samuel blushed uncontrollably. 'And that's good as well,' she continued, 'women love men who blush. Don't ever try to hide it.'

Samuel looked down at his breeches and then back at her, to gesture the question to her.

'It doesn't matter Samuel; for some reason it is acceptable for a man to retain his breeches while making love, you can unleash your member without removing them,' she said, 'but with a physique like yours I would again advise their removal. *I* certainly want to see you completely naked. Come stand before me so that I can look at you.'

With some embarrassment Samuel removed his breeches and stood before her in his draws and stockings. Once more she giggled and his embarrassment mounted.

'No-no,' she said, 'I'm merely teasing you. If the breeches come off, then so must the draws and stockings. Men in their draws are a comical sight, fit only for the music hall.'

He reluctantly removed the last of his garments so that they were naked together, but he felt as if she had him on parade like the lowliest of soldiers.

Dora's eyes widened; she marvelled in his masculinity for although she was a woman of considerable experience, she had never before beheld such a perfect specimen of athleticism as now stood before her. Nor had she had occasion to witness the evidence of his faith, which looked strange to her eyes. Her inquisitiveness, however, had interfered with his passion, and this became apparent to her. He had begun to raise an ardour within her that she had not expected and so she desisted from her examination and held out her arms to him.

'Come,' she said, 'return to my arms.

He thankfully reclined beside her on the sofa, and kissed her gently on the lips, but she put a finger in between them.

'Lips are all very fine,' she said, 'but kisses should not to be saved only for them. A carpet of kisses will be much appreciated by any lady.

Obediently he again followed her directions, and marvelled at the effect his actions had upon her. He began to understand the pleasure that can be obtained from the *giving* of pleasure, and he began to feel good about his studies. He covered her body with kisses displaying a gentleness that belied his brutal occupation.

Dora responded and allowed herself the consent to enjoy what was being done to her, for she normally denied it to herself. 'You have learned well, young Samuel,' she said.

'If I have, Dora, it is because you have been an accomplished tutor,' he responded.

'Good, good,' she said allowing herself to laugh as she did so, 'never let an opportunity to praise a lady go by. With whom is the liaison for which you so assiduously prepare, may I ask?'

'Lady Adele Fitzsymons.'

'Ahh,' she said knowingly, 'Adele.'

'You know her, Dora?'

'Oh yes,' her smile was tinged with regret. 'I am sending you into the world with this sophisticated new-found knowledge, and I fear it will be wasted on Adele. You will need little finesse with this lady, Samuel, but I hope you will keep in mind what I have taught you nevertheless, for it will serve you well.'

Feeling reassured that he would not be required to display the knowledge of a seasoned suitor for his forthcoming liaison, Samuel visibly relaxed, but Dora sensed it. 'We are not finished yet,' she said, 'your education would be incomplete without an intimate knowledge of Venus herself.'

'Venus?' enquired Samuel.

'Yes, Venus – you must know your way around a lady's most intimate part, young man.' Dora raised herself slightly and gestured almost imperceptibly with her pelvis. It was a subtle movement but it was enough to enlighten even as raw a youth as Samuel. What she was intimating was as earthy a suggestion as it was possible for a woman to make; yet she managed to achieve this with an accomplished grace that seemed to Samuel's eager eyes not in the least vulgar.

'Come and I will take you on a voyage of discovery,' she said, 'you must know the workings of every inch of this haven. It will be a key to unlock the very treasure that a woman has to offer you.' She beamed a mischievous smile at him and his misgivings drained away. 'Come Samuel,' she said, 'the ship is about to sail – the voyage is about to begin, and your navigator is keen to get underway.'

CHAPTER 10

Bob's Chop House was full of people, as it always seemed to be. It was an establishment that was much more that its name suggested, however, and attracted more than the diner. It was also a place for hard drinking and gambling. If wenching was on your particular menu to round off the evening, then this was also readily available. It was in short one of the lowest of establishments in London: its clientele however, was of a surprisingly mixed variety.

When Samuel arrived, John was already engaged at a card table as part of a hand of four. It was the highest stakes game in the establishment that evening and there was much interest in it from the other drinkers and diners, and a noisy, tousled, and unkempt crowd gathered around them. A number of women, whom Samuel assumed to be Mabels, had placed themselves close besides some of the players, no doubt believing that they would be prospective clients for themselves and, no doubt, also good payers.

'Ah,' bellowed John when he saw Samuel. 'Pull up a chair, Sammy lad. The cards are running kindly for me tonight - will you dare to take a hand and wager against me?'

Samuel sat down and gestured that he would, when another of the players also spoke to him.

'Evening Medina,' the man said, his voice slurred with ale. 'Are you an expert at this sport also? I'll look forward to emptying your purse if you're not.'

Samuel eyed this stranger who apparently knew him, but he couldn't place him at all. He pondered for a short time, and then, like a figure appearing out of the mists, he saw who it was. The man was dressed in common clothing, which had deceived him. But there was no doubting it – the man before him was none other than Sir Thomas Kettall.

John had already learned the art of impersonation: he could pass himself off easily as an officer or indeed anyone of rank for he had the knowledge and manners gained from his unusual upbringing. Kettall, however was undertaking this same deceit, but in reverse. He was dressed down in order to live the double life he enjoyed. Samuel was unaware of the strange life that Kettall led, and the strange world he inhabited. The man belonged to a privileged rank of society: he had a title and he had wealth. What he also had, however, was a taste for the basest of pleasures that life had to offer. The words 'disreputable' and 'degenerate' sat well upon Kettall's shoulders. Top of the list of his vices was gambling, but he was not to be confined to the genteel version practised by most of his peers - however high the stakes. Gambling in taverns had an edge that was not to be found in the drawing rooms, and he revelled in it. Big Charles Sweep himself had taught Kettall to fight with his fists, taught him the noble art of self-defence. He had similarly been taught how to fence and he knew how to use a cudgel. He did not fear for his physical safety and brawling with the most common of folk was not unknown to him. John had unwittingly chosen well when he had considered Sir Thomas as a sponsor for Samuel.

Kettall was deliberately unshaven as part of his disguise, and attired in a worn tunic over a dirty shirt. He looked older than his twenty-nine years, the excesses of his lifestyle beginning to show. His skin was sagging under his eyes, which in themselves were surrounded by darkened rounds, accentuated because his skin was sallow through lack of exposure to natural daylight. He drank ale, farted and belched without restraint as he sat and played cards, any semblance of his privileged upbringing having been cast aside. Yet, paradoxically, he had no interest in the world of these people. They were there purely for his perverse entertainment and he went in pursuit of whatever base pleasures they provided with a total disregard for the early grave that surely awaited him. Like many of the gentry who kept an eye on anything that might threaten their wealth, Kettall knew there was unrest in France. There was talk of rioting; revolution, even. Many feared it might spread to England – it was, after all, only five years since the Gordon riots had destroyed more than £180,000 worth of property. God forbid! It was in large part this anxiety that he might yet be denied his right to enjoy his wealth that led Kettall to live his life at a mad gallop: eat drink and be merry - and never mind tomorrow!

'Your servant sir,' said Samuel belatedly.

'I think *Tom* will be fine tonight, Medina,' said Kettall, pointedly.

Samuel nodded politely in acquiescence as two cards were dealt in his direction, along with two each for the four other players, who all picked up their cards to study them.

'What are we playing?' Samuel asked, looking at his hand.

'*Vingt-et-un,*' said Kettall.

'Huh?' said Samuel.

'Twenty-one,' said John, 'you *know* how to play.

'Ah,' said Samuel, 'yes I remember – this is the one that's very much a game of chance isn't it? You just have to decide whether to stick or..'

'That's enough, Sammy lad – you're not fooling me with your innocent victim routine.'

Samuel smiled broadly, playing the role that John had previously concocted for him. They talked as they played on.

'Did it go well today with Saul Wright, Sammy?' asked John.

'Aye it went very well John; he was most keen that his readers should know all about me.'

'*Boxiana*,' said Kettall, 'so that magazine has got around to reviewing you has it? You're about to join the ranks of the famous, young Medina.'

Samuel smiled proudly; he could never have imagined that he would one day be featured in an underground boxing magazine, never mind one that was so widely read across all strands of society as was *Boxiana*.

'Aye, Sammy lad,' said John, 'soon every young boy in England will know all about you, and every Englishman will want to shake your hand.' He looked at Samuel and smiled at the pride that was emerging on his face. 'So what did they want from you?'

'Mostly they wanted to measure me. They wanted a record of my height, weight, and reach, that sort of thing so that they have it available when they write the report of my next fight. But there is to be a small article before then about my style of fighting, and so I gave them a summary of my fighting skills.'

'Good,' said John, 'it will make your next fight easier to arrange, and help to raise your purse'

'Not good,' Kettall sneered, 'we don't really want him to be well recognised, nor well understood. The odds will stiffen against us if that happens. We want him *unrecognised* and *misunderstood* - that way we'll get better odds.'

'But we have to *get* him fights first,' said John.

'Don't worry about that,' said Kettall, 'I'll get him the fights – I have the contacts.'

'Two things,' said John to Samuel, but then interrupted himself whilst throwing a card down dramatically, 'and a seven makes twenty-one gentlemen. Pay the soldier in the red coat, I think.' He carried on speaking as though there had been no break in what he was saying, 'Firstly, your next fight.'

'Yes,' said Samuel, pulling his chair closer and folding his cards at the same time. 'Who's to be my opponent?'

'We haven't got a name yet, said Kettall, 'but your next three fights will be at the Fives Court on St Martin's Lane.'

'Aye Sammy, that's right,' said John, 'the Fives Court - the high temple of pugilism. Fighting there will make your name for you, that's for sure.'

'A name is fine, but Medina mustn't be seen to be too good,' said Kettall cautiously.

'I think Samuel can only fight in one way,' said John, 'and that's brilliantly. 'He doesn't understand any other way. The skill is in matching the opponent so that Samuel appears to be the underdog. And besides, he has won five in a row now. We won't be able to present him as the underdog indefinitely.'

'Aye, that's true enough' said Kettall, 'I suppose you're right in that, except that I need a couple more big wins, gentlemen. That must be part of our arrangement.'

For some time the conversation was overtaken by the rowdiness of the card game, and vulgar phrases were exchanged and insults swapped as the games unfolded. Kettall had been winning heavily, but now began to lose. Samuel was right in that this was not a game of skill, though it did require some degree of judgement, but any judgement Kettall possessed was being undermined by John Barleycorn. John had a similar problem, but Kettall was way ahead of him on the drink this evening. All four other players began to win heavily from Kettall and he became increasingly aggressive and antagonistic as the evening wore on. Kettall was a witty and charming man when sober, but a different, belligerent character emerged when he was drunk. He violently pushed away the Mabel who had been seated beside him, claiming that she was bringing him bad luck. 'You fucking scurvy whore,' he cussed at her.

The women fell heavily to the floor from where she cussed back at him. 'I'll *piss* on you, rat-arsed bastard!'

Kettall snarled at her, 'You fucking shit barn door,' he said contemptuously and then threw the ale in his tankard over her, before standing and raising the back of his hand as if he would strike her.

Samuel, hitherto open-mouthed at this display of vulgarity from a so-called gentleman, without thinking, did what he always did in such circumstances - for he would always move to right a wrong. He rose immediately, intercepted the blow, and with all his strength held Kettall by the wrist to restrain him, noting as he did so the rage evident in Kettall's glare. Samuel turned and looked down at the Mabel. 'Madam,' he said politely, gesturing with his head towards the door, 'this would be a good time to take your leave.'

Suddenly realising the danger of the situation, the prostitute scrambled inelegantly to her feet, trying to stay away from Kettall's reach as she did so, but she continued to cuss him as she reached the safety of the door. 'A fucking pox on you, Tom Kettall,' she yelled as she stumbled away. The same words could be heard repeatedly, muffled, as she walked away down the street.

In an effort to placate Kettall, Samuel called for the landlord to bring more ale to replace what had been lost in the scuffle, and when he felt Kettall's resistance diminish he released his arm.

Sir Thomas Kettall grunted resentfully as if he had been denied some good sport, but sat down grabbing the new tankard and swilling deeply.

Samuel turned to John in an effort to change the subject to lighter matters. '*Two* matters you said John – what was the other?'

'Oh, yes, so I did.' John realised what Samuel was trying to do, but unfortunately, the other matter was also of Kettall's making. 'It's about William Ainscough – well he's becoming a bit of a thorn in Tom's flesh – and mine too,' he added hastily with a quick glance at Kettall, who grunted something unintelligible and glowered.

'Do I take it he has been winning money from you then?' Samuel hid a smile.

'Well yes he has,' John nodded. 'It's just that he's a-'

'Very fine card player,' Samuel interrupted, 'and too good for both of you.' This time he was unable to hide his amusement.

Kettall grunted again, making no attempt to disguise his displeasure. The drink had brought on a meanness of spirit within him and he found Samuel's comments impertinent, to say the least, but since he was masquerading as Tom Kettall, a common man, his response was restrained by his deception to no more than a grunt.

'If only it *was* good playing,' said John, 'but he wins so consistently that we are beginning to think it is something more than that.'

'Cheating you mean,' said Samuel, 'surely not. He seems such an amiable, fine fellow.'

'*Fine fellow!*' bellowed Kettall, '*Knavery!* That's what it is - *bloody knavery!*'

'How is that, Tom,' said Samuel to Kettall, 'there seems little scope to cheat in a drawing room?'

Samuel, of course, knew that this observation was erroneous, having been enticed by John to do the very same thing himself, but he genuinely thought it unlikely of Ainscough.

'We think we know how he's doing it,' said John.

'It's that blasted daughter of his,' interrupted Kettall belligerently. 'She's signalling to him somehow.'

'Surely not,' said Samuel again. 'She's such a fragrant young lady.'

'Fragrant!' ranted Kettall, 'that's not what I'd fucking call her.'

'I would recommend caution, Tom,' said Samuel, 'for I have called on the young lady and she was gracious enough to accept me into her home. I will defend Miss Alice's honour if I have to.'

'Don't mess with me Medina,' said Kettall his voice guttural, his eyes wild with rage; his masquerade forgotten. 'You should know your place, *Jew*.'

Samuel's response was predictable. He had been attempting to play the role of peacemaker, but now he himself had been insulted. He reverted to a more primeval persona, the one that had motivated him for most of his life. He would challenge any man who insulted him. He would challenge any man whom he even *perceived* to have insulted him, whether real or imagined. In this case there was little doubt that the alcohol-fuelled, odious state Kettall had fallen into qualified as the former. The man had implied contempt for Samuel, not only as an underling for his common background, but also, and more importantly in Samuel's eyes, because he was a Jew.

Samuel pushed himself to his feet and took up the same posture he had displayed many times before, the chair falling backwards as he did so. The crowd about them moved warily a few steps back to be out of reach should either man lash out. They were not going to disperse, however; this was much too entertaining to miss. Many knew that this *Tom Kettall* had been involved in such brawls before and what to expect of him.

'The *Jew* does know his place, Sir,' said Samuel with all the indignity that he could muster, but retaining his elegance of speech, 'and I am proud of that place. If you want to *mess with me*, Sir, then I am at your disposal. Shall we step outside and settle this?'

Kettall also now stood, his own chair being thrust backwards and crashing against the wall as he did so. At once a silence fell over the whole establishment and all eyes now turned to the two men, as if they were two actors on stage about to perform the final act in a tragedy. The atmosphere was both disturbing and electric, as though every chair and table had been supercharged with static, and every hair on the back of every head had suddenly been raised. But then Kettall drew his sword. He was drunk and he had allowed an alcoholic meanness to override his behaviour, but he still retained that natural cunning that sustains such men in dangerous situations. He was not going to be drawn into a fair fight with a man who had far better fighting skills than he himself possessed. But neither was he afraid. He was fuelled by his own arrogance, but also by the courage of his recurrent companion, John Barleycorn.

'A Jew and an impertinent one at that,' said Kettall, 'I'll have your fucking hide *Jew*.'

There was hushed gasp from the crowd as he lunged forward to make his point with the point of his sword. The table was between them and Samuel moved backwards instinctively so that the tip of sword came to rest a few inches from his throat. It had not been Kettall's intention at that moment to strike but merely to reinforce his insult.

Samuel realised the danger he was in but he did not lack for courage. He returned the insult. 'An uneven fight, Sir, it seems. Yes I am a *Jew; a four by two - a Yid; a teapot lid,* – and it seems, Sir, a Jew that is far too formidable an opponent for you?' he goaded.

'I whip my dogs,' snarled Kettall, 'but I don't feel the need to give the beasts the opportunity to fight me back.' He pushed the tip of his sword against Samuel's throat.

Nervous laughter started from a few in the crowd, which then spread like wildfire so that within a moment raucous laughter enveloped the whole establishment. A satisfied smile split Kettall's features. He enjoyed his witticism and the response it had from the crowd. He relaxed the pressure on his sword and a bead of blood welled where it had rested.

Bravely, Samuel stood his ground and showed no fear. 'But this Jewish dog will not cower like a whipped cur before you, Sir. This Jewish dog has teeth to bite you.'

A roar went up from the crowd. Samuel too, was beginning to respond to the theatre of it all. He had his audience; there was no going back for him now. The meanness within Kettall would ensure the same for him.

John Campbell-John realised this for he knew both men. He had to act, but he feared them both when in this mood. He drew his own sword and brought it down right angled to Kettall's sword so that he forced the point down to the table. It was a decisive action, but when

Kettall looked around he saw that it wasn't a direct challenge to him. He didn't attempt to respond with his own sword.

'Gentlemen, gentlemen,' said John in a conciliatory tone, 'we are partners together, in a very lucrative venture. Let us not let a little misunderstanding spoil our undertaking. Our capital is at stake here.'

Rage was still emotionally uppermost in Kettall's mind, but debt was never far from his consciousness either. Since meeting Samuel Medina and John Campbell-John, his financial situation had been better than it had for many years, and with each fight and each betting coup he had moved into solvency, notwithstanding that his lifestyle quickly moved him back into insolvency again. John had been shrewd enough to mention that most significant of words – 'capital'. Kettall's financial capital was tied up with this man, this Jew, this pugilist. The word John had conjured released the cunning within him and that cunning now began to challenge the dominance that rage had established.

Kettall looked at John and then back to Samuel, and John could see that there was a way to resolve this dilemma, but he needed to find a means for both men to save face if that was to happen.

'Samuel!' said John, and again, 'Samuel', lowering his tone to reinforce the pacifying words that were to follow. 'I'm sure Tom will gladly apologise if we are being unjust to Miss Alice Ainscough.' He hoped that by returning to the original insult to Miss Ainscough, he could deflect the insult to Samuel's faith. 'So let me propose a commission for you to undertake. You shall be the judge and we will accept your pronouncement.'

'A commission?' Samuel glowered, resisting the urge to put his hand up to the scratch on his throat.

'Aye lad, a commission.' John's mind was running ahead, frantically trying to form a scheme. 'You will undertake to find out the truth, or not, of the matter. You will be our investigator – our inspector. There is to be a cards party this Friday evening, and both Tom and I will be present. The stakes will be high and we are keen not to be cheated. Will you be our eyes and ears this Friday?'

'I'm not sure that it would be an honourable undertaking to spy on this lady,' said Samuel.

John's heart sank as he thought to himself what a stuffed shirt, what a prig Samuel could really be at times. He held onto his temper with some difficulty, took a breath and continued.

'I see it as *honourable* in the extreme, Samuel,' he said, 'for you will be the guardian of her reputation. You will be doing her a great *service.*'

'Yes, I can see the logic in your words,' said Samuel pedantly. He was finally beginning to respond to John's lead but he still needed pushing.

'But that service cannot be tainted,' said John, 'you will be required to show that your enquiries were independent. You cannot take her into your confidence; for if you do you will leave it open for her reputation to remained tarnished. Do you understand that Samuel?'

'Aye, I see that,' Samuel nodded.

'And will you agree to perform this commission, then?'

'Aye, I suppose,' said Samuel. His chest was still puffed out and he was unsure if a *back-down* was being proposed.

'And you Tom,' John turned to Kettall, 'will you agree to abide by Samuel's findings?'

Kettall hesitated – rage had not yet totally left him. It was a frequent visitor and it wasn't used to being dismissed so lightly. But this solution would allow him to save face. He made a grunted response, 'Aye.'

The word was little more than a grumble in his throat, but John was not going to dwell on the indistinction of it. 'Good, then let us seal the bargain with a brandy.' He turned, shouted, 'Landlord. A bottle of your best Cognac if you please. We have business to finalise.'

Hesitantly, Kettall sheathed his sword and he and Samuel tentatively took their seats, both still uncertain of each other. Neither was pleased that the impasse had been avoided, but John had achieved his task. Satisfied, he thrust two glasses before them and without looking at each other, they both took a gulp. John now put down his own sword, but for the time being kept it out of its sheath, instead he put the point to the floor between his legs and rested his right hand on the hilt. With his other hand he lifted his glass and took a long, relieved swallow: the truce was still a fragile one, but it was nonetheless a truce.

The card party had all the elegance that Georgian society expected of it. Flip-top card tables had been brought from the walls to the centre of the room and set up so that the guests could play.

The hostess revelled in self-satisfaction at the fare she had provided for her guests. Wine, cheeses, fruit and bread were on offer on salvers at the pier tables, and the whole drawing room glowed in the radiance of the candlelight, which was highlighted by the glistening sparkle of light that glinted off glass and polished silver. It was primarily a social gathering, and several games were being played, mostly for the entertainment of the guests. *Vingt-et-un*, piquet, and loo were popular this particular evening, but little or no stakes were being wagered at this stage of play.

Samuel had introduced himself to Alice and she expressed her surprise at seeing him at this gathering. He struggled to put together an acceptable story because he couldn't, of course, tell her the real reason for his presence there, but his transparent honesty got in the way; he was an abysmal liar. Her delight at seeing him was such that she did not press him for a truthful response. They joined in with the playing and sat at the same table and Samuel enjoyed himself and her company immensely. She seemed every bit as fragrant as he had remembered, but this was now accentuated following his call upon Lady Adele Fitzsymons.

It had been a seminal experience for him. Dora had been right in her opinion of Lady Adele, for he had not been required to display any great sexual technique. He had set himself the task of becoming an accomplished lover, but Dora's advice had been to find a young woman of his own age so that they could learn together. These words had in retrospect been wise ones, but he had rejected them and continued in his quest.

It was apparent that Lady Adele had been interested in him only as a physical specimen, and his function had quickly been made very clear to him. He was there to pleasure her, much as a stallion services a mare. He had pleasured Dora when they were together, and in return she had pleasured him, but it seemed that Adele felt no such obligation. That is not to say that Samuel had not responded to her. He was a young man who was being offered sex by a beautiful woman – sex without any commitment - sex without any strings. That was in itself arousing and he responded to it as would any young, male animal, with his loins rather that his emotions. Any discomfort and misgivings he might have felt were temporarily subdued. He had rutted like a young buck, without any subtlety, all Dora's words of wisdom forgotten. He had rutted with stamina and strength, his muscles had rippled and his skin had sweated, and then he had rutted all over again for he was an athlete and he brought all that athletic ability to Adele's bed. But he had been performing for her. He had been a puppet and she had been pulling the strings. And when it was over all those subdued emotions had crowded back inside his head. A mire of anticlimax had taken hold of him and he felt its force. He was suddenly repelled by Lady Adele and repelled by himself and his own actions. He had wanted to get away from her as soon as it was over, but didn't know how to extricate himself. He need not have worried; Lady Adele was adept at such situations and that was exactly what she wanted also. To all intents and purposes he was dismissed as if he was a servant who had satisfactorily completed his task.

And now here he was playing cards with Alice, and this simple act somehow cleansed him of Lady Adele's carnality. Here was a sweet-scented young woman to restore his view of the delightfulness of the female gender. Her innocence was an attraction - it was charming, it was alluring, and it was enthralling. She was what he wanted women to be like and all Dora's words came flooding back to him. They chatted between hands of cards and talked of literature, for they were both avid consumers of popular fiction. They talked of society and of fortunes and of religion and she seemed keen to understand his faith. She expressed an interest in sport and confessed that she liked to ride, and they made arrangements to do so. She also expressed an interest in his pugilism and a wish to see him fight, but this disturbed him greatly. He explained that it could be a brutal affair and not for the delicacies of a lady, which was true but in reality he believed that the cruelty displayed would somehow taint her fragrant personality, and she would never again be the same person to him.

As the evening moved on more serious games were played and some of the tables were removed so that only one table remained. Sir Thomas Kettall partnering John Campbell-John took their seats. They were opposed by William Ainscough and another player, and the assembly applauded politely to register their appreciation for they were acknowledged to be fine players. Port wine and Stilton cheese were placed by each of the players for their refreshment during the game, and it was decided that the game should be whist, which was essentially a simple game played with partners, but with scope for considerable skill, and was a favourite among those who considered themselves to be players of merit. Such players earned their reputations in the drawing rooms and clubs of London and of them all, only John was little known to the audience that evening.

Samuel was keen to continue his conversation with Alice and suggested that she accompany him to the serving room so that they could talk and dine together, and after initial reluctance she agreed to do so. They talked and Samuel's fondness for her mounted with every minute they spent together. Blissfully unaware that he was seeing her through rose-tinted spectacles, she seemed to him the perfect image of feminine splendour. To his eyes she had a prettiness that made his heart fly, and he savoured every moment in her company.

But after a time, Alice became increasingly agitated wanting to return to the drawing room. She expressed a wish to see her father play, but it was Samuel's intention to keep her away from the game so that he could report that she simply had no interest in it at all. To his reasoning, that would be the most explicit denial of all, but it was not to be. She claimed that her father regarded her as a talisman, a lucky charm that brought him luck at the table. He would miss her after a time, and blame her if the cards didn't run for him. Samuel bowed slightly in acquiescence for he had an inherent decency and by this time he could not deny her anything, and so he offered his arm to escort her back to the drawing room. She took it politely but willingly, and they returned to the gathering to join in with the other spectators.

Samuel positioned them behind Ainscough so that they could see his hand. He reasoned that if she could see only her father's hand, then she could not be accused of signalling, but after a short time she gestured that they move to the opposite side. When he implied that she would not be able to see her father's hand from there, Alice said it was important for her father to be able to see her so that he would know his talisman was working for him. They moved as she had suggested, but even then he did not doubt her integrity, for in his eyes she was incapable of any such subterfuge as had been implied by Kettall and Campbell-John.

The game was evenly paced; the excitement was beginning to mount, and polite applause now greeted the winning of every trick. Ladies whispered to their partners on the expertise - or otherwise - of the play and their gentlemen whispered explanations when the intricacies of the play were not immediately apparent. But Alice needed no such explanations from Samuel for it was she who was the expert in this particular game; Samuel was a mere novice by comparison. He knew enough of the game, however, to see that one partnership now began to take ascendance. To his dismay it was Ainscough and his partner who were beginning to win the most tricks. Samuel still did not suspect Alice of any deception, but it troubled him that he would be unable to report on the lady's innocence, and that her incorruptibility could not be established. He suggested that they move back to other side of the table, but she would have none of it, saying that her father's playing had improved by the very sight of her. He tried to engage her in conversation so that her attention to the game would be lessened, but her focus remained resolutely on the cards being played, one by one, trick by trick.

Samuel's heart began to sink - and then into his mind sprang John's attempt to coach him in a similar deception: how a simple set of signals could be used to convey the strength or otherwise of your opponent's hand. In John's case the signals were from the player and Samuel had simply to convey verification or not. But Kettall and John had been unable to see any form of signal in Ainscough's gestures, so that if signalling was taking place then it must come from Alice, if she was indeed her father's accomplice. Samuel watched her as intently as she watched the game. He saw nothing to give him suspicion. All he saw was this beautiful young lady, this personification of blamelessness; this childlike figure of innocence. He saw only purity.

But then he saw her fluttering fan, and having seen it, his eyes were drawn to it and followed its every movement.

For highborn ladies in society the fan was an essential accessory, and they developed dexterity with it to the point that it seemed almost to become an extension of their arms. It was reactive and wielded without any obvious forethought on behalf of its owner. The fan transfixed Samuel's gaze, as it fluttered and flicked, twitched and trembled, shivered and shook It was unfolded and employed, and then expertly and rapidly refolded again; snapped shut for no apparent reason, as though involved in an intricate dance with its own unfathomable choreography.

Try as he might, Samuel could recognise no signalling in these movements, but he did not have to. The scales had fallen from his eyes and suddenly he saw Alice in a different light: he noticed the imperfections in her appearance, which were there before and apparent to everybody else, but which he had not seen for he had been smitten by her. In a heartbeat he was smitten no longer. She had attractiveness, but was by no means the beauty he thought he had seen. He dropped his gaze and looked endlessly at the ground. Abruptly, the world seemed a bleaker place. It was in his personality to see the best in people, and the let down was in consequence always so much more intense and harder to take. Her appeal for him had added a further intensity, so that he now experienced a sense of betrayal that ate into his consciousness. He had appeared to have the world at his feet, but that world now seemed to be a tainted one.

Swallowing his unhappy, bitter thoughts, Samuel decided that he would later tell John Campbell-John and Sir Thomas Kettall that he had seen nothing in Alice's behaviour to suggest that she was signalling to her father. This was factual enough in that he had not unravelled the way her signalling was operating - if one was operating at all, he added to himself, still in denial - but deep down he knew that it was. He would preserve her reputation, but she was a lesser person to him now, and the world was a poorer place because of it.

CHAPTER 11

1787 was becoming a very prosperous year for Samuel. He had fought twice at the Fives Court, and been victorious on both occasions. He had also fought at Epsom racecourse and this too had brought him a rapturous victory to the delight of a huge crowd. These three fights had made his reputation and also his status and he had achieved the rank of celebrity, both in the ring and about town. He was recognised wherever he went, and people from all parts of society would now stop him and insist on shaking his hand. It mattered not whether they were sporting gentlemen or road sweepers, for his style of fighting seemed to capture the imagination of all. He was the little man showing uncommon bravery against the more powerful foe. He was a living metaphor for all those downtrodden people who were bullied by life and he personified the belief that you could best the bully if you tried hard enough. It was part of the Englishman's psyche that he stood up for what he believed in: there was honour in stripping to the waist and fighting for your principles. Samuel Medina, embodied this conviction and his adoring public were content to overlook his Jewishness.

Samuel loved this celebrity: the natural showman in him was galvanised by every accolade, every compliment. He revelled in the fame and hungered for even more. He had also become a man of property, having purchased a residence for himself: a gentleman's house, for that is what Samuel aspired to be – a fashionable gentleman. The house was in a terrace of recently built houses, each one symmetrical and built in the classical style that was so admired, of stuccoed brick to look like stone, with columns, decorative plaster mouldings and paned sash windows. He had it furnished in the style of the late George Hepplewhite, whose light, elegant designs were so fashionable, choosing pieces with classical detail in the carving, and shield-back chairs, the seats covered in leather. He had arranged for the furniture to be made by Jewish craftsman to Hepplewhite's published designs, for he believed that he should bring some of his own prosperity to his community: to him, it was also at a fraction of the true cost. He now had three servants in his household – a housekeeper, a maid, and a manservant to do the heavy work, who was allowed to sleep on the flag-stone floor of the basement kitchen.

Once he was settled in his new house, Samuel began to entertain in the manner of a gentleman and his dining room was designed for the purpose: masculine, but at the same time, elegant. Plain green walls divided by a dado rail, a marble fire-surround, windows shuttered, not curtained, and with candles mounted in sconces backed by mirrors to reflect the light.

He also bought another property and gave it over to Ginny Farmer, who had so delightfully initiated him into the joys of sex soon after he had become embroiled with John Campbell-John. It seemed a long time ago now. Ginny and her cousin Moll shared the house, from where they traded as prostitutes. This generosity on Samuel's part was not for the purpose of pimping - nothing was further from his mind - it was an act of kindness motivated by his agreeable disposition and his sympathy for Ginny's plight. He was at heart a decent man who was aware that charity was in short supply, and if you had no means of supporting yourself, your options were limited. It was common knowledge that throwing yourself on the parish for support was only marginally preferable to starving. Samuel recognised that Ginny needed to earn a living and prostitution was all she knew, but a common street prostitute could expect only a few pence if plying her trade on the Strand. Having a property would at least enable her to keep off the streets and attract gentlemen of means, and it brought Ginny prosperity and safety.

Samuel had himself moved up the social ladder: he had a new affluence that previously he could never have aspired to, but that strange mix of personality traits was undiminished. Despite his own brutal craft, he still saw himself as a cross between Robin Hood and King Arthur. He was a righter of wrongs, and when he saw or perceived injustice he would stand against it, whatever his position in society.

On this particular day he had such an injustice on his mind. This time it was not one committed against a stranger, nor even an acquaintance, but an injustice against himself. He was owed his purse of sixty guineas from his last fight and his pride was injured. Despite the comparative riches that had come his way, his lifestyle demanded that his finances were continually replenished. He was living the life of a gentleman, and a gentleman of high profile what is more. He was generous and gave money away; he stood not only his own round but that of others as well - and this cost money. He had become a gambler under the influence of John Campbell-John, although unlike his mentor he was cautious in his wagering and not a heavy loser.

While Samuel's lifestyle had become one of easy-come, easy-go, it faded into insignificance when compared to the lifestyle of John Campbell-John. He had become profligate in the extreme. The expenses of his tailor and his wine merchant matched his penchant for wenching and gambling. He had rented a house that he rarely visited, the upkeep of which drained his funds, as did the costs of shooting, and livery for his horses. He was often in the company of Sir Thomas Kettall, himself a renowned profligate, but Kettall at least had an income to underpin some of his lavish spending. Today they were together again, this time pursuing their passion for cockfighting, and Samuel was intent on cornering them so that he could retrieve his sixty guineas. What Samuel did not know was that despite winning vast sums on the outcome of his fights, John Campbell-John was now seriously in debt.

Cockpits were attached to many a disreputable inn, but the most famous were on the south side of St.James's Park and near Gray's Inn Gardens. Samuel had been tipped off that John had gone to the cockpits, but his humour had been further soured by having to tour many of these establishments to look for him. He had so far failed to find him, but Samuel was not one to give up easily. It was early evening when he entered the Royal Cockpit in St James's Park and his mood was unnaturally dark. The dire atmosphere of the place met his senses and this did nothing to help his disposition. It was all piss and ale: it had the stench of human sweat mixed with animal excrement and primed with foul breath. Add to this the stink of decaying, half-eaten food and festering blood and mucus and it all added up to a noisome attack on the senses. But it was the noise that set such a place apart from the norm. Where fashionable entertainment was concerned, the norm itself was pretty raucous, but this paled into insignificance beside the bedlam at a cockfight.

The cockpit consisted of tiers of benches surrounding a raised platform and, as Samuel entered, a fight was in progress. Two cocks matched by weight and fortified with steel spurs on their feet, were in the process of maiming each other. The spurs lacerated the flesh until they were both heavily bloodied, and with each wound the crowd bayed its approval or disapproval, depending upon which fowl their money was wagered on. There was a crescendo of sound that rose with every stabbing of tissue, every gash, every abrasion, until all that remained was a wall of sound, unstructured, indistinct, which then reverberated back off the walls to further harangue the senses. And then, in a heartbeat, one of the combatants collapsed signalling that the fight was over, its body malformed by combat, its flesh hanging from its bones. It was close to death and its owner grabbed it quickly with the merest hint of compassion, although far more motivated by the bird's value than by any affection for the poor creature. The wall of sound diminished only slightly as the audience turned to the business of settling wagers. In benches that were crammed with people, so much so that gentlemen were forced to accept the close and immediate proximity of the common people, disputes were noisy and at times violent.

Samuel sighed heavily to himself at the scene that unfolded before him. This inconsequential, insignificant, miniature theatre had compressed within its undersized curtilege a performance that was primitive, almost primeval, and yet it was vital, pulsating and very much alive - except, of course for, the birds that met their deaths within its walls. Samuel had visited cockpits before; he had no qualms about joining in that revelry, had often enjoyed the stimulating bloodlust and excitement of the wager that a cockfight afforded, but right now he simply was in no mood to appreciate it. And then he caught John's eye at the same moment as John caught his and a broad smile crossed John's features as though he was genuinely pleased to see him.

John was a rogue at heart. He had an eye for the main chance, and was not averse to a deception or two – his entire life had been something of a deception - in fact, he positively enjoyed his waywardness. Roguery in pursuit of his preferred lifestyle came easily to him, and initially there was no doubt that he saw Samuel as someone he could exploit, but over the last couple of years his initial liking for Samuel had grown into a genuine bond that had built up between the two men. In many ways, John was caught between one place and another. He had the personality of a confidence trickster, but Samuel was somehow his antidote and the nearest thing to a friend that he had ever had. When John's face registered pleasure at seeing Samuel, that pleasure was indeed genuine.

'Sammy lad,' he bellowed, but his words were drowned by the cacophony all around him. He bellowed again, this time beckoning Samuel over with an eccentric hand gesture.

Samuel threaded his way through the agitated bodies and by the time he got to John and Kettall, the noise had eased enough between fights so that they could at least converse, if at full holler.

'*My money,*' shrieked Samuel, '*sixty guineas, my purse - sixty guineas.*

John feigned misunderstanding with a shrug and put a friendly arm around Samuel's shoulders.

Samuel shook him off. *'My purse!'* he shouted again, but John only gazed back at him with an inane expression on his face, still pretending not to understand. Samuel took hold of John's cloak by the shoulder and began to pull him away, gesturing that they should leave the cockpit and go into the inn to talk.

John sighed, and got resignedly to his feet, signalling to Kettall where he was going. Kettall followed and all three went through to the inn. Samuel ushered them into a spare booth and Kettall, having shouted at the landlord for ale, made no attempt to hide his impatience to return to the cockpit. 'What's this all about?' he growled.

'Sir!' said Samuel, 'it's about behaving honourably and being paid what is my due.'

'Sammy, Sammy,' said John teasingly, 'you know, if there was a parade of stuffed shirts then you would be the Drum Major.'

'And you can stop that!' Samuel knew what John was up to: he would use his humour and charm to defuse Samuel's resolve as he had so often in the past.

John ignored him, a grin lifting the corner of his mouth. 'You know, if there was a battle between all the pompous people of Europe then you'd be the British general.'

'That's quite enough of that, John, dammit!' said Samuel with all the gravitas he could muster. He fought off a smile but he was fighting a losing battle.

'You know if there was a *puffed up, starched* deck of cards, then you'd be the ace of spades,' said John, the grin now consuming the whole of his face.

Samuel's resolve cracked as a laugh manifested itself in a snort down his nose. John put his arm around him and slapped his face playfully.

Kettall was becoming irritated by this display of brotherly affection, not only because it excluded him, but more importantly, he was missing his sport. 'Commerce has nothing to do with honour,' he said dismissively.' Three pewter tankards arrived brimming with ale. Kettall put one to his mouth almost before he had finished speaking, so that the word 'honour' seemed to echo hollowly in the tankard.

'I see nothing honourable in failing to pay your dues in this world,' said Samuel his humour quickly disappearing at Kettall's tone.

'Then your quarrel is with Campbell–John,' said Kettall testily 'for he is your agent and has your money.'

Samuel turned to John. 'Have you?'

'Aye, I have your money, Sammy boy. Stop worrying.'

'Then I will thank you to give it to me now,' said Samuel.

'Look, I've heard this wizard riddle, Sammy lad,' said John trying to change the subject. Once again he put his arm around Samuel's shoulder and leant over so that their faces were close together, creating an impression of intimacy between them. 'Answer this riddle,' he went on as Samuel sighed in resignation. 'A wench begets triplets and then calls them Matthew, Nathaniel, and Tattersall. - *Mat, Nat and Tat.* Get it – *MAT, NAT and TAT,*' he repeated, sniggering. 'Now which one'll be the runt? Come on Sammy lad, what do you think, which one'll be the runt?'

When Samuel did not answer, John looked intently at his friend willing him to play his part in the story telling, but Samuel looked impatiently into John's inebriated eyes, smelt the stale smell of beer on his breath and refused to participate.

John continued undaunted. 'Why *Tat*, of course – and do you know why Sammy? Well 'cause there was no *tit* for *tat.*' John roared out loud, and Kettall joined him, slapping the table as he did so.

'Yes, very good,' said Samuel drily. At any other time John's rather witty - if somewhat vulgar - riddle might have amused him, but he was past that now. He held out his hand, 'My money if you please.'

'I don't have sixty guineas on me, Sammy lad. You will have to leave it in my charge.'

Samuel frowned. 'I'd wager you had it on you when you came into the cockpit. You did, didn't you?'

John made no attempt to answer the question. 'Look, why don't you go to seek out a lady friend this evening and I'll have your money for you by tomorrow night.'

Defeated, Samuel again sighed resignedly, his shoulders rounding in acceptance as his resolve left him. 'Tomorrow you say?'

'Aye, tomorrow,' repeated John.

Looking on, Kettall saw his opportunity to return to his gaming in the cockpit. He stood and took a few steps, but looked back at Samuel and John and said over his shoulder, 'Tough fight your next one Medina. Can you beat him?'

'Beat who?' said a puzzled Samuel.

Kettall raised his eyebrows at John, who looked away and mumbled, 'I haven't discussed it with Samuel yet.'

'Who?' Samuel asked again.

'Daniel the Gravedigger,' said Kettall, 'have you seen him fight?'

'The Bristol Bonecrusher? Yes, I've seen him fight. He's fit and strong, and he likes to wrestle, but I can best him.'

'Glad to hear it,' said Kettall, 'then it's at the Fives Court, first Saturday of next month. I'll see you there.' He turned to walk away, but John, who knew what was coming, screwed up his face and waited for the inevitable.

'Oh no you won't,' said Samuel.

'What!' Kettall swung round in astonishment.

'I don't fight on the Sabbath,' said Samuel.

Exasperated, Kettall snapped, 'But it's not the damned Sabbath. He seemed completely unaware of both the irreverence and incongruity of this utterance.

'I am a follower of Judaism, Sir - it is *my* Sabbath.'

'Nonsense,' said Kettall, 'it's all arranged, and that is an end to it.'

'It is not an end to it, Sir,' said Samuel puffing out his chest in that way of his when he was in full challenge mode. 'I shall not fight - you must get somebody else.'

'You will fight, Medina, and on the first Saturday of next month, or I'll be damned if I won't make sure you never fight again.'

'Then you must do your worst, Sir, for I will not fight on the Sabbath,' said Samuel. 'And that *is* an end to it.'

Kettall blustered and walked away, waving his arms as he did so, but then he stopped abruptly and came back. Like a chameleon's skin his features changed colour, going from white to vermillion, his body language signalling his fury. He opened his mouth to yell at Samuel, but his rage had left him inarticulate and no words attached themselves to the air that was expelled violently from his lungs, so that all that happened was that he shook his head, whilst at the same time his lips vibrated vigorously and saliva was catapulted in all directions into the air. He looked at John in desperation.

'You talk some sense into him, Campbell-John,' he bawled finally, and still shaking, walked away muttering the word 'Sabbath' over and over to himself.

John looked long and hard at Samuel without speaking, but his expression spoke volumes. It said: *why do you keep doing this; you've gone and done it again; you are a dunderhead Samuel Medina.*

Samuel read the unspoken words and understood the disappointment conveyed by John's expression. What he failed to read, however, was his friend's desperation. John was broke – worse, he was in debt and had no income to finance his lifestyle, let alone to pay off his creditors. Samuel's next fight was to have been his passage out of this predicament.

'Don't look at me like that,' said Samuel, 'this time it's different.'

'It always is,' said John disingenuously.

'But this is my religion.'

'It's always something or other, the reason changes but the reaction is always the same.'

'Maybe, maybe,' said Samuel, 'but you have always known that I will not fight on the Sabbath.'

'Sometimes it's necessary to bend before the wind, you know,' said John, peevishly. 'But oh no, not you – you'd stand tall against the worst tempest wouldn't you?'

'I know I can be a bit of a stuffed shirt,' said Samuel, with a touch of contrition, 'but the Sabbath is above all that. It's not right to fight on the Sabbath.'

'But this is London, Sammy, it doesn't stop for the Jewish Sabbath. Sometimes things are unavoidable.'

'So you didn't speak on my behalf then.'

'Yes I did, but they didn't want the fight on Sunday. This is a fight that everybody wants to see.'

'Then why can't they see it on a Sunday?'

'Because it will make more money on a Saturday,' said John.

'So I must compromise my beliefs so that someone else can make money – is that the size of it?'

'You are a name now, Samuel - a big draw - and I can get you big fights, but those fights come with conditions. I can get you a fine purse and I have. One hundred guineas I've got for you – think about it, one hundred guineas. But the fight has to be on a Saturday.'

'Then we have a problem John Campbell-John,' said Samuel, 'for I will not fight on a Saturday and nothing you can say or do will make me change my mind.'

CHAPTER 12

The frenzied noise from the packed terraces of the Fives Court was absorbed and sucked up by its walls and then it journeyed through the saturated structure of the establishment - beam-by-beam, joist-by-joist. By the time that noise had burrowed its way into the dressing rooms it had been muted and muffled, but nevertheless, it resonated through the walls, the ceiling and the floor. It signalled the expectation of the crowd to the combatants, so that the two antagonists could not escape the anticipation that was evident all around them. Samuel was normally calm in these circumstances, for he was abnormally confident in his own abilities, and he had only the expectation of the adoration that would surely come his way. He was brave, but in some respects his bravery was blind: a blindness that was deliberately fostered, for if he thought about it; *really* thought about it, he would never step into the ring. It was not a place for faint hearts: pugilists could be maimed for life, or even killed in the course of these pitched battles. They were called pitched battles for that was what they represented: a fight would continue for as long as it took, until one man was bested; beaten to the point where he could no longer go on. It was, in fact, not dissimilar to a cockfight – and the crowds who bayed for the bloody victory of the man on whom they had wagered, cared not a jot for his victim any more than they cared for the mutilation and death of a cockerel.

Today, however, Samuel was anxious. He was not afraid of the Bristol Bonecrusher: well, no more than any other opponent he had fought. What he feared was something much worse than a fellow pugilist. He feared that God would desert him, for he had succumbed to pressure and agreed to fight on the Sabbath. He fought under the banner of 'The Light of Israel', and he believed that this pleased his God, and conversely, that fighting on the Sabbath would anger Him. Samuel sat pensively on a bench and attended to the routine that he always adopted before any fight. He was oiling his upper torso when John and Kettall arrived, but he did not stop what he was doing, giving particular attention to his biceps.

'We can't get you at better that six to four on,' said John, 'it's two to one against the Gravedigger.'

'It was bound to happen,' said Samuel arrogantly, 'my reputation now goes before me.'

'Aye it does,' said Kettall agreeably. He was sober and he was adopting the charming, urbane side to his personality. 'They have come to see *you* today Samuel Medina, much more than the Gravedigger.'

'Then I will give them the display they have come to see,' said Samuel, adding, 'God willing, of course.'

'You haven't needed God's help before,' said John suspiciously noticing the tone of caution in Samuel's voice.

'I always take my God into the ring with me,' said Samuel, 'my skills come as a gift from Him.'

'Then it is time to display those God-given skills, Sammy lad,' said John.

'Aye,' said Samuel, 'and will you wager twenty-five guineas for me John? I will take six to four on.'

These words reinforced John's confidence in Samuel. He had been temporarily taken aback, but now he smiled inwardly to himself. He would take, as his percentage cut, twenty guineas from Samuel's purse, but he needed more than that to pay off his creditors. He needed to win. Despite the genuine bond he had developed with Samuel over the last two years, money and debt were powerful forces in John's life. This was a silver-tongued scallywag of a man, and at heart he was not a man of high principles. Samuel had been a good influence on him, but now he just needed money and while his friendship with Samuel demanded his loyalty, that loyalty was now subjugated by this need.

Samuel came to the ring with the cheering of the crowd sounding in his ears. He was no longer the unknown Jew who could fight a bit. He was a hero. Pugilists were men who embodied the virtues of what it was to be English: men who would stand up for what they believed to be right and who followed a noble pastime. They reflected what their contemporaries saw as a sort of humanity: a man's right to stand and fight for what was his. The fact that most pugilists were large, brutal men engaged in a pursuit of unmitigated brutality did not detract from this view among the boxing fraternity, and Samuel was a particular favourite. Because of his size, he seemed to reinforce the view that if your cause was right then it did not matter that your opponent was bigger and more powerful, for the English fighting spirit would see you succeed - that same spirit that had enabled the heavily outnumbered archers of England to defeat the French at Agincourt. Samuel embodied this perception and yet he was a Jew – an English Jew, but, nevertheless, a Jew. A Jew was not supposed to be part of this English perspective and yet paradoxically he had become the personification of it.

He was introduced to the crowd as Samuel the Jew, The light of Israel, and the crowd cheered joyously, irrespective of the fact that many of them would return to Jew-baiting the following day. He danced in a circle with his hands held high as his name was barked to the crowd, and he played with their emotions like the most skilled of thespians. The Bristol Bonecrusher was also well known to the crowd, and was favoured for his bravery and defiance for he was a man with a reputation for not being easily beaten. Today, however, he brought forth only the cheers of his own close friends and the subdued appreciation of the sporting gentlemen in the crowd. In terms of size there was an advantage to the Gravedigger, but he was not a giant of a man. He was only two inches taller that Samuel, but his upper body was exceptionally well developed from his years in the graveyard. His weight advantage was only about a stone and a half, for Samuel himself had filled out and his twenty-one-year-old frame was now more thickset than before. The Gravedigger was red-haired and his skin was pale and this distracted from his physique, whereas Samuel was eye-catching in his physical splendour. His dark, oiled skin glowed and his muscles rippled in the light, but the overall impression was of an athlete, rather than a muscle-bound hulk. He still wore his hair long and tied in the nape of his neck and was, as always, a remarkable and handsome specimen of the athletic male.

The bell sounded and Samuel took up his fighting pose, his left leg and left arm extended. The Gravedigger waded forward and threw heavy punches in a wide arc that Samuel easily evaded, and then Samuel responded by snapping his left into the man's face three times in rapid succession so that his head jerked backwards like a buoy bobbing in the ocean. After ten minutes the Gravedigger was heavily bloodied around the face whilst Samuel was unmarked. When he saw that his opponent was beginning to slow, Samuel began to plant his feet, as this gave him the purchase to land more powerful punches. He sidestepped to the left of another wild and round punch then placed his heels on the canvas stage and delivered a powerful right uppercut that sent the Gravedigger's head rocking backwards even more violently. A spray of sweat took to the air like a flock of frightened birds. The crowd roared their approval. The Gravedigger was stunned for a moment but Samuel did not follow up the attack, preferring to circle his opponent. He raised his arms above his head to emphasis the power of the blow, and the knowledgeable crowd needed little encouragement to cheer it a second time. Samuel loved to play to the crowd as if he was performing a duet with the spectators, but such lack of respect for his opponent was a dangerous strategy.

His senses having cleared, the Gravedigger came forward again, but he now decided upon a change of tactics and was not throwing wild punches, in fact he wasn't throwing punches at all. Samuel sidestepped to his left, but this time the Gravedigger merely reeled to his right in pursuit. Samuel repeated the sidestep but again the Gravedigger lurched to his right. Samuel changed tack and sidestepped to his right, but this time his opponent countered by moving to his left. Each time the move was completed Samuel's retreat was being cut off and he was being manoeuvred into a corner.

The Gravedigger then moved in, his legs in a wide stance and swaying from side to side so that he could oppose any sideways move from Samuel. The man still did not attempt to throw any punches, however. As he closed in, he put his open hands on Samuel's shoulder and his grip dug into his flesh, the thumbs digging deep into his neck. Samuel felt the pain penetrate his consciousness and that was something he had never felt before in a fight. Adrenalin was usually an antidote to pain, the pain itself being resurrected long after the fight was over.

The Gravedigger was adept at wrestling as well as fist fighting, and he saw this now as his best chance of success. Samuel, although multi-skilled was aware that he would not win a wrestling match against this man; he had trained himself in the manoeuvres necessary to escape. He thrust his arms upwards and inside those of the Gravedigger and then violently pulled them apart forcing his opponent's grip to be broken. He then brought his hands down and with his fists clenched, punched his opponent strongly on the ears, immediately sidestepped away and raised his hands again to the crowd so that they could salute him.

The Gravedigger was left with his ears ringing. He did not lack for courage, however, and he came forward again, shaking his head repeatedly as he did so in a forlorn effort to clear the buzzing in his head. The man had the sense to change his tactics but Samuel too had this ability, and he was not going to allow himself to be caught in a corner again. He knew he had young, fresh legs to outpace his opponent, and this was allied to greater speed and agility. He increased the tempo of the fight, abandoning for the moment the need to plant his feet in order to land heavy punches and the Gravedigger seemed to have no answer to this. For the next ten minutes Samuel danced and flicked punch after punch into the reddened, bloodied face that was now chasing him incessantly, until he felt that the man's resolve was beginning to evaporate. Samuel's movements now merged into a perfect harmony; feet and body and arms and brain in perfect synchronisation. A successfully delivered punch can create a surge of adrenalin to revive the most tired of fighters, but conversely a lack of success can have a devastating effect on the mind – this was the Bonecruncher's dilemma.

But doubts also suddenly entered Samuel's mind, for he started to blow. He was unable to sustain the pace that he had set himself. It came as a great shock to him, but the reality of the problem was that the excesses of his lifestyle were beginning to catch up with him. He was still only twenty-one and with that youth came lungpower and agility. He had always relied on that inherent athleticism; the need to train hard and keep his body in shape had never been a consideration before, but recently he had spent too many evenings in the company of John Barleycorn. He may not have drunk as prodigiously as John Campbell-John and Sir Thomas Kettall, but *they* were not required to be trained athletes. At this moment, however, he was unable to see that reality, for there was no room in his mind for anything but his own survival. His brain was calculating, but the subject of the tabulations was the mathematics of punches; of hits; of blows, not the damage his lifestyle was doing to his fitness. He determined to put the Gravedigger away as soon as he could, for whatever the state of his own reserves of stamina, his opponent's appeared to be all but expended.

At twenty-four minutes into the fight, the Gravedigger trundled forward, and Samuel planted his feet with no attempt to sidestep the lunge. He met his man head on, and let fly with a wicked left hooked punch and followed this with a right uppercut, the power of both punches being doubled because the man had walked onto them. The Gravedigger sank to his knees, but the man's pride was stung and he immediately and surprisingly got to his feet. His seconds called out, 'touch down,' for the agreed thirty seconds under the Broughton Rules, but their own fighter ignored them, lunging forward again belligerently, and the referee waving the fight on.

The Gravedigger was a proud man and he was being beaten and beaten easily, and to his perception this young upstart was ridiculing him. His wounded pride had summoned up some reserves of energy from some secret place and he redoubled his effort, but without any thought to his own self-defence. He led with his chin and it appeared to Samuel like an archery target; the bull's eye being marked as a direction finder. So Samuel obliged with another powerful upper cut, stopping his opponent in his tracks. Samuel saw the man's eyes blur as his senses were addled and temporarily detached from his rational mind; it also signified that his opponent was a beaten man and ready to be despatched. He was now helpless before him and Samuel raised his right hand high into the sky so that the crowd could witness his moment of triumph. He was playing to them the way he always wanted to do. The last punch would be with their lavish approval. It would be a spectacle and would feed that part of him that was a showman, and the showman's requirement for acclaim would be satisfied.

It was not to be however. The Gravedigger's seconds and two others of his cornermen dived into the ring. They grabbed Samuel's arm and then restrained him, claiming that their man had touched down, and was entitled to the thirty-second break to recover. They knew that if this final blow landed, their man would face inevitable defeat and not even thirty seconds of respite would counter that.

Pandemonium broke out and the ring was invaded from all sides. John Campbell-John jumped into the ring to try to protect Samuel, but he was unable to get to him, for so did members of the crowd, and most of them seemed to be followers of the Gravedigger. Claims were shouted and counter-claims bellowed, but this was lost in the roars of the crowd and no sense of order was achieved. For several minutes this melee continued. but in all this time Samuel was being held and was being manoeuvred away from the protection of his seconds.

And then someone grabbed the hair at the nape of Samuel's neck so that his head was pulled backwards forcing his vision skywards and his eyes protruded and gaped, brilliant with fear. A piercing pain then enveloped his lower back. It was the Gravedigger sinking punches into him. He was intent on taking as much advantage of the situation as he could, inflicting as much damage as he could, although it was unclear whether this was pre-planned or whether it was just opportunistic. Samuel cried out to John Campbell-John to help him but his cries were lost in the fracas. The strength was draining from him with every blow, and he would have sunk to his knees but for the men restraining him. And then he lost consciousness.

When the men realised what damage they had done, they released him but even then his fall to the canvas floor was not immediate, as the invading crowd had claimed his line of descent. When he did hit the floor the trampling crowd inflicted more damage, because his natural reflexes to protect himself were banished by his unconsciousness.

John looked around the ring, and panic took him like a bolt of lighting out of a menacing sky. He couldn't see Samuel and he was horror-struck. He jumped up and down shouting at the riotous crowd and pointing animatedly to those in the areas where he had last seen Samuel, roaring at those immediately around him. Eventually they realised what was happening; he engaged the help of a group of four men to make a human wedge and focussed it in the direction of the far corner. They heaved and tugged and pushed and the crowd ebbed and swayed before them, but they began to make progress and gradually they inched, step by resistant step across the ring.

When they arrived they found Samuel slumped still unconscious his lips blued by the lack of oxygen available to him in that cave of legs that had been his temporary prison. They hauled him to his feet, frantically shouting at the crowd to give their man air, but nobody listened. John held Samuel aloft with the aid of the ropes, whilst the four other men formed a barricade around them, and slowly Samuel recovered consciousness, but he was in a bad way.

It took more than twenty minutes for the ring to be cleared and John held Samuel all this time, but there was little sign that his friend had recovered sufficiently to take his own weight. When the ring finally cleared they took him back to the corner and sat him down and tried to revive him with smelling salts, which only had limited success. They drenched him endlessly with a torrent of water and whirled towels frantically in an effort to increase his oxygen intake. John examined Samuel's body and saw the bruising that had already begun to appear on his lower back.

'What have they done to you, Sammy lad,' he said. Instinctively he knew that all was not well.

Samuel looked upwards at John, his large, dark eyes registering comprehension for the first time, but that defiant spark had been extinguished so that they looked like the eyes of a beaten pup. 'They've done for my kidneys,' he said, his voice only just audible.

'This is an outrageous foul,' yelled John. 'We'll claim a foul and take the purse.'

At that moment however, the purse was the farthest thing from Samuel's fevered mind, but money was still a powerful force upon John. Sir Thomas Kettall had been appointed as Samuel's umpire to act in the event of a dispute, and John called him over and instructed him to claim the fight on a foul.

Kettall met with the Gravedigger's nominated umpire. A huddle was seen to form and animated discussions lasted a further twenty minutes, the crowd baying its disapproval throughout this whole procedure. John saw nothing sinister in this delay. It was the custom to choose gentlemen of rank who would act impartially for this task, but John nevertheless expected that the two umpires would disagree and stand for their own man. The Broughton rules would require them to appoint a third independent umpire to pronounce on the dispute.

But then the Master of Ceremonies took to the stage and raised his hands for quiet, and the crowd obeyed his gesture as they were themselves eager to know the outcome of the dispute.

'Gentlemen, gentlemen,' he pronounced, 'both the contestants, both Masters of the Noble Science of Defence, have claimed foul and have claimed the victory. I'm sure you will agree, gentlemen, that this is an unsatisfactory way to settle this contest. The umpires have come to an understanding therefore. Daniel the Gravedigger will accept the forfeit of his thirty seconds entitlement and Samuel the Jew will accept the interference from the Gravedigger's seconds. Both these acceptances will be without penalty. The fight will now recommence.'

John listened with stunned disbelief. Kettall, standing as Samuel's nominated umpire, had just handed the contest to the Gravedigger. 'The bastard must have bet against us, Sammy lad,' said John with resignation. 'Can you fight on lad?'

'I fear that I cannot,' said Samuel, 'my strength has been beaten from me.'

John signalled Kettall over and he arrived, shamelessly, without any visible sign of remorse.

'Our man is not fit to fight,' said John, 'why have you agreed for the fight to go on.'

'Both men have claimed foul,' said Kettall, 'and since Medina committed the first foul, it was the only solution for a sporting gentleman.'

'You've bet on the Gravedigger haven't you?' said John.

'You are impudent, Sir,' said Kettall evasively. 'Mind your manners and remember how much you need my support. You'll be back playing cards for farthings without me standing as surety for you.'

John took the warning to heart and dropped his head to hide his shame, for he knew that Samuel was being badly wronged. He had to do something but he knew not what.

'But Samuel is our man, is he not?' he said, attempting to sound contrite.

'Aye he is,' said Kettall, 'and bravely he has fought. The Bonecrusher was at the point of defeat and should easily be bested again.'

'But Samuel is unable to fight, we can't send him out again,' said John pleadingly.

'Nonsense,' said Kettall dismissively, 'our man is a pugilist, and that's what they do. They fight until one man is bested. Medina knows the rules of engagement – he understands that.'

'Aye I do,' said Samuel stirring his wounded and painful body, 'it is my duty to fight on.'

Samuel put his right arm on the ropes and painfully hauled himself to his feet, whilst his left hand held his side to try to ease the pain. Surprisingly, his legs held his weight and he turned to John.'

'I don't want you to throw the towel in,' he said, 'you must let *me* decide if I'm beaten.'

'You're a beaten man now, Samuel Medina,' said John, 'there's no more fight left in you. You're done for lad.'

'We'll see, we'll see,' said Samuel bravely, 'now let us prepare to fight on.'

Samuel and John were called to the square in the centre of the ring by the referee in preparation of the fight recommencing. Samuel looked at the Gravedigger and tried to hide the pain he was feeling. The Gravedigger was badly marked around his face but the blood had been cleared away. Bare fists cut and lacerated the skin with ease, but fights were not stopped because of this. Blood was an everyday experience for the pugilist, and they bore the scars to prove it. This fight had further mutilated the Gravedigger's face; it was misshapen with bumps and bruising and his right eye was almost closed. Although the blood had been wiped away, several cuts were beginning to weep red again. Nevertheless, one good eye looked back at Samuel and that look revealed the man's intent. It was a look of a man who knew he was about to win, a look that said he knew what damage had already been inflicted on his opponent.

The bell sounded and Samuel eased his way forward. He turned his stance around to lead with his right hand, keeping his left to protect his side. He flicked out a right into the Gravedigger's face but even that caused him pain. His opponent merely walked through the punch, making no attempt at this point to throw punches back. His objective was to cut off Samuel's retreat and back him into a corner. Samuel could see this, but his mobility was so restricted that he had difficulty in countering his adversary. He tried to dance and flick out punches but the man just kept walking through everything he threw. He felt the ropes on his back and this spurred him to move quickly before he was trapped, but he soon found himself back there - this time with nowhere to go. He was trapped.

The Gravedigger leered at him as he pounced. He grabbed Samuel by the shoulders forcing him downwards, but then he released his grip and grabbed him by the hair again. At the same time he started to punch, but those punches were directed at just one place – his back and his kidneys in particular. Blow after blow sank into Samuel but he was unable to free himself or respond. John cried foul but there wasn't anything in the rules that said the Gravedigger could not do this – the kidneys were not out of bounds. The holding of hair was not considered a manly thing to do and the crowd bayed its disapproval, for it was not part of that perceived noble pursuit that pugilists personified, but the blows continued. Samuel sank to his knees but was hauled up and held by his opponent, who then continued to pummel and to strike. Samuel again lost consciousness; the canvas should have been his liberation for this would require a thirty-second break, but the Gravedigger prevented him from falling and the pounding continued.

John mind was in turmoil. He had promised Samuel that he would not intervene, but Samuel was now in no state to make any decisions. He was clearly bested and in danger of being permanently hurt. John threw in the towel, crying repeatedly, '*YIELD!*' but the howling crowd drowned out his words. He dived into the ring and grabbed the Gravedigger's arm to stop the incessant blows. The Gravedigger's seconds then joined the furore and punches now rained down on John for his trouble, but he had achieved his objective.

The referee turned to John and enquired 'Bested?'

John nodded his confirmation, in an exaggerated fashion so that there could be no misunderstanding. The referee raised the Gravedigger's arm in victory, to the booing of the crowd. Samuel was left for a moment, slumped on the canvas in the opposite corner, unconscious and vulnerable. He was again being trampled on in the confusion. John hauled him back to his corner, but was still unable to revive him.

The surgeon examined Samuel, a grave expression on his face. Smelling salts were put under Samuel's nose again, but his senses cleared only slowly. He had been drifting in and out of consciousness for over an hour. He winced as hands again examined his back, and the surgeon muttered, *'Good'* for it meant that pain was being registered in Samuel's brain.

John leaned over to look into his friend's eyes, and when he saw comprehension there relief surged through him like an elixir. 'Sammy lad,' he said, 'you're going to be all right, Sammy - you'll see.'

Samuel responded only with his eyes, but the gesture was enough to acknowledge what John was saying.

'Look Sammy,' John continued, 'the Prince of Wales was in the crowd. He's sent his own surgeon to attend to you.'

The surgeon came into Samuel's vision, and gestured with a polite nod, but his countenance remained severe. He leant over Samuel, placed his thumb over Samuel's eyelids and pulled them up to look at his pupils. He mumbled, *'Good'* again to himself and then stood upright placing his hands on his side in a reflective gesture.

'Mr Allenby,' John addressed the surgeon by name, 'will he recover?'

'There are no broken bones, Sir. He is breathing freely and his brain is not addled.'

'You hear that, Sammy boy,' said John. 'You'll be alright in a few days, you'll see-'

'I fear not,' the surgeon interrupted. 'Your man has in my opinion suffered severe internal injuries. His lower back is badly inflamed and I fear that his system could collapse.'

'What can you do for him, Sir? John looked anxiously at the surgeon.

'I can do nothing, Sir, I have no physic for what ails him. I can only prescribe careful nursing. His recovery will be in the hands of God. But he has a strong constitution and with luck and his God on his side, then his system may heal itself with time.'

John looked at the surgeon and then back at Samuel. He did not know what to say or do. The silence was uncomfortable and the surgeon coughed in embarrassment.

'I'll bid you good day then, Sirs,' he said, 'the Prince has agreed to pick up my fee,' he added as an afterthought. He turned and walked to the door, opened it and looked back, as though he felt the need to add some words of encouragement but realised he had none to give. Instead, he gave a politely sympathetic nod and then left.

A silence fell on the little anti-room at the Fives Court that was Samuel's dressing room. John felt helpless – his carefree lifestyle had left him ill-equipped to act responsively or deal with an emergency. A knock on the door broke the silence and an equerry entered. He bowed slightly.

'The Prince of Wales would convey an audience on Mr Medina,' he said.

John looked at him blankly, failing initially to comprehend what the man had said. And then realisation hit him like a crashing wave and he grabbed at the interruption like a lifeline.

'You hear that, Sammy boy? The Prince of Wales wants to meet you.' Samuel, drowning in a sea of pain, forced a bewildered smile.

Six men now crowded into the small room, at length moving aside to enable George, Prince of Wales, to step forward from their midst and approach the wounded man. A large, rotund man with a reddened complexion, the Prince had an affable and jolly countenance.

John stood to attention and bowed with military precision while at the same time introducing himself as Captain John Campbell-John, Samuel Medina's manager and friend. The Prince acknowledged him gracefully, but his attention was focused on Samuel. He bent over him and smiled. Samuel struggled to rise, but the Prince put his hand on his shoulder to stop him.

'Mr Samuel Medina - and how is it with you, Sir?' said the Prince, which seemed to John a nonsensical thing to say in the circumstances, although he knew the Prince was just being polite.

'Very bad Your Highness, very bad,' answered Samuel speaking through waves of almost overwhelming agony.

'Aye Sir, I saw what happened,' said the Prince, 'and it's a rum do – a rum do indeed.'

'Aye; a rum do indeed, Sir,' winced Samuel, repeating the Prince's words. Weakly he attempted a smile, 'I fear my opponent has shown he possesses a cloven hoof.'

'Agreed, Sir,' said the Prince, 'his actions were base in the extreme. There was no doubt in my mind that you were the better man, and your defeat was the result of the basest skulduggery.'

'It is a comfort to hear you say so, Your Highness. Thank you, Sir.'

'Nonsense, Sir,' said the Prince, 'it is only the truth and plain for all to see.'

'Your servant, Sir,' Samuel coughed on a gasp of pain.

'Now, Samuel Medina' said the Prince, 'I have seen your last three fights and they have given me great sport, and what is more, they have swelled my purse for I have wagered on you.'

'Then I'm sorry to have let you down today, Sir.'

'Fiddle-de-de,' the Prince flapped his hand to wave away the apology. 'I haven't come here for that. I've come to tell you that I admire the way you fight, Sir, and I want to see you fight this Gravedigger fellow again, and show that you are the better man.'

'I would like nothing better, Your Highness,' said Samuel, 'but I fear it will be some time before I am able to fight again.'

'Tut-tut,' said the Prince, 'you are a fighter, Sir, and may I say, a damned fine one with an uncommon instance of spirit. I've seen you, and you embody all that is good in the British character. I'm sure that you will fight again when your wounds have healed.

But I am also a Jew, Samuel thought. Keeping that thought to himself, he gestured with a smile and a small nod of the head as graciously as he could and the pain would allow. The Prince patted him on the shoulder regally and then turned and was ushered out of the room by his entourage. The meeting had been brief and its end seemed as sudden as its beginning.

Silence fell again and John forced a smile to reassure Samuel. 'How about *that* Sammy,' he said encouragingly. 'The Prince of Wales himself is an admirer of yours!'

Samuel did not respond. He lay back with a grimace of pain and contemplated the ceiling. 'It's God's punishment,' he said quietly after a moment's reflection, 'for fighting on the Sabbath. I have displeased my God.' He tried to move but found it impossibly painful. Instead, he reached out with his hand and groped in mid-air searching for John's arm. Finding it, he pulled John towards him and whispered, 'Send for my father.'

Leaning over to hear, his ear close to Samuel's mouth, John felt relief cascading over him. Samuel had made the decision that he was plainly unable to make himself. 'Aye - aye Sammy lad, that'll be good. Your own people will look after you best.'

CHAPTER 13

It had been almost a year since his fight with the Gravedigger. Samuel had recovered, but that recovery had been in doubt for quite some time. His kidneys had ceased to function properly; they were not filtering the toxins from his blood. His face, his joints and is abdomen all swelled making his appearance grotesque. He spent many weeks vomiting, whilst his head pounded to the rhythm of his heartbeat. It had taken ten weeks before he was even able to leave his sick bed, and his doctor could do little, other than prescribe a physic to keep his temperature down to give his body time to heal itself. He had lost almost three stones in weight in this time as his body's own recuperative powers plundered his reserves of strength and energy, until finally his recuperation took a pace. His physical fitness and his youth were the only reasons that he survived. As his kidneys started to function properly again then so did the rest of his system, but the loss of weight had been accompanied by muscle wastage, and even after a year he was no way near the fighting specimen he had been before the fight with the Gravedigger.

The papers had been full of that fight and they had been clearly on his side feeding the public with the belief that he had been severely wronged. The letters' pages had been full of eyewitness accounts of the fight, and there was a clamour for a rematch. His condition had been purveyed to the public by many articles on the state of his recovery. This had been so slow however, that their interest in him had waned and he had been left alone by the press for several months now. He had been visited frequently by Miss Alice Ainscough, but he had not encouraged her and her visits had diminished. John, too, had been a regular visitor, but he had become increasingly agitated and finally confessed to Samuel the extent of his debt. He had amassed a small fortune, but this had all been frittered away by high-living and gambling, and his silver tongue was now unable to keep his creditors at bay. Samuel had loaned him enough to at least pay off his gambling debts, which being a matter of honour were regarded as preferential; his wine merchant, tailor and other traders would have to wait.

Samuel was a man of generous spirit. He would have fought John over a guinea if he thought he had been cheated, but he had loaned John money without a second thought, most of the funds that he had left, in fact. There was a need to start earning again very soon and the most obvious source of income would be from fighting as there remained a clamour from the public to see him fight again, and in particular to fight the Gravedigger - the Bristol Bonecrusher. Samuel, however, felt no such need, not only because the past year had given him time to reflect on the dangers he had faced, but also because Ginny Farmer, who had been a regular visitor, had repaid his own generosity of spirit. She continued to trade as a prostitute from the house Samuel had bought for her, but now she gave him money for the upkeep of his own house and made sure that his immediate needs were covered, which went a long way to alleviating his concern about his finances.

There was another and much greater influence on him, however. Whilst he had been ill his parents had arranged for someone to nurse him. They had sent for a second cousin of his, a young Jewish girl by the name of Rebecca Elias. At twenty-two, she was the same age as Samuel and she was well educated. As well as nursing him she had filled his mind with poetry and they read it together; wrote it together, and over the months he had become smitten with her. Rebecca was diminutive in stance but handsome. She was one of those people who speak with their eyes, which were strikingly large and black and flashed to convey her emotions. She had been his constant companion for almost a year now and they had developed a close relationship, to the point that she was the extent of his world and he thought very little about fighting: in fact, fighting was something of which she strongly disapproved.

Despite her disapproval, Rebecca accepted a proposal of marriage from Samuel after he promised that he would give up fighting. There was one proviso, however, and that was that he had to meet the Bristol Bonecrusher once more. So, almost a year after that horrendous fight and after a quiet Jewish marriage ceremony, the happy couple moved into Samuel's fashionable town house, which was to be their family home. This, of course, needed money to run it, and Samuel could not on rely on Ginny Farmer forever. It was agreed with Rebecca that he would set up an academy of boxing where he would teach the young gentry the noble science of self-defence. He rented premises in Chapel Court and he shamelessly traded on his reputation for boxing skills, but more importantly that the Prince of Wales himself was an admirer – indeed, he was Samuel's patron. It was a tradition that pugilists of the day set up such academies, but Samuel put the emphasis on the boxing skills that had made him so successful: *the art* of defence.

He also put his education to good use. Pugilists in general were not educated men. That was not to say that they were unintelligent men, as witnessed by Big Charles Sweep himself, but they were not men of letters. Samuel was to change all this. While he was recuperating, he started to write. Eventually, he submitted a manuscript of poetry to a publisher for consideration, along with a small volume entitled, 'The *Art of Boxing.*' The publisher showed little interest in the poetry, but was keen to publish the boxing manual, and agreed in the end to publish both. The latter was a sensation. For the first time there was definitive manual of the science (Samuel preferred the word '*Art*'). It became an instant best seller and was championed by the popular journals. Here was a manual setting out strategy, training techniques and even diet for the pugilist. It went further than that, however: it raised the standard of pugilism itself. It expanded its following so that it was not just the domain of the large and powerful professional, but it now encompassed boxing as a pursuit for the amateur. It tapped into the belief that it was honourable for an Englishman to strip to the waist and fight for what he believed in.

On the back of this book, Samuel's academy boomed. It was filled with young gentlemen keen to learn these skills, for this was not just common brawling. Over the next few months Samuel gave daily tutorials, sparred with his young gentlemen clients and gave exhibitions of his skills. This was in itself good training and gradually his fitness returned. His weight increased, but this was a natural weight gain as his body was now free from excess consumption, especially of alcohol. He was making a good living from this venture and it also gave him a good insight into business. With Rebecca's help he learned about profit and loss, about balance sheets, about debtors and creditors, about cash flow, about using his status as an asset and about maximising his income. The Academy was a resounding success, and the exhibitions he gave went some way to satisfying the need within him to be a showman. But it was never the same as the adoration of a large crowd, the thrill of a pitched battle, the euphoria engendered from the danger that it all entailed. Life was good, but for Samuel, there was something missing.

There was still a clamour from the general public for that rematch with the Gravedigger. At the end of every exhibition everyone wanted to know when that fight was to happen. John Campbell-John was courted by the showmen of the time eager to promote the fight because they could all see the prospect for profit. The delay in the rematch should have had a negative effect on the marketability of the fight, but the reverse seemed to have happened. As each month passed, the public's appetite seemed to be whetted even more. Articles were written, and speculation was rife. Showmen put up purses and then they were outbid by others. Some claimed that they were promoting the fight when they hadn't procured the rights, and all the time Samuel, to John's annoyance, held out. He would fight the Gravedigger when he was ready and not before.

When his mind was made up, he called for John Campbell-John, but rejected all the offers that had been made. He wanted to promote his own fight - or rather he wanted John Campbell-John to promote it for him. After an initial shock at this suggestion, John could see the benefit of such an arrangement. The potential returns would be serious money. Of course, they had to get the Gravedigger to agree to this, but it proved to be a trouble-free exercise and a contract was quickly drawn up. The Gravedigger, win or lose, would get ten percent of the gate in addition to a generous fee. He readily agreed, for he would not get such a deal from an independent promoter. Samuel was to get ninety percent of the gate. The venue was to be Marylebone Fields and all who attended were required to pay an entrance fee. There were to be no standing spectators allowed in for free at the back of the paid seats, nor were there to be any gatecrashers. Samuel was intent on maximising his earnings.

The fight was set for 14th July 1789, at two o'clock. At Samuel's instigation and against the wishes of John Campbell-John, the ticket prices were set at prices much higher than those for other big fights. But Samuel had been right for they sold like hot cakes. Dozens of itinerant workers were hired to erect the stage, set out the seats and police the perimeter of the Fields and the entrances so that nobody could attend without a ticket. A whole week before the fight they had enough gate receipts to be sure of a runaway financial success, and with the prospects of more than doubling that with the standing spectators who would pay at the gate on the day.

Samuel trained at his academy, although this did not prove to be an ideal venue as there was too much interest in him from his clientele and he found it hard to put in the hours he needed. However, his recovery was complete and he had slowly built up his body and his stamina and the sparring he had done had sharpened his reflexes. He was back to his fighting best and in fact, given the abstemious life he was now leading, was probably in better shape than when he had last met the Gravedigger.

It was the Sunday before the fight when things started to go wrong. Samuel had spent the morning sparring with a client and was sitting in a contemplative mood, his arms rested on his knees, the sweat dripping from his eyebrows, his nose and his chin making a small puddle on the floor before him, when John arrived. The academy was now quiet: the smell of sweat hung heavy in the air, but neither man found the odour unpleasant; it was familiar smell to them.

John was not his usual chirpy self. 'We have a problem,' he said. For once that permanent grin was not in evident on his face.

'We do?' said Samuel. 'What?'

'The Magistrate.'

'What about him?'

'He is are afraid of the crowd. It'll be large and he's worried about a disturbance.'

Samuel shrugged nonchalantly. 'We will be able to control the crowd, he needn't worry.'

'But he is worried - and he has banned the fight!'

'But he can't do that, can he?' Samuel looked up in disbelief, the seriousness of the situation suddenly dawning on him.

'They can and they have,' said John gloomily, 'which means we will have to return the gate receipts.'

'I don't like the idea of that.' Samuel ran his hand contemplatively through his sweaty hair, his fingers spread out like a comb. 'What do you think?' he asked eventually.

'I think the likelihood of me returning the gate receipts is as likely as me sticking on a hand of sixteen,' said John, a grin now returning to his face, 'and you know I always go for the twenty one,' he added impishly.

Samuel smiled in response. He ran his hand over his dripping face and cast the collected sweat onto the floor where it splashed into the small puddle that had collected there. 'All right,' he said, 'I'm with you on this one. So it seems that we must defy the Magistrate then?'

'Agreed,' said John, 'defiance it is. But we will have to come up with a strategy if the Magistrate's men arrive to close us down.'

'You got any ideas?'

'Oh yes – I've got ideas all right.'

'But let's talk to the Magistrate first,' said Samuel. 'Let's try to convince him that we will control the crowd. Can you get Kettall to back us? It will add weight to our case.'

'That should be no problem,' John said thoughtfully. He gave Samuel a knowing look; his eyes suddenly sparkled and then a toothy grin betrayed that mischievous character of his. 'Remember what I always say, Sammy lad, when things start to go wrong...'

'It's turning out to be a good day,' yes, I know, Samuel grinned back.

Sir Thomas Kettall did speak eloquently on their behalf. He put on his personable persona. It was a bravado show: he was affable and agreeable; charming and charismatic. Samuel and John presented their plans and explained that many men had been hired to control the event. They also argued that the mob were quick to riot when there was no cricket or football to take their attention. The mob saw the riot as a substitute for their afternoon's sport. Their argument was to the effect that this boxing match replaced the football and consequently reduced the likelihood of a riot rather than being the source of one. They even mentioned that the Prince himself might be in attendance.

It was all to no avail. The Magistrate disliked boxing and saw it as a source of unrest: a tinderbox ready to be ignited; the unleashing on the general populous of the unrest and evils manifest in the lowest persons of society. The mob was feared, there was unrest in France and the Magistrate was reacting to that. He issued an order banning the fight on Marylebone Fields on the following Sunday.

The morning of the fight dawned a bright and sunny day. An azure sky surfaced with the sunrise and only wispy clouds meandered lazily across the blue expanse, and there was no menace manifest in the vista; the Gods had sent no tempest to intimidate the good people of London. The weather was set fair. Samuel looked aloft at the skyscape and breathed a long sigh of relief. A persistent downpour could have seriously affected the takings, but the weather would not stop the fight going ahead. However, if the Gods were not intent on obstructing the contest, the Magistrate was and Samuel was uneasy at defying him. He had embarked on a course of action that could have serious consequences, motivated by the bravado that was manifest in his own personality, but now in the cold light of day apprehension crept up on him. Defiance could men jail - the rewards were colossal: the potential losses immense.

Samuel and John supervised the erection of the stage. Fights usually took place on an unfenced platform with several rows of seating for the gentlemen, separated from the platform by a gap where the middling classes stood, their eyes on a level with the boxers' feet. Today that gap would have to be widened to accommodate the increased crowd and likewise more seating was put out. A box at Drury Lane Theatre cost five shillings, and John had based his price on that and fixed these seats at the same price, with the front two rows paying seven shillings and sixpence. The front standing spectators were to be charged two shillings and sixpence, but those meanly clad spectators at the back, who would normally have watched for nothing, were to be charged a shilling. Two hours before the fight, the Fields were already teeming with people, all having prepaid or paid at the gate and special care made to issue them all with tickets.

One hour before the fight and the crowd had swelled further. Virtually all the seats had been taken and the front standing area was thronged with spectators, tightly packed and bustling with a mix of speculation and anticipation. Bets were being laid, with each other and the bookmakers, and there was a great crescendo of noise that was building minute by minute. The rear standing area was even greater, but because they had the space to move backwards, there was less compression and less crushing, though equal anticipation. The crowd was several thousand strong, much to the delighted disbelief of John Campbell-John, who stood on the stage marvelling at the size of the crowd, their clamour music to his ears. He could see his debts being satisfied from the takings, but then he saw what he was dreading.

The Constable and his troop of Watchmen could be seen picking their way through the crowd towards him. John Campbell-John, a naturally conniving man, had a strategy in place, however, and he now had to follow it. His first task was to delay the Constable as much as possible. He jumped off the stage and made his way through the crowd in the opposite direction, towards the tents erected for the fighters. It would take ten minutes or so for the Constable to find him, and he would then do all he could to delay matters further. His estimate was about right and he was with Samuel in his tent when he got word that the Magistrate's men were coming. He disappeared under the flap at the rear of tent, so that when they entered they found only Samuel and one of his seconds.

'I have an order here, Sir, banning this fight,' said the Constable.

Samuel looked at the Constable, and then at his second, and then both men looked back at the Constable, but neither spoke. The Constable looked at them with irritation evident on his features.

'Well, Sirs,' he said finally, the volume of his voice rising.

'You'll want the promoter then, Sir,' said Samuel.

'Aye, that is correct, Sir.' said the Constable, 'and which one of you two fellows is Captain John Campbell-John.'

'Neither, Sir,' said Samuel.

The Constable looked suspiciously from one to the other, 'But I was told he was in this tent.'

'Aye, he was,' Samuel feigned innocence, 'but you've just missed him, Sir.'

The three men stood and looked at each other for what seemed like an eternity, the body language betraying the Constable's mood. Pugnacity had welled within him, but unfortunately he saw no way to direct that emotion. Samuel and his second purveyed only exaggerated politeness, which the Constable was sure concealed dumb insolence and this increased his frustration.

'And where has he gone,' demanded the Constable belligerently.

'Gone back to the stage I think, Sir,' said Samuel.

The belligerence in the Constable mounted at the stonewalling, but in the end he could only stamp his foot. Glowering at Samuel, he barked out the word '*Doh*', turned and marched his men away. For the next half an hour he searched for John, but John kept hidden away from him, staying out of sight at every opportunity. If one of the Constable's men were to approach him, he would deny all knowledge of a Mr John Campbell-John.

Time moved on and when it was only half an hour to the fight, the Constable realised that if he were to stop it from taking place he would have to act. He decided to address the crowd directly. With his men at his back, he took to the stage purposefully, if inelegantly, and tried to quieten the crowd, raising his arms and bellowing, '*Gentlemen! Gentlemen!*'

Nobody took any notice. He bellowed again, but aside from a few sniggers in the audience, glad of any diversion to pass the time until the eagerly awaited fight commenced, still nobody responded. He held the banning order high over his head to signify his authority, but to little effect. John watched with mounting amusement and was joined by Samuel, who was looking down at his pocket watch. John pulled out his own timepiece and checked: it was one-thirty. They nodded to each other, concurring that it was now safe to move their plan forward. John clambered onto the stage and walked towards the Constable.

'I'm John Campbell-John,' he said, 'have you been looking for me?'

'I have, Sir,' the Constable flapped the piece of paper in his face. 'You are aware, Sir, that this fighting contest is subject to this banning order?'

'I am, Sir,' replied John, 'but I don't think that the crowd are. Hadn't you better tell them?'

'This is not a source of levity, Sir.' The Constable's face was crimson with rage, 'if you allow this fight to go ahead then I will detain you and take you before the Magistrate. You are looking at prison, Sir. Now then; is that a source of levity?

'No you are right Sir,' said John. 'Can I see that order?'

John took the order and studied it nodding his head as he did so, as if to show compliance. He then walked towards the edge of the stage and raised his hands. His military uniform seemed to have an effect that the Constable's uniform had not, aside from which many of the sporting gentlemen recognised him. There was an immediate reduction in the noise, which signalled to those who had not been paying attention to what was happening on the stage that something was going on. With a ripple effect, further eyes turned towards the stage and the noise fell away until it ceased altogether. John had achieved easily what the Constable had failed to do.

'Gentlemen, gentlemen,' he bellowed, 'the Magistrate doesn't want this fight to go ahead. What do we think about that?'

The crowd exploded with rage and cries of *outrage* were yelled. John raised his hands again and the crowd responded.

'Are we not freeborn Englishmen,' he said playing the crowd, which responded with a raucous show of support. The sporting gentlemen in their tall hats and white cravats yelled, '*Aye, that we are Sir!*'

'Do not incite this crowd, Sir,' said the Constable furtively into John's ear, 'it will be the worse for you if you do.'

'Gentlemen,' bellowed John again, waving his arms to get their attention, 'this order prohibits this pugilistic contest on today's date at Marylebone Fields. Now what do you think we should we do about that?'

'Defy the Magistrate,' yelled a sporting gentlemen and the crowd cheered their support.'

'But gentlemen, gentlemen,' bellowed John, 'are we not freeborn Englishmen with a duty to be law abiding?'

The crowd was suddenly confused and people looked at each other not fully understanding what was being proposed. The noise fell away again and only a few muttered comments persisted.

'I think we should respect this order and accept that there will be no fight at Marylebone Fields today,' continued John.

For a brief moment the crowd was silent, but then there were a few sporadic cries of '*Nay*', which multiplied until a united, thunderous shout of '*Nay*' went up. There was no doubting that the crowd was intent on having their fight.

'Gentlemen,' continued John, waiting until the noise died down again and he had their attention. 'This Order says that there is to be no fight at *Marylebone Fields* today - but it *does not* say anything about a fight at *St George's Fields* today, does it?'

Again the crowd fell silent for a moment until people began to realise what was being proposed. Cries of '*Hussar!*' started to ring out and were taken up by everyone.

John raised his arms again and the crowd responded. 'Gentlemen, gentlemen, a stage has already been erected, and you all have tickets. The fight will go ahead with a short delay of only one hour. I invite you all to make your way to St George's Fields where this staged battle will commence at three of the clock.'

'This is a sharp trick, Sir,' said the Constable caustically into John's ear. 'I'll get another order from the Magistrate you know – and you've not heard the last of this, Sir!'

'Then you have until three of the clock to get it, and then to get it to St George's Field, Sir,' said John, unperturbed, 'I think you'd better get moving.'

'Damn you, Sir!' said the Constable, knowing he was beaten as he stormed off.

'It's going to be a good day,' said John to nobody in particular.'

CHAPTER 14

In a good humoured mood, the crowd hurried for the exits. The gentlemen took to their carriages and the lower classes walked. John had reserved two carriages, one each for Samuel and the Gravedigger and their entourages, and within half an hour they were at St George's Fields and ready to fight.

'Are we going to get away with this?' asked Samuel as the carriages drew up.

'I don't see why not,' replied John. 'By the time the Constable gets the Magistrate to sign a new order, the fight will be well under way if not finished. And besides, he may have to chase the Magistrate all the way to his home, for I doubt if he will be at his offices, today being a Sunday.'

Within an hour, at fifteen minutes to three, most of the crowd had filed into the spectator area surrounding the stage in St George's Fields. It had been set up in secret and none of the public in the Fields had seen anything unusual in the work in progress nor drawn any connection with the much publicised fight taking place in Marylebone Fields. The set up was almost identical to that at Marylebone Fields and John looked out at the eager faces. The crowd was several thousand strong and the change of venue had increased the expectancy, if that were possible. The day's events would be the topic of conversation in the inns, clubs and coffee houses of London for many months to come. It was a day of notoriety. It was a day when everybody, from the contestants to the crowd, from the sporting gentlemen to the meanly clad, had cocked a snook at the authorities, and there was a primeval pleasure in that. They were all united in this shared gratification and the fight itself was still to come. It had moved from the main event to the bonus event, but was not diminished for that.

When the two contestants emerged onto the stage a great roar went up, and it was clear to everyone that the crowd was already won over. John was to be the Master of Ceremonies and had therefore given up his position as Samuel's second to Solomon. Big Charles Sweep had been persuaded to act as referee. Sweep was introduced to the crowd and they cheered their national hero. The man himself, however, seemed unusually sullen and when the cheer had died down a wag in the crowd cried out, 'What's up Charlie - you look as if you've got the stink of the Thames in your nostrils.'

The crowd laughed at the witticism but Charles Sweep acknowledged it only with the slightest raising of his massive hand and the smallest of oblique smiles - and even that quickly disappeared. Charlie was not a happy man: he felt that such a bravura occasion should have been for him. Today he did not have the major role - he was just an ensemble player, and his ego was bruised, if not his appearance. The big man cut a resplendent figure: he was wearing a knee-length frock coat in black satin with a cutaway front and a high stand-fall collar – a fashionable style he favoured - the decoratively buttoned cuffs designed to reveal his frilly, silk shirt. He wore black knee-breeches with white stockings and shiny black, buckled shoes. The attire was much too grand and quite unsuitable for the occasion since it would undoubtedly be covered in blood by the end of the contest, but like Samuel, Charlie was a showman; a larger than life character who was a self-invented man. His outfit, carefully chosen, reflected his personality. He carried a walking cane into the ring – it was really a cudgel, the top having been expertly fashioned into his own likeness. The carved head sat snugly in his massive hand as he retired sulkily to a neutral corner of the stage so that the two contestants could be introduced.

The introduction confirmed what the newspapers had been saying, and the crowd was clearly massively in favour of Samuel. They cheered him wildly at the barked introduction – *Samuel the Jew; The Light of Israel* -and he responded with his usual bout of shadow boxing and saluting with his raised arm. The Gravedigger was applauded with respect from a knowledgeable crowd, but clearly he was not their favourite and his reputation had been tarnished by the foul way in which he had bested Samuel in their previous fight.

The bell sounded thunderously, its custodian intent on not being drowned out by the throng; the carillon unleashed a resounding cheer from the crowd and the noise levels rose in expectation. Samuel instantly took up his normal fighting attitude, as did the Gravedigger, but unlike the first fight he was intent on saving his energy for a protracted fight and did not rush in. As before, his brilliant red hair and pale, freckled, scarred complexion was in stark contrast to Samuel's smooth, olive skin with no hint of damage. His raven hair was as usual worn long and he had once again entered the ring with it tied at the nape, much to the displeasure of John who was all too aware of the danger.

Samuel flicked out punches into his opponent's pockmarked face, but each time he did so, the Gravedigger merely took the punch and then sidestepped to cut off Samuel's retreat, trying to force him into a corner from which there was no escape. After five minutes both men had done little damage and the Gravedigger had hardly thrown a punch, never mind landed one. The crowd, surprisingly, remained transfixed, for they would normally boo loudly if they thought the antagonists were not getting on with the fight. Samuel was briefly backed into a corner but instead of throwing a punch the Gravedigger lunged at the pigtail at the nape of his neck. Samuel sidestepped away quickly, but his opponent had come close to grabbing him by the hair as he had in their first fight.

John, watching from the side of the stage, winced at this and glanced at Solomon; both men blew out their cheeks to gesture their anxiety. The Gravedigger had clearly signalled his strategy. He was not going to waste his energy throwing wild punches, he was going to stalk Samuel and hold him at the first opportunity, preferably by the hair if he could. But Samuel had his own strategy well worked out. He had relived that first fight endlessly in his mind. He had assessed what he had done right and what he had done wrong and knew that the key to his success lay in his speed. He knew his opponent would stalk him, but he also knew that that danger would diminish as the fight went on. No matter how much the Gravedigger attempted to save his energy he would tire eventually and with that he would slow. Samuel had the advantage of speed and agility, but he must have the stamina to keep that advantage going. He had trained with that in mind. He now danced around the ring with the nimbleness of a young gazelle, flicking punches into that disfigured face and soon the blood started to flow until the Gravedigger's face vied with his hair for ownership of the colour red.

Sixteen minutes into the fight Samuel saw the first signs of fatigue in his opponent in that he started to blow heavily. This was the signal for the second part of Samuel's strategy. He manoeuvred himself into the centre of the ring where he planted his feet firmly. He flicked out a stinging left jab into the oncoming face, but followed it up with a powerful right hook that went around the Gravedigger's defence. As the punch landed, Samuel twisted his arm to make it rigid, with all the weight of his half-pivoted body behind it. The man staggered back in surprise at the severity of the blow, but he smiled perceptibly to see that Samuel was standing his ground and came thundering back. He threw a mighty left hook followed by a similar right, but Samuel parried the first on his right forearm and then swayed backwards so that the right fell short. The power of that missed blow put his opponent off balance and wide open for a counter punch, which Samuel duly delivered. His own right hand came down in an arc, hitting his opponent on the side of the head and the Gravedigger dropped to the canvas.

The crowd roared in appreciation as Samuel looked down at the expression on the Gravedigger's face, which was not so much distress as disbelief. Dazed, he jumped to his feet, but Big Charles Sweep stepped in between the two fighters and then signalled for the bell that duly sounded. The Gravedigger's seconds rushed forward and took their man back to his corner, throwing water at him as soon as he got there.

Samuel went back to his own corner, turned and looked back at the Gravedigger in the opposite corner. His confidence paramount, Samuel grinned, said, 'I'll best him within thirty minutes.'

Solomon was not listening, however. Seizing the opportunity whilst Samuel was concentrating his attention on his opponent, he produced a pair of scissors and calmly cut off his brother's pigtail. Teeth bared, Samuel turned round and angrily grabbed Solomon by the collar, but before he could speak his brother held up the palms of his hands, one still holding the scissors and the other a tail of raven hair. 'Forgive me brother, but the Gravedigger will have you by the hair just like he did the last time - it's plain for all to see. We must deny him that advantage.'

Even though it was now too late to do anything about it, Samuel's vanity made him want to vigorously debate that contention. His looks were important to him and to his mind his appearance had been spoiled. He was more than annoyed, but before he could speak, the bell sounded again, so he merely grunted, released his grip on Solomon's collar, pushed him backwards and returned to the centre of the ring.

The Gravedigger had obtained a brief respite from the thirty seconds' break, and Samuel should have danced until its effects had drained from his opponent's legs and fatigue once again returned. But anger took ascendancy over his rational mind and he stood his ground in the centre of the ring. He parried two more round punches and then followed up with a muscular uppercut that ripped through his opponent's guard. The contact launched a cocktail of blood and mucus into the air and spattered the resplendent clothes of Big

Charles Sweep, so that his stunning attire changed from a contrasting monochrome to a complementary tricolour of black, white and red.

The Gravedigger took the blow without a backwards step and lunged at Samuel, reaching round the back of his head to the nape of his neck, but grabbing at thin air. Samuel, alarmed, stepped backwards and immediately realised that thanks to his brother's foresight, he had had a lucky escape. With that, his anger dropped away; his calculating fighting mind now reasserted itself and he returned to his strategy. He danced for five more minutes, but then began to stop and parry, his own heavy punches starting to hit home. Each time a powerful blow landed the crowd roared. Very soon Samuel was able to hit his opponent at will and the contest took on the appearance of an exhibition fight. The Gravedigger's face was a mess - his flesh mashed together with blood and smeared across his features so that he wore a vermilion mask. His right eye was already closed and his left was closing rapidly so that he could no longer see the punches coming. Samuel now played his matador role and walked up and down before his bested foe, flicking out left jabs that provoked his opponent to throw wild punches in response, but with his vision so badly restricted the Gravedigger had little spatial awareness and the punches just scythed through thin air draining away the last dregs of his stamina. The only thing he had left was his bravery.

But Samuel had a score to settle. To this point his mind had been calculating and his approach totally professional. He was not by nature a vindictive man, but the Gravedigger has wronged him gravely. He began to taunt him. He moved his weight to his right and sank a potent, gut-wrenching blow under the Gravedigger's ribcage, but he did not retreat out of danger. His opponent doubled up in pain and Samuel heard the air rip from his lungs with a guttural - *Ahhh*. Samuel leaned over, hissed, 'Is this all you fucking got?' and then sent another penetrating blow into the vulnerable man's midriff. 'Where's your fucking *cheating* now, eh?' Samuel crowed as another punch beat into the bent figure. 'You need to be taught a *fucking* lesson, my man.' Before he walked away a final punch was launched accompanied by the single word 'BASTARD!' which seemed enhance the power of it.

Samuel raised his right had high into the air to signal to the crowd that the matador was going to dispatch the bull and the crowd responded with a collective -*HUZZAR!* And the blow came crashing down. The Gravedigger wobbled but his courage kept him upright.

His guard returned as a reflex action, but there was little actual protection from it. Samuel's right hand rose high into the sky again, and again the crowd bayed – *HUZZAR!* The blow came swooping down like a hawk homing in on its prey. It hit home cruelly and the man staggered backwards and then fell back hitting his head on the canvas as he did so. The bell sounded and he was carried unconscious back to his corner.

His seconds tried feverishly to revive their man. Water was poured copiously over him and then smelling salts were waved before his nostrils but his nasal passages were too full of blood for any vapour to penetrate. After thirty seconds they heaved the Gravedigger to his feet, but those few flickering dregs of consciousness that had briefly surfaced had now evaporated again. His legs were dysfunctional; his head loped downwards, his mouth gaping wide open and his chin resting firmly on his chest. The only sign of vital activity was the gargled breathing emanating from his powerful lungs. Nevertheless, the seconds dragged their man to the centre of the ring in some deluded hope that he could fight on. They released him, but he just fell to the floor.

The fight was over and Charles Sweep held the victor's arm. A shout of adulation went up and gentlemen threw their tall hats into the air. Samuel bathed in the crowd's adoration, strutting about the ring both arms raised high in triumph. He visited each corner so that the whole crowd could see him and he could see them. He had proved himself to be the governor, but he had proved much more than that. He had proved he was a fighting man of unparalleled skill, but more importantly, he had proved to be a noble hero; one who had shown that the little man *can* prevail against the bully. In the midst of the drear, poverty-stricken, anxiety-ridden times in which they lived, it was something for downtrodden folk to cling to - the hope that somehow their lives *could* be bettered. And at the very least, it provided a splash of excitement and colour that for a brief space enabled the common folk to forget the endless, grinding misery of their days. If for no other reasons than these, Samuel was indeed their hero.

John took to the centre of the ring to announce to the crowd the result of the battle. It was a superfluous action but it was part of the show, part of the spectacle. He barked out an obvious statement, raising Samuel's hand again as he did so. '*The winner - Samuel the Jew, The Light of Israel*'. The crowd rose to give their hero a standing ovation, for they knew they had seen something special. Samuel

168

responded to the adulation once again. He bowed to the crowd respectfully, raising his arms again and shouting as he did so: 'The Light of Israel. I am Samuel the Jew – The Light of Israel.' Right now, they did not care what he called himself: he was just their hero. He was a pugilist of immense proficiency, a man of honour, a handsome man and a showman, but when the euphoria of the moment was over, he was still just a pugilist.

And then the Magistrate's men arrived and surrounded the stage, but this only brought forth laughter from the crowd. The Constable in charge took to the stage and addressed the crowd demanding that they disperse, waving as he did so the revised order. The crowd bayed and mocked him, and he turned to John and waved the order in his face.

John took it, read it carefully and with sarcasm dripping from his voice, said, 'Then the crowd must disperse, Sir. We are all law-abiding gentlemen here. Did you see the fight?' he added mockingly.

The Constable's face reddened still further, his temper adding to the colouring engendered by his lack of breath from scampering across the city and back again. He snatched back the order, observing now that the crowd were beginning to disperse on their own anyway.

'The Magistrate did not take kindly to this ruse, Sir,' he said, pausing for breath between some of the words. 'You will do well to remember that, Sir. Make no mistake; you have made an important enemy today. I fear next time it will be the militia.'

'And perhaps the Magistrate will do well to remember that there has been no crowd trouble, and that the event has been run without incident as we had promised him,' said John.

The Constable stormed away leaving John and Samuel to wallow in their achievement. John put his arm around Samuel's shoulder and they both viewed the scene before them. The crowd was dissolving, people streaming away from the Fields, but there were still cheers from certain quarters and Samuel acknowledged them all.

'I told you I would make your fortune Sammy boy, didn't I?' said John.

'Aye you did John,' replied Samuel, 'but I'm sure that I had something to do with it as well,' he added with a wry laugh.

'Aye you did. Aye you did,' said John. 'You are unique Sammy boy; you're unique alright.'

'Yes, I always remember that I'm unique,' said Samuel drily, 'just like everybody else.'

John laughed robustly. 'If jokes were horses, Sammy boy, then you'd be a donkey.'

Samuel smiled a warm and friendly smile. All the anxieties of the morning had drained away from him. It was only hours before, but it felt like a hundred years ago. He had bested not only the dreaded Gravedigger; the Bristol Bonecrusher, but he had bested the Magistrate too. In partnership with John he had become a promoter and what is more, he had been successful at that too. His star was in the ascendance but his mind was full of other plans as well.

John observed Samuel's bleeding knuckles: they were two shanks of raw, bloodstained flesh, the skin having been removed during the fight. 'Your hands look bad, Sammy boy - are they badly damaged?'

Samuel looked down at his hands and at the moment the pain in them registered in his mind. 'No. I doubt if any bones are broken, it's just flesh and blood I think.' He pondered for a moment, 'A fighter's supposed to take care of his knuckles. The Gravedigger kept offering me the top of his head as a target – it's an old tactic. He wanted me to break my knuckles on his head, but I saw through that.'

'But they must still hurt like hell,' said John sympathetically.

'Well aye.' Samuel paused, held up the offending hands and smiled, 'But then, I bleed gold don't I?'

'Aye, you do that Sammy – you bleed gold alright.'

'Have we made our fortunes then John?'

'We have that,' Sammy lad.'

'How much?'

John looked skywards as though calculating, grinned, 'I haven't had time to tally our net profit, but we have taken over a thousand pounds.'

'*A thousand pounds!* It's a fortune alright, John Campbell-John. God was with us today.'

'God was with *you* Sammy, not me,' said John, 'I fear he has long since given up on the likes of me.'

'Did not Jesus talk of shepherds and lost sheep,' said Samuel.

'Aye he did,' John laughed, 'but I fear that he long since tired of looking for me.

'Then I have a proposition for you,' said Samuel.

'And what would that be Sammy boy?'

'It's not for today, John, today is for - well it's for celebration. We have celebrating to do.'

CHAPTER 15

John Campbell-John rapped excitedly on the door of Samuel's town house. There was no answer and he stood back and looked up towards the bedroom windows. He consulted his watch, but had to squint at the dial to focus for his hand was shaking - he had had a night of celebration. He was aware that the morning shakes was becoming a common occurrence, but he thought little about his long-term health and in fact his mind had not connected the effect with his alcohol intake. He squinted again at the watch face until a time of ten minutes to eleven registered in his eyesight. The breeze rustled his hair; it was a sunny day and the air smelt uncommonly fresh, the wind having blown away the rank smells the Londoner was accustomed to. His chest expanded as he breathed in a large gulp of fresh air and looked up at the clear blue sky and the feathery clouds that raced across it. This was a good day to be alive. He was a late riser and Samuel Medina was usually up long before him, to pursue the business of running his Academy. It was the day after the fight against the Gravedigger and the celebrations had gone on long into the night. Even the servants were not in evidence.

John returned to the door and redoubled his efforts to rouse the household. He banged long and vigorously with the heavy brass knocker against the large front door; until he heard the housekeeper's voice from a window above, grumbling that she was coming. He stopped rapping, but he shuffled back and forth impatiently whilst the housekeeper found her way down from her attic room. He had under his arms some of the day's newspapers and journals and in his hand a copy of today's edition of *The World*. The door opened and Mrs Dawson, the housekeeper appeared, still wearing her nightcap and looking decidedly grumpy. He pushed past her and without invitation made his way to the drawing room on the first floor, shouting back to Mrs Dawson that she should go and raise her master.

The drawing room was the grandest room in the house, where Samuel and his wife kept their finest possessions. John spread the journals across the elegant table, but held onto *The World*. Samuel and his wife entered shortly afterwards, both wearing robes to cover their nightwear.

Scratching his head and yawning as he spoke so that his words were not clearly enunciated, Samuel asked why John had called so early. Unable to contain himself, John started to answer, but then his manners surfaced, prompted and rebuked in equal measure by Rebecca's disapproving stare. He broke off to address her.

'Madam; your humble servant and a happy day to you and to us all,' he said, bowing slightly. His body language acknowledged not only his manners, but also her rebuke, spoken as always with her large, dark eyes.

'I am rejoiced you are come, Captain Campbell-John,' replied Rebecca graciously, 'and will you take tea with us?'

'That would be most pleasant, Madam,' said John.

She turned and nodded to Mrs. Dawson, who was now hovering in the doorway. Charged with the task she disappeared, still grumbling to herself as she went. The drawing room was Rebecca's domain; she took charge from that moment, directing Samuel and John to sit and they both obliged. She enquired politely as to the reason for the call, and then the words spat from John's mouth as if a starting pistol had been sounded. The papers were full of the fight: hundreds of column inches, about not only the battle, but about the besting of the Magistrates as well. There were articles about the rights of an Englishman; about the power of the Magistrates; but mainly about Samuel. They had elevated him to the rank of traditional hero. He had triumphed over skulduggery and he was the centre of attention.

John insisted that they read *The World* first and Samuel complied, his chest swelling with pride as he did so. It seemed that he was a national celebrity, and it appealed to the showman within him. His cause had been taken up by *all* the journals of the day, which was certainly unusual, particularly given the rest of the news, which was momentous. John drew his attention to the inside page. A Parisian mob had stormed the Bastille. John knew this was hot news for a nation that was paranoid about revolution. He had seen for himself, the power of the mob, fuelled by cheap drink and inadequate policing. It was this that stimulated the paranoia and had coloured the Magistrate's view, causing him to try to ban the fight. The storming of the Bastille was an event that was sure to frighten the good citizens of London, and yet – and yet it was relegated to the inside page. The front page was reserved for an account of a pugilistic encounter – a staged battle between two powerful men. It was about the making of an idol.

Rebecca left briefly to change out of her night attire. She felt uncomfortable in anything lavish and rejected it, choosing instead a simple-styled dress consisting of a gown with a fitted bodice and a cutaway, draped and poofed overskirt worn over a petticoat of subdued grey cotton. The gown had a white silk collar and ruffled sleeves, and on her head Rebecca wore a muslin cap. Nevertheless, she retained her natural elegance and was the exact opposite of her husband. She was introverted where he was extroverted. She was uncomfortable with the limelight where he craved it. The things they had in common were their strength of personality and their love of literature.

Samuel was too excited to change out of his night attire. When Rebecca returned he thrust *The World* into her hand, pointing at the most adoring passages, and the three of them spent the next three hours poring over these journals. They were three educated individuals, previously without rank in society, but now elevated within it by Samuel's deeds of gladiatorial violence within a prize ring. They now seemed perfectly at home in their middling-class existence, and yet Rebecca disapproved. She was a woman of genuinely delicate sensibilities, notwithstanding that she was a Jew, for her life had not spared her the realities and harshness of that. She had encountered at first hand society's animosity to her culture. She had seen her male relatives return home beaten and bloodied for no other reason than that they were followers of Judaism. She was a Jew and she knew that violence was never far away, yet any longing for revenge had not shaped her personality. She did not revel in her husband's exploits in any vengeful way. On the contrary, her Jewishness had engendered distaste for violence in all its forms. And yet paradoxically she had fallen in love with a man who made his living as a prizefighter. She now enjoyed the spoils of his profession, but that did not distract her from holding a negative view of that profession. The irony of that did not escape her; Rebecca had her own agenda.

'We have to think about your next fight,' said John excitedly.

'No no, Captain Campbell-John,' said Rebecca, 'Samuel has made it quite clear to you that this fight was to be his last.

'But that was before he-'

Rebecca cut across him, 'Before what? Captain Campbell-John.'

'Before – you know,' said John, still unable to express exactly what he meant. He changed his approach, 'London has never seen the likes of such a fight. The crowd will be even bigger next time. We can't turn our backs on such an opportunity.'

'Samuel has other talents from which he can earn a living,' she said tartly.

'Not this kind of money he can't,' said John his exasperation mounting.

'Maybe not,' said Rebecca, 'but I will not continue to spend tormented nights worrying if my husband will come home maimed, or with his mind befuddled, or maybe not come home at all.'

'I understand, good lady,' said John, 'but Sammy has so much skill. He knows well how to defend himself. I wouldn't send him into the ring if I didn't believe that,' he added. It was a lie of course.

'But I have spent a year nursing him back to health,' Rebecca said, 'what good did his skill do him then?'

'But that was skulduggery - we won't let it happen again,' said John.

'But it was treachery that succeeded, was it not Captain Campbell-John?'

'Well yes it did, but we know better now.'

'Do you?' she asked looking directly into his eyes.

Her eyes burned directly into his consciousness and he felt his resolve dissolving. Helplessly, he looked away.

'Will you stand surety to me that Samuel will never get hurt, Captain Campbell-John? Will you do that for me?'

'But no one could do that my good lady – it's not possible,' John mumbled.

'Well then, that is an end to it,' she said. She sat back in her chair her body language suggesting a full stop – the end of a chapter.

John looked at Samuel for support, but none was forthcoming. With his eyes John pleaded with Samuel to contradict his wife, but he did not respond and the three of them sat for some moments in an awkward silence.

Samuel eventually cleared his throat and said, 'Do you have the final accounting figures John?'

'Aye – and they are spectacular, Sammy boy. We took £1,245.6s at the gate, and that gives us a net profit of £808, 15s.6d.'

'A fortune indeed Captain Campbell-John,' said Rebecca. 'I think my husband has a proposition for you.'

Samuel coughed self-consciously. John looked at him inquisitively, but there was an embarrassing pause before Samuel spoke. 'Now look here John,' he said uncomfortably, 'I know that I can make awful lot money from fighting, but I have promised my wife that I will not fight again and I intend to keep that promise. Do you understand?'

John shrugged his shoulders, but remained silent.

'But I'm not dim-witted and neither is my wife, Samuel continued. 'We are both aware of my celebrity and the earning potential that goes with it.'

'So what do you suggest?' said John.

'I'm suggesting a new partnership with an equal split of the profits. If I'm not to fight then I do not need an agent or a manager.'

John was intrigued. 'And in what profession will our endeavours be directed?'

'Why, mainly the entertainment profession, John,' said Samuel.

'In what way, Sammy?'

'I intend to go on the stage,' said Samuel.

'*The stage!*' said John in disbelief. 'And pray, what manner will this entertainment take?'

'Why I will give exhibitions of pugilism – what did you think I meant?'

'I wasn't sure,' said John, 'I just didn't connect boxing exhibitions with the theatre.'

'No,' said Samuel, 'but I do not see why not. The theatre has all the facilities for such an exhibition. Why should we not take advantage of it?'

'No reason at all Sammy,' said John warming to the idea, 'but won't it be too brutal for the ladies. If they will not come, then the theatre managers won't want to hire you.'

'Rebecca had the same concerns, didn't you dear,' said Samuel, turning to his wife. She nodded affirmatively and gestured him to proceed. 'She has considered that and has said that she will preview the performance to ensure it will not affect the sensibilities of the ladies. We will make it clear on the handbills that the performance will be suitable for them.'

'And how much were you thinking of charging,' asked John.

'I was hoping to get fifty guineas per performance,' said Samuel.

John's eyes widened in surprise and he shrilled a long whistle.

'But we may have to start with a percentage of the gate to get the managers to engage us,' continued Samuel. 'If we start to draw the crowds as I expect, then we can work up to such a fee.'

John leaned forward, 'And what will be my role in this venture?'

'Arranging the performances, negotiating the fees, organising the travel and accommodation, perhaps sparring with me on the stage, perhaps being my master of ceremonies, although I'd like to speak directly to the audience myself. I expect *that* to go down better.'

John thought for a moment. 'But that still sounds like a manager to me – why do you offer me an *equal* partnership?'

'Because...,' Samuel paused.

'Because,' Rebecca interrupted, 'Samuel has responsibilities to his people. He now has celebrity and that should not be wasted – it should be used to help them.'

'Your money will not go very far if he starts giving it away,' said John.

'No it won't, Captain Campbell-John,' said Rebecca, 'so Samuel has other business propositions in mind, and he wants you to manage those for him as well.'

'*Other* business propositions?' Once again, John was intrigued.

'Yes, 'said Samuel, 'what do you think of Box Clubs?'

'They're fine,' said John. 'That is to say, it's a fine idea to let poor folk contribute their hard-earned pennies to a club each week so they can eventually afford to buy whatever it is they are saving for, I don't have a problem with that. But as you well know, Sammy boy, it doesn't work when the organiser runs off with box – and that, as you also know, is by no means a rarity.'

'Exactly,' said Rebecca. 'The scheme is entirely unregulated. We mean to change that.'

John's jaw dropped, but before he could respond, Samuel nodded at his wife and added, 'I want you to set up a Box Club, John, under my name and I will personally guarantee the probity of it.'

'So you mean to use your reputation to guarantee its integrity?'

'Exactly,' said Samuel. It will be the one Box Club people can rely on; their savings guaranteed safe from theft. People, whether they be Jew or Gentile, will be falling over themselves to join it, you'll see.

'But where is the business opportunity in that?' John snorted. 'That won't make anybody rich, least of all you!'

'That's not its purpose, Captain Campbell-John,' said Rebecca, 'but in fact you are mistaken. As it gathers apace we expect considerable sums to be invested with us. We will need premises and honest employees, of course, but we will have money to invest in certain safe projects.'

John's face lit up as it gradually dawned on him what was being proposed. 'So we will take our profits in interest on the capital invested?'

'Exactly,' Rebecca nodded. 'But if we can also pay our investors a dividend, then we are likely to increase the business substantially.'

'But I have another business proposal,' said Samuel. 'It concerns counterfeited coinage. It's a great problem to poor but honest traders.'

'Well yes, said John incredulously, 'but surely you don't believe you can solve *that* problem, when even the Magistrates can't?'

Samuel smiled, 'Well actually I do.'

'But how? John's face was a study of scepticism.

'These new *bank notes* issued by the Bank of England - they avoid the need for large amounts of coinage,' said Samuel.

'That's as may be, but I have no truck with them - along with the rest of the population,' John sneered. Most people never even handle banknotes; like me, they prefer hard currency.'

'Unlike you, John, most people are too poor to have the option. The bank notes are too big - £10 and £15 denominations. What good is that to the average trader? And because he so rarely sees one, it's made it easy for counterfeiters to pass on their notes as genuine. Few traders can tell the difference.'

'And a counterfeit note is a disaster for a small trader,' Rebecca interrupted, 'so he'll try not to take a note at all in case it's a fake.'

'But I still don't see what *you* can do about it,' said John.

'Well I propose to issue my own notes, in denominations of a penny, three pence and six pence,' said Samuel.

John was stunned, the concept racing around his brain for a few moments. 'Isn't that a bit dangerous?' he asked eventually.

'I don't see why, if we take care only to issue notes that we can cover,' said Samuel. 'We'll check the authenticity of the coins we take, and only then will we issue the notes in return.'

'It sounds as if you are testing the water with both feet,' said John, 'I fear that we could drown.'

'It's a matter of trust,' said Samuel, 'it'll take time, but when people see that we will honour the notes, they will only bring them back to us when they are damaged and need replacing.'

'But won't *you* have the same problem with counterfeiters?' said John.

'Possibly, but the small size of the denominations will be a big deterrent. Even so, I suspect some crude attempts will be made and that will be your first job, John, to come up with a design that will be difficult to copy.'

'Phew!' whistled John. 'Well as a ruse it's certainly a novel one.'

'This is no *ruse* Captain Campbell-John,' interrupted Rebecca angrily, 'we intend to cheat no one. We are honest people.'

'My apologies Mrs Medina,' said John contritely, 'my words were chosen imprecisely. I did not intend to infer any impropriety or dishonesty.'

'Apology accepted,' said Rebecca, graciously. 'As you have said previously, Captain Campbell-John, charity would leave us penniless very quickly. We are proposing business ventures that will make us a modest profit, but will benefit the more venerable people in society at the same time. Do you understand?'

'Perfectly,' said John bowing his head politely.

'So, what do you say John – will you be my partner?' said Samuel.

John hesitated - it was an unexpected proposal. 'We'll need quill drivers,' he said.

'Aye, we'll need clerks; that's true,' said Samuel, 'and if you agree, then I will agree to backdate our partnership to include our venture as fight promoters, what say you to that, eh?'

'Yes, Captain Campbell-John,' said Rebecca before he could respond. 'And if my arithmetic is correct, then a one half share of £808.15s.6d is £404.7s.9d, whereas your twenty per cent share would be only £161.15s.1d.

John did not take long to think. He had wagered 50 guineas at 6 to 4 on and had winnings of £33.6.8. This amount plus the £161.15.01 would come nowhere near clearing his debts. Samuel's offer made him suddenly almost £249 richer; his reservations rapidly subsided. He pushed himself up from his chair and thrust out his hand. Samuel shook it vigorously. A new partnership had been forged.

CHAPTER 16

The next year was a golden one for the partnership. Samuel quickly became a stage hit; the showmen wanted him because he could fill their theatres. His fees rose as he had expected and within months he was being paid the fifty guineas he had wanted for each appearance, and he was at times performing three times a week. Songs were written about him and his name was included in the scripts of many of the plays that were on the boards at that time. The songs were sung wherever crowds gathered, and all this added to the cult of celebrity that surrounded him. He had to exhibit himself to the crowd wherever he went and the demand for him was insatiable. The performances he gave, however, were much more than an exhibition of pugilism. He was a gracious man and he had intellect and wit, together with the ability to play an audience. With that innate showmanship he beguiled the audiences with his commentaries, with anecdotes and stories.

John was a perfect foil for him, for they both shared that wit and John was a natural actor. A self-invented man; he played the parts of the gentlemen of rank within Samuel's yarns. Rebecca had meanwhile done her part, directing Samuel's performances so that they appealed to the ladies of refinement. Consequently both genders and all classes populated the audiences. By the end of their first year in the new partnership, the Medinas and Campbell-John were earning colossal amounts of money.

Samuel's fame also had a catapulting affect on the other business enterprises. As he had predicted, the Box Club had several hundred contributors within weeks of its launch, and this swelled to thousands when withdrawals were honoured and its reputation was established. In effect the partnership was running a small bank for the patronage of the common folk. Engraved notes were ordered from the printers with an image of Samuel in his fighting stance. These were then embossed before issue and personally signed by Samuel, and they quickly became good in trade – so good in fact that Samuel could hardly keep up with the signing of them. Each note contained a serial number, and batches were given a code, so that the serial number of a suspicious note could be checked against the codes that were known to only a small number of privileged employees. Within a year the

Box Club and the bank notes business had a workforce of fifteen, working out of three premises.

But that was not all as far a Samuel was concerned. Together with his wife he became a regular guest at literary evenings. He continued to write poetry and became a seasoned orator. Society was racist, chauvinistic and bigoted. It wasn't just class conscious, but super-class conscious so that even if you were accepted as a person of rank, within that rank there were echelons of rank. If you were invited to dine then you were expected to proceed to the dinner table in order of your rank, the higher the echelon the sooner you were seated. However, Georgian society also had immense respect for money, which overrode race, creed or other social disadvantages. So Samuel's wealth and celebrity overrode both his lowly upbringing and his Jewishness, and it seemed that there was no stigma to his inclusion in polite society. He stood beside some of the most renowned literary figures of his day and gave his readings without embarrassment, even if there was some resentment towards him in those ranks.

That same year, his wife fell pregnant with their first child to Samuel's absolute delight. It was a difficult birth but Samuel was presented with a beautiful baby girl that they named Miriam. The child looked like her mother and Samuel loved her all the more because of that. There was a Jewish naming ceremony and Samuel's heart swelled with satisfaction when he saw the pride in the eyes of his parents. His family had been close to him when he was a child, especially his father. But it was a Jewish fundamental to honour your father and mother, and Samuel believed that he had, in the past, let them down, so many times by failing to hold down the many jobs that he had had. Now he was a success. Instead of being a drain upon his father, who had other children to feed and educate, he was able to offer support to them. He paid for the education of his siblings. He provided a new house for the family.

All seemed to be perfect in is life - and the catalyst to it all was his ability to fight. In public he still played the role of knight errant and if he perceived that someone was being wronged then he would take up their cause – there and then, in the street if need be. But his fame was now so well established that he no longer needed to fight, for nobody would stand against him. His image as a man of character, a man of the people, a man prepared to fight the corner of the underprivileged, was enhanced with every encounter.

There was a sizeable spanner heading for his particular works, however: in the great frame of Big Charles Sweep. Sweep had showed Samuel nothing but respect in his early meetings with him. He had allowed his name to be linked with a young, unknown pugilist. He had sparred with this young upstart, and he had given him the benefit of his experience. He had stood as his second and he had refereed his fights. Sweep was the unofficial Champion of all England, and yet his fame was now completely overshadowed by this young Jewish boy. The result was resentment. It had started on the day of the fight with the Gravedigger when Sweep realised he had been relegated to no more than a bit player; one to whom the crowd gave only a passing attention. Every day since then, Sweep's resentment had grown. He felt that all the adulation that was now being given to Samuel was rightly due to him. It represented a lack of respect for who he was. With each newspaper article, with each stage performance, Sweep's resentment turned to bitterness and then to anger. His genial personality was infected with bile. Samuel Medina filled his thoughts day and night. He, Charles Sweep, was the Champion, not this young Jewish upstart. Medina was an ungrateful minion in his eyes who had failed to show him the proper respect that he deserved. He followed Samuel's example and put on a stage show, and he had some success with it: as an exhibition of the noble art it had all the skill that this great Champion had brought to his profession. It had showmanship and, unexpectedly, it had narrative and wit, but Samuel's show had so much more of both. In comparison, Sweep's show fell some way short.

Sweep decided that it was time to put the record straight. Along with his entourage he went to a stage show at the Pantheon Theatre on Oxford Street, where Samuel's show was being performed. A ring had been erected on the stage from which Samuel was performing his exhibition. The crowd was enthralled by his performance and were unusually quiet. Samuel was boxing and narrating to his audience when Sweep stood up theatrically and slowly swaggered down the aisle towards the front of the stage. Each step was taken purposefully so that the audience could see what was happening. Heads turned and people recognised him as he went; he made sure of it by stopping at intervals and looking about him, so that they had time to recognise that it was Big Charles Sweep. Not that this was difficult, for as usual he was magnificently turned out in his customary black satin coat and breeches, topped by a tall hat. In his right hand he carried his cane-cum-cudgel, and he touched it to his hat at intervals acknowledging the recognition of the crowd. A murmur began to spread through the audience in anticipation that something significant was about to happen.

Samuel sensed this from the stage, but the bright lights shining in his eyes from the many candles stopped him from recognising Sweep. He assumed it was a drunk: intoxication was a regular feature at the theatre and drunken interruptions were common. Samuel had quickly learned how to handle them. He stopped his narrative and turned to the silhouetted figure below him.

'Come Sir,' he said mockingly, 'if you feel that the audience has come to see you, then get into the ring with me and we will debate the matter.' Samuel expected the audience to laugh and then applaud him, but instead gasps sounded in the auditorium. Samuel, confused, squinted at the figure before him - and then Sweep spoke, and it was in a voice projected as much to the audience as it was to Samuel.

'Sir,' he said, turning to the audience for dramatic effect before turning back and continuing, 'the master does not debate with the apprentice.'

Samuel and John both recognised the Cornish tones. The cunning inherent in John's personality sensed danger. Samuel, however, responded instinctively with a display of immaculate manners. He climbed through the ring ropes and walked to the edge of the stage so that only only a few feet separated him from Sweep, though Samuel was on the stage so was standing some six feet higher.

'Ladies and gentlemen,' announced Samuel, 'we are privileged indeed to have a great Champion amongst us.' Turning to Sweep, he bowed and said, 'your servant Sir, I am rejoiced to see you.' He then clapped his hands vigorously and encouraged the audience to do likewise. They obediently did so, and cheers began to ring out.

Samuel's impeccable behaviour took Sweep by surprise for he had rehearsed his speech in his mind many times, and this was simply not in the script. He felt obliged to turn and bow to the audience in recognition of their affection for him. Samuel had stolen his thunder. In the sidelines, John breathed a premature sigh of relief.

'Mr Sweep – and how is it with you Sir?' Samuel continued.

'Very bad, Sir,' bellowed Sweep.

'I am sorry to hear that, Sir,' said Samuel, 'I am at your service if I can be of any help.' Samuel had unwittingly given back to Sweep the opportunity to launch his prepared speech.

'Aye you can that, Sir,' said Sweep, 'you can return to me what is rightfully mine.'

'I am an honest man, Sir,' said Samuel indignantly, 'if I have something of yours then I will gladly return it to you.' The crowd had gone quiet as to hear a pin drop, so enthralled were they to hear this exchange.

Every bit as indignantly, Sweep shouted, 'You have a reputation that is rightfully mine, Sir, for *I* am Champion of all England, not *you*.'

'I do not understand, Sir,' said Samuel, 'I do not claim to be Champion of all England.'

'But you claim everything else that goes with my title, Sir,' said Sweep.

'I assure you, Sir, that I claim nothing that isn't rightfully mine.'

The hackles rose on the back of John's neck. He knew what Samuel's response was likely to be to any suggestion that he had behaved dishonourably, and he feared that Samuel would immediately challenge Sweep there and then. If he did so, with a ring already erected on the stage there seemed to be nothing that could stop a fight. John, however, was convinced it was a fight that Samuel could not win, for Sweep was not only much bigger and stronger than Samuel, he had the skill to go with it. The cunning in John also wanted reward for such a fight, because it should not be put on free for an audience who had paid only for an exhibition. He looked to the heavens as if pleading and Samuel caught sight of the gesture. He understood immediately what John was trying to communicate, but he was powerless to change his own personality.

'I repeat, Sir,' said Sweep, 'you have my reputation. It is not yours to trade on.'

'Sir,' said Samuel, 'then we must settle this like gentlemen. I am prepared here and now to fight for my honour and my reputation.'

John put his hand over his eyes and hung his head, shaking it in dismay. Samuel had allowed himself to be easily manoeuvred into a challenge and John had somehow to intervene, but he was unsure how to do so. He need not have worried; Sweep was now in control of the situation and of his temper.

'I agree, Sir,' said Sweep, 'that we both need to fight for our reputations. We owe it to the public to see who is the better man. But this is neither the time nor the place.' With that he took off his tall hat, raised it high into the air and turned to the audience so that they all could see it.

The crowd understood the gesture and a cheer went up as Sweep turned back to the stage and theatrically tossed his hat into the ring. It was a symbolic challenge from one pugilist to another, and the audience now stood, applauding and shouting its approval.

Samuel was now on the horns of a dilemma. He had promised his wife that he would fight no more pitched battles. He saw no dichotomy in being prepared to fight Sweep then and there, yet not being prepared to fight him in a pitched battle. It was about the parameters of a promise, about the definition of a fight, about perceptions of honour. But the only person to whom it made any real sense was Samuel himself. He walked up and down the front edge of the stage as he wrestled with this personal crisis. The crowd fell silent and the tension mounted. And then Samuel resigned himself to do something he had never done before – he would simply have to accept the loss of face.

'Sir,' he said loudly, but with resignation in his tone, 'it has been well reported in the newspapers that I have made a promise to my wife that I will fight no more pitched battles. We will have to find another honourable way of settling this dispute.'

There was an audible groan from the audience, and Sweep turned to them in response. 'Does the public want to see such a fight?' he bellowed.

Cries of 'Aye!' rang out in response. 'You hear that, Sir?' Sweep turned back to Samuel. 'I want this battle and the public want it too.'

'But as a man of honour,' replied Samuel sadly, 'I cannot lightly break the pledge I have made to my good wife. I'm sure the public will understand that, Sir.'

'But you are also *honour* bound to accept my challenge, Samuel Medina, or forfeit your right to trade on my reputation as a great Champion.'

'I trade on my own reputation, Sir,' said Samuel indignantly, 'I have no need to trade on yours.'

'Then you must prove your reputation, Sir, and as we are both pugilists the answer seems to be most obvious to me.'

Samuel felt backed into a corner. Time seemed to freeze, but was in reality only a few seconds; he struggled to find a safe passage from this entrapment. The silence was uncomfortable and some of the audience leaned forward in their seats in anticipation. Some thought Samuel was afraid to fight this great Champion, and perhaps he should have been, but he had an arrogance about him that precluded fear. While his lack of fear was quite genuine, paradoxically he was encumbered by his wife's dominion. She was a woman who expected him to keep a pledge and he was acutely aware of that.

And then John came to his rescue. 'Mr Sweep,' he hailed as he walked to the edge of the stage. 'Mr Sweep,' he continued, 'you know me, Sir. I am Captain John Campbell-John.'

Sweep bowed imperceptibly but politely to acknowledge him.

'I am a personal friend and the business partner of Samuel Medina,' John went on, 'and I have acted as his second in the ring.' Nonchalantly, he stepped into the ring, retrieved Sweep's hat and bent down over the edge of the stage to hand it back to him.

Taking the hat, Sweep again acknowledged the truth of this statement with a slight bow.

'Sir,' continued John, 'if you will arrange for your seconds to call upon *me*, we can discuss a means of settling this dispute. But for the moment we have a show to complete for these good people,' he gestured to the audience who sat with bated breath straining to hear what was being said.

It was an imprecise statement John had made, deliberately choosing his words so that they were noncommittal. There was room for manoeuvre and both men realised that, but it gave them both an exit route so that there was no loss of face. Some of the audience, however, interpreted *'the meeting of seconds'* as an acceptance of the challenge, and a cheer went up around the auditorium. Sweep turned and bowed to the crowd to reinforce that perception. Samuel looked at John with bemusement, and John shook his head to signify that Samuel should say nothing.

Unaware of this unspoken exchange, Sweep raised his voice theatrically, 'My seconds will call upon you tomorrow, Captain Campbell-John.' The two men bowed to each other politely. 'Please now continue with your *performance*, Sir,' continued Sweep, 'for we are all in need of *entertainment.'* His tone was sarcastic, as if to suggest that Samuel's exhibitions amounted to no more than that. He then swaggered back up the aisle of the theatre, acknowledging with a raised arm the applause of the audience and holding his cane and hat high in the air. He continued past his seat and left the auditorium, his supporters quickly shuffling after him.

Inevitably, a sense of anticlimax surrounded the remainder of the performance.

Sweep's seconds did indeed call upon John the next afternoon. John, however, had met with Samuel and Rebecca in the morning and they were both adamant that Samuel should fight no more pitched battles. John's silver tongue would therefore need to be at its best and in truth it was employed manfully. He suggested that Samuel act as Sweep's second in forthcoming battles to return the favour that Sweep had done for him, so that the public would see that Samuel endorsed Sweep as the rightful Champion. He suggested that an exhibition bout be fought between the two, but all his suggestions were rejected, for Sweep wanted nothing less than a pitched battle.

The loss of face that Samuel had accepted, however, was much worse than he had expected. The challenge at the theatre was reported in one of the newspapers, and picked up by most of the others when the challenge was not accepted. Over the next few weeks Sweep turned up three more times at the theatres to interrupt Samuel's performances and the clamour for the fight began to take on a momentum all of its own. In response, Samuel wrote a letter to the Editor of the *Globe,* who published it with glee. Samuel explained once again that he had made a pledge to his wife and felt honour bound to keep it. He acknowledged Big Charles Sweep as the unofficial Champion of all England, but it failed to quell the clamour for this fight. On the contrary, the letter prompted a response from Sweep that impugned Samuel's honour and again accused him of stealing a reputation to which he was not entitled. This was to be the start of correspondence between the two men that would grip all England.

CHAPTER 17

Over the course of the next few months the correspondence to the Editor of *The World* became a sensation and each time a letter was printed, the public clamoured to read it. Samuel had started the correspondence, confident that his literary expertise would enable him to save face in the eyes of the public – that was important to him. Big Charles Sweep, however, proved to be a worthy and wordy adversary himself and an accomplished advocate on his own behalf. Each letter prompted a response and these replies became more and more stinging, much to the delight of a voyeuristic public. The first letter from Samuel, which had prompted all the correspondence, was polite and conciliatory and that politeness, at least, was to last, for it was expected in society - but the conciliatory tone was quickly replaced by provocative words and then it spiralled down through the aggressive, to the confrontational and finally to the downright offensive: and yet all that bile was couched in the civility of the day.

To The Editor, The World.

Sir

Those of your readers who are of a sporting persuasion will know that I have traded as a pugilist over the last few years, and that I have been successful in my endeavours. I have lost only one of my pitched battles, and that after an outrageous foul by my opponent. That result was reversed easily in July in this year of 1789. Now your readers will also know that a challenge has been issued to me by Charles Sweep, a man who is acknowledged as the unofficial champion of all England.

Now, I concede without reservation that such a fight would be welcomed by those sporting gentlemen amongst your readers, but however much as I want to oblige your readers, I must declare publicly that I have made a pledge to my wife that I will undertake not to fight any more pitched battles.

My time is at present chiefly spent instructing gentlemen in the science of self-defence at my Academy from whence I derive the means of supporting my family. I am also now giving exhibitions of the science and have recently become engaged in the field of business.

I declare again that I will not break my pledge and will fight no more pitched battles.

I remain Sir, etc.

Samuel Medina.

To the Editor, The World.

Sir

You have seen fit to publish a letter from Samuel Medina in which he declares his intention to fight no more pitched battles. His declaration at first glance seems to be from the most noble of motives, having given a pledge to his wife not to do so. However, let us examine his motives in more detail.

This a man at the height of his fighting powers. He has fought none but a handful of contests and is in the best of fighting health. My own career has lasted many years now and my reputation stands for itself and I feel justified in declaring that I am the best man in England. In my time many a prospective opponent has been feared to stand against me. I see no shame in that because I know, and they know, that they cannot best me. Such men do not dishonour themselves as they merely face the truth that is self-evident.

Samuel Medina, however, does not tread such an honourable path. He continues to earn his living from the noble science. He trades on his reputation as an unbested fighter, but that reputation rightly belongs to me. Those sporting gentlemen amongst your readers may question whether his motives are as noble as he suggests. I invite him to now take the noble course and declare that the true reason he will not fight me is that he is afraid of me.

I remain Sir, etc.

Charles Sweep

This letter of course was a thinly disguised attack on Samuel's courage, and this burned deep into his consciousness. His personal pride was wounded by the accusation and it would not allow him to take the insult on the chin. He was not, by nature, a man to miss a good chance to speak up, given that he had always spoken his mind in defence of his honour. Indeed, he even spoke his mind in defence of someone else's honour – it did not matter to him - he did so even if the person concerned was unaware of the injustice. In Samuel's mind he was Robin Hood - he was King Arthur. He was a knight errant in search of a damsel in distress. As Samuel was to discover, experience is something you learn just after you need it. In reality he needed to walk away at this point and let all the fuss die down - but he simply could not bring himself to do it. He would respond to the indictment against him for he could not bear the thought of the finger pointing if he did not. With each letter, however, Sweep drew him in, deeper and deeper.

To the Editor, The World.

Sir

In your recent publication you have printed a letter from Charles Sweep that makes several allegations that cast serious doubt upon my honour. I cannot let this pass without responding to put the record straight.

Those who know me can bear witness that I have always striven to act honourably in all my endeavours. I believe that I have the highest of reputations for principled dealings, both in my private life and in my chosen profession of pugilism. I consider that my reputation stands for itself, but I also consider that my honour would be sullied if I resiled from my pledge not to fight again.

I wish to publicly declare however, that although I may fear God, I fear no man. In my life I have always been prepared to stand for what is right without fear for my own personal safety. This is something that I will always strive to do.

I remain Sir, etc.

Samuel Medina.

To The Editor, The World.

Sir

I refer the your publication of a letter from Samuel Medina where he once again proclaims that he will not meet me in a pitched battle to decide once and for all who is the better man.

He talks about his honour and reputation but I see no honour in his persistence of hiding behind his wife's petticoat as the justification of his refusal. He proclaims that he fears no man, but it must seem obvious to all of your readers, who are sporting gentlemen, that he clearly fears me.

It is well documented that my hat has been thrown into the ring to challenge him, and I dispute his right to trade on his reputation until he has proved his worth. I declare that my challenge still stands, and I invite him to meet me at a convenient date so that this matter can be settled to the satisfaction of the sporting public.

I remain Sir, etc.

Charles Sweep

To The Editor, The World.

Sir

Mr Sweep's letter published by you on the 5th of this month once again makes scurrilous accusations against my honour. Such accusations are without foundation and I regard his behaviour in this matter to be reprehensible.

This is a man that I once admired greatly but who now stoops to such a base level in the hopes of goading me into breaking my solemn pledge. I hope, Sir, that you will not sully the reputation of your fine journal by publishing any more of these slanderous letters.

I remain Sir, etc.
Samuel Medina.

But of course, the Editor had every intention of publishing as many letters as he could. His circulation was increasing dramatically because of them. He was writing articles based upon each letter, and inviting his readers to judge whether Samuel's actions were honourable or not. There was a public clamour that far outreached the normal interest of the sporting public. It was the topic of conversation in the coffee houses and the pubs, supplanting those discussions of politics or business. Theologians and academics debated the proposed contest. It became a topical tale of morality and everybody had a view of the most honourable course of action.

Then Big Charles Sweep raised the stakes.

At his Academy, Samuel was completing his tutoring sessions for the day, and as was his custom he finished by sparring with a fellow pugilist to demonstrate the various moves he had been teaching to his pupils. Today he was sparring with Daniel Ben Adi, who was also a Jew and who had followed Samuel's lead into the ring. Other members of the public had arrived to witness this and had swelled the audience. Seats were now erected around the stage ring, and Samuel was narrating as he boxed. He did not notice the entrance into his Academy of eight men led by Big Charles Sweep.

With them was Sir Oliver Ruddle, who still bore a grudge against John Campbell-John for taking money from him at cards. More than that, John had denied him his little subterfuge at the gaming table, when Ruddle, at the point of holding the best hand, had attempted to raise the stakes . To compound that, this incident had been in front of people of society - at Sir James Kettall's no less. Ruddle had lost face as well as money. To a lesser extent – and quite illogically - he also held a grudge against Samuel for winning boxing contests; Ruddle had lost money on those fights. He was now sponsoring Sweep as a way of exacting his revenge against both John and Samuel. The eight men who had so unexpectedly entered Samuel's Academy also included a journalist, but his presence was unknown at this time. The audience shied away from the pack of troublemakers, moving from the benches at one side of the ring and Sweep and his cohort menacingly took the vacated seats.

The air in the Academy was always thick with the smell of fresh sweat; of manly physical exertion, but with the arrival of the audience it mingled with the fusty reek of stale body odour emanating from the largely unwashed press of onlookers. To make matters worse, Sweep's party included common street thugs, few of whom had ever seen a bath. The stench accosted Ruddle's nostrils and he pulled a sour, distorted face as he sat down, as much to display his displeasure at being forced to sit with likes of the common folk as at the objectionable smell. Exaggeratedly, he freshened his nostrils with a wave of his silver vinaigrette, placing it purposefully back into his waistcoat pocket in a manner that suggested his innate–superiority over all those present. The atmosphere was heavy with body odour, but a new and less tangible ingredient now entered the brew. Fear and anticipation spiced the concoction and prickled in the air like bursting champagne bubbles, adding a zest to the smell.

At first Samuel did not realise what was happening, but then he broke off from his sparring, disturbed by the clatter of the movement of wooden benches on the floorboards. He looked down and saw the beaming face of Big Charles Sweep and the leering features of Ruddle. In contrast, he frowned perceptibly at the sight that befell him and the beam on the face of Sweep broadened in response. Samuel composed himself and greeted Sweep with all the poise he could muster. 'Gentlemen of my Academy,' he barked, 'I am honoured indeed to have at my Academy the great pugilist, Big Charles Sweep.' He then led the applause for the sporting idol, and Sweep stood to acknowledge the applause, responding to such flattery. 'I do hope, Sir, that you were not required to pay your shilling at the door, for you shall be my guest this day,' Samuel spoke with a flourish.

'Aye,' said Sweep, 'I was, but that is the least of the injuries that you have done to me, Sir.'

The other men in Sweep's party joined in the insult by shouting 'Shame' and 'Disgraceful' and 'Rogue'. The commotion grew and it was clear to Samuel that it was all premeditated. He also knew that if a disturbance took place the City Magistrates might ban him from future exhibitions, which would take away his livelihood. But then, he figured, Sweep also ran an academy so that a disturbance might put his *own* livelihood at risk as well. If his actions today were calculated, then a disturbance surely was not the intention.

But Samuel was wrong: a disturbance was exactly what Sweep had in mind, for he now had a sponsor to support him financially. Ruddle would now underwrite his losses and would, in addition speak on his behalf to the Magistrates.

'If I have offended you, Sir,' said Samuel with all the charm he could muster, 'then I offer you my sincere apologies, for I assure you that no insult was intended. Your shilling and those of your companions will be refunded.'

'To hell with you, you bloody scoundrel,' thundered Sweep, shaking his distinctive cane in the air as he did so, and the words *'bloody scoundrel'* were repeated vociferously by his companions. 'I'm not concerned with the recompense of a shilling, you braggart. I'm talking about the theft of my reputation.'

'I am on record, Sir,' said Samuel genuinely affronted, 'of being your most strident admirer. I salute your abilities as a pugilist. I covet *nothing* that is yours, Sir – I have stolen *nothing* that is yours, Sir.'

'Your indignation is a falsehood, Sir,' bellowed Sweep, 'the whole of London knows that you cower from the thought of doing battle with me, yet you exhibit yourself as the champion you are not.'

'You scurvy coward,' yelled one of his companions, a scruffy man with missing teeth who stood and shook his fist at Samuel as he did so. 'You should fight Big Charles Sweep like a man,' he continued, the words being accompanied liberally with voluminous spittle escaping through the gaps in his blackened teeth.

Richard Sutton, a young gentleman, came to Samuel's aid and castigated the man for the use of the word *'coward'*, but the scruffy man, emboldened by the presence of Sweep, told him to go to hell, at which Sutton challenged him to a pugilistic contest there and then. But there was to be no fight according to rules, and the man just walked over and threw a punch without any further invitation.

Young Sutton parried this and then bloodied the insolent man's nose. It was then that things got completely out of hand; a common brawl ensued. Samuel attempted to quell it from his raised position in the ring. He bawled his instructions to his patrons not to be drawn into the fight, but it is difficult not to defend yourself when punches are being thrown in your direction. Chairs were raised by Sweep's men and smashed down as weapons, but also in an attempt to wreck Samuel's Academy. The young gentlemen saw it as degrading to brawl with the lower classes – it just wasn't done. Since it was beneath their dignity to exchange punches with people such as these they began to draw their swords - and then things looked to be getting very ugly indeed.

Through it all Sweep sat impassively with Ruddle at one side, and a small shrew-like man on the other who was scribbling away in a notebook, long bony fingers appearing to propel his charcoal across the page, as if some spider was the scribe.

As he caught sight of the swords Sweep rose and entered the affray. He was such a big and powerful man that he did not need to employ his pugilistic abilities, his strength and his cane were enough. In a common brawl Samuel would have been disadvantaged, and his potency diminished - he could not have compensated for his lack of stature by using his manoeuvrability and his knowledge of the science. Sweep had no such problems. His potency was based on size and strength as well as technique, but in addition he was also an expert in all forms of fighting, including the cudgel. His cane became his cudgel, striking down his own men and opposition alike as if he were Samson amongst the Philistines. He was shrewd enough, however, to spare the young gentlemen who might have had influence with the Magistrate. His blows made an impression in more ways than one and the head of his cane left Sweep-shaped contusions as his legacy. Within half a minute he had separated the two sides and most now cowered from his raised, cudgelled hand.

'Enough,' he roared, and instantly most people stopped, recoiled and turned their eyes in his direction. He was in complete control, his body language expressing his dominance. He was clearly the alpha male and everyone else was subservient to him, much as wolves will turn over and expose their throats to the pack leader, offering their lives because they are vanquished, the brawlers waited for Sweep to command them. And like the dominant wolf, Sweep accepted that gesture of subservience and allowed them their freedom. A great smile now traversed his features and he held the fracas in suspension as if it were frozen in time. He turned his head slowly in the direction of Samuel, who was still on the stage gripping the ropes so that his knuckles were whitened against the rest of his olive-skinned appearance. Anxiety was sculpted all over his face. He had lost control and Sweep had sensed it.

'It is time the talking stopped,' Sweep said, lowering his voice to a menacing growl. 'I challenge you once more, Samuel Medina, to stand against me in a pitched battle to decide which one of us be the greater master of the noble science. To decide which one of us is worthy to be called a champion.'

Samuel shrugged, 'And once again I repeat that I am bound by a pledge. There will be no fight between us. But I am more than happy to acknowledge you as the great champion that you are.'

'Not good enough, Medina,' said Sweep, 'this is a matter of honour.'

'Honour?' said Samuel. 'You castigate me for the supposed theft of your reputation, but then you take improper liberties with my name. It is clear to all, Sir, where the dishonour lies in this matter.'

'You dishonour your own name, Jew, and I merely point it out. You call yourself The Light of Israel, but you bring dishonour to your own people.'

'How *dare* you,' fumed Samuel, for this was an insult too far, '*you* dishonour *yourself* by such an accusation. I have never brought dishonour to my people. I call upon you to withdraw that remark at once, Sir.'

'Never,' roared Sweep, 'I'll piss on you first.'

'You show yourself to be damned knave, Sir,' said Samuel, outraged.

'So what are you going to do about it, you poxy coward?' Sweep goaded Samuel ever further.

'I think that I need to teach you some manners, you slanderous dog,' said Samuel resorting to his usual response when provoked. The absence of John Campbell-John meant that there was no restraining influence on him.

'And how will you do that?' chortled Sweep realising that Samuel was rising to the bait.

'Why I'll thrash you, Sir, for your impudence.'

'Then come let us set the time and place so that honour is served,' said Sweep.

'Now Sir! Here and now,' Samuel had now relinquished all forms of self-restraint. 'Come and get into the ring and let us settle this right *now.*'

'Aye Sir, that I will; I will fight you for the love of it, you damned Jew boy. I'll fight you for nothing.' Sweep threw down his hat and cane, and pulled off his black satin frock coat as a cheer went up from both factions of the audience. They were to witness what every man in London wanted to see. The confrontation had been calculated and premeditated, but there was no fabrication in the emotions of both men – at that moment they were genuinely antagonistic; there was nothing but hatred between them; the hostility was indisputable and unadulterated.

Sweep jumped into the ring and took up his fighting stance and Samuel followed him involuntarily. They circled each other in a state of anger, but both parties had lost all self-control. Samuel advanced forward and threw a straight left followed by right hook, but both punches were parried easily by the big man. Samuel retreated quickly evading the counter punch from Sweep's massive right fist. Samuel advanced again, throwing the same combination and again the punches were parried, but this time as he tried to retreat a great right from Sweep caught him on the chin just before he had backed out of range. That punch and his backwards momentum sent him to the ground as a cheer went up. There was no referee but Sweep retreated to his corner gallantly, and the other pugilist, Danny Ben Adi, helped Samuel to his feet as if he had become his second by default.

Samuel's head was clear but the power of Sweep's punches was evident and it did not bode well for him. Sir Oliver Ruddle, being a devious man by nature, feared that the fight would be over in no time and it was not his intention to sponsor Sweep without the opportunity to wager on the outcome. If money was to be made it was not going to be in a small academy in front of a handful of people.

Samuel made no attempt to take his allowed half-minute and his second took him straight back to the scratch. 'Fight on,' Samuel bellowed and he upped the pace immediately and circled away from that great right hand, leaning backwards when Sweep attempted to lead with his left, so that it fell short. Then Samuel lunged forward and led with his own left, landing it on Sweep's eyebrow and the blood began to flow. Once again, however, Sweep counter-punched with his right, fractionally missing Samuel so that the blow whistled past his chin as if it were some phantom riding on the wind.

Ruddle now jumped to his feet, shouting '*Gentlemen! Gentlemen!*' But the two adversaries were not to be stopped so easily. Seeing this, Ruddle signalled for his companions to enter the ring. They did as they were bid, for Ruddle was to be their paymaster for the day. Some of Samuel's young gentlemen clients, fearing for Samuel, also entered the ring, their swords drawn; forming an impromptu guard around him, and the fight was effectively stopped. Ruddle now retrieved Sweep's cane and raised it into the air like a beacon and it had the necessary effect, the crowd looking to him to take charge.

'Gentleman!' he yelled again and then his voiced dropped as the noise level fell away in anticipation. 'This is clearly not the time nor is it the place,' he said and a groan of disappointment went around the Academy as everyone realised that the fight would not be allowed to continue. 'This fight will be the talk of all England, but-' Ruddle's voice was lost as the crowd cheered in response. He flapped his hands for quiet, shouting above the buzz, 'But it must not degenerate into a common brawl, it must be the great occasion that the public demands.'

'Here here!' shouted Richard Sutton, to Samuel's surprise, and the audience cheered their agreement. There was now an assumption that Samuel had agreed to a pitched battle with Sweep.

'The Jew, Medina,' said Ruddle, his devious eyes denying his true intent, 'has clearly indicated his willingness to fight. Mr Sweep will send his seconds to call upon Medina's seconds so that this mightiest encounter can be staged for the gratification of an eager public.'

Another roar of approval greeted his words, and as it died away so did the charge in the air that had sparked the adrenalin-fuelled furore. There was a sense of anti-climax and with it the crowd began to disperse, each man taking away a tale to tell to this friends. News of the encounter would spread like wildfire. Within minutes Samuel was left alone, apart from his sparring partner, Danny Ben Adi.

In the sweat-reeking silence of the Academy, Samuel realised he had been out-manoeuvred. He gave a knowing look to Dan, who returned the look in confirmation of what he was thinking.

Samuel grimaced, 'Dan, who is going to tell my wife? I fear she will kill me when she hears of this!'

Dan hid a smile. Samuel was one of those men who feared no other man, but it was also true that he *did* fear his wife, or to be more precise he feared her reaction.

Samuel was not to be disappointed, for this polite and gentle woman could dip her tongue in acid if the occasion demanded it – and in her view this was such an occasion. Rebecca was incensed by Sweep and Ruddle and their ruse to provoke Samuel into fighting again, but she kept her most virulent criticism for Samuel himself. She felt he had let her down badly and forgiveness was not going to be tendered easily. It would take time. In her eyes Samuel was a very special man, not for his fighting abilities, nor for his intelligence, but for his righteousness. She saw in him a man of principle and decency who would live up to his principles whatever the cost to himself. He was as honest as the day is long - he was virtuous and upright. In her eyes he was all this and more, for if the truth were known, she loved him to distraction.

While much of what she thought about her husband had the ring of truth, no man could live up to the image that Rebecca had built of Samuel in her mind. When he failed - albeit unintentionally - to reach the great heights she had set for him, she felt slighted. She was a courageous woman in her own right, however, and was not going to give in to the pressures of some unpleasant members of the public. Samuel had assured her that he had not agreed to a pitched battle but had merely offered to fight Sweep there and then in protection of his reputation. Rebecca duly drafted a letter for Samuel to send to the Editor of *The World*. Here was their escape clause and she planned to exploit it – but before a letter could be sent, the newspapers hit the streets.

The first article was a front page exclusive in *The World*: a major article by their correspondent who had witnessed at first hand the incident at Samuel's Academy. The slant was heavily against Samuel, and purported to show that he had agreed to a pitched battle to defend his good name. The other papers then came in with their own take on the story – but they all started from the assumption that the match was made. John Campbell-John was called in for his advice and he suggested that they should call Sweep's bluff. As John pointed out, in the heat of the moment Sweep had declared that he would fight Samuel for nothing – for love of the sport. They would challenge him to make good that pledge. He should give up all claims to a percentage of the gate, and in addition, he should put up a thousand pounds.

This was a *prodigious* sum of money; John's intention was to strain the relationship between Sweep and Ruddle. Ruddle was acting as sponsor and had agreed to underwrite Sweep, but if they agreed to fight on those terms then he faced a loss of several thousand pounds. On the assumption that Sweep would start any fight as odds on favourite, then Ruddle would need to wager several thousand pounds more just to break even. John assured Samuel and Rebecca that Ruddle would not agree to the fight on these terms and that if they stood their ground, honour would be upheld without a contest taking place.

It was a clever idea; typical of John, but he was being disingenuous for in reality he was just as keen as everyone else for the fight to go ahead. He had ostensibly put forward a strategy for the fight to be stopped, while believing that it was in fact no more that a stumbling block, and that it would contribute to the momentum now gathering pace like a runaway coach that could not be stopped.

Sweep's seconds, led by Ruddle, did indeed meet with Samuel's seconds, led by John Campbell-John, and the proposition was put forward. Ruddle's reaction fell just short of apoplexy, but John

Campbell-John failed to move his position, and much to his dismay, the meeting broke up in acrimony. It seemed that his ploy to do no more than embarrass Sweep and Ruddle financially, while *appearing* to support Rebecca's need to stop the fight, might succeed too well!

Rebecca now drafted another letter for Samuel:

To The Editor, The World.

Sir,

Your article of the 7ᵗʰ inst. purports to be an eyewitness report of the encounter that took place at my Academy at Chapel Court. I feel I must put on record that this article is replete with absurdity and falsehood. My offer to fight Charles Sweep there and then was to protect my reputation and in no way was an offer the take part in a pitched battle.

However, I am sure that your reporter will bear witness that Sweep offered to fight me for nothing; for the love of it. I have to tell your readers that I have challenged him to make good this statement, but his seconds have declined to honour it, and by that action, as I think all right thinking men would agree, he dishonours himself and the science of pugilism. By his own words he has entered into a contract, but he now declines to fulfil it.

I call upon him again to stand by his offer. I will fight him at a time and place to be agreed, under stipulations of engagement to be agreed. He shall put up a thousand pounds against nothing from me, the purse to go to the victor, but with the gate money going to me.

I remain Sir, etc.

Samuel Medina.

Sweep was indeed embarrassed by the letter and angry with himself for making such a nonsensical statement in the heat of the moment; unfortunately there were too many witnesses for him to deny it. It left him in an iniquitous position: the fight would hold no financial gain for him unless he pressed for a share of the purse, but to do so would leave him open to claims of dishonour, for he had so publicly claimed that he wished to fight only to preserve his reputation as the true champion.

The World, ran a leader article confirming that Sweep had indeed made such a statement and Sweep seemed to be caught between a rock and a hard place. John's strategy, even though it had not been his true intention to stop the fight, seemed to be working and Rebecca's opinion of him softened to be *almost* favourable.

For a while nothing more was heard from Sweep. He was an intelligent man but not by nature a devious one. Ruddle, however, was a different kettle of fish - he was conniving and underhand. What happened next was unsuspected, to say the least. Ruddle knew the City Magistrates personally and had a good deal of influence. He petitioned them to ban the activities at Samuel's Academy, and this they duly did, issuing a charge on grounds that were as incongruous as they were laughable. Sparring caused suffering to others, they said, and therefore to spar on a public stage was an illegal act. Samuel and John took their case to the Lord Mayor, but he too was open to influence by Ruddle.

The Lord Mayor went further and refused Samuel permission to receive money for publicly exhibiting the science of self-defence. In a stroke, Ruddle had taken away Samuel's main source of income, on which he depended to support his family. Samuel, of course, had his other business activities, but he was effectively trading as a banker and he needed circulating capital for that. The business was successful and he was able to take drawings on account of profit, but it represented a fraction of his previous income and he had a household to run. John Campbell-John urged him to supplement his income by dipping into the trading reserves, in effect lending the investors' money to himself, but both Samuel and Rebecca were too honourable for that. Besides, such were the political tensions - emanating largely from the situation in France - that any rumour could set off a run against the bank and if this were to happen Samuel would need the reserves. His business had started successfully, but it was new and it was vulnerable.

Samuel was nothing if not resourceful, and prompted by the strain of his reduced income he came up with a plan to get around the Magistrates' order. He employed a man who was a Freeman of the City to sell outside his Chapel Court Academy, engraved portraits of Samuel for a half crown, and then to invite each purchaser into the exhibition room, mentioning at the time that no money was required to see the performance. The ruse had moderate success and what is more, it received extensive coverage in the newspapers and journals. The general public liked nothing better than to see someone put one over on the Magistrates. Unfortunately, it also had the effect of alienating Samuel even more from the Magistrates and this would come back to haunt him. At first, the notoriety of the ruse filled his Academy with paying customers, but as the notoriety wore off so the number of customers began to dwindle and his financial worries returned.

The ban on his sparring applied also to his stage show and he was forced to take this outside London, putting a further strain on his marriage. Rebecca could see that Samuel was wavering in his pledge never again to fight a pitched battle. The tactic of backing Sweep into a corner had itself backfired and as a consequence there was now an offer on the table for Samuel to fight. She had not forgiven him for what she considered to be his failure. She remained in London to look after the baby, but he was away for such long periods now, that the natural healing of the rift between them became impossible and they began to drift apart. It was only a matter of time before he entered the ring again. A pitched battle was something that she feared, and a pitched battle with Big Charles Sweep filled her with dread. That fear manifested itself in her relationship with Samuel, driving a wedge between them.

CHAPTER 18

Lady Constance Forbes-Wingfield would have been a very remarkable woman by the standards of any era. She had arrived in London twenty years previously to pursue a career as an opera singer and had quickly – and apparently effortlessly - achieved that goal. She had supposedly arrived from Salzburg where she claimed to be a recognised performer, but this was untrue. Born plain Constance Oakham, she was actually the daughter of an impoverished rural minister from a village in the Yorkshire Dales. The young Connie was unlike the other children of the parish and saw herself as somehow superior to them. As the daughter of the minister she was deemed to be from the middling class and there were very few children of her own station to play with, so she lived a mainly solitary life, spending hours in her room in a dream world of her own creation where she was usually the Queen, the Empress, or the prima ballerina or whatever creation sprang from her fertile mind as long as she was centre stage.

When she did play with other children, from whatever class, she made no distinction for station, they were all deemed to be her playthings rather than her playmates. She manipulated them with a natural ease that was pure instinct to her. She was the automatic stage manager who also happened always to be the lead player in her performances, for playing to her was always performance - she could act instinctively and she was a natural mimic.

Her father had been unable to provide for her the lavish life style that she craved, but he had given her a fine education and also coached her in her musical education and encouraged her fine singing voice. He had hoped she would put such a fine voice to the service of the Lord, but such a restricted life was not for the young Connie and she ran away at the age of eighteen to marry Arthur Prideaux, the local squire.

For a time she enjoyed the status that went with being the wife of the richest man in the neighbourhood, but the bright lights of London acted as a magnet for her and she quickly tired of her husband when he showed no inclination to move to the capital to satisfy *her* lust for fame. Arthur was twenty years her senior, and was besotted with her beauty, her intellect and her wit, for they were an unusual enough combination for any woman in the restrictive society of the time, and virtually unheard of in a rural setting. In most matters he was putty in her hands. She had that power of manipulation that she had developed as a child, and she used it on him expertly. She knew intuitively how to use her favours as an inducement; how to entice her husband and then reject him if he did not give in to her whims. Arthur, of course, knew he was being manipulated, but he was powerless to stop himself. He even knew that deep down she did not love him, but that again was something with which he was prepared to live.

A move to London was one indulgence too far, however. He may have been the wealthiest man in the neighbourhood, but he knew that such wealth was only modest by the standards of London society. He also knew that his wealth was based on being a landowner. His income came from being a gentleman farmer: he could not rely solely on the rents from his tenants to support his lifestyle, and certainly not with the increased expenditure required by a move to London, either full time or even for the season - and besides, he liked his lifestyle, his status and his influence within the local community and he wasn't going to give it up.

And so one morning whilst he was performing his duties as the local Magistrate, Connie upped and left, taking with her some money and much of Arthur's family jewellery. When she arrived in London she transformed herself into Constance Von Schleckter, complete with what she hoped was an Austrian accent, one that she had heard as a child when a visiting minister from Vienna had stayed for a time with her father. She concocted for herself a bogus history that could have come straight from the libretto of one of her beloved operas. She was a young widow whose husband had been killed fighting a duel over her. She had fled from Salzburg to avoid the advances of the victor, for she believed it now improper to succumb to him knowing that her husband's blood was on his hands. She blagged her way into an operatic production when a performer was taken ill, making sure that the newspapers carried the story, and despite never in her life having appeared professionally on a stage, she pulled it off with aplomb. She had a fine soprano singing voice and a knack for accents and revelled in her stage appearances, but more than that, she thrilled in her powers of deception. The management had then offered her a leading role in their next production and within months she had gone straight to stardom as a leading lady at Covent Garden Theatre - where Handel's oratorios had first become so popular when male sopranos reigned supreme. But thankfully, female singers had been permitted on the London stage since the 1750s, and Connie, with her rich voice and extraordinary beauty, went from strength to strength.

She did not take lodgings to match her new status – she went beyond that. She rented the finest house she could find, notwithstanding that her earnings were insufficient to finance such a place. Initially, she sold off Arthur's family jewellery and then she hatched a plan that needed to come to fruition before the money ran out. The stage still held a certain stigma for women, at least as far as polite society was concerned, and from the very start Connie was intent on bridging that gap. She wanted to be part of polite society and for that she needed a conduit. Not only did she need a conduit, she needed to find one before the bailiffs came to call. The role of mistress to a rich man was the goal of many a successful actress, but Connie regarded herself as something more than an actress, and she had set her sights much higher than that. Notwithstanding that she was still wed to Arthur, she wanted marriage and with it, a title.

Enter at this point one Sir George Forbes-Wingfield – hereditary peer and a man of substantial wealth. Sir George was a widower - having lost his wife to diphtheria - and a very lonely man. His marriage had been a great success; he had loved his wife intensely and her loss had brought him great heartache. His two sons had followed military careers, one to the army and one to the navy. His life was empty and forlorn. He was neither a womaniser nor a gambler, but he did have one passion in life – the opera. If Constance had written a wish list for a potential husband, then she could not have found a better candidate – quite simply, he ticked all the necessary boxes. At the age of twenty-two she became the second Lady Forbes-Wingfield to the forty-eight year old George, much to the displeasure of his two sons.

For five years she was a surprisingly good consort to George. He made few sexual demands upon her, being content simply to have her company, and he had no need of a further heir. Connie was his intellectual equal, well read, and witty, and she provided the companionship that he craved. More than that, however, he took great pleasure in her singing and liked nothing better than being able to show her off. Sir George re-entered polite society with Connie on his arm, and as might be expected she was a great success at this also. She was simply playing another role, and the couple became a *must* on the social scene. The fact that she was supposed to be Austrian, somehow - however illogically - negated the stigma of her career in the theatre. She had accomplished that childhood dream of being permanently centre stage, and it brought her happiness and fulfilment. She loved her title of 'Lady Forbes-Wingfield' and revelled in what came with it in a society obsessed by rank and privilege - and of course, it opened doors for her, both professionally and socially – but there was one drawback. Her marriage was bigamous for she was still married to Arthur Prideaux.

She kept this dark secret to herself, but then at the age of fifty-three Sir George died suddenly of a heart attack, leaving Connie, in the eyes of her society world, a widow again at the age of twenty-seven. Surprisingly she grieved for his passing and her period of mourning was not in any way hypocritical for she genuinely missed him. The bulk of Sir George's fortune passed to his sons, but he had not forgotten the five years of happiness that Connie had given him and he left her a generous annuity. More importantly, however, he left her a life interest in his substantial town house – one they had bought and furnished together. The property would revert to his sons on her death, but for as long as she lived Mapletree House, was hers. For a time she continued her operatic career, and she entertained from this fine spacious London property. She continued to be accepted by polite society and in fact was one of its leading lights – but Connie began to tire of this lifestyle and she looked around for something else to do that would stimulate her. But what could replace the public acclaim she received as an operatic star and the admiration of polite society for her beauty, wit and intellect?

Originality was also part of her makeup. She began to throw parties, but these were no ordinary parties. Mapletree House became the venue of parties on a scale never before seen in London. She established the party season from mid-November until the end of March and charged the unheard of sum of five guineas, per guest, which excluded from her parties all but the conspicuously wealthy and well connected - and she established a membership committee to keep it that way. Nevertheless, Mapletree House was full every night. She tuned into that passion of the times; that desire to dress up in fantastic clothes, and her Masquerade Balls became more and more extravagant. These parties brought her vast wealth, but this was not the source of her ambition - what she really craved was fame. Fame on a scale far above that she had achieved as an opera singer and gradually the opera engagements waned to be replaced full time as a party hostess of the most expansive of parties. She was a natural publicist and she had her own column in the newspapers, where she made sure that the widest possible audience read of her parties' notoriety. Her celebrity and reputation grew, and her parties were the *must* place to be, if you were lucky enough to be invited.

Connie also understood the fickle nature of fashion. She had to guard against being last year's fancy; she needed to be permanently in vogue. So year on year she ploughed her profits back into Mapletree House, making it ever more extravagant. There was an Arabian room with real camels, and an Alpine room complete with a mineral spring. There was a Japanese room, bedecked in the finest silks, and in the banqueting hall there was a table that could seat several hundred. There was a function room with silk marquees and thousand of candles were used every night to light the chandeliers. These were parties on the grandest scale and brought her the fame she coveted. It was a celebrity, however, that walked a fine line between fame and infamy. Those restrictive unwritten rules of society were in part blurred at these parties, and in part totally overridden. This was a society that said men and women should only ever meet formally and a single woman must always be chaperoned or risk her reputation. Nevertheless, it was generally accepted that men could and did keep mistresses and visit prostitutes. At Connie's parties, however, upper class women could conduct illicit love affairs, safe in the knowledge that the gentlemen concerned would have the good breeding to maintain discretion. There was something about dressing up that gave a degree of anonymity, and with that anonymity those invisible strands that held together accepted social behaviour were somehow stretched to give the partygoers a sense that they had a dispensation from the unwritten rules. Bedrooms were made available and the maids were kept busy making the beds endlessly throughout the night, for these parties started at eight o' clock and went on until dawn. The most celebrated musicians and composers in London were hired, as were the best chefs, and champagne was drunk by the gallon. Year on year the parties became more and more excessive, the dresses more revealing and the behaviour increasingly decadent. The parties had themes: devils and nuns, sultans and slave girls, Abbots and novices, and all this added to the spice. Constance was a woman before her time: she had created a fun palace for the rich and famous and she had done all this in the Eighteenth Century.

Needless to say, John Campbell-John longed to go to one of these parties, but he had never got past the membership committee.

His own creation of the army captain and second son of a country squire were not considered to be of sufficient rank for such a function. He had met Connie on several occasions, since they were both devotees of the card table, and despite the age difference - she now being forty-two to his twenty-eight - he had found her enticing and had pursued her romantically. They had been lovers for a short time, but even this did not qualify him for admission to one of her parties. There is nothing as alluring as something that you cannot have, but not even pillow talk could get John that invitation, and she merely kept referring him, to her amusement and his irritation, to the membership committee. But John Campbell-John was nothing if not resourceful, and he hatched a subterfuge. Samuel Medina did not have the required breeding either, but he did have fame and notoriety, and John was able to get Samuel's name passed by the committee.

He presented Samuel and Rebecca with two tickets as a wedding anniversary present. The tickets were accepted with due courteousness and gratitude, but John knew that when it came to it Rebecca would never attend such a function. Nor would she really want Samuel to attend. But John then proceeded to remind them constantly of the invitation; with the intent of putting them under an obligation to attend since it would be ungracious not to do so. Rebecca's relationship with Samuel was still strained at this time, but she was also acutely aware of a potential breach of etiquette and could see only one way out - she offered her ticket to John to be her husband's partner for the evening, which John accepted with due reluctance.

When John and Samuel arrived at Mapletree House they did so in a carriage; they did not want to dirty their costumes with the grime of the London streets. It was probably best that they did so for they were both dressed as a sultan for the theme of this night was sultans and slaves. Their costumes had been acquired, with the help of Connie, from a local theatre that had used them in one of their productions. There were yards of silk in both costumes and both men cut a fine figure in their outfits, standing out from the many bloated nobles who were present. John wore a turban in vermilion red, with a large fake emerald at its centre. His robes were a mixture of the same shade of vermilion, tied at the waist with a jewelled studded belt, which carried a large curved eastern scimitar, similarly fake. A black satin over-robe completed his outfit, together with slippers of purple that were pointed and curled.

Samuel, however, took to the role as a natural, his large dark eyes and olive skin adding to the masquerade. The impersonation of a sultan seemed to be made for him. He wore a turban of ivory silk with long flowing robes in a combination of jade green and emerald green colours. He too wore a fake scimitar and jade slippers pointed and curled.

As they alighted from the carriage, they were met by a crowd of the lower classes that had gathered to gape at the elite of London society in their dazzling costumes. When they entered Mapletree House the grandeur of the event took their breath away, notwithstanding that both men thought they knew what to expect; they too had read the articles in the newspaper and journals. It was not so much the opulence, the sumptuousness, that invaded their senses, but also the colours – they were so vibrant, so vivacious; primary and pulsating, as if the pastel shades of all the colours had been banned from making an appearance.

John Campbell-John soon noticed appreciatively that all the ladies seemed to have their breasts exposed to some degree or another: from half exposed to almost fully exposed. The relaxation of the rules that came with the masquerade seemed to be fully engaged. Most of the ladies hid behind traditional masquerade masks, either fixed to the face or perched upon sticks, although the latter offered little in the way of anonymity.

John and Samuel explored the house together like two generals reconnoitring a battlefield to decide upon their deployment strategy. Each man approached his survey with a different objective in mind. John wanted to sample all the delights that were on offer, including sexual encounters, whereas Samuel now saw himself as a married man restricted in what was available to him. Nevertheless, Samuel saw John as an exciting companion, even if he did not wholly trust him not to get him into trouble. Trouble always seemed to follow when they were together – and yet, somehow he had fond memories of those occasions

Each time they passed a lady guest, John eyed her provocatively and in turn his own appearance was similarly surveyed. Such behaviour was normally outside the perceived rules, but even if those rules had been abandoned the normal rules of politeness were still in play, and both genders bowed courteously to each other to reinforce their good breeding. On the landing of a swirling stairway that led to the Persian Room, the two men encountered two ladies masquerading as slave girls. Both John and Samuel bowed courteously, confident that their masks gave them anonymity. The slave girls responded with an acknowledging nod, but then John was taken by surprise.

'Why Captain Campbell-John,' said one of the slave girls. Her outfit had been made of particularly fine materiel, but its construction was scandalous – it was scandalous because the outline of her body was clearly visible through it. A woman's legs were *never* on view in a public place: it was unthinkable. But there was little doubt that a pair of finely sculptured legs was evident beneath the slave girl's costume. Her bosom was also well exposed, but her features were supposedly hidden behind a yashmak of fine muslin folded in such a way that one edge covered the mouth and the lower part of the nose. Because the veil was so thin the features could quite clearly be seen. Peering through the muslin haze John recognised Constance. His gaze then darted to the rest of her costume and he admired the form that was on display. His gaze shot to her bosom, and then back to her face and then to her torso, and finally to her legs where he lingered a short while drinking in what was on view. Samuel however, looked only once and upon realising with alarm that he could see the slave girl's semi-nakedness, strove manfully to keep his gaze in the northern hemisphere. She was forty-two years old, but her torso was still resplendent for all to see.

John noticed a knowing smile in response to his ungentlemanly stare and was emboldened. 'Lady Constance,' he said, 'now I don't think you are playing by the rules of the masquerade, are you? Tonight I am a Sultan and not Captain John Campbell-John.'

'But it's my party Captain; I'm at liberty to change the rules to suite my caprice.' They laughed together at the retort, but the surprises were not to end there.

'Why Mr Medina,' said the second slave girl, 'well you *are* coming up in the world aren't you?' She was the taller of the two masquerading slave girls, and although her costume was also finely made, it was less revealing than that of her companion. Her features were also concealed, for instead of a yashmak her face was hidden behind a more traditional masquerade mask that covered most of her face: overlapping, iridescent feathers, of green and bronze with a peacock pattern that suggested the repetition of eyes around the mask. From the eye openings, two piercing blue eyes were visible, but little else. She nodded her head gently, firstly to Samuel, and then she turned to John and nodded again, and there seemed something provocative in her body language even though they could not see her face for confirmation. John was puzzled as he had failed to recognise this lady guest, but Samuel recognised her from her voice and had realised her true identity as soon as she spoke. It was Lady Theodora Fulworth, the Marchioness of Thame.

'Ah, Lady Fulworth, you recognise me,' said Samuel to John's surprise, 'but not *so* far risen,' he continued elegantly, 'for I still have to look up to such a heavenly star as yourself.'

'Why I recognised you instantly,' she said provocatively. Her features were not visible but nevertheless there was the perception of a smile, 'but it wasn't from that elegant tongue of yours,' she continued.

'If not his elegant tongue, Dora,' said Constance mischievously the innuendo obvious to them all, 'then pray say from *what*?'

'Why from his thighs my dear Connie – are they not magnificent,' said Dora.

They both took a step backwards to look at Samuel's legs, aping the way in which the gentlemen had looked at theirs. These were not darting movements of the eyes, however, and their eyes lingered to admire what they saw. The ladies were intent on teasing their male counterparts by looking at them with more than equal lustiness. Samuel blushed. These were two worldly women, and were everything he was not. They were not to take pity on him, however.

'Touché,' said John attempting to come to Samuel's aid, but the ladies had not done yet.

'Are they not magnificent my dear Connie,' said Dora.

'They are indeed,' said Connie. 'They're *rutting* thighs are they not,' she continued scandalously.

The present fashionable style was for men's frock coats to be cut away at the waist, so that everything below the waist was on display. It was considered attractive and desirable for men to have powerful thighs. Breeches that hugged the legs without any pretence of concealment put men on display and if a man did not have powerful thighs he would wear padding to conceal his deficiency. Samuel's thighs were prodigious by anyone's standards – athletic and powerful and therefore much admired by the ladies and envied by the gentlemen. And now here were two well-bred ladies admiring a man's thighs openly without any hint of the impropriety that should have been acknowledged. Their language was coarse and outside the unwritten rules of etiquette, but all restraint had been removed and Samuel felt decidedly uncomfortable.

'Pon my word Connie,' said Dora, 'I can vouch for that. This is a young stag ripe for rutting I can assure you.'

Samuel's face reddened further as his embarrassment mounted. They found his shyness attractive, but not enough to curtail their assault on his discomfort. They were amused but also excited by the complete control that they seemed to have over him. Samuel tried to regain the initiative, but that persona that he was wont to adopt if he felt he was being insulted, merely got in his way.

'My dear Lady Fulworth,' he said haughtily, 'you must forgive me for being so familiar in my conversation, for I now remember that you made in quite clear to me, that I was not to speak to you in polite society, my station being so far below yours.'

'That is true my young buck,' said Dora, 'but tonight is not about polite society. You are pardoned for your familiarity.'

At a stroke she had rendered Samuel's counter offensive toothless. 'And you are certainly pardoned for your thighs,' Connie added, and both ladies laughed out loud.

'But I'm not wearing my breeches,' said Samuel nonplussed, 'I'm in costume, and my thighs are hidden.'

'Any normal thighs would be hidden by those pantaloons, but, *Sir* you have even managed to fill those, so prodigious are they,' said Dora, 'Am I not right Connie?'

'Pon my word you are right,' answered Connie teasingly, but then holding out her arm for Samuel to take. 'And for that I think our young buck needs a reward, does he not?'

'I do indeed concur,' said Dora. She too held out her arm. She had enjoyed her mischief making but they had now decided to end Samuel's ordeal

Each lady moved to his side and he graciously offered an arm to each of them. They both looked at him and smirked. Looking round to John for reassurance, Samuel was met by a sheepish response and became suddenly aware that John knew more that he was prepared to reveal.

'Where are we going?' Samuel's bewilderment was etched on his face.

'Why, just follow our lead,' Connie reassured.

Samuel was led by the two slave girls up another flight of stairs to the second floor and from there down a long corridor to a closed door at its terminus. The party of three stopped and Samuel looked behind to see that John was still following them. The two ladies waited for Samuel to escort them into the room, but he was unsure of himself.

'Do I knock,' he said to nobody in particular.

'There is nobody within Mr Medina, said Connie, 'you may open the door for us.'

Samuel did as he was bid, unsure of what he would find. He released Dora's arm and opened the door slowly hoping that this was not a bedroom. To his surprise, however, the door opened, not into a bedroom but into a large reception room that clearly had been several smaller rooms originally, but which Connie had had knocked through into one to become a function room to accommodate her themed parties. Samuel's anxieties were quenched temporarily, but then he looked further into the room and what he saw surprised him, and set his mind racing ahead. Annoyance mounted and then turned into anger. In the middle of the room had been erected a boxing ring, and it was surrounded by chairs for an audience to view. He surmised that he was to be the performer. Now normally this would not have bothered him, for he was infected with that disease that compels people to perform before an audience. What so upset him, however, was that he now believed his invitation, which had so excited him, was a sham. It did not represent recognition that he had come up in the world; his invitation was not as a guest but as servant and he hated the thought of that.

'And what am I to make of this pray?' he said, his tone resonant with accusation.

John realised immediately that he was adopting his, *I am a man wronged*, persona and rolled his eyes so that Samuel could see him. 'What now?' John sighed as he spoke, 'what's offended you now?'

'Isn't it obvious?' asked Samuel.

'No, not really,' answered John, 'you are so easily offended that there must be a queue of people standing in line to do it.'

'I thought I was invited as a guest not as a performing monkey. I am more than a pugilist – I am a... .' he stuttered to a stop, as if the words had hit an invisible barrier between his brain and his mouth and would not let them pass. 'I am a poet, I am a businessman, I am a writer,' he spurted out eventually.

'Yes; yes you are all of those things,' said John, 'but I am sure that you wouldn't give up an opportunity to recite your damned poetry here if you had half a chance. Stop being such a stuffed shirt and show some appreciation, some graciousness.'

'What's wrong with my poetry?' asked Samuel snootily.

'There you go again – if insults were guineas, Sir you'd have a vault as big as the Bank of England.'

'No, no Captain Campbell-John,' said Connie, 'I understand Mr Medina's chagrin. I too am a performer and I do empathise with his displeasure. One does not like to be pigeon-holed in this way.'

'You are indeed gracious, Lady Forbes-Wingfield.' Samuel bowed perceptively, having rediscovered his graciousness.

'But I assure you Mr Medina that you will be no performing monkey. The decision of course, rests with yourself, but I was most saddened to hear that those silly Magistrates had banned you from sparring, and deprived you of your living. I was to propose that you give to my guests an exhibition of your art and then I was to arrange for a subscription to be taken up on your behalf.'

'That is most gracious of you Lady Forbes-Wingfield,' said Samuel, 'but I fear that the Magistrate would still object.'

'I think you can leave the Magistrate to me, Mr Medina,' said Connie, 'for, as a party thrower, I can assure you that I have a long experience in dealing with such creatures.'

'And what is your proposal in this instance, Lady Forbes-Wingfield?' asked Samuel.

'Oh it's quite simplistic really, Mr Medina, I merely invite them along. The Magistrate is here tonight as my guest.'

'But surely that would make my situation worse, Lady Forbes-Winfield?' Samuel's face registered his confusion, 'there's no way that I can exhibit with the Magistrate present.'

'You must start to think like a woman Mr Medina,' said Dora. 'Your ruse to sell an etching of yourself instead of charging an admission was... let us say, clever and designing, but it takes a woman to be really cunning and deceitful.'

Connie smiled her agreement, 'I have arranged for a lady friend of mine to keep the Magistrate - shall we say amused, whilst *you* entertain us.'

'So he will not be able to account for breaking an order without incriminating himself,' Dora chipped in.

'He'll just have to grin and bear it,' Connie added.

The realisation of what was planned now took Samuel's consciousness and a broad smile began to traverse his face.

'Now Mr Medina,' Connie continued, 'come what do you say? Can I rely on your good offices to oblige me and perform for us?'

Samuel looked around at the others and felt that he was being ungrateful in his reluctance. He pulled himself up to his full height and then bowed nobly in confirmation. 'Your servant Ma'am,' he said.

CHAPTER 19

The boxing exhibition was a great success. It was more than that – it was a triumph. Samuel rose to the occasion and punctuated his athleticism with a commentary of fine wit and intellect. It was a bravura performance of brain and brawn in harmony and it captivated his illustrious audience. John, acting as his sparing partner, chipped in with just the right amount of coarse humour, the Magistrate being the butt of most of his jibes. When the performance was done the *huzzahs* rang out, and Samuel accepted the appreciation with his chest swelled with pride. Connie started a series of speeches and after every acclaim she called upon Samuel to respond: he was required to respond to the action of the Magistrates, he was required to respond on the question of the benefits of training in the fighting arts for the young gentlemen, and he was required, if reluctantly, to respond on when the fight with Big Charles Sweep would take place. He rode all the questions with aplomb. He was on a high

Connie then proposed a subscription to compensate him for his loss of income following the Magistrate's order and at this point something remarkable happened. A cocktail of factors conspired to remove any restraint from those called upon to make a donation. The audience was, of course, the wealthiest in London. In addition, prodigious amounts of alcohol had been consumed. This however, could not account for what happened. The dislike of the Magistrates was an added ingredient; the desire to cock a snook at them obviously played a part, as did a form of auction hysteria. In frenzy, bidders tried to outbid each other and a whirl of donation fever erupted, with each donor trying to outmatch his predecessor to justify his station in life. Whatever the reason, nearly eight hundred pounds was raised by the subscription. But it came with a price, for many of the donations were made on the assumption that they were providing Samuel with a purse to put up against Big Charles Sweep. For now, however, this notion did not enter his consciousness and he became infected by the elation, the excitement that was all around him. All inhibitions left him. He ate and drank copiously and all roundly patted him on the back wherever he went at the party. His identity having been revealed already, he threw away his mask and basked in the glory that was poured upon him.

At this time the glances of the ladies were all over him. Here was a young, athletic and handsome man; a man of fine words and intellect but with that hint of danger - that danger that came with his violent occupation. He now had the fame and celebrity to go with that and he became the target for every titled female who felt that she had left her honour, her restraint at the door on entering the party. They became a pack of predators taken over by blood lust and the blood they lusted after was that of Samuel.

John was initially green-eyed with envy, but then his natural cunning kicked in so that he resolved to feast upon the pieces that were left. Rejection for these women was not a bedfellow they were used to encountering, so John resolved to be their bedfellows instead. A women who is rejected in this way suffers not only the emotion of rejection, but in a society where status is everything, they lose face as well, and somehow that badge of anonymity that the masquerade gave them did not extend to the loss of face. So then John was on hand to fill that gap.

Dora perceived very early in the evening that a pursuit of Samuel was manifesting itself. She acted as a quasi chaperone, but this hid the fact that her own desires had also been aroused. She had goaded him like a little boy only hours before. Treated him like a young and inexperienced subaltern. And now suddenly a transformation had occurred – he was the most desirable man that she had encountered for such a long while. This was a metamorphosis that she could not have explained rationally, but nevertheless it had gripped her totally. Recollections of his naked muscle-rippling body filled her now fevered thoughts and she began to long to touch him again – to run her hands up and down his torso as if he we some Greek God descended from Mount Olympus. He was indeed God-like. His large, brown, doleful eyes and his aquiline features, which sat atop his sculptured physique, were reminiscent of Michelangelo's David and he had become somehow irrationally transfigured in her mind's eye.

She took her duties as his self appointed chaperone seriously because she was not about to concede possession of him to anybody else. She manoeuvred him around the party so that he could drink in his applause, his celebrity, his acclaim, but she remained in total control of him, to the annoyance of many a covetous and envious eye. Her chaperonage was painstaking and meticulous for as each moment passed, her own desire increased. She caught sight of herself in a mirror, and suddenly she disliked what she saw. She had prided herself that she had become an independent woman no longer to be beholden to any man and that she would be in control of any future intimate relationship. What she saw in that mirror, however, was a woman driven by her passion, her ardour having overruled her intellect. This was not the Theodora Fulworth that she wanted to be, but her lust had taken control and it again overrode her reservations. She had a hunger – an empty stomach hunger - a gut wrenching hunger, an aching so profound that she longed for him and that veracity within her was mounting minute upon minute, hour upon hour until she could control herself no longer. She went into denial with herself. She somehow rationalised that she was being herself and that she was the controller, the dominant partner in this liaison. In some ways that was true and she certainly was the ringmaster calling all to perform to her will. It was not a will based on reason, however, it was a runaway stagecoach of emotion that had somehow snared her, lured her with such a terrible craving. She wanted him as a lover. She had not had any such thoughts when she had arrived at the party, and her first reactions had been to pet him like a puppy dog. But then she had seen him fight and suddenly carnality had replaced those earlier feelings. Her mouth was dry and her heart began to pound. She had now had enough of this socialising and wanted privacy – she wanted him – and she wanted him now.

He was, of course, a man of honour and she realised that. She needed a strategy to take control of him – she needed a strategy that would overrule his own reluctance to cheat on his wife. Alcohol was at the heart of this strategy. It was not a subtle strategy. It did not rely on her womanly cunning; a talent that she had in abundance. Nevertheless it was effective and she had allowed him to take wine in plenty for she knew that wine would nullify his resistance to her carnality – but she would need more than that.

Samuel was manoeuvred to a part of the house that he had not seen before and then to a closed door. Only at this point did any realisation become evident to him, for he had been happy to take Dora's arm and allow her to lead him around the party. He had allowed her to introduce him to the partygoers and she seemed to him to be more than able in this task, and he had mentally conceded the task to her. Now suddenly he did not understand why he was here.

'Where are we?'

'Open the door and see Mr Medina,' she said, and then added more intimately, 'Samuel go in, for I have had enough of people for the moment.'

He opened the door and bowed imperceptibly as she strolled past him, but she continued to hold his arm so that she gently tugged at him and out of politeness he was obliged to follow her. He quickly realised that this was a bedroom, although he did not enter any state of alarm, the strategy of alcohol being proved a correct one. Not only had it blunted his senses it had also increased his own desire. The feelings that had manifested themselves within Dora had been impossible to hide, despite the strict courtesy code that was required of them. He had not consciously realised that she had an extreme yearning for him, but on some subconscious level that connection had nevertheless been made – and he wanted her as well. She had expected him to object to being manoeuvred into a bedroom, and she had her strategy in place to counter this, but he did not object at this time. She closed the door behind them and she brushed intimately past him as she did so. To her surprise he grinned back at her, lasciviously signalling his willingness.

She continued with her manoeuvrerings and they sat on a couch in front of the curtained windows that had been drawn to keep out the night. The room was dimly lit with a candle chandelier and although the light was weak it nevertheless sparkled off the glass droplets, so that the room seemed soft and muted and romantic rather than uninviting and bleak. She reclined backwards raised her legs and draped them across him. She toyed playfully with her feet in front of his face as if she were conducting an orchestra. At the same time she ran her hand over the full length of his fake scimitar, which had been forced upwards like a phallus when he sat down, and she smirked provocatively back at him as she did so. It was a complete departure from her normal sophisticated behaviour, but by now she had abandoned all pretence of that other person. She was wearing authentic Turkish cedik on her feet – slipper boots of yellow Moroccan leather, and the aroma of leather mingled with her perfume to enhance the eroticism of the moment. He took one of her feet in his hands and caressed it gently and she purred in satisfaction. He drew the foot to his mouth and kissed it gently and the purring intensified and her body squirmed in harmony and it writhed in the seat.

The enigma that was Samuel's personality excited her. Here was this powerful man who engaged in a brutal profession – and yet he had gentleness about his nature that was truly noble in its naturalness. This was not a man who was superficially honourable within the constraints of the etiquette of the day, whilst beneath dwelt something far baser. He was genuinely noble, a decent and righteous man, and he was attractive to her because of that.

This attraction, however, was not as simple as that. The sight of his bare-chested performance in the exhibition ring had enriched it. It had been enhanced by that delight that some women find in danger - an attraction that compels them to search it out, despite their better rational judgement. She had had no interest in prize fighting. To her it was one of those silly pastimes that her errant husband, and other men of his ilk, engaged in. It was a source of gambling losses, and gambling had brought her husband - and by association herself - to the edge of penury. And now here was a *pugilist* displaying all the nobleness of a knight of King Arthur's court, and it was beguiling and it was tantalizing. This other side of him was just as enticing, however. The sheer brute strength of this man excited her. She wanted to be taken by *that* man, not the honourable noble one. This was an experience that was new to her and it alarmed her and thrilled her in equal measures. It was an expectant and sweet delight and her mouth now watered in anticipation.

'Do you remember the skills that I taught you?' she said.

'Aye,' he replied, 'I was a good student, but I have not really had the opportunity to put them into practice.'

'Well now here is your chance, I shall be your examiner. Do you remember your lessons in the art of disrobing?'

'Aye, I do that, but you weren't wearing anything like this costume,' said Samuel.

'No I wasn't,' she said laughing as she did so, 'so this is a test for you, isn't it?'

'A test I fear that I shall fail Lady Fulworth,' he said.

'No more Lady Fulworth,' she said, tonight I am your Dora.' Samuel smiled a knowingly smile. *Tonight I am your Dora,* he thought to himself and it gave him pleasure. She had told him once that he was not to presume that they could meet as equals for his place in society was so far beneath her. In addition he was a Jew and that came with its own social stigma. Yet here he was being invited to break all those rules that she had herself imposed.

'I still fear Dora that I will fail this test.'

'Nonsense, she said, 'this costume is simple compared with the complexities of ladies' fashionable attire. Why I swear an engineer not a couturier designs some of it. I'll give you a hint Sir – if you find the right spot then the whole costume will leap into your arms exposing me to your glance. I will be left with nothing to cover my modesty at all.'

She reversed her position one hundred and eighty degrees so that she could lean forward – she did so and kissed him gently in encouragement and then sank into his arms. He responded by returning the kiss but with more passion, and she believed that she had total control over him.

'Why Dora, I do not believe that you and modesty are common companions,' he said breaking away from the kiss.

'Pon my soul Sir, you cannot be in earnest,' she said mockingly, 'for if so you hurt me grievously.' As she spoke she put her hand around his neck and pulled him downwards so that the kiss was re-engaged.

His hand explored the costume that she was wearing, lingering on her breast, gently at first and then more passionately. As his grip tightened she rose in his arms exhaling involuntarily as she did so. She then relaxed as his hand moved down across her abdomen, and she sank back tranquilly into his arms. He tugged at the silk ribbon that was tied around her waist and to his astonishment what she had promised him proved to be fact. The costume seemed to disintegrate before him as if the ribbon was in reality the keystone that held the whole ensemble together. In reality that is exactly what it was. He now only had to slip the silk off her shoulders for the garment to fall away completely. He then stood and took her by the waist and raised her from the couch effortlessly, his immense strength making light of the manoeuvre. She should have been angry with him for she had taught him these skills using the most refined of techniques and now here he was using brute force - but then no anger rose within her for paradoxically he used his brute force with such gentle effect – and besides, it was his brute strength that she craved. He lifted her skywards, as a normal man would lift a child, and she felt suddenly as insignificant as a child in his arms. That feeling was only transitory however, and was cast out by more earthy feelings. Feelings of raw passion took her like a thunderbolt. They were powerful and frightening feelings and then her whole body suddenly shuddered in the thrill of it. She had perceived him as innocent only hours before and now he had released such uncontrolled passion within her. She was crazed and she abandoned herself to the moment and this was something that she had not done for many years. He brought her down from that lofted position and as he did so he allowed her breasts to glide down his chest marking a trail of delight as they went.

Finding that he liked it he lifted her again effortlessly into the air and repeated the process again, and then again and finally again. It sent Dora into a frenzy of orgasmic excitement and eagerness overtook her. She clawed at his costume with that same paradox - without any of the genteel skill that she had tried to instil in him, but she succeeded in exposing his bare chest and her hands explored his undulating muscled physique.

He placed her feet tenderly back on the ground, creating a small gap between them, so that he could drink in the sight of her nakedness. As he did so, however, other emotions suddenly resurrected themselves. These emotions had been cast aside by the passion of the sexual arousal that had totally overtaken him. Alcohol had acted as a sedative, anaesthetizing these more noble emotions, but suddenly they had returned, assaulting his consciousness like a ray of sunshine piercing through a chink in a curtain. Fidelity gripped him powerfully, as faithfulness was something to which he had aspired. He genuinely loved Rebecca and since their marriage he had never before been tempted to take another woman. The proposed fight with Big Charles Sweep, however, had driven a wedge between them – their relationship was strained, and he was now sorely tempted. He knew that he should rise above it, but he was alone with a beautiful woman, and driven by uncontrolled sexual desire. He was also driven by his desire for status, for in some absurd way, the taking of such a highborn lady- the sexual conquest of her, was a prize to be won. They had, of course, had sex before but his status had been made quite clear to him. That coupling had been no more than a transaction between them. It was little more than commerce and he was clearly the subservient partner in that contract. But now he felt her equal, if not her superior and this in itself was a powerful aphrodisiac.

She looked at his face and read the subtle change in his manner, but she misread the reasons for it. She thought the sight of her nakedness repulsed him. Insecurity swept over her and she imagined that her forty-year-old body was a disappointment to him. She placed a hand in front of her pubis and an arm across her breasts, suddenly aware of her nudity, modesty overtaking the unashamed brazenness that had been so flagrant only a split second before. In a scintilla of time this dominant, strong, self-empowered woman was reduced to a timid self-conscious mouse, hesitant and apprehensive. Her posture responded and her body recoiled. Her shoulders hunched and one knee bent and that bold, tall upright stance that was evident at the height of her sexual passion was replaced by the demure bearing of a virgin presenting her untouched body to her lover for the first time. He noticed the obvious change and for a moment his own conflicting emotions were distracted.

'Why Dora,' he said, 'is all not well with you?'

'My body repels you, Sir, that is obvious,' she said, ' I once told you to go and find a woman of your own age, and you obviously have, for my ageing body now cannot compare.'

'I don't understand, Dora,' he said,' for you have a body like an athlete. All that riding has sculptured your physique – we have that in common.'

'You are being gracious Mr Medina, but I can see your true feelings - your eyes tell the truth.'

'That may be true, but if my eyes tell a truth Dora,' he said, 'then it's not the truth that *you* perceive.'

'Then what, Sir?'

'Well,' he hesitated, 'well, I am a married man now and...'

'Ah,' she interrupted him, *'fidelity* - a noble cause.' Her whole demeanour reverted instantly, for this was something she could handle. The thought of sexual rejection had almost brought her to her knees, but this – this she *could* handle. She had expected it. She stood tall again, her nakedness now no longer something to hide away, but something to display like a badge of honour. She stepped forward and cupped his face tenderly with her hand. Her strategy was simple – she would give him permission to be unfaithful to his wife.

'There are many forms of faithfulness Samuel,' she said. He looked back at her without speaking, but his face confessed to his confusion. 'You have entered a world where things are not so simple - you are now living two separate lives, and each of those lives comes with its own prospects and its own obligations.'

'I'm not sure that I understand that, Dora?'

'Well, was not the Duke of Marlborough a great soldier and a national hero?'

'Why yes, that much is obvious.'

'But doesn't my Old Testament and your Bible say, thou *shalt not kill,*' said Dora.

'Ah, I think I see,' said Samuel, 'you mean that because Marlborough had a responsibility to protect the nation, then it wasn't wrong to break the commandment.'

'I think it is better that we say he had been given a dispensation,' said Dora, 'you see he lived in two different worlds. He would not break that commandment in his private life.' Samuel nodded his understanding. 'So you can be a good husband to your wife in that other world of yours, but you must separate it from this new world that you have entered. I'm told that you have even had a personal audience with our future King – are you the first Jew to be formally introduced to him?'

'Yes I think so,' said Samuel, 'and I am very proud of that distinction.'

'There you see – you are beginning to understand that this new world of yours has a whole new set of rules,' said Dora, 'in this new world a Jew can talk to a King.'

The logic was flawed of course. It was a logic that had been the cause of many injustices down the ages. It was a logic that gave powerful men the right, in their own eyes, to commit terrible wrongs. It was a logic that Samuel himself would have stood against if confronted by it in others, but at that moment all he wanted was for someone to say, *go ahead – everything is all right – you are doing the right thing.* And Dora was doing just that.

'Now Mr Medina,' she continued, undoing the buttons on his costume as she spoke, to fully reveal his chest, 'we have unfinished business together. You have hired my services as a tutor in the ways of Venus, and it matters not that you have married since the contract was entered into. The conditions still apply and you are obligated to it, until all its clauses have been fulfilled.'

She pulled at the collar of his costume, so that the top half fell away, and ran her hands roughly over his torso in an implicit invitation. He smiled and took her in his arms and kissed her forcibly and she knew that her strategy had been successful. The doubts were cast from his mind because she had authorised their banishment. He had allowed himself to be convinced that her words were true. He abandoned himself to her, but he acted physically as the dominant partner for he was subconsciously asserting his new found status. He was taking his prize – he was taking a marchioness. Her words, if they had any volition at all, about the previous contract being unfulfilled, did little more that sound a starter's pistol. This was not about a previous contract, this was about rank, and it was about status and privilege. He took her in the way a gentleman of position would take a servant, because position enabled him to do so, and for him to take a titled lady in that way reinforced in his own mind that his status was bona fide. Samuel was an honourable man, but this was not the most

honourable of motives. Nevertheless this was something that he had
to do.

When the carriage arrived home the dawn had long since made
its appearance. The morning air was far from fresh, however, as the
air in London was nearly always polluted. Samuel was still drunk but
he was elated, the adrenalin still flowing through his veins from the
night's events. Thoughts of his exhibition and the collection taken up
on his behalf, fought in his mind with the vision of Dora's naked
body. He stumbled as he got down from the carriage but he grasped
tightly to his chest the heavy casket containing almost eight hundred
pounds. When he regained his balance he reached into his overcoat
for his purse and with one hand managed inelegantly to find a coin to
pay the carriage driver. He stood for a moment in the far from
fragrant atmosphere, and watched the carriage disappear round the
corner at the end of the street, and he then turned on his heels, but
stumbled against his own front door. He shushed himself, as a drunk
will, raising a finger to his mouth. He did not want to wake his wife,
but his servants occupied the top floor of his house and for a while
he leant against the wall because this dilemma seemed
insurmountable. Then the door opened and his housekeeper, sour-
faced, beckoned him to enter. She was disagreeable at the best of
times, but somehow this was different. She spoke in a hushed tone,
which he initially put down to a reluctance to wake the rest of the
house, but a feeling of foreboding began to overtake him. There was
something about her demeanour that was not quite right.

'What is it, Mrs Dawson?' he said, fright now casting the
intoxication from his system, 'Is there ..... has something....?' His
words did not actually make sense but nevertheless they were
understood.

'You had better go through to the Mistress,' she said to Samuel's
alarm. He looked round in total confusion, unsure what to do.
Intoxication was not replaced by any clarity of thought, but by a sense
of shock. 'Where?' he said suddenly, seemingly unable to remember
where he was in his own house. 'Where is she - err the Mistress?'

'She's in the drawing room, Sir,' said Mrs Dawson, casting her
eyes up the stairs as she did so. She was unusually civil, which further
heightened Samuel's sense of apprehension.

'Dammit! What is it woman?' he hissed venomously, and the
harshness of the words made the housekeeper jump with surprise.

'It is not my place, Sir,' she said, her voice falling away and tears suddenly welling in her eyes.

Samuel froze; an icy coldness crept over his skin and he felt the hair stand on the back of his neck. 'Miriam,' he whispered to himself, suddenly wracked with an all-embracing dread that stemmed from the immensity of his emotions; emotions that came with the responsibilities of parenthood and family. He looked up the dimly lit stairs that were starved of sunlight and he was transfixed with fear. And then he exploded into action and he bound up the stairs bellowing Miriam's name as he went. *Miriam! - Miriam! - Miriam! - Miriam.* The casket fell from his grasp; coins cascading back down the stairs. He burst through the drawing room door to find his wife seated quietly, perched on the edge of a chair. She looked small and insignificant staring into space, and then she looked up at him. Her skin was reddened and her face puffed from hours of crying but those eyes were now empty of emotion and looked back at him as if she were a corpse.

'Where is my Miriam?' he gasped.

'God has taken her,' Rebecca said in a composed and almost tranquil voice. She looked down to her side where a baby's crib stood. In it lay the body of their baby girl. It had been bound from head to foot so that no part of the little body was now visible. Rebecca looked up from the crib but her eyes did not fall on Samuel –they just looked straight ahead again, impassively, as though all her last dregs of emotion had been sucked from her.

'When?' said Samuel and when Rebecca did not reply immediately he added, 'what happened?'

'She had been fractious all afternoon if you remember,' she said eventually, 'but then I noticed a rash on her arms and belly. I was so fearful that I sent out for a doctor. He said it was the brain fever, and that the next twenty-four hours would be crucial.'

'He was here, the doctor was here? Could he not do anything?'

'He tried but the fever just got worse and she was dead by the early hours of this morning.'

'Couldn't you have sent a message for me?' He was now consumed with guilt but she did not immediately answer him. He put his head in his hands and sank into a chair and then began to sob uncontrollably.

Rebecca looked at him but at that moment she had no compassion for him. For her there was no supportive arm, no shoulder to cry on, and for him no bosom to sink into and be reassured. She could not cuddle him and say that everything would be alright – for everything was not alright. She could not do this. This was the man she had loved, and still loved but he had not been there for *her*. He had let her down. This was a time when they both needed each other, but they could offer nothing to fulfil this need.

Samuel sobbed for many hours, and when that sobbing had eventually dried up, they both sat, together and yet not together, almost tranquilly; never talking to each other or anyone else. They became two empty husks of human beings, without even an echo of the love that they had had for each other. This tragedy should have brought them together: but it did not. It was a hammer that drove that wedge that existed between them, deep into their souls.

CHAPTER 20

To the Editor, The World.

Sir,

I beg leave through the public channel of your paper to say that I have heard no more from Charlie Sweep for several months now. It seems that he will not be bound by his own pledge to fight me for nothing. The sporting public must make up its own mind about the honour in such a denial. In addition the rogue has insulted me in my own Academy without provocation and without an apology. I am convinced that, in despite of all his protestations, the man never intended to fight me, and I hereby declare him a coward.

I am aware however, that there is a substantial interest from the general public to see this set-to and much pressure has been put upon me to accede to this fight. I have been persuaded therefore, that this fight will be in the best interests of the sporting public and that I should release Charlie Sweep from his own verbal contract to fight me for nothing.

I therefore propose that the fight be at the first Spring Meeting at Newmarket of next year 1790, and that I will fight him for 500 guineas a side, the winner to take all and that the gate be split evenly between us. I invite his seconds to meet mine so that the final conditions of the fight can be arranged.

I remain Sir
Samuel Medina

This letter signalled many things. The main obstacle to the fight had been his promise to his wife, not to engage in any further pitched battles. And yet Samuel was now proposing to do so. It seemed that everybody else, however, from the lowest in the land to the highest, from the illiterate to the columnists of the journals, wanted the fight to go ahead. It had captured the hearts of the nation. He had resisted these pressures for such a long time but now he had succumbed to them. It was a combination of circumstances that had conspired to change his mind. His own Jewish community had petitioned him. They had noticed that a change in attitude was apparent following his rise to fame. There was now less likelihood that they would be assaulted in the street – for the mere crime of being Jews. But it was more fundamental than that: it was tribal. Samuel was their man – a man to stand up for them, and they wanted him to fight and they wanted him to win.

Ruddle had also made contact with John Campbell-John through an intermediary. The proposal was that if the fight went ahead on an equitable basis, then he would use his position to have the Magistrates' order lifted. The fight would still make both boxers rich men. The obstacle of the promise to his wife still remained, however, and the letter, sadly, signified a significant shift in their relationship. In fact following the death of their child the marriage had broken down completely. Rebecca had withdrawn into herself and had kept Samuel at arms' length. They maintained their house together, but that was all that was left of their relationship. At a time when they needed each other most they could not give of themselves to each other. The promise not to fight seemed to fail - merely by forfeit.

And then, paradoxically, when the Magistrates' order was lifted and he could legitimately reopen his academy and earn his living, Samuel took to the road: a tour of theatres and exhibitions, leaving Rebecca to oversee his business interests. She threw herself earnestly into this task with all the enthusiasm that she could muster, but the reality was that this was no more than a smokescreen. It was merely her way of grieving, or perhaps her way of avoiding grieving. But this time, for Samuel, the rules of engagement would change. Following the death of his daughter and the breakdown of his marriage, the world was somehow a bleaker place. He would not be a faithful married man away from home. He and John Campbell-John took to the road as two bachelors free, intent on capitalising on fame.

They started their tour at Exeter and then moved to Teignmouth and then on to Plymouth. Samuel now refined his act and introduced into it a particular exhibition whereby he mimicked the manners and attitudes of other boxers: – Big Ben; Johnson; Broughton; Sweep and Figg and then exhibited his own original 'attitude.' It introduced much levity into the performances and the shows were even more successful than they had been in London. John and Samuel, however, were intent on much more than mere employment: Samuel sent money home regularly, but with John as his partner the pair had mischief on their minds. On arrival in Plymouth, events took an unexpected turn. John introduced Samuel to one Jeremiah Cotton, the manager of a travelling theatrical company who had a proposition for him. Jeremiah Cotton was acutely aware that if Samuel exhibited in the city then it would have a severe detrimental effect on his own house-takings.

'Sir,' said Jeremiah Cotton in an affected plummy tone. 'I must apologise for intruding upon you in such an abrupt manner.' He offered his hand to Samuel as he spoke, as if to purvey friendliness and openness, and Samuel took it willingly. It was a curious handshake, however. It was both bold and extensive in its movement, rising and falling a good eighteen inches from top to bottom, but the grip was limp, so that it said neither one thing nor the other. He was a large, rotund man with ruddy cheeks that were interspersed with pronounced spidery red veins. He was, plainly and simply, a fat man yet his movements were those of a slim and nimble ballet dancer. His clothes were garish but he had outgrown them so that all the buttons pulled against their holes as if they were holding on for their lives. He was a *player* and it was hard to tell if the image he now presented was the real Jeremiah Cotton or whether he was playing the part of a theatre manager.

'If we both open at the same time,' he said, 'then it will operate against both our interests Do you see that?'

'Aye,' said Samuel, 'that is plain enough.' Samuel knew, however, that it was likely to be an uneven contest in his favour.

'Well Sir,' said Jeremiah, 'My troop of players is contracted to perform for the next two weeks, and it would seem to me that if we could come to some agreement between us whereby you did not oppose us and delayed your own performances for that time – well, it would be for the benefit of both of us.'

'It is true, Sir,' said Samuel, 'that we are not at present under any engagement to perform, but my reputation for filling theatres goes before me. I feel confident that any theatre manager will jump at the opportunity to engage us.'

'Your performances are admirable, Sir,' said Jeremiah, 'I myself travelled to Teignmouth to see it for myself. You are a natural, Sir, and you can take it from me that I know my business.'

'Too kind, Sir,' said Samuel responding to the flattery, 'and if it is possible I would not wish to deprive you of the profits that you would otherwise derive from your own performances.'

'You are a gentleman, Sir,' said Jeremiah.

'Your servant, Sir,' said Samuel with a polite bow.

John, watching the exchange, hid a smile. It seemed that both men were intent on outdoing the other in their posturing display of good manners.

'But we have expenses to meet whilst we are in Plymouth,' Samuel continued.

'You do indeed, Sir,' said Jeremiah and I have therefore, a proposition for you.

Samuel looked round at John who was remarkably quiet through all this exchange. Samuel read the expression on his face and realised that there was some collusion here. 'Go on,' said Samuel knowingly.

'Well Sir,' said Jeremiah, 'my troop is greatly short of performers - so much so that every one of my players is obliged to sustain two or three characters every night in the same piece.' He paused for a response; when none came he continued, 'Well even by this contrivance, Sir, I have not sufficient players to enable me to perform several pieces that I would wish to bring forward.'

Samuel looked at him with a puzzled expression, 'I'm not sure that I understand your proposal, Sir.'

'Well, Sir, you are no stranger to theatrical pursuits yourself, and I would propose that your good self and Mr. Campbell-John here, join our troop for the next two weeks.'

Samuel bellowed an unrestrained laugh at the proposal. 'You cannot be in earnest, Sir.'

'I assure you I am, Sir,' replied Jeremiah. He looked crestfallen for a moment before resuming his performance.

'But I know nought about play acting,' Samuel said.

'But you know how to play an audience,' said Jeremiah, 'you have a presence on stage, and I will be your guide in all other matters thespian.'

'But...' Samuel stumbled for there were so many buts, 'but surely there is no time to learn the lines.'

'You will only be required to play minor roles. There are very few lines to learn. And then you will also be required to help build and move the scenery. All my players must help; be prepared to, *roll up your sleeves*, so to say.'

Samuel stood for a moment shaking his head at this proposal. It was as unexpected as it was unreal. And yet in some deep down place it had an attraction. He suppressed such thoughts, however, and tried to find reasons to decline the offer. He looked around again at John for reassurance, but was presented with the opposite. John's expression seemed to plead to Samuel to accept, as if he were a small boy peering into a sweet shop window at the sugary delights on display. Samuel sighed heavily.

'You will pardon me, Sir, if I consult with my colleague,' said Samuel. Jeremiah nodded his approval graciously, and Samuel walked John to the corner of the room and spoke in a hushed tone.

'I take it that you want to do this?'

'Aye,' said John.

'But why? Why earn shillings when we could be earning pounds?'

'Adventure Sammy boy, it'll be an adventure.'

'But can we afford such an adventure?' asked Samuel.

'There you go with your *buts* again. Just release yourself from always having to do the right thing. Do something for yourself for a change. And besides, we'll get free board and lodgings so we won't be out of pocket.'

'Maybe not, but I suspect this is about something that *you* want, not something that I want.'

'Aye, it's true that I want to do this but I also know you. Deep down so do you.'

'And I know you, John Campbell-John. You're a devious bugger. There's another reason isn't there. Come on spit it out – what are you up to?'

John's expression at first feigned injury, but as Samuel's eyes peered back at him, he could not keep up the pretence and a small smile betrayed him. He saw the recognition in Samuel's eyes and the small smile then broadened full across his face. He put his arm around Samuel's shoulder so that he could whisper confidentially to him. 'What's the main attraction at the theatre Sammy boy?' he said, but he didn't wait for an answer. 'Girls Sammy – wenches. That's why men go to the theatre. We'll have our own harem to pick from, Sammy.'

'I thought as much – it had to be something as base as that, didn't it.'

'Oh stop being such a stuffed shirt,' said John. 'If stuffed shirts were apples then you'd be a pippin. You can be just as lusty as me. I just don't try to hide it.'

Samuel smiled recognising the truth of what John had said. It had deflated his ego in a moment.

'Come, let's have a two-week holiday,' continued John, 'but let's make it a two-week tupping holiday, eh?'

Back stage was an exercise in ordered chaos. There was obviously some *raison d'être* to the hive of activity but it was hard to see it. Things seemed to get done, however, or only *just* get done in most cases. The changing rooms were cramped and filled with semi-naked bodies frantically trying to change their costumes or applying their make up. It was a room of hustle and bustle, of commotion, of goings-on and of sweat. It was poky and overcrowded and Samuel loved it. It was vibrant and alive; it pulsated with emotion and passion.

The first piece in which they were to perform was a Grecian Tragedy and Samuel searched for a piece of unused mirror to see himself in his costume.

'It doesn't fit,' he said to John.

'No,' said John, 'but then it wasn't designed for somebody of your build.'

'But won't it spoil the performance if it doesn't look right?'

'You're only playing a messenger, and you've only got one line!' said John. 'And besides the ladies in the audience will be looking at your legs and not your costume,' There was a giggle from behind them from two of the young actresses.

Jeremiah and one Mabel Royale took the leads in the play. They were both much too old for the roles, but they had the pick of the parts in all the pieces. The younger actors and actresses fought over the remaining roles, which gave Jeremiah a hold over them.

Samuel looked down at his legs. The costume was too short, just covering his loins, so that his heavily muscled legs were indeed on display. He felt uncomfortable. Before he could muse further, however, he got his cue and he was bundled to the side of the stage. He took a deep breath and thrust out his chest and boldly made his first entrance. His one line was, *'I bring news from Thebes my Lord'*, but as he pursed his mouth to say it, a cheer rang out from the audience. He had been recognised. He said his line, but the audience drowned it out, and Samuel stood awkwardly on the stage not knowing what to do.

Jeremiah stepped forward and took him by the hand and walked him to the front of the stage. 'Always acknowledge your audience Samuel,' he whispered. He then took a step to his right and held out both his arms in Samuel's direction to direct the audience's acclaim to him. *'Mr Samuel Medina,'* he proclaimed and then whispered again to Samuel to take a bow.

He did so tentatively at first, but when the crowd's applause increased he repeated the bow theatrically and the applause continued. The piece was stopped for a full five minutes, and when it resumed Samuel uttered his line again to a further round of applause before making his stage exit. As he left John said, wryly, 'It's thee legs you know.'

A pattern had been set. Audiences were rowdy at the best of times and it was not unusual for interruptions to occur in a performance. Jeremiah was unconcerned at these repeated interruptions, accepting that it added celebrity to the performances. He did have concerns, however – he was concerned about the effect that John and Samuel began to have on his troop. At the completion of each performance the tavern became the first port of call, sometimes followed by the cockpit or the gambling den. Drinking, gambling and wenching were part of John's normal lifestyle, but now he was on holiday he became completely unrestrained. The younger members of the troop became his co-revellers drinking into the night, and they began to arrive at the theatre still hung over from the night before. The quality of the performances began to suffer, but Jeremiah metaphorically shrugged his shoulders and just hoped that the female side of his troop were not all left pregnant in some months' time.

John knew that young actresses had a reputation for being little more than prostitutes. Such a reputation did have some basis in fact, for the stage gave them a perfect shop window. If a *gentleman* member of the audience took a liking to one of the girls it was expected that he would pay for her services. Casual sex, therefore, was part of their lifestyle. Into this lifestyle John immersed himself with relish, and after some reservations Samuel soon followed him. Sex was available to them both and they drank deeply from this cup of fornication. They were both a physical attraction to the girls of the troop: John playing his role as the dashing young soldier, but that vulnerability was not something that Samuel now displayed in the troop, however. He was the celebrity and he traded on that celebrity. He spent money on his companions and drank to excess, gambled and, of course, he wenched.

The sheets on Samuel's bed were crumpled and dishevelled. They mingled with two bodies that cared nought for any tidiness. The bed was not being used for sleeping. A long, female leg protruded from beneath one side of the sheet whilst a head and painted face protruded from the opposite end, and a large breast projected from an off-centre half-way point, its owner without even a scintilla of coyness.

With no embarrassment, Samuel sat upright holding a book in his hand. His large powerful finger followed the text and he laughed out loud as his companion struggled to recite her lines. Emma Green was an actress in the troop. She was twenty-eight years old and older than

Samuel, but that did not seem to matter. Samuel's physical appearance was that of a mature man. She had enough seniority to command good parts and she saw no problem in learning her lines in bed, with sex as an extra-curricular activity.

'It's all your fault anyway,' she said.

'Why?' He grinned back at her. She stroked his thigh provocatively, directing the movement towards his loins, but then terminating the stroke abruptly before heading south again. Her large, heavily made up blue eyes looked sheepishly back, but they were only mocking him.

'Well, I wouldn't have to learn these lines if it weren't for you. You give the dancing fat man the opportunity to perform different plays. I haven't needed to learn new lines for years,' she said.

Samuel chuckled. 'The dancing fat man – is that what you call him?'

'Oh yes, haven't you seen the way he moves. It's as though all that weight somehow doesn't quite make contact with the floor. He ought to be called Jeremiah Lighfoot.'

'Aye, you're right,' Samuel laughed at the mental picture. 'It's as though he's a puppet and he's dangling on the strings.'

It was Emma's turn to laugh at the image. 'They'll need to be bloody strong strings,' she mocked.

'And a bloody strong puppeteer,' said Samuel. They laughed again but this time together.

'Talking about strong,' she said teasingly, 'these thighs...' She looked down at his legs and back again. 'How on earth did they become so...?' She paused as she searched for the right word. She grinned. 'muscular,' she said at length. It was a euphemism. She was the latest female to be amazed by them. Thighs were regarded as a sign of a man's virility. It was a risqué thing to say – she was in reality referring to his manhood.

Samuel by now was sufficiently worldly to understand the euphemism, but he pretended not to. 'Part of it is a natural athleticism,' he said casually, 'and part of it is training to fight. It builds up my power.' She ran her hand up his thigh again and her two large eyes beamed back at him as she did so. She sat up and caressed his torso with a look of wonderment on her face. Her thoughts had moved on from learning lines. The task had been cast from her mind by the sight of his athletic body. Likewise his own thoughts were a million miles from his family responsibilities. He was a bachelor again and intent on sampling the delights that fame and bachelorhood had on offer, and which he had missed out on the first time round by marrying so young. She straddled his torso, reciting lines as she did so and he attempted to continue following the lines in the book. She rose on her knees and reached behind her to guide him inside her and then started to rise and fall on him. She continued to recite as she did so, and he continued to correct her, but the words became increasing punctuated with laughter and giggling. As she continued, each word became a laugh in its own right and it became a contest as to who could keep reciting or correcting the longest. The volume rose as the task became harder and the laughing became more hysterical. She stopped abruptly with an audible squeal as a sudden surge of intensity spread outward from her pubis, and overrode her efforts. She stopped briefly, but then she rose again, re-instating the rhythm – rising and falling and reciting the words again.

There was a bang on the wall, from the next room and muffled words were audible. '*Will you fuck the whore and get it over with,*' they screamed. It was Mabel Royale who occupied the next room. She was learning her own lines and she believed herself to be a real actress not a whore.

Samuel and Emma stopped abruptly and both shushed each other with a finger to the mouth whilst holding their breath. After a few moments, however, they simultaneously released it with a voluble snort and then again laughed loudly. There was another bang. Ignoring it, Samuel rolled over powerfully so that he was on top of Emma, and she had little option but to comply with his much superior strength. He rose aggressively on his powerful arms and increased his rhythm intent on bringing a swift end to their copulation.

'Hey lover,' said Emma, 'you don't have to rush for Mrs poxy skin next door – just take your time lover boy – take your time.'

He smiled back at her in acknowledgement accepting that she was right. There was another bang, but Emma somehow managed to belligerently bang the wall herself, without any interruption to the coupling. 'Go and get *yourself* fucked,' she yelled uncouthly, and Samuel's eyes widened in surprise. She noticed his reaction and was initially puzzled. 'Well what did you expect?' she said, 'I'm no fucking lady, you know.' A robust laugh spurted from Samuel's mouth and then she joined in the laughter. 'Poxy woman,' she said and then laughed again, but then the fervour within her began to mount. She bit her lip and then reached up and put her hand round the back of his neck and gripped tightly so that she pulled herself up from the bed in reaction to the mounting sensations. She began to make small yelping sounds and was carried away from rational consciousness on the wings of the ardour that rose within her. She closed her eyes and gave herself to the sensations that were overtaking her. The yelping turned into squeals as the mounting continued and he allowed himself to give way to his own climax, and they clung to each other vigorously though the process. Their muscles tensed in response and they both held their breath for what seemed like a time without end – and then he exhaled and relaxed but she didn't respond to his lead. Her climax was prolonged and persistent and she held on to his torso with both hands while he took the weight of them both on his powerful arms.

'Sounds and sweet airs, that give delight and not hurt,' he quoted. The quote took some time to enter her consciousness but when it did, it triggered a relaxation of her muscles. She eased herself down the bed, with a long, drawn out exhalation and he rolled away to recline next to her.

'Shakespeare?' she said eventually with some puzzlement.

'Aye, Shakespeare,' he replied, *The Tempest* I think.'

'An educated pugilist is a rare fellow indeed,' she said, 'but-'

'What's the relevance?' he interrupted, anticipating her question. 'Why, the sweet little sounds you were making.'

She still looked puzzled, 'What sounds!' she said.

'You make sounds when Cupid takes you.'

'No I don't... what sort of sounds?'

'You know - fucking sort of sounds.'

'You mean the yelling.'

'No, before that, before the yelling.'

'What?' she said.

He yelped like a puppy as the nearest impersonation that he could do. She hit his arm playfully in disbelief. 'I do not,' she said. He raised an eyebrow as if to say, *you do* and she hit him again, and they both laughed.

'Where did you learn Shakespeare anyway?' she said going back to the quote.

'I have had a good Jewish schooling – it included Shakespeare. What is so unusual about that?'

'Well - because you're a fighter. You just don't expect brutal fighting men to be able to quote Shakespeare. It don't seem right, that's all.'

'I'm a poet as well as a fighter – and a man of business- and a man of charity,' he said.

She looked at him with wonder in her eyes. She had never met such a man before. She had met gentlemen who had been well educated but they did not display that education in their dealings with her; she was just a wench they used. 'You're a strange cove,' Samuel Medina,' she said.

He shrugged his shoulders, 'People always seem to say that.'

They returned to their labours: the learning of lines. They would be together for the best part of the two weeks – the two weeks in which he was a member of the troop. They talked and ate and fornicated. They acted together and fooled about together like overgrown schoolchildren. John Campbell-John was behind this, but for once Samuel was a willing participant. It was a relationship of sorts, but it was not based on love. Both knew that it was temporary but neither of them cared, for this time they were still within the rules of society – the rule that said young men could indulge in sex with the lower classes. Samuel and Emma knew that and revelled in it. It was a period to be adored.

CHAPTER 21

Like Samuel, John Campbell-John had also made a liaison. There was one girl in particular who had caught his eye. It was a given that actresses were pretty; prettiness was more important than acting ability and Abigail Fitzherbert fell squarely–into that category. She could act a bit and she had a fine soprano singing voice, which unfortunately was used by Jeremiah only as a vehicle for the bawdy songs that he knew his late night, drunken audiences wanted, but in the main it was Abigail's attractiveness on which she traded. Like John, she was not all that she seemed, for Abigail Fitzherbert was not her real name. She was in fact plain Abby Smith from St.Giles. Abigail Fitzherbert was her stage name and the choice said much about her aspirations. The name was chosen to suggest a high status, a lady of rank. If you put Lady in front of her name, they seemed to belong naturally together. Lady Abigail Fitzherbert could be the name of a lady in waiting to the Queen herself. Abigail had learned to replace the harsh vowels of her coarse London street accent with the affected vowels of a society lady and she had always thought that she could ensnare a gentleman admirer into her bed with a view to becoming his mistress. Indeed, the name she had chosen for herself was taken from the most celebrated mistress of all: Mrs Maria Anne Fitzherbert was the mistress and close confidant of the Prince of Wales, and rumours were rife that he had in fact wed her clandestinely.

Abigail had not set her sights as high as marriage, her goal had been merely to be a kept woman – she was being realistic, or so she had thought. She was twenty-nine now, however, and although many a gentleman had been attracted to her bed, none had been prepared to set her up as his mistress. In her mind's eye she had seen herself as a companion on the arm of a gentleman in society, but the reality was that no gentleman was prepared to risk his place in society by taking such a chance, for there was still a stigma against women on the stage. Abigail would have been satisfied to be a secret mistress, kept in a convenient house somewhere – which was what many gentlemen did - but she had not achieved that either. In the eleven years that she had been an actress, not only had she failed to achieve her goals, but she had no savings and she knew what little she had to look forward to when her looks began to fail.

That was not to say that life had been all bad to her in those eleven years. There had been times when she had gone hungry, but generally speaking she had lived in relative comfort, certainly far better than she could have hoped for on the streets of St.Giles. Those were mean streets indeed; one of the poorest of London parishes: there were few expectations in life for the good - and not so good - citizens of St.Giles. Abigail was a bright girl however, and had a cunning that she brought with her from those streets.

In John Campbell-John she did not so much see a meal ticket as a kindred spirit, and tonight she was on his arm. It was a role she had wanted to play for such a long time, but John was no *real* gentleman. Abigail somehow sensed this, but it did not detract from the delight she felt in his company. They were at a house party, and she strained every sinew to play her part as convincingly as she could. She nodded gracefully and displayed all those barely perceptive gestures of body language that passed for refinement - a minute nod here and a raised eyebrow there. She uttered little snippets of wit when they were called for; taking her lead from John whose own wit was far bolder, as was acceptable for a man. She recognised acceptance in the eyes of the other guests and revelled in it, for she saw it as vindication that her dream was attainable: if only a *real* gentleman had had the courage to engage her.

Paradoxically, after an hour or two, gentlemen began to flock around Abigail. She was pretty and witty, and she outshone most of the society ladies present. This was only part of her task, however, to play the role of lady companion, at least until the more respectable guests had left for home. John Campbell-John and Abigail Fitzherbert had made a pact. They had devised a plan, a money making scheme. It was to be in two parts, the first designed by John and the second by Abigail herself. When the gaming tables were brought out John took his place and Abbey took up her own prearranged position. She was nothing if not astute: she took the arm of a non-playing gentleman and acted the role of the innocent lady who did not understand the rules of the game.

'I'm such a dunderhead fool when it comes to cards,' she remarked, 'they just seem to bamboozle me.' She flashed her eyelashes as if to invite help and her escort responded enthusiastically, but then she carefully manoeuvred him into the prearranged position allowing the man to believe that he himself had picked the ideal vantage point. John was a skilled gambler, but he was not the only skilled player present. He wanted an edge at the gaming table and he had found in Abigail a willing ally. Quite simply they were to cheat. He had schooled Abigail diligently and she was an enthusiastic pupil. He had been losing heavily recently, mostly because of his liaison with the fruit of the vine, but that was a consequence that he was not able to admit to himself: it was everybody's fault but his own.

When John had tried, without success, to recruit Samuel Medina as his stooge, the signals that Samuel was supposed to have given were simplistic. In Abigail however, John had found a skilled card player in her own right. The signals they had worked out were extensive and subtle, and now in action her performance was masterful. She peppered her supposed guide with question after question and he answered attentively, trying to impress her. All the time, however, subtle signals were being passed to John. It was an exercise in what a magician would call 'misdirection' - whilst the right hand was taking the viewer's attention the magician's left hand was completing the sleight.

As the evening wore on, John's chips began to mount up. He was winning heavily; more importantly he was also winning subtly. But then the tide began to turn. His wine glass was being constantly refilled, and John saw no reason to hold back on his drinking. Glass after glass was gulped down, firstly between hands and then during hands. He had become a well-known card player over the last few years and his reputation was now established. His skill was accepted, but his drinking was also common knowledge. The other players bided their time expecting to win back their losses. Abigail was making the right signals, but John began to miss them as the wine dulled his senses. Abigail had not expected such a turn of events, but she was not going to allow the scheme to fail simply because of John's inebriation. After another hand was lost, she excused herself from her gentlemen guide and then approached the gaming table. She put her hand elegantly on John's and gestured him away.

'Now come, John, you have been neglecting me all evening,' she said. She moved a step away holding his hand as she did so. A *gentleman* would have had no option to follow, but John resisted and remained seated. Abigail noted the displeasure on the faces of the other three players at the table, but she was to have none of it. 'I insist, John,' she said again, 'I need some air.'

The comment was well judged. Politeness now demanded that he accompany her, and he rose hesitantly. He looked back apologetically.

'I must take my leave gentlemen,' he said. Gruff voices reluctantly accepted his withdrawal with feigned politeness - they were to be denied the opportunity to win back their losses. Like a schoolboy sent out of the classroom by the master, John gestured for his chips to be cashed in as he left the table. Abigail was still playing her part and with a show of affection she took his arm and led him into the garden. Their breath made trails in the chilled evening air; summer had passed now into autumn and condensation was forming on the last of the flower petals. Abigail shivered, but she had requested the fresh air and she had now to see this performance through. John made no attempt to hide his displeasure; his face was emblazoned with petulance.

'Bad show old girl,' he said after a time, 'I was on a winning streak there. You should've let me play on.' She looked at him incredulously, and that look was enough for him to embrace reality. It chased away all his resentment and replaced it with contrition. 'You had stopped signalling,' he whispered apologetically, not really believing those words himself, 'that's why we lost a few.'

'I stopped!' she exclaimed and then looked around the garden to see if they were alone, before continuing in a whisper. 'The signals were there but you were just too drunk to see them.'

Sorry old girl,' he said penitently.

'I should think so,' she said. 'I've played my role expertly, even if I say so myself.'

'Oh you have, you have,' agreed John readily, 'you were bang on, old girl.'

'I was in character,' you mean, 'and don't call me old girl.'

He coughed a sort of non-verbal agreement. She looked at him for a few seconds before going on, still making no attempt to hide her displeasure.

'Look,' she continued, 'I've sweated long hours to learn my part in this ruse, not only learning signals but integrating them into my performance, and I'm not going to stand by whilst you…' She paused in frustration for he had put on his naughty boy face that usually made her break into laughter, but this time it did not work. 'I am not going to all this effort for you to piss it up against a shit barn door,' she continued, now well and truly out of character and reverting to her street language. The sudden realisation of that hit her and she looked around again anxiously, but saw that nobody else was around to share the chill night air. 'Half of those winnings are mine, so don't you forget that.'

'Half less the original stake...' he replied, the words tailing away as he realised it was not the time to correct her. It was time to be quiet.

'Do we, err...' said John tentatively after a time, 'you know - carry on with our other scheme, or should we just cash up and call it a night?'

She thought about this for a couple of minutes. She was angry but she was not going to give up a chance to make some real money. 'We'll continue,' she said eventually, 'but you need to play your part well. Are you up to it?'

John sniffed, relieved, 'Oh I won't let you down I promise you.'

A footman yawned behind his white-gloved hand. The last of the couples had just left as the hall clock had struck two o'clock; the chimes echoing now in the relative emptiness of the rooms. He was ready for his bed but his day's work was not yet done. There was always an underbelly to polite society, and a few expectant gentlemen remained, their interest having been primed by John who had instigated whispers of something interesting by way of a nightcap. Abigail was the only woman now present, and all eyes were staring at her. She smiled provocatively back at those inquisitive probing eyes, for she had now taken on a quite different role. She would still play the respectable society companion of a respectable gentleman, but that role would now be subtly changed.

John had arranged with his host for an auction to take place for the benefit of a few sporting gentlemen, but this was to be no ordinary auction. The goods to be auctioned were not gold or silver, nor livestock, nor jewellery even. The commodity to be auctioned was clothing. The plan had not come from John's own devious, avaricious and degenerate mind. It was a simple money making scheme that had been devised by Abigail herself, but John was proud of it nonetheless for it was the sort of scheme that was worthy of him. Its concept was simple, yet its execution had all the spicy delights that would tempt the overindulged gentleman. Quite simply, the clothes to be auctioned were the clothes that Abigail was wearing.

Abigail saw herself as an actress and not a whore, but she also knew that her dream of being a mistress was not far removed from whoring. She was also no stranger to nudity and she had often worked as an artist's model when her funds had been spent and her belly groaned from hunger. Daily the costumes she wore on the stage meant that she appeared in semi nudity anyway, and certainly for the back stage changing between scenes it was accepted that she would be exposed to the theatre staff. But the gentlemen who were ogling her now could get a whore for a few shillings, so why should her scheme so entice them to bid for her clothes? The answer was that she was not perceived as woman of the streets, nor was she perceived as an actress, or a whore. She was, to all intents and purposes, a lady of society and that added a honeyed sweetness to the event in the thoughts of these gentlemen. This was a chance of seeing something that was forbidden by the rules of society. It was a taboo that was being broken. Certainly there were some highborn ladies who were infamous in their behaviour, but none had stooped to such exhibitionism. It was a temptation that was irresistible to such men, and Abigail had a performance to master. She must play the part of a cultured and gentile lady, playing the part of a whore. A part within a part, a play within a play - which would expose not only her nakedness, but also that underbelly of a society within a society.

John opened the auction in a subdued and respectful manner, conscious of the rebuke he had recently taken from Abigail. He was trying hard not to let his inebriation run away with him. 'Gentlemen,' he said gesturing with his arm in the direction of Abigail, 'may I introduce my companion Miss Abigail Fitzherbert. Some of you will already have had the pleasure of meeting this charming lady earlier this evening. The gathering nodded politely in her direction and she acknowledged them with a feigned ladylike blush of embarrassment. 'She is a fine and cultured lady as you can see, but there is another side to this charming lady.' He bowed slightly in her direction and she nodded back again in return. 'The lady has a most unusual party piece that she performs for her friends, but she has never before performed it for...' he paused and looked around the room with a mischievous smile, 'shall we say for gentlemen of the town such as we.' He paused again allowing the tension to mount. 'I beg your indulgence, gentlemen, for I need your help in trying to persuade Miss Fitzherbert to perform her party piece for us.'

'Oh Captain Campbell-John - I couldn't, really I couldn't' confessed Abigail with all the embarrassment she could muster.

'Come my lady, we beseech you – pray do share your party piece with us.' said John. 'We would be honoured Miss Fitzherbert – wouldn't we gentlemen?' implored John, clapping politely and then turning to the others for encouragement who took their prompt like good sheep and joined in the applause. It was all, of course, pre-planned. It was the way of the street entertainer who entices his audience with promises, but then makes them wait. And with each pause, the anticipation rises and the audience swells. The performance of the trick may take only a minute, but the choice of that minute is in the performer's command. Samuel understood this naturally and John was showing that he too was a disciple of the art.

Once again Abigail turned away with contrived innocence. 'Sirs, you wrong a poor innocent girl,' she said. The bait was taken. John and Abigail had successfully introduced an added ingredient – that of illicitness. To the eyes of the audience not only was she a lady of society but also she was now an *innocent* lady of society. This was becoming an irresistible mix of expectation.

'Come, my dear,' said an ageing gentleman paternally. His fatherly tone was a deception, of course, but he was quite unaware that it was *he* who was really being deceived. 'You have our word that you will be treated honourably,' he added. A cry of *here-here*, then stuttered around the room.

'Do I have your word on that, gentlemen?' said Abigail coyly.

'You do Miss Fitzherbert,' led John and the others followed suit. Abigail paused for moment, and then extended that moment looking around at her audience like the actress she was. She realised that she had never put so much into a performance before, and it gave her an extra thrill. She opened her mouth to speak, but closed it again, and hid her head in pretended shyness. She then saw the look of irritation beginning to appear on John's face and she had to try hard to stop a smile from ruining her performance.

'Oh very well gentlemen, if I have your word that you will-' She did not finish the sentence as a cry of *Huzzah!* erupted spontaneously from her audience. John bowed politely to her and then took a chair and placed it in the middle of the room and gestured her to sit in it. She obliged elegantly and demurely.

Abigail had chosen her outfit carefully. The trick was to look seductive but yet retain that air of respectability. She had chosen a pink silk gown figured in red spots. The collar had bound Vandyke edging that exposed an open neckline. Her bodice would then normally have thrust up her full bosom, but the gown had frills that ameliorated most of the exposed cleavage. She crossed her legs elegantly, exposing a black and white satin shoe and the merest hint of white-stockinged ankle. She looked around the room again as her audience jockeyed for the best vantage point. It was time for John to adopt his role of the auctioneer.

'Gentlemen, gentlemen,' he barked, but then adopted a more restrained volume, 'the auction will now commence. Miss Abigail

Fitzherbert has agreed, for your personal delectation, to offer to the highest bidder, not only her personal attire, but the actual attire that she is wearing. 'Huzzah,' cried a number of gentlemen. John let the noise die down before he continued. 'We will start, gentlemen, with her right shoe.'

'Huzzah!' went up again but this time with much less bravado. John slipped the shoe off Abigail's foot, held it aloft as a trophy and called for the opening bids. A crown was offered, but this moved only slowly to ten shillings. John used all his persuasion to raise the bidding, but the assembly was slow. He coaxed and cajoled his audience telling them that the auction could not go on until the shoes were sold. Eventually he gave up, realising that the gentlemen were saving their money for later lots. The shoes were sold for a sovereign and thirty shillings respectively, which hardly covered their original cost, but John continued unrestrained.

'The lady has frills around her neckline, gentlemen.' John turned slowly around as he spoke so that he made eye contact with all his audience. 'I'll wager it's worth a pretty penny, is it not gentlemen? Who will start me at a new golden guinea?'

'A guinea it is Campbell-John,' a voice came from his left.

'Two guineas, Sir,' reposted a voice from his right. The auction was beginning to move at a pace, but then stalled again at five sovereigns.

'Come gentlemen,' cajoled John, 'five sovereigns for such a fine garment. Do I hear five *guineas*? I will sell at five guineas to the first gentleman to offer five guineas.' His wheedling worked instantly and an offer of five guineas was quickly made: 'Sold!' John cried in true auction style.

Abigail removed the frills demurely, but this exposed her constricted bosom to full sight. She saw the eyes all around her respond to the sight, and she accentuated the effect by breathing deeply and rapidly in an out, as if she was in a state of anxiety to be so exposed before these gentlemen. Her bosom rose and fell in rhythm to her breathing but she continued to play the part of the modest young lady. This was quite a feat bearing in mind that she was semi-naked.

The performance continued in virtuoso fashion. The bodice part of her gown was sold for eight guineas, and then John assisted the disrobing of it by unhooking the myriad of buttons with an unhurried precision so that the tension mounted. The skirt of the gown was sold for twelve, and when she stepped out of it she did so with a charmed innocence that the most accomplished of actresses would have been proud of. The price of her stays was raised to sixteen guineas, and her petticoat rose to a price of twenty guineas. The evening was to reward Abigail with a purse that a prizefighter would have envied, but John and she had anticipated all eventualities. Abigail returned to her seat for a brief moment. Her only attire now was a long chemise that fell to mid-thigh level, and her white stockings that terminated just below the knee. She tightened the pull-chord that controlled the collar of the chemise and this had the effect of recovering her bosom that had been partly but deliberately exposed when she had removed the stays. She gestured imperceptibly to John and that was his prompt to conclude the auction.

'Thank you gentlemen,' he said boldly, gesturing his arm in the direction of Abigail, 'a round of applause for Miss Fizberbert who has entertained us most royally with her *party piece*.' There was consternation around the room. John had dangled illicit delights in front of them, but now he was snatching them away again. Abigail nodded politely to acknowledge John's acclaim, and a courteous, if muted applause followed. Abigail likewise acknowledged her audience while still, incredibly, playing the role of the naive young girl despite being half naked. But the applause was accompanied by whispers and muttering. John heard this and smiled inwardly to himself. He put his great coat about Abigail's shoulders and led her to a corner of the room. They looked knowingly at each other, but did not speak: they had rehearsed their parts well and the performance was far from completed.

An impromptu huddle formed in the vacated performance area, and expressions of dissatisfaction wafted towards their corner. The phrases 'Bad show', and 'Not playing the game', rose above the grumbling, and then all the faces turned in their direction, stared for a few moments and then turned back again and the mutterings continued. The gentlemen were making their dissatisfaction plain and the polite restraint of moments before was now beginning to drain away as fast as the waters from an opening lock gate. A delegation of three was appointed and came to the corner to negotiate on the others' behalf.

'Now look here, Campbell-John,' said Lord Scalby, a former judge who now sat in the House of Lords as a Law Lord. He had been appointed to lead the small delegation, being a man of the law. He had no intention, however, of putting forward a reasoned legal argument. 'Now look here, Campbell-John,' he said again, 'this is a bad show, don't y'know'

'What is?' said John innocently.

'The auction, that's what.'

'What was the matter with it?' said John.

Lord Scalby found it hard to say the words that they all knew were relevant. He was on the horns of a dilemma. This was not some whorehouse where the rules of society did not matter. It was a society party, albeit the rump ends of one. Aside from Abigail, it was now men only, but he still had a responsibility to his hostess. He was still encumbered by his responsibility as a gentleman, and in addition, by his perception that Abigail Fitzherbert was a lady. He leant across John attempting to whisper in his ear, but his booming voice was not made for whispering and his words rose into the air for all the assembly to hear. 'The filly, err...' he said and then coughed in embarrassment his discomfort plain for all to see, 'well - she 'aint finished - what! What! If you take my drift, Campbell-John.'

'Finished?' John again innocently feigned incomprehension 'Was it not a naughty party piece from this delightful young lady?'

'Dammit, Campbell-John, you know what I mean. The filly has been put in the stable before the race has finished.'

'Lord Scalby!' interrupted Abigail with mock shock, 'what are you suggesting? You gentlemen promised me that I would be treated honourably. And now you suggest...' She turned away without completing the sentence, as if overcome by the implied suggestion. John put his arm around her, they took a step away from the delegation and he whispered reassuring phrases in her ear. But that was not all he whispered.

'Don't overdo it Abi, or we won't be able to back track.'

'You underestimate me,' whispered Abigail wickedly in response, momentarily allowing an impish expression for John's eyes only.

Lord Scalby stepped forward uneasily and bowed respectfully whilst muttering a throaty, 'Your servant, Ma'am,' at Abigail. He took John by the arm and manoeuvred him away from her, gesturing that they needed to talk man to man. 'We're all men of the world here, Campbell-John,' he said.

'Aye we are, Sir,' said John,' and we are all *gentlemen* as well are we not?'

'We are Sir, we are Sir,' said Scalby heartily, instinctively responding to the prompt. He was then speechless for a moment realising that he had been backed successfully into a corner. He could not immediately see a way out that would not reflect badly on his honour as a gentleman 'Well of course, we're gentlemen, Sir,' he mumbled unintelligibly not quite knowing where this conversation was going. 'We're gentlemen,' he repeated, 'but we're gentlemen of the world, what! God damn it Campbell-John!' Scalby's gravelly voice bellowed in frustration. 'We want to see what the filly's made of, what!'

'Oh, I see,' said John rubbing his chin as if he was being presented with an insoluble problem. 'You mean you want to see her *naked*, Sir? Do you think we can ask such a thing of a *lady*?'

'The gal looks a decent sort, a good sport and all that,' said Scalby. John realised that Scalby was not going to be manoeuvred into suggesting the right solution himself. He wanted it to be Scalby's suggestion, but it was simply not going to happen. Scalby, for all his experience as a judge, simply did not have the guile to suggest a way out of his perceived dilemma.

John sighed genuinely and rubbed his chin again. 'She's already shown us that she is a good sport Lord Scalby,' said John, 'but you ask a lot of her, Sir.' He looked again into Scalby's eyes, but no sign of comprehension met the look. The man's grasp of the situation was clearly somewhat limited.

'We could appeal to her sense of fairplay,' prompted John.

'Fairplay, how's that?' said Scalby.

'Well I could say that I – as her agent so to speak - have led you gentlemen to believe that her performance would be...'

'More explicit,' interrupted Scalby enthusiastically.

'I was going to say, full-blooded,' corrected John.

'Good, good,' said Scalby, 'd'ya think the gal will oblige?'

'It's going to be difficult,' said John. 'I'll have to say that my honour is at stake and that only she can redeem it.'

'Yes, yes,' said Scalby the reasoning suddenly becoming apparent to him.

'And it'll need all you gentlemen to play your part - be enthusiastic when she resumes - if you take my meaning, Sir.'

'Of course, of course,' said Scalby, his voice losing the last pretence of privacy. They nodded to each other to signify that they had agreement. John then walked Abigail away so that the charade could continue. He put his arm around her as if to comfort her from the shock of the proposal.

'That was hard work,' whispered John, 'the old bugger tends to lag behind in the conversation, if you take my meaning.'

'I have to looked shocked now do I?' said Abigail.

'That's about the size of it,' said John, knowing that on command Abigail would oblige with a performance of no little skill. 'What next, then?' she asked.

'My turn,' said John, 'I have to pretend to look dishonoured.' He put the back of his hand to his forehead.

'Suppose that will have to do,' whispered Abigail sarcastically.

'What now,' said John?

'Oh we just keep repeating this for ten minutes to show that it was difficult for you to persuade me.'

'You're a diamond, Abigail,' said John.

When the auction resumed Abigail returned to character. This time, however, she had to add a sense of duty to that subtle mixture of sauciness and virtuousness that she had originally displayed. The addition was delicate, but nevertheless significant. It heightened that sense of illicitness and the already charged atmosphere was enhanced. It amused her considerably to observe that a number of gentlemen were attempting discreetly to rub at their groins. How easy it was to bamboozle a man! She was wearing only her stockings and the long chemise that she and John had prearranged to sell as one lot. They would go for the big finale to rouse their audience. The gentlemen, however, had deviously got together to put ten guineas apiece into a voting fund and would bid collectively a hundred guineas. They meant to continue the charade of an auction and bid up to that amount. The deceived and the deceivers were now becoming confusingly blurred. It would be a classic sting, however, in that the marks – the gentlemen - would not know they had been taken.

Scalby's grating voice boomed the first bid at a handsome ten guineas, and the charade quickly took the bidding to the prearranged hundred guineas, and then to John's cry of '*Sold!*' This took the night's takings for John and Abigail far past their intended target and in fact far beyond their wildest dreams when they had hatched their little scheme. Such sums had become commonplace in John's life and his share would not cover his accumulated debts, but the best part of a hundred guineas was far more that Abigail had ever had at one time. It gave her options for the future. What's more it gave her the opportunity for further earnings. The scam had worked better than she could ever have expected. She was approaching the age of thirty and she knew that she had to cash in quickly, for even the greatest actress could not conquer the march of time. A powdered face could not forever hide those lines of life that Mother Nature inflicts so vindictively. For the moment, however, Abigail felt triumphant - not only for the money, but also for her performance. She had shown to herself that this street urchin from the slums of St.Giles could walk hand in hand with the privileged of society. She had bridged a chasmic divide to mock that very structure that told people to *know their place*. In her mind a plan formed. She would purchase a half share in the theatre company from the fat puppet who employed her, and much to the annoyance of Mabel Royale, she would be able to take the leading parts. Suddenly, Abigail's ambition of becoming the mistress of a wealthy man seemed less important for she now knew that she could attain her goals in other ways: she would make provision for her old age by becoming a woman of property.

But for now she had a performance to complete. It was to be a difficult performance for she had to strip completely naked, whilst at the same time remaining in character. She toyed with the idea of full-on sauciness, but then decided that this would be a betrayal of her performance so far, of which she was now supremely proud.

She twirled slowly, looking at every pair of eyes as she did so and saw expectation all around her. She had painted a canvas of anticipation and now she set herself to fulfil that expectation. She slowly crossed her legs, granting one onlooker a fleeting glimpse of her pubis. '*Tallyho!*' he cried out in recognition of his good fortune. She then commenced to peel down one of her stockings, slowly, pausing at intervals; a silence fell as with bated breath the gentlemen watched her gathering fingers easing the stocking down her leg, until it slipped off her toes. The silence was broken with a roar of *Bravo!* And then the silence fell once more. She looked around again and feeling like a maestro conducting the performance of an orchestra, she repeated the routine with the other stocking. She now stood and crossed her arms, bending so that each hand took hold of the hem of the chemise. She paused again, but now held that pause, for she knew the importance of timing. And then – she pulled the chemise quickly over her head in one rapid movement. She then twirled around vigorously waving the chemise above her head, her breasts bouncing as she did so.

A raucous cheer erupted spontaneously and shouts of *Huzzah!* again echoed, but this time around the whole assembly. 'Game little filly,' roared Lord Scalby, clapping his hands vigorously as he did so. She was exhilarated by the response of her lascivious audience.

The scene was one of pure sauciness, but now Abigail knew she must return to character to maintain the illusion. Suddenly, she pulled the chemise down in front of her, holding it hard against her body as if overwhelmed with embarrassment. She covered one breast, but was clever enough to leave the other one exposed; she then fled to the corner, holding her chemise in such a way as to allow a delectable glimpse of her bottom before covering herself with John's coat.

The performance was now complete. Still in character, she stood in the corner, the applause ringing in her ears; she was a player and she had just given the best performance of her life.

CHAPTER 22

Samuel's muscles ached and cried out for relief. It was February and it was bitterly cold outside, but the bright winter sun, which had shone for many hours, warmed him through the expansive skylight, supplementing a rigorously burning fire inside. But now his naked body began to shiver as the warmth of the sun began to fade and with it that warm glow that had nourished him through the long hours of holding an unnatural pose, also began to dissipate. He longed to climb down and exercise his arms and legs so that the blood would start to flow freely once again around his body and refresh his weariness. Here he was, an athletic and powerful man, yet without doing anything his limbs and muscles had been reduced to that of the feeblest child. He was unable to move, however; strung up and held in position by ropes and pulleys, his right arm hoisted above his head. The unnaturalness of the pose was being preserved in this most brutal of ways. The artists of the day were meticulous in their pursuit of accuracy, and if this meant extreme discomfort for their models, then that was the way of it: they were paid to put up with this discomfort.

Samuel's fingers were beginning to go numb. His arm had been raised above his head now for many hours and the flow of blood to the hand was beginning to fail. His mouth was parched; he had not taken even a sip of water in this time. He waggled his fingers in an effort to bring them back to life, but the artist coughed loudly to register his dissatisfaction. A long, thin, gaunt face seemed to show permanent irritation, and a deep furrowed forehead and rounded shoulders supplemented this expression, the result of many hours spent concentrating over his easel. Samuel Medina was a deferential man and the eminence of the artist was not lost on him. Out of respect for the great man, he had endured extreme discomfort for many hours but his impatience and his discomfort were now reaching such epic proportions that he could endure no longer.

Emma Green had introduced Samuel to an artist friend for whom she modelled, after convincing Samuel that his athletic physique would be much in demand and he could earn a bob or two. The artist for whom he was now so painfully posing, Sir Joshua Lazenby, was one of the most famous portrait painters in England.

He was also a well-accepted man in society, his patrons of the very highest echelons within it, and he exhibited at the Royal Academy. The artistic community however, was a very narrow one, and when gossip had reached him that a beautiful young man with the face of a saint and the body of Adonis was new to the modelling scene, he had made it his business to see for himself.

The problem for Samuel was the lowly status of an artist's model. A fee of a few shillings was all a man could expect to be paid, for there was less social stigma attaching to male models. Women, on the other hand, could earn a half a guinea as a reward because it was recognised that a female model was regarded as even lower than a common prostitute; such women were scandalous! It followed that many of the women were in fact prostitutes, but it was an additional source of income, which Emma, in common with other actresses, relied on when funds were short and hunger took her. She had introduced a reluctant Samuel to her regular patron, who had at once marvelled at his physique and been most eager to paint his portrait, being generous enough to offer a full half guinea. This was, of course, far below what Samuel's could now earn, but he was nevertheless aware of the difficulties in earning a living – his parents would jump at such an amount for a day's toil. Besides, his vanity was massaged by the thought of being painted and he needed very little persuasion to accept the half-guinea. Sir Joshua, however, was a much grander artist than usual, and with a much grander canvas: his reluctant subject was to be St. John baptising Christ in the River Jordan. There had previously been another model for the role, but Sir Joshua had been prepared to remove him from the canvas and paint over his image for this marvellous specimen that now presented itself. In fact, Sir Joshua believed he had found the *perfect* man.

'Can you release me, Sir?' asked Samuel. Sir Joshua did not respond, the concentration evident in his face was undisturbed. 'Sir Joshua, Sir,' said Samuel again, but this time more stridently.

'Uh,' said Sir Joshua after a short moment. He looked at Samuel over the top of the canvas, his expression now changing to one of surprise.

'I fear, Sir, that I cannot hold this pose a moment longer,' said Samuel.

Sir Joshua looked at his skylight and saw the light was beginning to fade. He sighed a deep sigh and then rose up to his full and considerable height, stretching his arms and pushing his rounded shoulders back as far as they were now able to go. He was an imposing figure; sixty-four years old with a shock of white hair swept back from his forehead but, unlike Samuel, not tied at the nape. He had a large hooked nose so that in profile his own features had a biblical look about them. He could have been his own model for he could surely have portrayed Moses. Although age had bowed him, he was still that imposing figure. A pair of spectacles pinched his hooked nose, for his fading eyesight meant that he now needed assistance. Despite these glasses he was still required to hover only inches from the canvas in order to execute the more delicate of brush strokes.

'You're quite right my dear fellow,' he said remarkably amiably, the concentration now draining from his features. Most of his models arrived shabbily dressed, but Samuel had arrived dressed as a gentleman, and this had not gone unnoticed by this grand old man. He recognised that Samuel was a man of substance. 'You poor man you must be in need of a break,' he said, as he walked to the pulleys to release Samuel.

Samuel's arm fell down violently. Although propelled only by gravity it slapped his naked thigh as if a firecracker had just fractured the atmosphere. He bent forwards and rested his arms on his knees to support himself, and gradually, little by little, the fatigue began to ease and drain from his limbs. After a few moments he felt able to straighten up, but as he did his joints creaked from the stiffness, and he too stretched accompanied by an involuntary elongated groan.

'My dear fellow,' said Sir Joshua handing him a robe to cover his nakedness, 'you must be parched, will you take some supper with me? It'll only be some bread and ham, for I eat very frugally but if can offer you a good glass of burgundy, or a fine cognac?'

'You are most kind, Sir,' said Samuel, rubbing the pins and needles from his limbs, 'but my religion will not allow me to eat ham. A glass of cognac would be most acceptable though.'

'You are a Jew?' said Sir Joshua the name Medina suddenly coming into focus in his mind.

'Aye,' said Samuel proudly, 'I am, Sir.'

A knowing smile now navigated Sir Joshua's face. 'Splendid – that's absolutely splendid,' he said, 'that's why you look so perfect as The Baptist. I couldn't put my finger on it before.'

'Because the Baptist was a Jew like me?'

'Exactly,' said Sir Joshua, 'but you don't realise how surprising that is. You see, historically, artists have always portrayed religious scenes in the image of their own experience, but they didn't realise that they were doing it. They thought they were portraying a true image of Palestine, but all the faces were of white Europeans. The Italian Masters of the Renaissance put the faces of their patrons into their canvases. The English have traditionally shown Christ with blue eyes and blond hair.'

'Which of course the Prophet could not possible have had,' said Samuel.

'Precisely, my boy – you see they had no sense of history. And artists are still doing it today.'

They genuinely interested each other and became easy in each other's company, but then Sir Joshua remembered his manners.

'Cheese then?' he said, 'I can offer you some cheese.'

'Cheese will be fine,' said Samuel, but then his overwhelming thirst nudged his mind and he added, 'but I fear I must drink the best part of a gallon of water, Sir, to nourish my aching muscles.'

'Ah.' Sir Joshua handed him a glass and a flask of water. 'It's the athlete in you. You are obviously dedicated to keeping your body in such a magnificent condition.'

Samuel paused, suddenly overcome with a realisation: it was an innocuous comment and was meant as nothing more than a compliment, but he *did* have an understanding of what a pugilist needed to do to keep in tip top condition. He had used that knowledge to best much bigger and stronger men. He observed the strength in his opponents and knew that if they did not have that conditioning, he need do little more that use his own athleticism, avoiding their strength until exhaustion overtook them – their fatigue and lack of condition were his allies. He also knew something of diet and nutritious foods and, from his own experience, the need for a temperate and regular mode of living; he knew to avoid beers and liquors. And yet he had abandoned all this well held knowledge. Sir Joshua's nonchalant compliment made Samuel suddenly aware that he had been living the life of the young gentleman about town; that he had allowed John Campbell-John to lead him into a way of life that was far from ideal for a pugilist - and he had to admit to himself that he had been a willing follower. Drinking, gambling and whoring had been part of his everyday life for some months now, and after an initial reluctance he had pursued them all with enthusiasm and relish. But he had seen for himself how once great fighters came to the ring: their bellies bloated; their reflexes shot. Under-prepared and ill-equipped to sustain their effort for more that a few minutes, they would attempt to use their strength to affect a quick knockout. They knew that their legs would soon give out on them, and their lungs would burn and wheeze from exhaustion until they could offer no more resistance than a newly whelped pup. Terrible beatings occurred, for pride would keep them upright to be pummelled, pounded and beaten into eventual collapse, and then poverty would force their return to the ring some months later, still carrying that lack of conditioning, but now with their faculties reduced by the previous beating and only another beating to look forward to. The prize money was then frittered on more liquor, until an aching, hungered belly forced them back into the ring to continue on their downward spiral to a pauper's grave. The thought made Samuel shudder. He suddenly saw this future yawning before him; a future that was inevitable unless he stopped his joyful, unthinking pursuit of debauchery.

Sir Joshua noticed his reaction. 'You were saying, Sir?' he prompted.

Samuel, who had drifted into a dark daydream, snapped back into reality. He looked at Sir Joshua for a moment before saying eventually, 'Forgive me, Sir. It is just that you have reminded me that I'm supposed to be an athlete, but I have not been behaving like one for some months now. Indeed, I have been tempted away from my chosen path by the delights of the flesh.'

'Ah,' said Sir Joshua, 'the curse of the young man with a roving eye and coins in his pocket. You're by no means the first, I assure you.'

'No, but I should know better. I have an education, and I have the discipline of my religion.'

'You need a good wife to keep you on the straight and narrow, young man.'

Samuel was again taken aback. He had put Rebecca to the back of his mind, and now thoughts of her came flooding back to him.

'To my shame, I have to admit to you, Sir, that I already have a wife,' he paused for a moment as the words formed disagreeably in his mind. 'And yes, I also have to admit that she kept me on the straight and narrow as you say.'

'So what went wrong?' said Sir Joshua.

Samuel stared into the distance and sighed heavily as he did so. He then looked back at Sir Joshua and noticed the artist's kindly expression. He felt a sudden overwhelming need to confide in this man – this man who was almost a stranger to him. He took a long gulp of water, swallowed and then sighed again. 'It would be disagreeable to burden you with my problems,' he said.

254

'Nonsense, it would be good to share your company over my vittles,' said Sir Joshua, 'I have little educated company these days. All the clever people I knew seem to have died.' He pulled the cord to summon his housekeeper who was then dispatched for the brandy and cheese.

They talked for many hours and Samuel told his story. The old man showed a keen interest in Samuel's poetry as well as his boxing. He had previously employed pugilists on a number of occasions but had merely dismissed these men, whether rightly or wrongly, as ill educated and ill-equipped to converse on his art, but Samuel reciprocated Sir Joshua's interest and they talked about the techniques and disciplines that they both needed in their chosen professions. Samuel had some knowledge of art but the old man had little knowledge of pugilism and was amazed at the dedication and skills required. They had things in common. Most particularly, they had both reluctantly been required in their time to use patrons, and they knew the anguish of having to be subservient to less intelligent, but nevertheless rich and powerful men: men who knew nothing of art or style, but who could nevertheless call the tune simply because they paid the piper. Similarly, they both had that shared experience of negotiating fees and then facing the difficulty of actually getting their patrons to pay them. A bond between them had been forged – two unlikely candidates who on the face of it should not connect: and yet they did. Shared experience and intellect were their common companions.

Lady Adele Fitzsymons's house parties were notorious for their revelry: both infamous and risqué. Samuel Medina and John Campbell-John had returned to London specifically to attend her party and had spent the earlier part of the evening gaming and drinking and eating. The party was ostensibly a card evening but for a select few, other delights were available to them. The cards had run kindly for Samuel but John Campbell-John had lost heavily again. He had again negated his undoubted skills as a card player by over consumption of alcohol. It was now three o'clock in the morning and most of the guests had gone home. The card games had now finished to be replaced by other, more earthy games.

A dozen partygoers remained. Adele, four of her lady friends and seven gentlemen. The ladies were all of rank in society, if notorious within it. Their ages ranged from twenty-nine to thirty-five and they were all prima facie married, but fidelity was something they had long since abandoned. For the gentlemen, of course, fidelity was not so prized and an evening's whoring was not seen as anything too scandalous. These gentlemen had been carefully picked, and in this respect the use of the accepted definition of gentlemen was somewhat blurred. As well as Captain John Campbell-John there was another young army officer, Captain George Granville of the Horse Guards. George was a handsome and athletic man, if not the sharpest pencil in the cavalry box. He had a small income from his father but this was only just enough to meet his mess bills. He did, however, tick all the other boxes as far as the ladies were concerned. He was attractive, a fine physical and muscular specimen, with powerful thighs on display through his figure-hugging breeches. He rode, and he had developed a charm that was much appreciated by the ladies. He had worked on this for he knew that it was the key that would open doors for him, for he was nominally only on the fringes of society. He had even developed a passable wit, or enough of a wit to satisfy many of the ladies of society. He was a Don Juan, a libertine: or at least this was what he tried to be. In this respect he was in direct competition with John and, to a lesser extent, Samuel, for their chief function this evening was to stand at stud for the ladies.

The other four gentlemen were men of genuine wealth, if not all genuine gentlemen. Three of them also considered themselves to be sporting gentlemen, but for tonight they had other pleasures on their minds. What all four had in common was that they were *squires of dame*, voyeurs, rakes intent on carnality, debauchery, harlotry, or any other form of sensual delight that might be on offer. Their ages ranged from thirty-eight to – in Lord Cowden's case - sixty-four.

The party had repaired to a reception room where the furniture had been pushed back against the walls to leave a large area for the games to be played out. These games were in reality little more than variations on simple parlour games and tonight a game of *Newmarket Stakes* was in progress. All the gentlemen had removed their frock coats, but some were in more of a state of undress that others. A course had been laid out to simulate a racetrack, and obstacles placed at intervals to replicate the fences. Samuel, John and George Granville were playing the part of the horses along with a fourth, Gilbert Furley. Furley was a fifty-five year old, wealthy merchant but also a well known ne'er-do-well whose only redeeming feature was his ready wit. That was enough to make him a popular party guest. Each horse carried a lady as the jockey. The object was to get around the course, clearing the obstacles, but with each race, the last one over the finishing line had to pay a forfeit and that forfeit was the removal of an item of clothing by both the lady jockey and her horse. If any part of the lady jockey touched down on the way round then they automatically came in last with the appropriate forfeit to pay. Gilbert Furley had played the game robustly from the start, and with great enthusiasm, but his age was catching up on him. His face was now crimson red as he toiled with the weight of his lady jockey, and sweat formed freely on his forehead and then cascaded down the rest of his tomato face so that it dripped profusely off his nose and his chin. His jockey was now perched precariously on his back, having slipped down from the original high starting position so that she now splayed lopsidedly, her right leg held high against his hip, but with the left leg only just held so that it hung low below his rump. She grappled at his neck frantically with her right hand trying to hold on, but this increased Furley's discomfort, by pulling his head backwards in a choking movement. Her left arm was unable to reach his throat or even his collar, and so it hung down accentuating the asymmetrical riding position. She had pulled her gown forward and then up through her legs before mounting, but she had been obliged to discard her right shoe and then her stocking as previous forfeits. Her riding position had caused her legs to be exposed to the upper thigh and she cut a comical figure with one leg bare and the other shod and stockinged. Her bodice had also been lost to forfeit and her semi-exposed bosom fought a losing battle with the top of her chemise to keep it from escaping altogether as a result of the exertions. Both horse and jockey were drunk, but they played the game enthusiastically and loudly and she encouraged her mount on to even greater efforts by shouting and whipping it with her riding crop.

All four horses lined up for another circuit and Lady Adele put a hunting horn to her lips and blew it vigorously, if unprofessionally. A strangled toot escaped the bell end of the instrument but this was enough to encourage Lord Cowden to cry out *Tally Ho,* and the race was away again. Gilbert Furley set off as wholeheartedly as ever but he was quickly passed by the other horses at which point he eased to a walk realising that he could not catch his opponents, but Lady Adele came to his aid, tripping Samuel as he went by so that both horse and jockey fell headlong across the floor. Samuel jumped up angrily but his annoyance was calmed when laughter broke out. Gilbert Furley came home, tailed off but still valiant, to the cheers of the others.

Samuel and his mount paid the necessary forfeit, Samuel removing his waistcoat, having previously only removed his neckcloth, and his jockey removing her bodice. She prepared to remount again, pulling her dress forward through her legs and then held it up as she jumped on his back. On doing so, however, her gown snagged against Samuel's back so that it was caught and as her body rose the gown did not, with the result that her bosom was released and overflowed, and she frantically tried to pull the drawstring of her chemise top to reinstall it. A great cheer went up from the spectators followed by bellowed laughter. She failed at first to achieve the manoeuvre however, and Lady Adele took the opportunity to embarrass her further by tooting on the hunting horn to start another race. The four horses bolted at the sound of the horn, Samuel's jockey shouting 'Whoa', as he galloped away, but her horse did not respond. After a few moments she gave up trying to adjust herself and she returned her arms to Samuel's collar and throat to ride her mount wholeheartedly and without inhibition. Her ample breasts now rose and fell extravagantly to her horse's gallop, slapping Samuel around the head with every stride. This provoked even more laughter from the spectators and all restraint now began to dissipate from the gathering.

After another half an hour or so, only three competitors remained and they were in an advanced state of undress. Gilbert Furley had already taken his jockey to a bedroom intent on fornication, despite his body being in a state of total exhaustion. John was now so disrobed that he was wearing only his draws and his jockey was dressed in only her chemise top and one stocking, which covered little of her body, and even less of her modesty. When her horse took off, her Rubenesque rump was on full display to the gathered onlookers. Samuel and George had at least still retained their breeches, but both men were now bare-chested and bare-legged.

It was now decided that the game needed a winner. It was agreed that a final race was required. This would last five full laps and if any horse or rider touched down then they would be eliminated.

Three sweat-stained men lined up with their equally clammy jockeys eager to charge away for one last time. Bets were placed and Samuel was installed as the clear favourite. They looked fervently down the course that itself had been saturated with sweat and punctuated with moist bare footprints, so that it held dangers for the over-enthusiastic horse, which might easily lose its footing and skid uncontrollably at the corners. None of the horses were alive to such dangers however. Another strangled toot from Adele fractured the tension and the galloping began. At the first corner all the horses arrived simultaneously with Samuel on the outside. It was clear that someone had to give way but no horse would yield and it was left to centrifugal force to decide the outcome. George had the inside lane and as he turned he was forced outward by his own momentum. There was nowhere for him to go and he cannoned into John forcing him even wider around the bend. In turn John had no way to go and he cannoned into Samuel, who was then propelled off the course completely, and when he tried to compensate his bare feet lost all grip on the sweat-stained floor and he slewed uncontrollably and overbalanced. He was saved from falling, however, by the wall that he was rapidly approaching and both horse and jockey collided with it fiercely. The other horses now galloped away, but at least he was still in the race. His burning passion to win was in no way diminished and he took chase of the other two horses, but he was now nearly half a lap behind.

George had taken a lead from John, but both maintained a steady pace. Samuel strained to catch them and galloped after that naked rump that seemed to wave at him from John's back like a hot-cross bun, glowing with freshly baked colour. Slowly but surely that imitation confectionery came back to him, inch by inch until by the third lap, those buttocks, now even more rosy red with endeavour were right in front of them. Samuel cut to the inside at the next corner to the shouts of *foul* from the bystanders. He cared not however, and took the inside and shortest route around the corner. He bumped John away as he did so and John swore in response, 'Fucking cheat sir!' Straining frantically to stop himself from overshooting the lubricated corner, John managed to come to an inelegant stop just in time; his jockey perched precariously over his right shoulder, her ample buttocks now pointing upwards and her legs flaying behind him.

They righted themselves gracelessly and set off again, but this time only at a trot, the race obviously lost to them. Samuel had just over a lap in which to catch the cavalryman and he willed himself on to greater efforts. His bare feet paddled the wooden floor like a beaver's tail in the water, his powerful thighs pumping up and down like pistons. He hated losing at anything and the fact this was little more that a sex game made little difference to him. Rationally he knew that it did not matter but winning was part of his persona. He was competitive with a capital C – this is what he did. This is what turned a gentle man, a kind man, and a man of honour into a raging and brutal fighting machine. He was gaining and a cry of *Tally ho!* went up from the racegoers. His jockey was urged to use the whip and she responded by accepting that screeched advice and brought her crop down hard on her mount's rear. Samuel was oblivious to the pain, his mind consumed only by effort, by exertion, by endeavour – by winning.

With half a lap to go, he drew level in the straight and pulled alongside George in an overtaking manoeuvre. Those sporting gentlemen who had wagered on George, pleaded with him to respond and he did so. He knew that if he made it to the last corner in the inside position then he could deny Samuel the shortest route, Samuel would be forced to take the long way around. George accelerated to Samuel's surprise and he strained to match him. It became a question of whether George could maintain that effort until he reached the corner.

Both men knew that and they strained against each other. Samuel was the athlete but George was a fit young man and he would not concede his advantage. They reached the corner still shoulder to shoulder, but now the bend worked in George's favour. Samuel dropped his left shoulder to go for the inside berth, using the same manoeuvre as with John, but the cavalry officer would have none of it. He too moved to the inside to block that particular course and Samuel had no alternative but again to go the long way round. To make matters worse, when he did so, George then moved to his right forcing Samuel even wider, and he struggled to keep his equilibrium. As they came off the bend George led only by a couple of feet, but the finish line was but yards ahead. Another great cry went up from the onlookers who were delighted by the fine race, and which, of course, had been spiced by their own wagers. *'Come on Granville!'* competed with *'Come on Medina!'* and both horses laboured even harder in response. Samuel came up to George's shoulder but his effort was in vain, and he crossed the line inches behind the cavalry officer. Both horses were exhausted, and dripping with sweat. Their jockeys attempted to dismount, but then fell off inelegantly as the horses let go in pure exhaustion. They both bent over gasping for breath, their efforts reflected in the condensation that had built up on the windows, as the air, warmed by human endeavour, reacted with the outside February cold.

'Well done, Granville,' snorted Lord Cowden. George stood up momentarily to wave an arm in recognition of the acclaim, but then reverted to his recovery position, his back bent and his hands gripping his knees, his lungs sucking in huge quantities of air. 'Good show though, Medina,' said Lord Cowden by way of consolation, which Samuel acknowledged from his bent over position. The other onlookers, however, were less that generous, particularly those who had wagered on him.

'Samuel Medina!' taunted Lady Adele. She was mocking him. 'Look at you – why you're wheezing like an old scullery maid smoking a clay pipe.' It was not an analogy that she made from first-hand knowledge, as her own servants were always out of sight when not attending to their duties. It would suffice for the purpose of ridicule, however.

'Aye,' said, Samuel, trying to maintain some dignity, 'it was an energetic race, and George ran well. I must congratulate you, Sir.'

'Pon my sole, Sir but you did,' said Lord Cowden, addressing the cavalry officer. He then turned back to Samuel and a mischievous look took him. 'Are you not due to fight Big Charles Sweep in May sir?' he said sardonically.

'Aye, Sir,' said Samuel still breathing heavily, 'that I am, and God willing I hope to prove my worthiness.'

'But, Sir,' said Lord Cowden, 'if you haven't enough air in your lungs to beat young Granville here, how will you possibly be able to match Big Charlie?' The onlookers laughed heartily at his expense. Anger built up within Samuel. His normal reaction in such circumstances was to call out the offending gentleman for satisfaction. He could hardly call out Lady Adele, and Lord Cowden was far too old. Samuel felt impotent and his anger mounted. This anger was also fuelled by the realisation that the jibes had a truth about them. It was the second time within a matter of days that his fitness had let him down. He wheezed for breath and he remembered how fatigued he had been when posing for Sir Joshua. He was still a fit man but this level of fitness would not be enough against Big Charlie and he knew it. The fight might last an hour and one half or even more, but those two capricious friends, John Barleycorn and the fruit of the vine had jaded his athleticism enough for him to know that he could not fight for that length of time. He sat on an isolated chair at the other end of the course from the finish where the onlookers had been watching. They wanted a new race by reversing the roles – the ladies would be the horses in this race and the gentlemen the jockeys. The race started with great gusto but Samuel took little interest in it. He sat isolated in contemplation. The race itself fizzled out quickly. The role of the jockeys was taken by the older and less fit gentlemen and they were keen for the race to be completed. It was great fun for them, and they shouted their encouragement heartily, but the ladies quickly tired of carrying these bloated profligates. At the end of the first lap only one horse had strength enough to carry its jockey to the finishing line, and by the end of the second none were left standing, and the race card was deemed to be complete.

Jeers and hisses mixed with roars and cheers; Samuel gulped down another glass of burgundy. It was a fine wine and was really a waste being used now as part of a drinking game. John had encouraged Samuel to join in and he did so, if for no other reason than to rouse himself from his own melancholy. He was consuming alcohol profusely, because it was a competitive game, and he was one of life's natural competitors. But his mood had swung from one of jollity and high spirits to glumness and dejection, and the alcohol had the effect of accentuating this. The more he drank the more *down* he became, and the more down he became the more he brooded and the worse he played the game. He was required to down the glass in one as a forfeit for his loss, rather than to savour its obvious charms. They were all playing Taps – two card tables had been put together and the decanter of burgundy placed in the middle. Taps was a simple game really, but it did require skill and dexterity. Each competitor was equipped with a sovereign, and one player started by tapping his coin once. The person sat immediately to the coin-tapper's left was then required to likewise tap his coin once. The process was then continued around the table. Tapping the table once maintained the current direction of the play, but by tapping the coin twice the direction was reversed. If the coin was tapped rapidly three times that was a direction to skip the next player. The penalty for getting the turn wrong was to drink down a glass of the burgundy in one. This was a favourite game for most of them and the game was played at a pace, the coins tapping speedily in response to their neighbour's directions.

Samuel returned his empty glass upside down to signal that he had paid his forfeit and the game was ready to restart. He now had the honour of the first tap and he double tapped so that the game went to his right rather than his left. A single tap came from his right indicating that the player on his right had correctly played his turn and now Samuel tapped again on the basis that the game had come immediately back to him. Another cheer went up but now there were more jeers than cheers. The game should have gone to the player next to the right, as there had been no double tap to change direct. The problem was that Samuel had now lost quickly three times in a row and he was beginning the spoil the game for the other competitors who were unable to display their own skills at the game. Some had not even had a turn in the last three games.

Samuel's mind was elsewhere. He was brooding on his own fitness or the lack of it. He had been teased about it, and he did not respond to teasing at the best of times. But this time the teasing had struck a nerve, for he saw the truth in the taunting. His fitness levels had fallen and he was not where he should have been in his preparations to fight Charlie Sweep. An elbow hit him in the ribs and he looked around at the culprit. No words were spoken but the expression told him that they were waiting for him to pay his forfeit. He righted his glass and reached for the decanter, and filled his glass clumsily and it over spilled so that the baize of the table was stained red, but his hostess was too drunk to care. He swigged down the wine in response, to the chanting of *forfeit, forfeit, forfeit,* and he upturned his glass again. He tapped his sovereign again, sending the game to the left, where it went away to the delight of the other payers. *Tap, tap, tap, double tap, double tap, triple tap, tap, tap, tap, double tap.* The game was being played with gusto, and much noisy banter, but again Samuel's mind wandered away.

Tap, tap, tap, double tap, and then there was a pause. Eyes darted around and a tense silence mounted as the competitors waited for the next tap. It brought Samuel's mind temporarily back to the table and he assumed that it was his turn – he tapped again. He had not followed the game, but his tap turned out to be right, and the game went speedily to his left again, *tap, tap, triple tap, tap, tap, double tap, double tap.* His mind wandered again, racing as fast as the game that he was now ignoring. Another cheer went up to signal some fine play and he looked around but when he saw that the game was at the other side of the table he switched off again. *Tap, tap, tap, double tap, double tap, tap, tap, tap,* and then there was another pause, and eyes again darted as the competitors held their breath. This was a tactic, however, as the incumbent player knew that it was his turn, but he paused to bait another player. It wasn't intended to catch Samuel, who was far from the point of the game. The silence bit into his consciousness temporarily again and he tapped.

This time there was a universal moan because it was such poor play. Samuel sighed heavily realising his own shortcomings. 'My apologies,' he said dejectedly, and refilled his glass. He drained the contents and replaced an upturned glass again.

It was the end of the game for him - melancholy had overridden his competitive instincts and he feigned his own inebriation and conceded the game to the other players. 'My apologies again,' he said, 'but I am too drunk to play the game properly.'

Samuel had reached a crossroads in his short life. He knew that he had to abandon this degenerate lifestyle or fear public humiliation when he fought Big Charlie. He was still a young man and young men did immature and foolish things, until maturity caught up with them. For some, of course, maturity never did catch up with them; witness the wastrels at the party tonight. The perceived wisdom would be that he was still too young to have acquired that wisdom, but he had already known responsibility in his young life. He was a father, and he had known the pain of losing a child. He ran businesses and had the livelihood of his employees to consider. But most of all he was Jewish and he felt an obligation to his people. He knew it was time to leave such festivities as these behind him. He needed to train and to train hard. He would call on that stubbornness that was inherent within him – he would call on that tenacity that characterised his success in the ring. He would revert to that Samuel Medina who was unrelenting, and cast aside the rake that he had become. Fate had raised an eyebrow in his direction. It had not gone unnoticed. He would respect and heed that reaction.

CHAPTER 23

The April of 1790 started so very un-spring like. There were buds on the trees but they seemed reluctant to venture forth into the chilly world. Heavy frosts greeted each new morning but the temperatures failed to rise through the rest of the day, and it seemed that winter was intent on overstaying its welcome. The year's new crop of wild daffodils stood erect but stubbornly failed to bloom and the only colour that could be seen came from scattered outcrops of crocuses, which had blotched the linen land with dabs of yellow and purple since February. As they always did, they had arrived early to the spring party, but no one else had followed them and each one stood lonely and shivering, like a lovesick young girl yearning for her soldier boy who had failed to come home from war. The scene was dismal and discouraging and the tardy spring had let down its followers who longed for its reappearance.

Samuel ran across the frozen, unforgiving ground of Lord Cowden's estate, mile after miserable, wretched mile. He had started his run well before the dawn had broken, but with the daylight had come a freezing drizzle that replaced the intermittent nocturnal snow flurries. It stung his cheeks, as if the wind carried a thousand tiny needles to prick his wet, chapped face. His fingers throbbed with numbness and his toes, despite his stockings and shoes, echoed that icy feeling. His discomfort, however, was not a source for abandonment - such thoughts were simply overridden. He was punishing himself. He was punishing himself for months of overindulgence, for months of drinking and wenching, for months of gambling and gaming. But most of all he was punishing himself for months of forgetting who he was, and for months of failing himself and his people. He had a responsibility on his shoulders and he had ignored that.

Lord Cowden had joined in ridiculing Samuel's lack of fitness at Lady Adele's party, but he was a sporting man himself, and he had recognised Samuel's problems. He had gone to see him the next day and offered him this estate as his training ground in order to prepare for his fight with Big Charlie Sweep. In fact, Samuel had not needed such a spur, but he was happy to accept it anyway; the offer afforded him free board and lodging, as well as a place to train, and it avoided his having to ask Sir Thomas Kettall to provide such facilities. For six weeks now he had pounded his lonely way around the estate, paying his debt to himself - a debt that had to be repaid with exorbitant interest. His daily vigil had been a solitary affair. His loneliness had been self-imposed as he had sought seclusion as part of his penance. He spoke to the cook about his daily requirements, but other than that he kept himself to himself. He was not yet sparring, but with each mile his stamina was replenished and his lung power was enhanced. He worked with weights and medicine balls to increase his strength and he sweated out the impurities that he had allowed his body to absorb.

He trudged the last few yards of his lonely run and entered by the front door of the Gothic mansion that was Cowden Hall in the heart of rural Oxfordshire. In his eyes he was a guest and the tradesman's entrance was not for him. Other than that he made few demands on his host. An impromptu gym had been prepared for him from a storeroom near the kitchen, and he dragged his sodden, steaming body to it, for his day's work was far from done. He asked the cook, as he did every day, for a drink of hot cider, coriander and caramel, and then in the privacy of the gym he wrapped himself in blankets, pursed his face and drank the noxious mixture. The drink was an emetic – its purpose was to purge the body. First would come the profuse sweating, and this was accentuated by wrapping himself in the sweat-stained blankets. A purging sweat erupted from his skin as though a tap had suddenly been yanked on, and the blankets then sponged it up - they were now reaching saturation point from days of this treatment. And then the vomiting started. His stomach was emptied in violent pulsating retching, the sounds being overheard, with raised eyebrows, by the cook and her staff in the kitchen. He was treating his body cruelly, but he reasoned it deserved it – *he* deserved it. His days were spent in disagreeable toil and he made no effort to enjoy his training. It was a cycle of running; sweating, vomiting, exercising and weights, followed by eating huge quantities of protein, fruit and vegetables, and then the whole cycle would start again. In the evenings he refused the invitations to dine with Lord and Lady Cowden, and preferred to read and write his poetry by the dim light of a single candle. He was dour in his determination and nothing was going to deter him from his purpose.

The weather broke unexpectedly on the twelfth of April, and bright sunlight flooded the grateful fields. All of a sudden the scant and monochromed vista burst into life with vibrant colour. The spring plants were all suddenly there, as if they had just been in hiding, waiting for that bully that was winter to limp away for another year. But it had not limped away dragging its heels, it had just seemed to disappear in the night and the next day it was gone. Bright bursts of yellow exploded from the daffodil stems and they shared their displays with plants that would normally have been blooming weeks after the daffodils had died away. The temperatures soared from freezing to sweltering in a matter of days and balmy afternoons brought refreshed spirits to the household. Spring, as it always did, brought forward feelings of renewal, and everyone's spirit was lifted – but Samuel continued on his dour way as if the springtime had passed him by.

Samuel agreed eventually to dine with Lord and Lady Cowden at their insistence; it seemed they had a proposal for him. A house party was to be held at Cowden Hall and Lord and Lady Cowden would be hosting it on behalf of their nephew. The party was to last for six weeks and the Hall's complement of forty staff would be put at the disposal of six eligible young men and six eligible young women. The whole purpose of the house party was matchmaking, presided over by a hostess and that would be Lady Cowden. Lord Cowden in reality had little to do and he was happy to let his wife take charge of the gathering. Her job was to keep the party respectable within the rules of society, but Lady Cowden's main role was to find a match for her nephew. Lord Cowden had never been a good companion to her, being more interested in his sporting pursuits than his wife's welfare, and she had developed a life of her own with friends of her own.

Lady Cowden liked nothing better than to throw house parties. All the girls would be chaperoned, but each chaperone would be trying to get a match for her charge and would be looking after the interests of her own girl. Not only did it fill the house with people and give Lady Cowden the chance of entertaining, it also gave her the conversation that she could not enjoy with her husband. There was an edge to these house parties as the chaperones vied with each other to put forward the cases of their charges. Lady Cowden loved them.

'Now look here, Medina,' said Lord Cowden, 'Fraid there's a bit of a billeting problem.' Samuel looked at him with resignation, guessing what was coming. Status was everything and the best rooms always went to the men and women of the highest rank within society. In fact there was a strict pecking order and a title would command the best room; others would be allocated downwards according to their status in society. The same would apply at dinner; the order by which the guests would enter the dining room was governed by their status. Samuel knew only too well where this would leave him.

'You want me to leave,' said Samuel with a tone of acceptance.

'Pon my sole, no,' said Lord Cowden.

His wife interrupted him. 'The young gentlemen will need entertaining, Mr Medina,' she said, 'we'd like you to arrange some athletic pursuits for them. I know you don't shoot or ride, but Henry and the groom can take care of that.'

'I could school them in the art of self-defence,' said Samuel, 'boxing and the cudgel. Take them running as well.' Samuel had closed his Academy when he went on the road. He realised that he missed the camaraderie and the thought of tutoring again unexpectedly pleased him.

'Capital,' said Lord Cowden.

'But where will I stay?' asked Samuel.

'Ah,' said Lord Cowden, 'back to the billeting problem, don't y'know.'

'Leave this to me, Henry,' said Lady Cowden scowling at her husband, and irritated by the ineptitude she perceived in him. He looked down at his knife and twiddled with it like a rebuked schoolboy, but in reality he was more than pleased for her to deal with such problems. 'Mr Medina,' she continued looking back at Samuel and forcing a smile as she did so. Surprisingly, the harshness of her stern, wrinkled face disappeared temporarily. 'I am sure you can see that your room will be needed for my guests.'

'Aye, I can Ma'am,' he was resigned to that.

'I think the best solution would be for you to double up with Tobias, one of our footmen,' she said, 'would that be satisfactory for you?'

Samuel sighed heavily without any attempt at circumspection. It was enough to signal his dissatisfaction, much to Lady Cowden's surprise. She was not an unkind woman and was regarded by her servants as a superior sort of mistress. However, the offer of a shared room with a servant represented her view of Samuel's position in society – which was not very high.

'But *I'm* not a servant here, Lady Cowden,' said Samuel, reading her thoughts and voicing his dissatisfaction. He was offended by the offer, but then again he could find offence in many things. His tone did nothing to hide his feelings.

Lady Cowden was astonished by his comment, which she regarded as highly impertinent. She was lost for words for some moments. After an uncomfortable pause she said, 'Mr Medina; are you in earnest, Sir? May I remind you that you have been staying here at our expense for some weeks now?'

The tone of rebuke was obvious to Samuel and his feelings were now ambivalent. He was by nature a principled and considerate man; he did not wish in any way to be impolite to his hostess. But he had been wronged – had he not? – and it was in his nature to challenge anyone who wronged him. He wanted to leap to his feet, throw down some coins in payment for his board and lodgings, and stride away, but for once he caught himself.

'My apologies, Lady Cowden, I am at all times your obedient servant,' he said with all the politeness he could muster. 'You have indeed been a most gracious hostess to me. Pray grant me an opportunity to offer a solution.'

Lady Cowden nodded almost imperceptibly, reassured that the correct social order had been restored.

'If a cot could be provided,' Samuel continued, 'I will be happy to sleep in the room that you have kindly provided as a gymnasium for me.'

'But surely a bedroom will be more comfortable, Mr Medina?'

'Your servant, Ma'am,' he said, nodding respectfully, 'but it's not really about comfort.'

'Very well, very well; if you will be content with that, Mr Medina, then that is the end of the matter. But surely you would be more comfortable sharing with Tobias?'

'No, that won't be necessary,' said Samuel, happy that his standing as a guest had been preserved. 'I am content to sleep in my gymnasium, Ma'am.'

'Good show!' Looking furtively at his wife, Lord Cowden leant towards Samuel in a conspiratorial manner. 'That is good, for I have another proposition for you,' he spoke in a theatrical whisper.

'Oh for goodness sake, Henry,' snapped Lady Cowden, irritated by her husband. 'I don't want to know about your gambling schemes. It's a wonder you haven't led us both into penury years ago.' With that she stood and threw her napkin down in an exaggerated display of disdain. 'I shall retire to my room and leave you to your schemes, Henry.'

Both men stood out of politeness until she had left the room, but then Lord Cowden leaned over and filled Samuel's glass without any invitation. 'Now look here Medina. I've always maintained a string of thoroughbreds and I've had a number of champions over the years, though I've never had a champion boxer.' He grinned at Samuel, 'I have every expectation that this will change.'

Samuel looked at him with puzzlement for he wasn't sure what Cowden was getting at. 'But I'm my own man,' he said doubtfully.

'No, no not *you*, Medina,' Lord Cowden said, *'Tobias.'*

'Your *footman*, Tobias?' said Samuel.

'Aye,' said Lord Cowden, 'what do you think of him?'

'I don't know. I haven't seen him box. But he certainly has the athletic physique for it. Has he fought at all?'

'Aye, twice and won both times. But he took a lot of punishment. He only won because he was fit and outlasted his opponents.'

'He has no understanding of the noble science of self-defence, I take it?' said Samuel.

'None at all, but he just keeps on coming; never gives his opponent a respite. If he is knocked down he gets up and comes again and again until his opponent is exhausted. Even if you hurt him badly he just keeps coming at you.'

'Sounds as if he's got a fighter's heart, but who's he been fighting?

'Oh, only local stuff,' said Lord Cowden disparagingly. 'He fought Sir Giles Pope's groom, and the blacksmith from the village, but I want to take him to the fairs and race meetings to bring him on, so to speak.'

'So you want me to teach him some method?'

'Aye', said Lord Cowden, 'I thought you could include him with the young gentlemen.'

'Aye, I can, and he can also be my spar when I'm teaching. That'll avoid the young gentlemen getting too bruised.' Samuel chuckled, 'The young ladies won't want their young gentleman's looks to be mashed, will they?'

Lord Cowden laughed heartily and re-filled Samuel's glass.

John Campbell-John arrived at Cowden Hall in a hired carriage. He was the last of the party to arrive and he had done that deliberately. He would now put on a display of ostentation for the benefit of the other guests. His rank, as the second son of a country gentleman, put him at the bottom of the social ladder as far as the house party guests were concerned, and to make himself a potential catch he had to appear to be wealthy. It was John's game to trade on

270

the fact that it was quite acceptable for people of rank, but without wealth, to marry new money. John's deception, however, was much more complicated than that. While he needed to dupe the others that he was wealthy, marrying above himself to someone without money was not an option. He needed to find a young lady of means and he would find it easier to deceive her if the lady in question saw him as a suitor who had his own money.

John Campbell-John continued to be in debt despite his considerable earnings and gambling winnings. Money passed through his fingers like water: he had a wardrobe of the finest clothes, and a string of horses to show for his profligacy, but the debts for household expenses, and to his jeweller, lace maker, bookmaker, gun maker, shoemaker, book-seller, saddler, coach-maker, embroiderer, hatter, watchmaker, wine merchant, and his butcher all represented gluttony to excess. For this house party, however, he would appear in his finery as part of his subterfuge. He met his hostess and was charm personified. This was repeated when introduced to his fellow guests, both male and female. He was going to be all things to all men – and women. He kept a special welcome for the chaperones, for they were the secret to any success in the matchmaking stakes.

In his impromptu gymnasium, Samuel sweated with a medicine ball. He lay back on a bench and strained his muscles time after time as he lifted the ball from his chest until his arms were extended and locked. He was working on his strength now to add to his stamina training. He grunted with each strained movement, expelling the air from his lungs through his teeth as he did so. It was cold in the room but he was wrapped in several layers of clothing and so he sweated profusely. He had taken his daily emetic just before lunch, but now he was well into his afternoon training, when there was a rap on the door. He stopped and listened intently, unsure if he had heard it over his own grunting. There was a second rap. 'Come' he shouted and heaved the ball skywards again, locking his arms and then holding it. He had expected it to be one of the servants, and had not bothered to stop what he was doing or even to look around. He became aware that somebody had quietly entered the room, closed the door and now leaned against the doorway. He tried to look without releasing the ball but the strain was growing. 'Speak up then,' he croaked, but there was no answer. He yelled again, 'Speak up,' but then had to release his effort and the ball descended to his chest and then rolled over and on to the floor with a muffled thud. He swivelled in his seat and sat up, about to give somebody a piece of his mind, when the identity of the caller became evident to him. Leaning against the doorframe and smiling mischievously was John Campbell-John.

'Oh it's you,' said Samuel casually, trying to hide his surprise. 'What are you doing here?'

'Come to keep my eye on you Sammy boy.'

'Don't need you to do that,' said Samuel wiping the sweat from his arms and neck.

'Have you missed me Sammy lad?' said John roguishly.

'It's certainly been quiet without you,' Samuel, laid back again with the medicine ball on his chest.

'You mean it's been dull?'

'Aye, it's been that as well, but perhaps dull is what I need at the present.'

'Nobody needs that,' said John. 'Remember Sammy, laugh and the world laughs with you, cry and...'

'I know,' said Samuel finishing for him, 'cry and you have to blow your nose.' He had heard John say it so many times before.

'Why did you run away?' asked John.

'I didn't run away. I left you a note.'

'Oh, the note,' said John, 'need to take care of this and take care of that.'

'I take my responsibilities seriously even if you don't.'

'Stop trying to carry the world on your shoulders,' said John, 'you're only twenty-four; wait till you're twenty-five.' He chuckled to himself, but Samuel didn't respond. 'So what have you been doing about *your* responsibilities then,' he added.

Samuel frowned, 'I've been giving Rebecca some support with the businesses - a job, I might add, that you are being paid to do.'

'And what help have you been able to give?' John asked mockingly.

'Yes, you're right,' said Samuel, 'not enough because I've been training for the pitched battle with Charlie Sweep.'

'And is your training going well?'

'It is now that I've sweated John Barleycorn out of my system, no thanks to you.'

'He's good company when he's around, though isn't he?' said John. 'Old Johnny is always good for a merrymaking.'

'Aye he is that, but he always overstays his welcome,' said Samuel laconically. 'The bugger doesn't know when to go home,' he added, smiling at John's robust laughter 'So why are you really here?'

'I'm here as a guest. I'm looking for a wife *don't y'know*,' John added affectedly.

'Oh la-di-da,' said Samuel, but then he paused as he realised what John had implied. He continued with surprise evident in his tone. 'You're *not* part of the house party are you?'

'And why should that surprise you, Sammy lad?' John feigned indignation.

'Yes you're right - nothing you do should surprise me,' said Samuel, 'but it's a bit out of your league isn't it?'

'Pon my sole,' said John, using his affected voice again, 'what are you suggesting, Sir?'

'I'm suggesting, Sir, that you are a gambler, a drunkard, and a wastrel and you've no title either!'

'Got me in one, Sammy,' John laughed with mock self-deprecation, 'but what's the point you are making?'

'The point is that even your silver tongue can't change the rules of society.'

'You underestimate me, Sammy lad – old titles and new money are common enough companions.'

'But you've frittered away most of your money – it won't be long before it's all gone,' said Samuel, unaware that it was not only all gone but that his friend was again in substantial debt.

'But *they* don't know that. I'll behave as if I'm new wealth - and I have the finest wardrobe to assist me.'

'And I bet you haven't paid for that either.'

'A wicked suggestion,' mocked John. 'You'll be saying next that I'm only here for the free board and lodgings, and to eat Lord Cowden's food, drink his wine and de-flower his delectable guests!'

Samuel's face broke into the smile he was trying to withhold. 'You're a poxy scoundrel,' he said affably, adding, 'but you can forget about the de-flowering. As I understand it, all the eligible young ladies will be chaperoned.'

'I look upon it as challenge,' said John tongue in cheek.

'A challenge that even you won't be able to achieve.'

'Care to wager on that?'

'Oh no,' said Samuel, 'knowing you, you probably already have some cunning plan in mind.'

'Pon my sole, got me in one again,' mimicked John, 'if the *gals* are out of bounds, then I shall have to bed the chaperones, *don't y'know.*'

CHAPTER 24

Samuel was a mile into a three-mile cross-country run across Lord Cowden's estate. The spring sun shone brightly on a crisp April morning and memories of those foul winter runs were now diminishing in his mind. The sun was on his face and Tobias, the footman, ran at his shoulder and Samuel reluctantly admitted to himself that the company and the sunshine were inspiring. Over recent weeks his motivation had been purely from guilt. That sense of shame had been powerful though, and the hard running had acted as a form of exorcism. For the first time in weeks he smiled as he ran, and he looked around at Tobias to see that smile reflected back at him, mirrored in his companion's African features. The two of them were now beginning to leave behind the young gentlemen who trailed in their wake. An evening of over-indulgence: an excess of wine and a late night playing billiards and gambling, had left their mark and some of the young gentlemen were now struggling badly. The main house came into view, however, and the sight of the young ladies assembled to greet them had its own motivating force: none of them wanted to be seen as failing in the eyes of a prospective wife.

With about four hundred yards to go, Samuel's natural will to win surfaced, and without thinking he began to increase his pace, but Tobias matched him step for step. Imperceptibly the pace increased until Samuel's rational mind realised that Tobias had thrown down a minor challenge. He looked around again at the African to be greeted by a broad smile that confirmed his conclusion: 'Let's see what you're made of then,' Samuel thought to himself.

Tobias was twenty years old. He had not known that himself, but Lord Cowden had established it from the plantation's bloodstock records. The slaves from which his lordship derived his income were considered to be part of his livestock. Records of their origin, birth dates and vital statistics added value to any sales that were made, so were meticulously kept by the overseer.

Tobias was a naturally athletic specimen and he had been well nourished since being brought to England to work as a footman. He stood five feet eleven inches in height, three inches taller than Samuel, and he did not carry that massive bulk favoured by the pugilists of the day. Those men brought strength and resilience into the ring and the better ones brought good technique as well, but Tobias had been forged in a different furnace. He had linear and angular strength rather than bulk; Tobias's athleticism was built for speed and endurance and was very much in the mould of Samuel himself.

Samuel started to sprint when he was about a hundred yards from the impromptu finishing line, expecting to forge ahead, but Tobias again matched him. They ran step by step and Samuel looking around at his competitor now thought to himself: '*Let's see if you have that heart that Lord Cowden says you have.* The answer was to be immediately obvious. Samuel could not shake him off and in fact Tobias's longer stride took him inches ahead at the line. The ladies applauded politely, but their attention was more directed at the young gentlemen who were now coming into view and led surprisingly by John Campbell-John. Samuel's pride was bruised, but he also recognised that Tobias had run well. He slapped him heartily on the back, 'Well done, Sir,' he said. Tobias had never before been called 'Sir', and his brow furrowed in puzzlement. 'In the ring, Sir,' Samuel continued, panting heavily, 'when you think you are spent and you have no more to give – you have to find some more from somewhere. Do you think you can do that?'

'Aye, Master,' said Tobias enthusiastically, his rich bass tones resonating in just those two words.

'Then let us see,' said Samuel. 'Do you think you can do another circuit right now?' The idea was not attractive to Tobias. He had made no attempt to save anything as he had fought for the line. He was not going to reveal that, however. 'Aye, Master,' he said again.

'Then let us go, Sir,' said Samuel, setting off immediately and looking behind him to see if the footman responded. He hoped that he would not, for likewise, Samuel had not paced himself to go another circuit. The challenge had not come from any desire to further his protégé's training; it was just his natural will to win. He wanted to be the superior man, even at this level - though he would not have admitted that fact to himself.

Tobias also had that natural will to win – they were in fact two sides of the same coin. Whereas Samuel's background meant that he had always been in physical danger on the streets of London simply because he was a Jew, Tobias likewise, had always been in physical danger from the overseers, simply because he was a black slave. Such menace chipped away at most men, their spirit diminished, bit-by-bit, beating-by-beating, until they were cowed and servile and their spirit broken. A very few, however, reacted in the opposite way. With each beating another layer of obstinacy was put down, which by necessity may have been suppressed, but it was there nonetheless, festering below the surface like a reservoir of antagonism and when the sluices were opened it would flood forth in a cascade of uncontrolled violence. Even at this minor and agreeable level, Tobias did not want to concede, so he set off in pursuit of his tutor – neither man wanting to race, but both compelled to.

They tramped around the estate again, their levels of reserves diminished and tested to the full. Samuel had been in hard training for several weeks now and that conditioning put him at a definite advantage, enhanced by the fact that Tobias was running in ordinary shoes - but even so, the African would not concede and they ran side by side for another agonising two-and-a-half miles. They approached the Great Hall for a second time with the African spent, but he forced himself on step by step. He was weaving now, his gait rendered inefficient by fatigue and his unsuitable shoes, and Samuel eased himself a few yards ahead and maintained his lead to the finish. The young ladies and gentlemen applauded, the young gentlemen in particular, now aware of the effort it must have taken to reach the finish. Samuel acknowledged their applause, the showman within him still able to react, before falling to his knees in exhaustion. Tobias noticed this; showmanship had never been part of his fighting ethos, but he was envious of what he saw. He wanted more of it.

The two men retched for breath, their bodies demanding great gulps of oxygen. Samuel looked around at Tobias with respect for his athleticism, but even more so for his spirit. He held out his arm to draw the attention of the house party guests to him and they responded by redirecting their appreciation, now quite strangely, to the servant. Samuel gestured to Tobias to acknowledge that applause and he did so modestly raising is right arm slightly, but shyly, knowing his place as a servant.

Tobias also wanted to reciprocate that respect to Samuel, but he found it hard to display it. All his life he had had to hide his feelings, being taught never to look a white man in the eyes. Now here was a man who was his physical equal, and had even called him 'Sir'. It was the start of a bond that would form between the two men over the next few weeks.

An impromptu ring had been erected on the lawn in front of the great house and for the next hour Samuel schooled the young gentlemen in the noble science. He was used to such schooling at his

Academy, of course, but he also proved to be a considerate tutor, aware of the needs of these young gentlemen in the marriage stakes. He did not set man against man so that some would be seen to be lacking. Each man sparred against Samuel, knowing that he had the ability to block any punches that they could throw at him. If a demonstration was required he used John, who had been part of his act and knew the routine. It also gave John Campbell-John an advantage in the eyes of the young ladies, not that Samuel was concerned about that.

Samuel normally took his luncheon alone with a specially prepared high protein meal, but today he invited Tobias to join him. The African was uncomfortable in sharing victuals with a white man, though had come to terms with it below stairs; he had come to realise that his place was with the other servants. This white man was not a servant, however, and so he sat as far away from Samuel as he could, avoiding eye contact and staring at the floor as he ate.

'Do you know what a Jew is?' asked Samuel sensing his discomfort.

'No Sir, Master,' said Tobias shaking his head.

'I am a Jew, Tobias,' said Samuel trying in vain to engage him in conversation, but Tobias did not respond. Samuel tried again, 'Do you believe in God?'

'Yes, Master.'

'Have you read your Bible?'

'I'm just learning to read, Sir, but we went to services on the plantation. I know my scriptures, Sir.'

'So you know what a Hebrew is?' said Samuel.

'Yes Sir, Jesus was a Hebrew – it was them that crucified him.'

Samuel sighed heavily. It was an age-old accusation of Jews that led to the anti-Semitism Samuel had witnessed so many times, but he could see that this naive man had made it in innocence and, unusually, he did not take offence. 'Well a Jew is a kind of Hebrew, Tobias.' When the African looked at him, unsure of himself, Samuel added, 'You are a Christian, Tobias, I am not.'

'You are a heathen!' Tobias was horrified.

'Well, not exactly,' chuckled Samuel, 'my people worship the same god as you do, but we see Jesus only as a prophet. Do you understand?'

'I think so,' said Tobias, not sure where this conversation was going.

'Christians tend not to like Jews very much and that's why I learned to fight – I had to protect myself. I think we have that in common.'

Tobias was not convinced, but he kept his council to himself.

'Fighting can bring you respect Tobias – I have found that. It gets you past people's prejudices. Do you understand what I am getting at?'

The African again did not respond, and for ten minutes or so they ate without speaking, in an uncomfortable silence. The respect the African had felt for Samuel only an hour before had somehow cooled as the adrenalin in his bloodstream dissipated, to be replaced again with caution and suspicion. Aware of this, Samuel felt that he needed to renew his efforts.

'What is your family name?' he asked. The African looked at him blankly, his lack of understanding plain to see. 'Your other name,' Samuel prompted, but again the African did not understand. Samuel tried again: 'What were your parents called?'

'Jonah and Martha,' said Tobias.

'Jonah and Martha what?' Tobias still did not know how to respond.

'Just Jonah and Martha,' he stuttered after a few seconds. 'Slaves only have one name, Sir.'

'What name is shown here in the Master's wages book for you?'

'I'm just Tobias.'

'What do the other servants call you?'

A broad smile now crossed the African's face. 'Toby, Sir,' he said enthusiastically.

'You like that name don't you?'

'Oh yes, Sir – that's what my momma used to call me.'

'Then Toby it is,' said Samuel, 'but you will need a proper name if you're going to be a famous fighter - I think "Toby Tobias" has a ring to it. What do you think about that?'

The African grinned back at Samuel for a few moments. 'Toby Tobias,' he mumbled to himself and then repeated it over and over again changing the emphasis on the different syllables as he did so. He then turned and looked directly at Samuel as if seeking permission. 'Can I do this?' he asked respectfully.

I don't see why not,' said Samuel. He then stood and walked over to Toby and held out his hand. Toby had seen men shaking hands before but had never been offered someone's hand himself. 'Mr Toby Tobias, how do you do, Sir,' said Samuel.

Toby took his hand and shook it exaggeratedly five or six times. 'Mr Samuel Medina, Sir,' said the African, 'how do you do.'

'Bravo, Sir,' said Samuel and both men laughed.

John Campbell-John looked intently at Lord Cowden trying to catch his eye over the dinner table. When he did so he gestured with his glass and both men raised their wine glasses to be joined by the other diners. He knew that at the dinner table it was not the custom to drink alone – one had to catch the eye of another diner and then all the diners would drink together, the gentlemen draining their glasses in one go since it was regarded as the manly thing to do. Samuel had agreed to dine with the other guests and was forced to drain his glass out of politeness, but was secretly angry with John who clearly had no intention of considering his needs. Samuel wanted to cleanse his body of alcohol, but John wanted nothing less than to indulge himself.

John Campbell-John dominated the conversation over dinner. He was clearly by far the wittiest of the young gentlemen and the most handsome, as well as the best dressed, and the young ladies giggled at his yarns. If wealth and status had not mattered then he would have been the leading candidate in the marriage stakes. In fact he was causing some of the chaperones problems as their charges were beginning to look enviously at him rather than at the young gentlemen of higher status with whom they were intent on making a match. But then John had gone out of his way to charm the chaperones as well, as he had boasted to Samuel that he would.

Toby was helping to serve the meal. He was now well groomed again and in his smart green livery and white wig. He leaned respectfully beside Lord Cowden placing the next course in front of him. Thus reminded of his protégé and keen to know of his progress, his lordship addressed Samuel, 'Pray tell me how the young buck got on today, Medina.' His wife, dismayed, glared at her husband, but he affected not to notice.

Toby looked at Samuel with embarrassment, and then at Lord Cowden, who continued, 'I hope you acquitted yourself well today, Tobias. I'm not feeding you with the best of everything just to fatten you up y'know.'

'Yes Master,' mumbled Toby, not sure if he was supposed to respond or not.

Samuel came to his rescue. 'You were right about his spirit,' he said. 'He seems to have a fighter's heart alright.'

'Splendid, splendid,' boomed Lord Cowden. 'You sparred with him yet?'

'Tomorrow, My Lord, then we'll see if he can learn some technique to go with that spirit.'

'Ya hear that Tobias?' said Lord Cowden condescendingly and without waiting for a response, 'now see that you do, d'ya hear.'

'Yes Master,' said Toby.

'This is no subject for the dinner table,' said Lady Cowden, 'the ladies have no interest whatsoever in men fighting.

'You're so right,' smarmed John playfully, 'but let's spare a thought for poor Tobias here.' All eyes turned to John sensing the mischief in his tone. 'I know Samuel Medina well and he is a stout fellow, but I fear the poor black boy will be rigid with boredom after a few days in his company.'

'Why so, Sir?' asked one of the other young gentlemen.

'He is always in so much earnest - he is such an intense sort of chap. Why if pistols were seriousness then he'd be a blunderbuss.' The quip brought forth laughter and the gentlemen slapped the table to show their approval. It was a cruel jibe, but delivered with aplomb. Samuel's reaction to such a taunt would normally have been to offer a challenge, but he was used to them from John and he accepted them from his friend. He searched for a suitable riposte.

'And if wit was a pistol John Campbell-John, then you'd be pea-shooter,' he said. It wasn't the sharpest of responses, but it was a statement that throughout the meal he would not be the butt of John's acerbic tongue.

'Touché,' said John charmingly and slapped the table. The other guests responded and Samuel nodded his acknowledgement. 'Of course the venerable Mr Medina is right,' continued John, now intent on combining his wit with his charm, 'before you criticize someone, you should walk a mile in their shoes.' All eyes fell on John in anticipation, expecting a follow up line. He did not disappoint them: 'That way, when you criticize them, you're a mile away and you have their shoes.'

Laughter broke out again for John was on good form. 'Good show Campbell-John,' snorted Lord Cowden.

'Why thank you, My Lord,' said John, milking the accolade. He saw the look on the faces of the ladies, both the marriage candidates and the chaperones. Multiple eyes fluttered in practised modesty, but in reality John saw desire in them. Even Lady Cowden, who was too old to be a target and was throwing the expensive house party for the purpose of making a match for her nephew, revelled in his performance. It was bordering on adoration. He knew that wit was a much prized quality in a man and he had clearly demonstrated that quality, but now he wanted to widen his performance to show that he was a man of honour.

'Pon my soul though,' he said, 'but I fear my jibe may have wounded my good friend Mr Medina, and he is the most admirable of men. I think I must put on record that I know him to be a man of the highest character.

'Well said, Sir' said one of the young gentlemen, and the others joined in. John saw his opportunity to milk this further. 'And you know ladies and gentlemen – do you know what you would get if you sold *this* man's character.'

'What would you get Campbell-John?' asked Lord Cowden, instinctively playing his part in the charade.

'Why sir it would be sold at a premium,' said John. He was manipulating the conversation like an artist creating a work of art. This was his territory and he could paint with words to fashion the most imaginative of canvases. But those canvases were not representational or allegories. His canvases were an illusion and represented a reality of his own making. Everything about John Campbell-John was a fake, but he believed in his own superiority and the gullibility of those of high rank. His performance was one of light and shade. He had used acerbic wit to put Samuel Medina down, but then by praising his character he was able to wallow in a kind of reflected honour. The night belonged to him.

After the meal they were entertained by a silhouettist who skilfully cut out their images in black card. The evening was genteel and both sexes played their part by behaving with the best of manners. John Campbell-John was keen that a pair of silhouettes be done of Samuel and himself and Samuel was happy to oblige.

The gentlemen repaired to the games room after the ladies had retired: their boots clip-clopping on the wooden floor as they filed in. A long carpet runner bisected the floor, but it did little to muffle the sound of boot on wood for they simply skirted around it. The room was naturally bright, with a cream and patterned wallpaper, but now that the sun had gone down, the brightness was negated by the inadequacy of the candlelight. There was an aroma of wood and polish, mixed with tobacco and candle wax. Great portraits of male ancestors looked down sternly upon them from their elevated hangings so that the room had a masculine ambiance.

Lord Cowden leant against a large globe on a stand and called for wine. A servant arrived almost immediately having anticipated the request, and placed a well-stocked tray on a side table. Under Cowden's weight the globe spun slightly in its hefty stand and he stumbled forward, his awkwardness accentuated by his inebriation. Undignified, he righted himself clumsily and waved the servant away. 'Help yourselves, gentlemen,' he slurred, but no one cared that he was already drunk; they were all now intent on an evening's gambling and drinking. The Prince of Wales had shown the country how to party, and these young men needed little encouragement to follow his lead.

A game of billiards was started, but the card table was the main attraction and they gathered round it. Before they began to play, however, all the vulgarity within them that had been restrained at the dinner table was intent on bursting out. They knew that swearing in front of the ladies was considered a breach of good behaviour, but now that the young gentlemen were alone together they were free to talk dirty, get drunk and gamble – that is what they did. The cards would have to wait for this.

They all talked about the young ladies as if they were livestock: who had the best bosom, who had the best rear and who had the best thighs for the marriage bed. Bosoms were on display; legs were not, but the young gentlemen had taken great pleasure after the afternoon's race, in eying the respective female torsos – particularly when the wind pressed their clothes tight against their delightful forms. This was in no way a precise study, of course, but it gave an indication of the female thigh beneath the dress and this was enough to fill their fevered minds, so that their fantasies ran wild. With extreme vulgarity the young ladies were now openly and rudely compared with each other. The gentlemen shared pinches of their own blends of snuff as they talked and an air of rowdiness quickly took hold.

Samuel smiled to himself as he watched those prized good manners quickly drain away. The sound of the snorting of snuff was interspersed with the rasps of farting and the gulping of wine. John spiced the evening with a vulgar joke and the obligatory guffaws rang out. If a joke was vulgar somehow it required a different form of laugh in response; a chuckle, a giggle or a snigger was strong enough. It required the full-blown guffaw to do it justice. Samuel knew where the evening was heading. A few short weeks ago he would have been a willing participant, but now he made his apologies and retired to bed.

John ribbed him mercilessly but he was not upset to see him go; the evening would be less restrained without him. Lord Cowden felt no need to keep the young gentlemen in check or remind them of their manners. He was himself a man who had never really matured and he was intent in joining any such revelry. Maturity was the province of his wife; he would have been penniless years ago had it not been for her.

The card game was started, but was interrupted after a few hands. John had returned surreptitiously to the games room after a visit to his private room. On his return he carried under his arm a large leather-bound book. His demeanour was furtive - like a naughty boy up to no good. In reality that was exactly what he was doing; the book contained pornography. Numerous drawings of scenes of erotica were enclosed for the *discerning* gentleman. This was expensive and quality merchandise, but it was crudely published underground for the contents were explicit.

It was pawed over by all those present, the gaming being temporarily forgotten. The drawings were representations of ladies of social standing, not coarse wenches. They were exposed in salacious detail, usually in the act of intercourse with gentlemen of rank. The more shocking it was the better they like it. Vicars and nuns were especially popular. Pages that were already well dog-eared from previous maulings now had another evening's pawing added to them. Language descended down into even more crudity. 'Why that nun has a quim like a ripe date,' said a young gentlemen, 'who could have imagined such a thing.'

'Why, the rampant vicar,' said another to boisterous laughter and the swilling of wine; 'why, his member is stood like a gunner's ramrod.'

'Why, I think I recognise this lady,' said another young gentleman turning a new page. 'I think the model could be Lady Adele Fitzsymons, don't y'think?'

'But is it her face or her quim that you recognise, Sir,' snorted Cowden to more guffaws.

John Campbell-John could not let such an opportunity pass him by and mocked the young gentlemen with a riposte. 'I'll wager ten guineas that the young sir wouldn't recognise Lady Adele's quim if he saw it. Why, such a quim would surely be too much for an inexperienced knave such as him!'

Hoots of derision erupted at the put down and John waited until it died down slightly before producing the tag line. 'Why, I do believe that such a quim would devour him whole should he attempt to mount such a voracious creature.'

John revelled in his wit and the fact that he had established dominance over the others. He slapped the young gentleman on the back to show that he was a stout-hearted fellow and meant him no harm, then clinked his glass so that they drained their glasses together. The mood was re-established; the revelry would continue into the night.

CHAPTER 25

There was a morning chill in the air, but the sun had begun its day's work and the lingering mist was now beginning to burn off. It was just after nine, and Samuel was throwing sand on the turf that served as the floor of his impromptu ring that had had been assembled on Lord Cowden's lawn. It was slippery with the morning dew, and he did not want to injure either himself or any of the young gentlemen. They were scheduled to start at half-past-eleven, and Samuel therefore had time to work out with Toby.

The African had arrived on time after completing his breakfast duties, and had been given the rest of the morning off by Lord Cowden. He had discarded his livery frock coat and his powdered wig and wore only his breeches, stockings and a shirt, the sleeves of which were rolled high up his powerful arms so that his biceps bulged tightly against them. He had taken to shaving his head, after repeated scoldings from the butler for scratching his head through the wig; his wiry hair made it itch uncontrollably. His black skin shone in the morning sunlight as if he were a bronzed statue freshly polished to reveal its patina. There were similarities between the two men in physique. Neither was barrel-chested, their power coming from below the waist, which also gave them their mobility. But there the similarity ended. Samuel's power was in his thighs, whereas Toby's was centred in his commanding buttocks. He had that natural athletic build that turned eyes in admiration.

Samuel gave him some shadow boxing exercises and liked what he saw. He watched intently as Toby moved about the ring, his agility and natural hand speed suggesting that he would be a formidable pugilist. As the sweat began to form on Toby's arms and face, it reflected the glinting sunlight so that he appeared to twinkle like a bright star in the night sky. But then - all the grace and elegance of the natural athlete disappeared in an instant the moment Samuel entered the ring to spar with him. At the command of *Box!* Toby lurched at his opponent with a frenzy that initially took Samuel by surprise. His attention had been momentarily diverted as he was still adjusting his mufflers: the padded gloves Broughton had invented for use in training and exhibitions were a useful protection and Samuel insisted they were worn for sparring. Nevertheless, he parried the first of the punches aimed at him by Toby, and then retreated backwards along a diagonal to take him out of range. The second punch was a crude round arm swing that punched thin air and missed Samuel by at least two feet, but the effort put into the punch spun Toby round and off his feet so that he sprawled uncontrollably to the floor. Samuel offered a hand to help him to his feet, but the African, declining the offer by his actions, sprang to his feet and launched himself again at Samuel. Samuel swayed away from another attempted punch, but his gentlemanly offer had brought him within range and he could not totally avoid it this time. The punch glanced off the top of his head, but it had been delivered incorrectly with the inside of the hand so that the venom was negated and it represented no more than a slap.

But the relentless attack was maintained without respite and Samuel took to retreating and parrying the shots so that he could observe his opponent as he did so. He prided himself that he was a master of balance; he could move backwards or forward effortlessly, but Samuel was also confident that he could control his opponent at close fighting because he had the parrying skills to negate any punches thrown in his direction. The attacks were crude and easily controlled, but it quickly became apparent that Toby had two major advantages that he took with him into the ring. The first was his stamina, for after twelve minutes of sparring at full velocity there was no let up in the attacks, however unsophisticated they were. The second was the length of Toby's arms that gave him a distinct advantage over Samuel, and would over most of his proposed opponents in the future. His guard would keep them at a distance, and would allow his own blows, by reaching further, to be struck with more force.

For a while Samuel observed all this and made no attempt to throw back any meaningful punches, being content merely to parry and observe Toby at close hand. Sweat dripped from both their faces for the workout held nothing back. After fifteen minutes Samuel cried, 'HALT!' raising his arm as he did so. He looked into the eyes of the African and saw, from the raw aggression still reflected back at him, that a further strength was apparent - focus. This amiable and good-natured man had the ability to focus, to put his natural characteristics into a box and bury them in some dark, shadowy place for the duration of a fight. He was able to concentrate fully on the fight and cast everything else from his mind.

For some moments Toby did not respond to Samuel's cry and maintaining his fighting stance he raised his fist to punch. Samuel reinforced his instruction with a barked, 'TOBY - END!' and at last the black man relaxed his posture. Samuel approached and put his hand on Toby's shoulder, his body language conciliatory trying to reinforce his position as the tutor and not the opponent.

'Have you ever had any instruction before?' asked Samuel. He had not observed any indication of technique in Toby's performance.

'Aye,' Toby said, 'the overseer on the plantation.'

'And what did he teach you?'

Toby looked puzzled for a moment as he struggled to find an answer to that question. 'He – he told me to be the *guvna*, Sir.'

'The governor,' said Samuel, 'and were you the governor just now?'

'Oh yes Sir,' Toby replied, a proud smile lighting his features.

'And how many times do you think you landed a blow on me?'

'I don't know - did I hurt you, Master, Sir?' Toby said almost apologetically.

'You didn't land a single telling blow, Toby,' said Samuel harshly. 'You have never been taught any technique. We have a lot of work to do, you and I. You have to learn to parry and defend as well as attack.' Samuel looked and saw the disbelief in the African's eyes. 'We will spar again, but this time every time you leave yourself open I will counter and hit you.'

Toby nodded his agreement, for in his own mind his invulnerability was undiminished.

At the command of *Box!* Toby again rushed in. His actions could not have been more announced if he had published them beforehand. He had spent his whole life being unnaturally subservient and compliant. That was what the plantation owners had demanded of him, reinforcing their demands with the whip if he strayed from the path. The pain had taught him to be submissive, but it had never removed that spark of defiance within him. It had made him a problem for the overseers for that spark would sometimes ignite and unleash a spontaneous response before his conscious obedient mind could resist it. His punishment was a whipping, but because of his rebelliousness the overseers had introduced him to fighting! They had not done so out of any altruistic motives, but paradoxically his behaviour had improved. They had given him an opportunity to release all the suppressed aggression within him. When he was fighting it would burst into life. It was not just that he was allowed to beat his opponent – he was positively encouraged to do so. Samuel thought he was like a caged animal suddenly released into the wild.

But he also saw that it was a problem; Toby had developed a boxing style that was totally one-dimensional. His opponent would be able to read him like a book; know exactly what he would do.

Toby's first attempted punch was a great swinging overhead right hand. Samuel was not taken by surprise this time, but he made no attempt to move backwards out of range. He simply moved slightly to his left and easily evaded the punch. This left Toby almost defenceless, the missed punch having turned his body away from his opponent. To regain any sort of guard he would have to recoil his body, but Samuel would deny him any such luxury. By remaining in range he was able to counter and he did so with a short downward right of his own that hit Toby on the side of his head just above his ear. Samuel had not used full force and the punch would not have downed an opponent, but it supplemented Toby's own momentum and he was sent sprawling to the floor. The same manoeuvre was repeated three or four times, with both the left and the right hands, but each time Toby responded by becoming more and more uncontrolled and consequently even easier to hit. His eyes bulged with rage as he redoubled his efforts but his rational brain was not working and he was learning nothing from the experience.

'Halt!' Samuel cried, and then again, 'HALT!' as his first instruction had not been assimilated. Toby eventually rested his stance and reason again entered his consciousness. A small crimson trail of blood snaked down from his mouth to his chin and dripped onto his gleaming chest. The gloves, however crude, had saved him from further punishment. Bare knuckles would have left him much more lacerated. Toby looked down at the blood droplets and then involuntarily wiped the blood from his lips with his glove and stared down at it. He was transfixed for several moments by this crimson stain on his gloved hand, and with that his own inadequacies crystallised in his mind. He turned and walked to a corner and bowed his head, shame suddenly taking him. In his mind fighting was the only thing that made him special and that had been taken away from him by a sound beating. It did not matter to him that they had only been sparring.

Samuel sensed the man's dejection. What he had done to Toby may have seemed unkind, but it was what he had intended. If he was to succeed as the African's trainer he had to dismantle his modus of fighting and then rebuild it again. But he also had to prove to Toby that aggression on its own was not enough and that whatever methods the overseers had taught him were inadequate. He walked

288

over to the African and put a soothing hand on his shoulder. 'Take a rest awhile,' he said gently.

Toby put his arms on the top of the ropes and hung his face between them. His feeling of shame was overpowering and he felt that he could not show his face to his opponent. His ancestry had been denied him by slavery but his bloodline was intact and had given him an inheritance. For generations his people had been warriors, and victories had been worn like badges of honour. Status in the tribe was based on such valour in battle, and conversely status was denied by a lack of it. Samuel had stripped him of his status and he now bore that dishonour heavily.

'Toby,' said Samuel soothingly, but again the African did not respond. 'We need to talk, Toby.' Toby ignored him, unable to look him in the eyes. Samuel physically turned him round and put his hands on his shoulders. 'Look at me,' he said, but Toby just stood before him, his head bowed, contrite and now totally malleable, the perspiration dripping from his chin turned slightly pink by the blood it encountered on its journey. But then Samuel noticed that it was tears and not sweat and that Toby's shoulders had begun to heave as his despair became uncontrollable. To an Englishman such a display of emotion would have been regarded as unmanly. Samuel was English, but he was also a Jew and his Jewishness was sufficient to override this. 'What is it Toby?' he asked kindly.

At first there was no response, but then it was as though a floodgate had been opened. 'I can't fight, Master, that is now obvious to me,' Toby said, his gaze still rooted on the ground. 'I know that now. Thank you for teaching me that.' He was trying to behave like an Englishman should, and in his mind he felt that he was not even doing that with any manliness.

Samuel searched for the words to console him. 'Have you ever been to the races Toby?' he asked.

'Yes Master,' said Toby, puzzled by the question, 'I've been with his Lordship.'

'Are the horses not magnificent animals?'

'Aye Master, they are that,' Toby sniffled, dabbing his runny nose with his gloves as he spoke.

'Aye, they are bred to it, Toby - but they still need training. Breeding has given them natural talent, but it has to be brought out of them.' Samuel could see from the African's expression that he did not understand the analogy. He tried again, 'Don't you see? An untrained racehorse will not win races but it's still a racehorse. It's not

289

a pack horse – you can train a pack horse, but you can't make it win races. Do you understand what I am saying, Toby?'

Toby began to see what Samuel meant and was able at last to look his tutor in the eyes, the glimmer of a new respect shining in the depths of his own as slowly he nodded. 'Aye, I think so, Sir – I'm not a pack horse?'

'No – no, of course you're not. You are a magnificent racehorse, but you have to be schooled in the profession that you are entering. Do you know what they call fighting?'

'Aye master, it's called pugilism.'

'Aye it is that, but it's also called "The Noble Science", Toby - and we need to teach you that science. You will have to study hard but you can do it. You are being taught how to read and write aren't you? And I'll teach you the science of fighting.' The words brought the hint of a smile from the African – he was desperate to be a fighter.

For the next hour he was schooled in boxing techniques - how to move in and out of range, how to parry, and how to counter. Toby had mixed emotions about the experience. He so desperately wanted to learn, but he found it so hard. He had always fought by instinct and these techniques seemed so unnatural to him. Samuel tied his hands behind his back and asked him to avoid punches by movement along a diagonal and the side-to-side movement of his upper body. This was a help, but even then instinct took over and at times he would surge forward using his head as a weapon rather that try to avoid his opponent. He was beginning to learn, however – he was now on the road to fighting enlightenment, he just did not know it yet.

With no sign of embarrassment, John Campbell-John lay naked on top of the bed. He was sharing a room but this was neither his bed nor his bedroom. The sounds of blows and grunts drifted into his consciousness and brought him out of his light sleep. He could hear the sounds of toil coming from outside the window on the lawn in front of the bedroom where Samuel and Toby were sparring. Shafts of sunlight pierced chinks in the voluminous curtains, one of which fell on a large long-case clock that ticked away unhurriedly and unrelentingly in the corner. John twisted his neck, straining to see the time, his head falling back on the pillow with a muted thud, disheartened to see it was already fifteen minutes to eleven. He was due to make an appearance at half past in that same ring, but he had

had a heavy night and his body was rebelling against the thought. Alcohol, gambling and wenching were no strangers to him, but they took their toll, even on a naturally athletic man such as he.

But it was more than an appearance that was called for. It was an inspection. The young ladies would be there and supposedly so too would the chaperones. He took a deep intake of breath in an effort to fill his lungs and bloodstream with oxygen, and then attempted to rise. He failed. He was pinned to the bed by the ample, and also naked, rubinesque body of one of the chaperones. He tried to move her arm so that he could slide sideways out of her bed, but she roused herself just enough to put the arm back again, holding him more tightly than before. She then also rolled over so that now her leg straddled his legs and the restraining was more complete.

Margaret Moorhead was the wealthy widow of a wool merchant. Her widowhood had commenced five years earlier, at the age of 35, when her 62-year-old husband had passed away, having cut a finger whilst checking the condition of a wool consignment. It had seemed such an inconsequential wound and he had thought nothing about it, but then it turned bad: started to irritate and then to fester, but much worse was to come and it developed into full-blown blood poisoning. He died within days, leaving Margaret an extremely wealthy woman. Wealth was no stranger to her, however; it was something she had grown up with. Her father had also been a wool merchant and her marriage had been one of convenience – a merging of family businesses and wealth. Nevertheless, he had made her a good husband and likewise she had been a respectable and dutiful wife to him, bearing him two sons along the way. She had been forced to marry a much older man out of duty and it was accepted that it was a good match, but now her affluence and new status presented new opportunities for her: money was also acceptable for a match with a gentleman of higher status and this was now her quest – she was to aim high. She would remarry, and she had an aristocrat in mind. Acting as a chaperone was a step along the way. It brought her into contact with the titled people she was targeting. Acting as a chaperone, however, was paradoxically, on the face of it, not the obvious way to do it. These house parties were about finding partners for young gentlemen and ladies - not their chaperones - but it took her out of her world of provincial commerce into another world of privilege and refinement.

'I have to get up,' whispered John attempting to move, but Margaret clung to him. He tried again, 'You're supposed to be there as well you know – along with your charge?'

Margaret opened her eyes in resigned acknowledgement and released her grip on him, but before he could move she changed her mind and snuggled up to him again. 'Let's stay here,' she said into his chest.

'We have to play the game, Margaret,' encouraged John.

'Why,' said Margaret, 'It doesn't matter how much *you* impress the ladies, the chaperones don't see you as a good match. You have no money and little status.'

John had reluctantly also come to that conclusion, but it nevertheless came as a shock to hear it spoken out loud by a chaperone. 'But I *have* money, I have accumulated a great deal of money,' said John. He was lying.

'What – from gambling!' said Margaret disparagingly.

'Aye, I am an accomplished gambler,' he retorted.

'There's no such thing as far as I'm concerned. And anyway, look at your clothes, the finest quality I would say.'

'Aye they are that,' said John proudly, missing the point she was making.

'I thought so - you have that need to spend, soldier boy. You're a gambler *and* a spendthrift. *I'd* like to wager you've spent all you've won and that's the reason you are here. Am I right?'

'But the others don't know that,' retaliated John sardonically. 'And anyway, Miss Georgette is a possible match for me, don't you think?'

'No she's not – she's as poor as you are.' said Margaret. She looked at him wondering if he was serious. 'She's just the one that you'd like to bed most – and you know it. Her chaperone will be looking to marry her to a gentleman of higher status. It's much easier for a gentleman of wealth to take a pretty young thing like her as his wife than it is for a wealthy young lady to take an impoverished gentleman, no matter how handsome or witty he is.'

'But she is *such* a pretty young filly is she not? A fine bosom and a finely turned ankle,' said John coarsely. 'Wouldn't mind some horizontal refreshment with her, don't you know,' he added mockingly.

'Aye, and that's your problem. You and her are by far the most gifted and attractive, but you both want to improve yourselves, and so you must both rule each other out.'

John thought for a heartbeat. He already knew that truth. But he also saw an opportunity and he wasn't going to let it go by. 'I could marry *you*,' he said without further hesitation, but without really thinking it through. He would gladly trade the age difference for a secure and wealthy future. Margaret raised her head and looked at him with incredulity and he responded to that look with an indignant, 'Why not?'

'I had assumed we had an understanding, Captain John Campbell-John. You are a dalliance that is all. Where does marriage fit into this?'

'Aye, a dalliance on both our parts, but the thought just popped into my head,' said John. 'Is it so outrageous though? I promise you it wouldn't be a dull marriage.' He grinned at her with his naughty boy face.

Margaret, unable to stop herself from laughing, said, 'You'd have me bankrupt and stood before the King's Bench within eighteen months!'

'You wrong me, Madam,' he feigned indignation, but then that grin reappeared.

'Good try Sir, but you must know that I have other plans in mind on the matrimonial front.'

'Do tell,' said John intrigued. He turned over and rested himself on his elbow in anticipation.

She stared at him again for a few seconds knowing that it was unwise to confide in this man, but nevertheless she did so. 'Look,' she paused, 'I'm a wealthy widow. My late husband was much older than me, but he was a good man and I have two sons still to bring up – they will soon be young gentlemen. But I have done my duty once – I married for the sake of the business. Now I want to serve my own interests.'

'Then marry *me* this time round,' said John again, seizing on an opportunity.

'I wouldn't want you anywhere *near* my sons,' she said with a smile. 'You'd turn them into wastrels like you in a matter of weeks.'

'Why thank you, Milady,' he said turning an insult into a compliment. She too raised herself up on her elbow, laughing at his sassiness and slapped his face playfully. Her ample bosom vibrated to her laughs and his hand was somehow magnetically drawn to her nipple, which he caressed gently with his thumb. It was pleasurable and she looked down at the union, but she was not to be swayed by such transient pleasures.

'Look, John Campbell-John,' she said, 'I can see you for what you are. You are a rogue sir, a likeable rogue, I'll grant you that, but still a rogue all the same. You are looking to marry money and I wish you every success in your endeavour. But I am not to be your meal ticket.'

'But you are a-bed with me Madam - you cannot deny the attraction.'

'I deny nothing, Sir,' she said, 'I am a widow in a small Cotswold wool town. I live as a prominent person in a small community. My life is ruled by society's demands and I live as a widow is required to live. I have done that dutifully. I have mourned my late husband both privately and publically. I have raised my sons to be good Christians, and I have brought no shame on the family name. That means celibacy, sir, and I go alone to a cold bed each night.'

'So now you're off the leash, so to speak,' said John. He saw the look on her face change from amusement to disapproval and he realised that he had said the wrong thing.

'I am not a bitch on heat, Sir,' she said scornfully, 'if you see me as a desperate dried up old hag frantic for a good tupping then you are sadly mistaken.'

They were naked together, but suddenly she had evoked the rules of society and he now had to respond. He somehow managed to suggest a bow from his prone position, and with a smile and all the politeness required of a man of his station he said, 'Madam you humble servant. I did not intend any offence, but if I have offended you, then with all my heart I apologise for I have the utmost respect for you.'

She too bowed imperceptibly in recognition of his act of contrition. The rules of society had been fulfilled. 'I will admit to nothing more than a dalliance with you, Sir,' she reflected. 'This house party has given me the privacy to share a warm bed with a handsome young soldier. It's a pleasure that is denied me in my real life.' She paused for a heartbeat, 'but of course even that comes with dangers.'

'Dangers?'

'Aye dangers, Sir. Certainly a pregnancy out of wedlock would be a catastrophe for me.'

'Ah,' said John raising an eyebrow, 'the reason for the lamb's skin for my cock - you came well prepared Margaret.'

'It's called a "condom",' she said.

'Yes, I've heard of them, but never had the need for them before.'

'Then you should acquaint yourself. A gentleman should consider such things. You may keep that one. It will stop you from getting the pox.'

'Your humble servant Madam,' he said and then he tried his luck again with his naughty boy smile. She responded and against her will a smile fleetingly materialized in the corner of her mouth. She immediately and consciously did all she could to eliminate it but the damage was done and he knew that he had once again managed to wriggle himself away from trouble like an accomplished escapologist.

'You are such a rogue Sir,' she said with resignation.

'Why thank you again Madam,' he said pausing for that faint smile of amusement that would be the green light for him to probe further. It appeared as if on command and she emphasized her permission by again playfully slapping his face. 'And what are these marriage plans that you have?' he duly asked.

She knew it was unwise tell him, but she did so nonetheless. She sighed before she spoke. 'I'm no stranger to money, Sir - I was born into a wealthy family and I know the power of it. But my people are in trade and that has its own limitations. Status is a very elusive spirit. Just when you think you have its recognition it somehow climbs up some invisible ladder and is once again out of reach.'

'Ah – but we should all know our place,' said John drily. She looked at him with disbelief until he smiled impishly back at her.

'You rascal, Sir,' she said, before continuing her reflections. 'As you say, we are supposed to know our place, but…' she paused and looked at him as if those words somehow made her look at John in a different light. A realisation crystallised in her mind as if some truth was suddenly obvious to her. She realised the truth of it but then filed it away for a later occasion. She continued, 'but some people, some very few people manage to find loopholes and I want to be one of those very few people. I want my sons to rise to the very *highest* of rank.'

'Phew,' whistled John, 'you aim high Madam.' She smiled as if it were a compliment.

'Yes I do sir,' she said, 'I want to marry a title.'

'There is precedence I'll grant you that Madam. Impoverished aristocracy and new money are sometimes seen as acceptable by society. But it would be easier to do it through your children, surely – isn't that what these house parties are all about?'

'I'm aware of that, Sir,' she said, 'I have not wasted my time acting as a chaperone. I have studied how the system works.'

'So what's the problem?'

'The problem, Sir, is that I have no daughter.'

John looked at her puzzled for a moment, and then he realised what her dilemma was. 'Oh I see,' he said. 'If you marry your son to a duke's daughter, your grandchildren will not inherit the title – it'll go to the eldest son's children.'

'Exactly Sir, I want my son to inherit a title and my grandchildren and great-grandchildren to continue to inherit it.'

Margaret Moorhead was nothing if not astute and she had a clear plan in her mind. She was the eldest daughter of a wealthy wool merchant who had no sons. She had married another wealthy wool merchant and the joint business had prospered. The family had prospered further, becoming property owners in Gloucester, Stroud and Cirencester, but they had led a prudent provincial life. They had not maintained a London house nor had they travelled there for the season. Margaret was not just comfortably off, she was extraordinarily wealthy, and that wealth was intact, free from any debt. She had far more wealth than her hosts could have imagined, and she reasoned that the extent of that wealth gave her leverage. She was on the look out for something quite specific. She was looking for childless, unmarried titled man, who was desperately on the verge of bankruptcy. She knew that the law recognised that a wife's property belonged to her husband, so the degree of desperation must be sufficient for her to demand that the targeted title legally recognise her sons as his heirs before she agreed to the marriage that would clear his debts. She would get the lawyers to nail that down with the appropriate entailing deeds. She would also have the bulk of her wealth put into trust for her children until they came of age. This would have two beneficial effects: it would mean that the profligate aristocrat could not bring his new family to penury since it would deny him access to the bulk of that wealth. In addition, it would mean that when her sons reached their majority and inherited their mother's wealth from the trust, they would have a power over their stepfather since he would need their continued financial support.

There was no place in this plan for a dashing young military man. She could go right now to the debtor's prison and take her pick from any titled man there, any of whom would be prepared to take her in marriage, for that would clear their debts and obtain their release. Yes, she could that, and this was the proof of her reasoning. John

Campbell-John did not tick any of the boxes - she had a *mark* in mind, someone very specific.

Watching her face as she thought these things through for the hundredth time, John smiled. They were kindred spirits; he recognised her game plan and imperceptibly he nodded that recognition to her.

She smiled equally imperceptibly in acknowledgement of their mutual understanding.

That evening after dinner an entertainment had been arranged for the ladies and gentlemen of the house party. A young lady was to sing for them. The servants had arranged the chairs around the piano so that the facade of a small theatre had been intimated. The young lady played the piano delicately and with all the refinement that she undoubtedly possessed. John Campbell-John had recommended her to his hostess. She was a young lady of good breeding, from a good family, well educated and refined in the ways of society. But the family had fallen on hard times, and she was now forced to sing and play the piano to make a few guineas, for society afforded young ladies of her class little opportunity to earn money. Lady Cowden recognised the curse of falling on hard times; her own husband had threatened to do that to her all her married life. She readily agreed that the entertainment was a fine idea and the girl now playing before her was no disappointment.

She was such a slip of a girl, Lady Cowden thought, and much too delicate a creature to be forced to supplement her income in this way. She pondered whether she should find a husband for her. She did not set her sights very high for the girl. Yes, she was pretty enough but she brought no wealth to any union. Lady Cowden's estate steward was as yet unmarried; he was about thirty-five and that was a good age for prospective husband. A plan germinated in her mind as she listened.

The young lady cleared her throat delicately behind her white-gloved hand, in preparation for the first song. The first notes sounded pure but her sweet soprano voice had a quiver betraying the nervousness that she felt at appearing before her audience. Lady Cowden smiled to herself; she found it charming. Perhaps, she pondered to herself, the young woman could be hired as a governess to her great nephews and nieces – that was, of course, supposing that the house party was a success and she found her nephew a bride!

After a few couplets the young woman's voice strengthened, the quiver disappeared and her fine voice resounded around the room, its purity being enjoyed by all present. Abigail Fitzherbert was giving yet another masterful performance. If her singing was fine it was still overshadowed by her talents as an actress. She had created this persona of the delicate society maiden whose future had been torn from her by her squandering father. She was in no way, physically, a delicate woman herself, yet such were her powers of characterisation that she appeared to be just that.

Abigail glowed inwardly with pride at her own abilities. This performance however, was a prologue, an overture to a much grander performance – her party piece. This later performance was to be played out when the ladies had retired and the gentlemen's minds, fuelled by abundant alcohol, turned to baser thoughts and deeds. Aided and abetted by her erstwhile lover, John Campbell John, Abigail Fitzherbert had on her mind more that the few guineas she had been promised for singing and playing the piano. She smiled to herself, lowering her eyes demurely and allowing another small quiver to enter her voice.

CHAPTER 26

Edgar Jasper was born into a privileged aristocratic family, the third son of an Earl. He had had a start in life that most would envy. He was intelligent and well educated and he had the family wealth behind him. Yet, at the age of eighteen he had been disowned by his father – cast out penniless to fend for himself the best way that he could – and this is exactly what he had done. Now, a mere fifteen years on, he lived in a new, large and imposing building in the West End. His crime, for which his father would never forgive him, was to be a sodomite – he was a 'Molly'.

Although frowned upon, homosexuality was tolerated if discretion were used. Edgar was by no means the first nobleman to want to tup another man, and there were circumspect ways in which such men could satisfy their appetites. This option, however, was not open to Edgar Jasper; he was wildly effeminate and circumspection played no part in his character. To say that his homosexuality was *in your face* would be to substantially understate this. His own face was heavily powdered and he wore the most outrageous piece of felt on his cheek masquerading as a beauty spot. There was no blemish to cover as was the habit of many a lady; he simply revelled in the outrageous. His clothes were garish and gaudy and his cuffs were so long that they surpassed his heavily jewelled fingers and painted fingernails. His voice was not only effeminate it was loud; there was nothing subtle about Edgar Jasper – even his mincing gait was effeminate. He did not so much walk, he pranced and flounced. He was the living caricature of an effeminate man.

Whatever his appearance might suggest to the contrary, Edgar Jasper was no fool. He was a fine swordsman, a crack shot and an astute businessman. In his earlier days he had had to protect himself many times from the outrage that his homosexuality caused, but now he had wealth he paid for that protection and surrounded himself with large, burly men, who coincidentally were his particular pleasure. He existed on the edge of society, yet he was famous throughout London as 'Molly Jasper'. Everyone who was anyone knew of Molly Jasper's rooms.

Trouble was not tolerated at Molly Jasper's rooms: visitors were met first by a huge man at the front door; then by the footmen, who likewise were all heavily muscled. All the attendants were dressed in the finest livery, magnificent in black satin with gold braid and epaulettes. White stockings, white gloves and powdered white wigs were worn to set off the ensemble. Everything at Molly Jasper's was of the highest standard. It was a place where gentlemen could go to eat a fine quality meal. But it was much more than that – it was a brothel and a gambling den. The gambling and the whoring went on upstairs. The girls were the best in London. Gentlemen–could get a girl of any nationality, any colour and any race. Molly Jasper brought to his establishment a style that was unique throughout the city. Everything that was fashionable could be found at Molly Jasper's rooms: the best Dutch china; goldfish in large glass bowls; caged song-birds; exotic fruits such as pomegranates and pineapples to tempt your palate. Even the most depraved of activity was somehow given a veneer of culture. This was where the young bucks came to play, to gamble and to whore – whatever their tastes.

Molly Jasper was a natural businessman. He kept immaculate books, especially as to the gaming. The house took a percentage of all the gambling – they held the stakes and took a twelve-and-a-half per cent cut. But if a gentleman gambled at Molly Jasper's, he knew that his debts *had* to be paid. A debt to Molly Jasper was not comparable to debts a gentleman customarily owed to his gun maker, his saddler or his wine merchant. There was no shame in a gentleman owing money to the lower classes and it was not uncommon for such debts to be outstanding for many years. If he owed Molly Jasper, however, that debt had to be paid for it was bad for a gentleman's health if he did not pay his dues. This was an establishment where huge side bets were laid on horse races or pugilistic set-tos. Racehorse owners would put up their horses against each other and the house would hold the bet and guaranteed payment. Likewise, the patrons of the fighters would gamble their man against another's.

It was hardly surprising therefore, that such an establishment should be a lure for John Campbell-John. On the surface he fitted in perfectly. His clothes were of the finest that could be bought in London. He had dropped the pretence of being a soldier, with the new pretence of having sold his commission, but for effect he retained his fictitious rank of captain. Tonight he wore a maroon silk frockcoat, delicate lace cuffs flowing with his every arm movement. His style matched the opulence of the great room in which he and his contemporaries gambled. It was a collage of gilt and onyx and leather and murals and goldfish bowls and fine furniture. It had a myriad of smells, of wood and leather, musk, spices and incense. It was what John Campbell-John was all about. It was a fantasyland for a man who lived in a fantasy. Despite his massive debts, he continued to live and to spend with abandon. Today he had the best part of a hundred pounds as a stake - his cut of Abigail's auction- and he wanted to play in the highest stakes' game in town.

A footman led John to his table and he ordered claret for himself. His three opponents were already seated and his eyes lit up to see that one of them was Sir Oliver Ruddle. Ruddle thought himself a fine player, but in reality John knew that he fooled himself. If lady luck gave him a good hand the man would play it with reasonable competence and this was enough to sustain his delusion. John was a cunning man and saw Ruddle as a mark whom he could systematically bleed as the evening wore on. The other two were unknown to him, but the game would be for high stakes and he afforded them respect. 'Welcome gentlemen,' he said.

'A pox on you Campbell-John,' said Ruddle with his usual belligerence, 'just sit down and let's play cards.' The man was rude and antagonistic at the best of times, but he was also a vengeful man and he saw John Campbell-John as a man that was owed. In that balance sheet of life, John Campbell-John's name was firmly in Ruddle's liabilities' column – and Samuel Medina's was not far behind. In his jaundiced eyes, both men had cost him a good deal of money, not to mention humiliation.

'Capital idea,' said John, meeting rudeness with charm so that Ruddle looked vulgar and boorish. John flicked the tails of his frockcoat purposefully behind him as he sat and then adjusted his cuffs. 'Whist is it to be, gentlemen?'

The cards were dealt, but Ruddle was still intent of goading John. 'Talking of the pox, Campbell-John, I hear that you have had a visit from Senor Gonorrhoea.' He wheezed a laugh. He knew nothing of the sort but he enjoyed the put-down and his shoulders rose and fell in unison with his laugh. 'Senor Gonorrhoea, what!' he wheezed again.

'The Senor is a friend of the lower classes, Ruddle,' said John dismissively, 'I move in much higher circles. I do find ladies of breeding have such good conversation after a good tupping, don't you? Such delightful company too.'

'I always suspected that of you,' said Ruddle, 'got more by your prick than your practice.' Ruddle again wheezed at his own wit.

'But a gentleman nowadays must respect the lady and look after himself as well,' said John. 'We all know, as you say, that cupid can leave us with that nasty sting.'

'What on earth are you blathering on about man?' Ruddle frowned.

'Why, condoms, Sir,' said John.

'Condoms! What's a blithering condom,' said Ruddle.

John feigned surprise that Ruddle had not heard of them. 'They prevent a pregnancy and at the same time protect a gentleman from both the French pox and the Senor, don't y'know.'

'Do they indeed,' said Ruddle his curiosity suddenly aroused. He had heard that syphilis - the French pox - addled the brain and being able to protect oneself against it seemed like a good idea. As it happened, unbeknownst to him he already had the disease having contracted it many years ago. It still lurked inside him and had yet to show itself, but it would eventually take his brain and his sight.

'Indeed they do, Sir,' said John mischievously, 'I'll get my merchant to send you round a dozen. Lambskin is the finest, but if your funds are short then linen will suffice, but you have to soak them in brine before you use them. What shall I tell my merchant?'

'Don't be impertinent Sir, tell him lambskin if you please,' barked Ruddle. He then thought for a moment and leaned across and lowered his voice, not wanting to show his ignorance. 'What exactly do you do with them, Campbell-John?' he said in his nearest approximation of a whisper.

'What do you *do* with them, Sir!' barked John mimicking Ruddle to exactly emphasize his ignorance. Eyes turned and looked at them from the other tables, so John repeated the words to embarrass Ruddle further, 'What do you *do* with them, Sir! – Why, you put them on your piercer, Sir.'

'Pon my sole,' said Ruddle, clearly amazed. 'On your piercer do you say?'

'I do indeed, Sir,' said John looking at the amused faces of the two other players.

'D'ya hear that,' barked Ruddle to one of them, 'you put them on your piercer, Sir,' his voice now wheezing as he laughed. But then his shoulders eased down and a furrow appeared on his forehead. He leaned across again to John conspiratorially. 'Why would you want to do that,' he said in his growled whisper.

John leaned into him as if to play the conspirator game, 'It creates a sort of barrier, if you take my meaning,' he said pretending to whisper when he was in reality audible to all. 'You see, it keeps cupid's juices *in* and the Senor *out.*'

Ruddle tended to lag behind in conversations on subjects other than gambling and horses, but the penny finally dropped and his shoulders again hunched and fell in unison to his wheezing laugh. 'What will they think of next,' he gasped.

The hands of cards were played at a pace, but that pace would stutter as Ruddle was clearly intent on goading John at every opportunity. Ruddle was not, at the best of times, a skilful player but now his concentration was roaming like a gypsy's vardo. After an hour or so, he was losing heavily to his three opponents, John being a particular beneficiary. Ruddle could not stop himself, however.

'How's your Jew boy,' he said, 'ready for the set-to, is he?'

'Yes, well into his training, Sir,' said John, trying to concentrate on his hand.

'I've given Big Charles Sweep the run of my estate as his training camp you know,' said Ruddle.

'Aye I'd heard that, Sir,' said John.

'Where's your Jew boy training then?'

'Lord Cowden's Estate.'

'Cowden always did like a long shot,' said Ruddle.

'And so far Medina has been a good long shot for him, if you'll recall,' said John.

'Big bugger, Sweep, you know,' goaded Ruddle.

'Aye he is that.'

'I always take a look at my estate workers' hands don't you know,' said Ruddle, 'if their skin's not hard and calloused then the rogues are not working hard enough.'

'Mmm,' said John, playing a card and then looking at Ruddle to follow him. *Oh get on with it man,* he thought but Ruddle was intent on more mischief.

'But Sweep's hands – never seen anything like 'em Campbell-John,' said Ruddle holding up the game. 'Hands like a pair of saddles to start with, but you should see the backs of 'em! Skin as thick and as hard as old leather.' He played his card with little thought and another player took the trick. 'The skin's tougher on the outside than the inside you know.'

'Yes I've heard,' said John laying a card following the lead from his right. He looked again at Ruddle to play but the man just leaned over to him again.

'D'ya know how he does it Campbell-John?' confided Ruddle.

'Your play,' said John, gritting his teeth.

'Punches the bark off trees y'know. Stripped the bark off three of my best oaks, so he has. Never seen anything like it Campbell-John – punches the bark right off trees. Swear that man could fell a brick wall so I do.' He looked back at his hand and played a card, again without much thought.

'Yes, he's a powerful man,' mumbled John picking up the cards after taking the trick.

'Your man's too small, Campbell-John. Never stand up to Sweep you know.'

'We'll see,' mumbled John again.

'Care to wager, Campbell-John, a side bet between us?'

Not with you at evens, thought John. 'What odds are you offering?'

'No odds,' said Ruddle, 'just a bet between gentlemen. Winner takes all. Not afraid of that are you Campbell-John?'

'Not at all,' said John, 'but you are only offering me evens and the house will take twelve-and-a-half per cent of that anyway.'

'You *are* afraid, Campbell-John,' said Ruddle.

'On the contrary,' said John, 'it seems to me, Sir, that if you are confident in your man then you should be prepared to offer me odds better than I can get elsewhere.'

'Come on Campbell-John, we'll get Molly Jasper to hold the stakes. What do you say to a hundred guineas each?'

'It's much easier to take a hundred guineas from you at the table,' said John. This caused an outbreak of laughter from the other two players, much to Ruddle's chagrin. Temporarily he returned his attention to his hand of cards. The game wore on and Ruddle continued to lose heavily.

Two hours into the game, and there was a moment when John took stock. Ruddle was using the piss pot and the attendants took the opportunity to bring candles to light the game as night was beginning to fall outside. The games table was made of rich red mahogany covered in green baize. At each edge there was a circular corner designed specifically to take the candlestick. At each side there was also a sunken hollow to take the players' game chips. John took the opportunity to lean back in his chair and count his stake. He had lost his winnings and was now back to his original stake or just behind. He was surprised as he thought he was still in front. He lifted a glass of claret to his lips without thinking, gulping the reddish purple liquid and then swirling it around his mouth, swilling it

between his teeth to enjoy its flavour. Into his mind suddenly
flickered a reminder of his huge and growing debts. Two hours ago
he was in a position to reduce those debts by a hundred guineas or
so, but he had decided instead to use the funds as his table stake. One
hour ago he was in a position to reduce his debts by nearly two
hundred guineas if he had taken his winnings. But now he was back
where he started. He was disappointed but by no means
disenchanted. He still believed in himself as a card player, and he
certainly did not see drinking as having a detrimental effect on his
skill. In fact the more he drank the more he believed in his abilities.
He swallowed the swirling claret with an audible gulp and gestured
with a dismissive hand to the liveried waiter to fill his glass. The
waiter obliged and he repeated the process swilling the wine in his
mouth, reclining contemplatively.

The next hand of cards was dealt as Ruddle rejoined the table,
and John pulled the cards close to him lifting the edges with his
thumb to look carefully at his hand. He was pleased with what he
had drawn. He was, however, taken aback by Ruddle's next
suggestion.

'Time to increase the stakes gentleman - what do you say?'

Huzzah, you dunderhead, John thought to himself. The other two
players readily agreed. John saw only greed in front of him and a man
to be taken to the cleaners – to be fleeced like a spring sheep recently
brought down from the hills. He coughed an approval and led with
his first card. But he was about to underestimate Ruddle. What the
man lacked in intellect and in card skills he made up for with an
unpleasant cunning, a sly and wily deviousness. It was not Ruddle's
intention to win back his own losses, but to dupe John into bigger
losses.

'I fancy a change of game gentlemen,' said Ruddle, 'what do you
say to that new French game, *Bouillotte*?' The other three players
looked at each other and they all had the same thought. They all saw a
chance for substantial winnings with Ruddle as the sacrificial lamb.
Bouillotte was an early form of poker. Unlike whist there was betting
on each hand and the hands could last only a few moments. The
possibility for large winnings was immense. There was scope for
bluffing and raising and all the dangers of being outplayed. The game
had an edge that was not present in whist. Conversely, the scope for
large losses was equally savage. The other three players nodded their
approval believing they had found a dupe.

Whist was the favoured game of gentlemen. It had style and skill, and all the finesse that made it perfect for a house party, but *Bouillotte* was a game made for a place such as Molly Jasper's.

'Chips!' barked Ruddle rudely. An attendant scurried and returned with a highly polished mahogany box. He bowed attentively, his white-gloved hands placing the box beside Ruddle as if it contained some precious substance. They agreed the stakes as proposed by Ruddle. There would be eight white chips to the pound, the red chips would be worth a pound and the blue would be worth five. These were rich stakes indeed: a white chip worth half a crown was enough to provide victuals and wine for a gentleman for a day. No money changed hands. They were playing as gentlemen - and gentlemen settled their gambling debts. As always, the attendant entered into the ledger the chips they had bought. All the gambling at Molly Jasper's was entered into the revered ledgers.

Ruddle was first to deal and dealt four hands of three cards, from a twenty-card pack made up of only aces, kings, queens, nines and eights. A thirteenth card was dealt face up as a common card that all the players could use to improve their hands. Each player threw in a white chip as the *ante*. The betting went round the table and they bet on the strength of their hands. They were all cautious so soon into the game and the hand was won with two kings. All players but the man opposite John folded, and he took the pot. The ranking was simple; four of a kind, three of a kind, and two of a kind – there was no ranking for runs or flushes.

As the game unfolded it became apparent that Ruddle had deviated from his normal strategy. For the next hour he played with an uncharacteristic caution. He bet sparingly, throwing in his hand if there was any display of opposition. His tactic was simple. He was not playing to win, but to negate his losses. He was trying to goad John into gambling above his means.

Ruddle now looked at his cards and saw that he had a pair of aces with an eight: a solid hand, but by no means an unbeatable one. He could be beaten by any prial or any four of a kind. The floating card was a nine, which was of no help to him. It was Ruddle's turn to bet first, at this point the pot contained only four white chips, being the ante that they had all been obliged to put in before the deal. He raised the stake immediately to a red chip - a sovereign - and sat back in his chair and raised a glass of claret to his lips, but then had second thoughts and put the glass down again. He looked around the table, his cunning mind gauging the situation and taking a perverse pleasure in his subterfuge. All the other players matched his bet. He threw in his cards to minimise his losses, but he still intended to have a say in the outcome of the game. For the loss of a sovereign his contribution had been to inflate the betting immediately and consequently the stakes in the pot. He leaned sideways in his chair as though he was a confidant of John. He tried to see John's cards but they were firmly held tight to the table, with only John's thumb able to raise them for his eyes-only. John was now the first in rotation to bet in this next round of betting, having been sat immediately to the left of Ruddle. He did not raise but made another bet of a red chip, which his opponents readily matched –they called, eyeing each other while trying to gauge the strength of each other's hands, but at the same time Ruddle eyed John. John leant forward and raised the bet, throwing two red chips into the pot. It was, he thought, time for a significant move.

'You'll never win back your losses with piddling little wagers like that Campbell-John,' said Ruddle. Two sovereigns was not in reality a small bet, but all things are relative and Ruddle had made it his business to know the size of John's debts for he had a score to settle. He knew the bet would hardly scratch the surface of John's debts and he saw his opportunity here.

'I have no losses, Sir.' With his right hand, John stacked his chips into towers and then lifted a white tower allowing the chips to fall, each one clinking on top of its neighbour. He quickly restacked it and repeated the procedure in quick time; it was a display of his irritation at Ruddle's chatter.

'Never did have any daring at the table did you, Sir,' goaded Ruddle again.

'I am a soldier, Sir,' said John, 'I know all about daring. I also know about strategy. There is a place for bravery and a place for tactics.'

'Hah! Tactics hey – is that what you call it?' said Ruddle, 'I think I'd call it spineless. Come on man, if you've got a good hand then attack the table - take the spoils.'

I'll attack you in a minute you poxy rogue, thought John. His two opponents matched the bet. John lifted the corner of his cards with his thumb while still holding them firm to the table with his other fingers. He reminded himself of his hand as he contemplated his next move. He had a pair-royal, a prial of kings. It was indeed a handsome hand, and the only other pair-royal that could beat him was a prial of aces. *Where his opponents bluffing or trying to hide the strength of their hands,* he thought to himself – they had not raised him but just matched his bets

'You're infantry aren't you, Campbell-John?' said Ruddle. John grunted a confirmation. 'Go on, pretend you're a cavalry man. Draw your sabre and charge.' Ruddle wheezed a laugh directed right at John. John gave him a sideways look of contempt but this only served to amuse Ruddle further. The man leant back in his chair and took his jewelled snuffbox from his waistcoat pocket. He tried carefully to position the snuff on the back of his hand, but it shook to the rhythm of his wheezed laughter and some spilled on to his frock coat adding to the existing stains. His clothes were expensively made, but were unkempt and did little to enhance his dishevelled appearance. His greying hair was long and thinning without any real style and just fell lank at either side of his head, his two large ears protruding through it. It looked as though it had not been brushed for days – which it hadn't. Profuse tangled hair emanated from his ears and his nostrils, the only difference being that his greying nose hair was dyed brown by the snuff. He brushed the rogue snuff away nonchalantly from his frock coat with his other hand, but managed to do no more than rub most of it into the material of the coat, leaving a brown-trailed stain. He raised the back of his hand to his nostrils, still wheezing. He forced himself to stop long enough to sniff up the powdered tobacco, but his wheezed laugh was now uncontrollable and half the snuff came immediately back down his nose. He wiped his nose and face with one movement of the back of his hand, still laughing at his supposed wit, leaving another brown stain on his unshaven face to match the one on his frockcoat. 'Charge!' he taunted again, waving his hand in the air as if he were holding a sabre.

A pox on you, thought John as he studied his hand again. He was a naturally bold card player but he also thought he knew when to be bold. He gulped down another glass of claret in one go, blowing out his cheeks so that his mouth had room to accommodate it before swallowing. The alcohol was dulling his senses and his judgement. It was also dulling his immunity to Ruddle's taunting, which was now beginning to annoy him intensely. Sober, he would deal with Ruddle with little difficulty; he had that silver tongue and natural wit. But now all he wanted to do was to shut the man up. He succumbed to the taunts. He tossed a blue chip into the middle to raise the stakes to five sovereigns and sneered an aggressive look at Ruddle. *Is that bold enough for you,* he thought to himself.

The player next to him called, matching the bet, but to John's surprise the player opposite him called and then raised another blue chip. Suddenly the game had changed and John knew he must re-evaluate his position. He had expected that at least one of his opponents would fold, but neither had. One could be bluffing, but he doubted it; bluffs were more common one on one. It was a possibility that he had to consider, but he suspected that the most likely scenario was that each of his opponents did indeed hold a handsome hand. He tried to calculate the odds. He could be beaten by a prial of aces, but it would be a rare hand indeed if both a prial of aces and kings had been dealt together. He must, he calculated, be able to beat at least one of his opponents, but that would count for nought if the other had those elusive aces. What he did not know, and Ruddle did, was that there could be no prial of aces as Ruddle had folded two earlier in the play.

Bouillotte was not a game where one was required to remember any sequence of previously played cards. Neither were any cards discarded during the play, so John could not eliminate the chance of aces by having seen them previously played. After each hand the cards were shuffled and players were always blind as to what their opponents may hold. All John could be certain of was that they could not possibly have been dealt the same cards as he had. It was clear to John that he had a very powerful hand indeed and the opportunity to maximise his winnings. He stroked his chin as he contemplated whether he would go 'all in' or let the game unfold in front of him and react to the play. For some moments he was engulfed in his own thoughts and was oblivious to his opponents. And then that concentration was speared by Ruddle.

'Charge!' he yelled again startling John. It was as though he had been hit by the percussive kick of a musket, yanking his thoughts back to the table with a start. Ruddle then mimicked the drawing of a sword lunging forward and bouncing in his seat as though he were riding a horse. He mimicked the slashing of a sabre and then a lunge across the table disturbing the stacked chips so that they fell and several lines scattered across the green beige. Preoccupied with his own hand, John was unaware that Ruddle had leant across to his right to see the strength of the hand that had prompted John's opponent to raise him five blue chips. What he saw caused another bubble of wheezing laughter to erupt from Ruddle's throat, along with a foul gust of bad breath. He did not know the strength of John's hand, of course, but he now knew the strength of his opponent's, which was formidable indeed.

Anger rose uncontrollably in John. He threw his cards down on the table. 'Damn you for a son of a whore, Sir,' he said, but Ruddle just continued to wheeze his laugh, his shoulders rising and falling to its rhythm. John picked up his cards again still leering at Ruddle, but the damage was done. He had accepted the goad. He would go *all in*. 'I call your five Sir, and I raise you twenty,' he said, throwing four blue chips in front of him.

'Tallyho!' cried Ruddle mixing his activities and using a hunting expression, 'we'll make a cavalryman of you yet, Sir!'

The player to John's left now studied his hand carefully. He too had a powerful hand, holding three queens. For an hour deals had been won by nothing more than a high pair, but also occasionally by good hands such as prials. Now the player contemplated his cards and was required to re-appraise the situation. He went through the same thought processes as John. He considered that one of his opponents may be bluffing, but thought it unlikely that both were. He had a really good hand and was not accustomed to folding cards of such power. On the other hand, it would cost him £25 pounds just to stay in the hand, and three hands could beat him: three kings, three aces and four of a kind. He called, throwing five blue chips into the pot.

The betting now moved to the player opposite John. He quickly called putting twenty pounds into the pot to match John's bet, but then without pausing threw five more blue chips into the pot, 'and I raise you twenty-five,' gentlemen,' he said boldly. John took a deep breath and eyed his opponent, flicking his own cards with his thumb as he did so.

'Your horse not beginning to blow is it Campbell-John - run out of steam has it?' sneered Ruddle. He then leaned towards John and with a snide serpent-like look hissed, 'or is it the man-atop who is gutless.' He was now playing John like a violin. It was no more than schoolyard baiting and yet John had succumbed to it, and his opponents had seen it too.

'Your twenty-five and raise you twenty-five,' said John throwing caution to the winds and the blue chips into the pot.

It would now cost the player to John's left £50 just to stay in the game. He thought for a few moments and then folded leaving only John and the player opposite him. Without hesitation he called John's twenty-five and then said, 'and I raise you…' he paused while he counted his chips. He looked John straight in the eye as he finished. He saw a ridge of sweat appearing on John's forehead. The tension was charged and other members of the club were leaving their own games aware that something special was going on.

A crowd was forming around the table and the spectators mumbled to each other as the latecomers were appraised of the state of play. Molly Jasper himself had been told of the game and he too joined the onlookers. 'More chips I think,' said John's opponent eventually. The attendant looked at Molly Jasper who nodded his authority and a second mahogany box was brought. The servant opened his ledger to record how many chips to register against the two players' names. The servant's white-gloved hand was raised and the quill hovered awaiting to note the amounts to be entered. 'I will take them all if you please,' John's opponent said, to gasps from the assembly, and turning to John he said, 'and I raise you - two hundred, Sir.'

A collective gasp rose again, but this time the level was intensified. This was the level of wager that two dukes might bet against each other on the merits of their racehorses. It was uncommon to say the least for such a wager to turn on just one card. Molly Jasper again nodded and the amount was entered into the ledger.

'He's trying to buy the hand from you Campbell-John,' goaded Ruddle, 'he's bluffing it's plain to see.' He was not, as Ruddle well knew.

'Pon my soul, Sir, I do believe the bet is with you,' said John's opponent mockingly leaning back in his chair to a round of applause.

'He's bluffing I tell you,' goaded Ruddle again.

John tried to think straight, but his mind seemed unable to respond. His debts were already considerable and he was really in no position to stand these losses. On the other hand, such a win would surely change his fortunes. He raised his hand and it shook plainly for all to see. He extended a shaky finger in the direction of the attendant who registered the required chips in John's name. 'I will call your bet, Sir,' said John to a '*Huzzah!*' from the crowd. 'Let us see if you can beat my three noble kings.' He turned his three kings over spreading them across the table in front of him, 'A pair-royal of kings, Sir,' he added with satisfaction.

A collective gasp went up. John's opponent sat back in his chair, but his expression did not change, and to John's surprise he was unable to tell if his three kings had won or not. His opponent milked the moment, leant forward and very slowly turned the first of his cards over. It was a nine and John was engulfed by a surge of relief. It was not an ace – surely now he was safe. The second card was turned and it was another nine. *It must be a prial of nines*, he thought, and then his opponent turned the final card over to reveal – the third nine.

A rousing cheer went up from the assembly together with shouts of *well-done, Sir*. Clapping replaced the cheers and John turned to acknowledge them, but when he did so – to his surprise the applause was directed to his opponent. For a heartbeat his mind struggled to comprehend what was happening, and then the full horror dawned on him. Ruddle's taunting and the alcohol had conspired against him. He had taken his eyes off the game. He felt suddenly like a chess player finding himself in checkmate when he had not seen it coming. He was on the attack, but unexpectedly all was lost. How could he have been so stupid? He was a seasoned gambler. His mind calculated the odds – the permutations without prompting. He had played so often that such judgements were instinctive and instant. But his instincts had failed him. Dulled by inebriation; diverted by goading and provocation. His eyes turned slowly and anxiously with trepidation and apprehension towards the thirteenth card – the common card. And there it was sitting alone on the green baize - it was the fourth nine, mocking him. It had no face, of course, but nevertheless it was mocking him. It represented a catastrophic error of judgement. There was only one possible chance of a four of a kind, and that was to bring in the thirteenth card – the common card. He had been fixated on aces when he should have considered the nines. His opponent had been betting on a certainty and John knew he should have seen that from the unprecedented raise of £200. He should have seen that his opponent had an unassailable hand. He *should* have seen it: but he had not.

He had lost £289 on one hand: on one turn of a card. His opponent would be famous amongst sporting gentlemen and John, conversely, would be infamous. His reputation would be shattered. He looked up incredulously and saw the smug face of Ruddle looking back at him. The man had exacted his revenge, paradoxically not by beating him at the card table, but by a scheming manoeuvre. It did not matter to Ruddle that he was not the winner, for his revenge was sweet. It was a luscious, sweet revenge. For not only was John now deeper in debt, he had lost this money at Molly Jasper's. The house took responsibility for any gaming losses at their establishment notwithstanding that twelve-and-a-half per cent belonged to them.

His name and his debt were now inscribed in their ledger, the all-knowing ledger. This was a debt that he had to pay back and pay back quickly.

CHAPTER 27

The last Monday of May 1790 was, on the face of it, an unremarkable day. An early morning shower had freshened the air and the sun had appeared at around half past nine and started its day's toil. The overnight mist of the London parks came under its glare and readily capitulated, leaving the watered grass to stand-alone against its rising strength. The parkland had been well stocked with the ammunition of rain and each blade of grass sparkled with its own droplets of rainwater. They quickly gave up their precious consignment to the ever-hungry sun and a fine spring day was set fair.

The parklands were peaceful in their early morning finery, their green springtime lushness undisturbed by the bustle of the city itself. The city parklands were popular and a morning constitutional was one of the pleasures of the Londoner. Likewise, those who were better off would ride out, displaying the Englishman's love of his horse. But for some reason the parks were almost deserted this fine spring morning, leaving the open spaces undisturbed for the rabbits to play and the birds to sing, for this day was to be a remarkable day indeed.

The last Monday in May was the day of the first spring race meeting of the year at Newmarket. It was popular with all the social classes, not just Londoners, but the inhabitants of other cities, as well as those in the smaller towns and shires. Many of the working classes would take a holiday, for the race meeting brought with it many other entertainments. There was a fair, there were jugglers, there were contortionists and there were puppet shows. There were strolling players to entertain and hog roasts to eat. There were vendors of all kinds selling food and drinks and there were games to play. In addition to all of this, there was the spectacle of boxing: all levels of skill - from the very limited to the very best pugilists in the land - would be on display.

The set-to today was to be something extra special. Today was the long awaited fight between Big Charles Sweep and Samuel the Jew, The Light of Israel. The newspapers had been full of the on-off contest for many months, but the week leading up to the contest had surpassed anything that had gone before. It was the sole topic of conversation in the alehouses and gentlemen's clubs. From the coffee houses to the cock pits and from the meat market to the Houses of Parliament, the newspapers and journals fuelled it all. Both boxers were extremely popular in the eyes of the public, but the newspapers now fed their readers with a portrayal of the contestants' differences. The aim was to polarise the support for each boxer, to drum up interest in the fight. Samuel was depicted as the ordinary man who would stand up for what he believed in at all costs. Big Charles Sweep was portrayed as the epitome of 'John Bull', that *'honest plain-dealing fellow, choleric, bold, and of a very inconstant temper'*, as the political satirist, John Arbuthnott had written of the generic Englishman. Sweep personified this popular view of English superiority.

For Samuel, the fight took on an unusual slant. As it approached it became clear that he was not the people's favourite as he had been in his previous fights. The boxing fraternity had been obliged to choose their man and a reprehensible view manifested itself, propelled by the newspapers, that the champion boxer of England should be an Englishman – not an Englishman who was also a *Jew*. The contest may not have been an official championship fight, but there were no dissenting voices to the universal recognition that the winner would be the champion fighter of all England. Sweep would not only be the bookies' favourite, he would also be the favourite of the crowd.

In fact, the drumming up of interest was never a requirement: the public had already decided that this fight was something special and one they wanted to see. The actions of the newspapers, however, would put Samuel at a disadvantage for his motivation would not be inspired by the adulation of the crowd, which had always been so important to him. He would have to win them over. But he would be up against a man who was equally skilled in crowd manipulation. Samuel would need every one of his showman's abilities to manipulate the crowd if he was to get them on his side.

But something extraordinary was happening on this fine May Day. Large crowds were not uncommon at Newmarket race meetings. They could swell to several thousand if the weather and the attractions were right. Racing had taken place at Newmarket since 1622, and after the Restoration, Charles II, an ardent race supporter, had moved his entire court to Newmarket for the spring and autumn meetings; he it was who commissioned the building of the two-storey pavilion. Today the conditions were right for horseracing and it was still a massive attraction, but today it was by no means the *premier* attraction – it was not a horse race at all, but a pugilistic encounter that had taken hold of the nation's psyche. The reason the parks of London were almost deserted was because an exodus had happened; one which was repeated in towns and shires up and down the country. There was no accommodation to be had within miles of Newmarket, but this had not quelled the numbers for the vast majority of the crowd was prepared to sleep rough in order to see this encounter. In the eyes of the public everything else took second place to this contest. Political intrigue and manoeuvrings were relegated to the inside pages of the newspapers; public unrest was temporarily deferred; business matters were put on hold. The fight had caught the public's imagination and engendered a euphoria that crossed the class barriers. Not since the public hanging of Jack Sheppard on 16th November, 1724, had there been such a spontaneous outburst at this level. Shepherd had been the original working class hero and on the day of his execution the *London Journal* had reported that two hundred thousand people had lined the route.

Such was the magnitude in the public's expectation of the set-to between Samuel Medina and Charlie Sweep that by the time of the fight the crowd would swell to well over two hundred thousand, eclipsing even the Shepherd hanging, but *this* crowd had been drawn from all sectors of society. The small town of Newmarket had been invaded – it was totally overwhelmed by the multitude that assaulted it. It was a town that knew about crowds, its prosperity so long intertwined with the sport of horseracing, and yet today it was a town that could not cope. Every road into Newmarket was choked – the life of the town stifled by a multitude of humanity. It was as if a dawdling caterpillar of people had squeezed its way into every thoroughfare and every alleyway, as it sluggishly edged its way, inch by inch, yard by yard towards the racecourse.

Samuel and John were by now skilled in the art of promotion. This was not to be a fight for noggins - for coins thrown into the ring in appreciation of a good fight - as many a fight at the racecourse was. A natural hollow in the rolling countryside had been cordoned off to make a temporary enclosure with seating for the wealthy, with the object of maximising the takings. Everybody who entered the enclosure would be required to pay. But even they had underestimated the size of the crowd. Over ninety per cent of it would now be outside the enclosure, but luckily the hollow in the downs created a natural amphitheatre so that the throng would have an uninterrupted, if distant view. They alone would watch the fight without paying.

There was an unexpected consequence in that the crowds were so very large and they spilled backwards so very far, that they not so much encroached on the racing line, they totally obliterated it. People overwhelmed the Beacon Course. Choak Jade was a popular vantage position to observe the racing, but the ever-swelling throng now swallowed this up. Frantically, the Jockey Club and the race organisers tried to reorganise their schedules. The fight had been scheduled to take place at five o' clock after the last race of the meeting, but it became clear after the first race that the crowd swell was becoming a major problem, so much so that the jockeys in the second race had to take a different line to avoid the ever-growing throng. The remainder of the races were suspended, and after negotiation the fight was brought forward to fifteen minutes past two. And then, strangely, a remarkable order took over the eager crowd. There was no military to control such a gathering - if this had been in London the Magistrates would have dealt with it as a mob and sent out the military to keep control. Also, there were few stewards at the meeting, although there were stewards paid for by Samuel and John to control the enclosure. It was a recipe for chaos and mayhem – and yet no chaos or mayhem occurred. Astonishingly, a collective mindset had somehow materialised, a collective state of mind, a collective way of thinking. It was as if everyone knew what he must do in order that the fight could go ahead. Everybody could see the massive problems and could see that there had to be order. In a time when the mob habitually ran riot at the slightest provocation, extraordinarily the opposite seemed to occur. If there is such a thing as a mob mentality then such a concept now happened in reverse. This was because they all desperately wanted the fight to go ahead. Those who had not the funds to buy a ticket naturally gathered outside the enclosure, leaving room for the paying spectators to enter. The wily, who would always try in the confusion to gain access without payment, had this day left their guile behind. The gentlemen who had gathered to watch their horses race, now easily made their way from the pavilion to the preferential seated areas without encumbrance from any mob. It was like a well-oiled machine - it was as if it was a well rehearsed gathering for a military tattoo. They had all travelled such a long way and nobody wanted anything to stop this fight going ahead. They all wanted the bragging rights when they got back home – they all wanted to say, *I was there. I was at the great fight. The day Big Charlie Sweep fought Samuel the Jew.*

'I've just seen the size of the big bugger,' said John as he entered Samuel's changing tent. He must have put on a good stone.'

'I suspected as much,' said Samuel matter of factly. Without looking up he carried on with his preparations. John now looked at Samuel's physique and a realisation took him. He should have seen it before. Samuel was lean and muscled and looked in wonderful condition. His olive skin rippled and glistened with health and vitality, a compliment to his training regime. He had purged his body of all the toxins that he had allowed to build up - all that high living that had begun to negate his natural athleticism. The body hair had been shaved from his back, his arms and his chest, and his skin oiled so that the blows would have no purchase - like a stone skimming on ice – and he had cut off his pig tail. But something was not quite right. Somehow it just seemed – what was it? He seemed so much – smaller...

'What's your fighting weight?' said John.

'Eleven stones and ten pounds,' said Samuel equally matter of factly.

'Eleven stones ten!' exclaimed John, 'Jesus - but you're nearly down to what you weighed as a nineteen-year old when I first met you.'

'Nearly,' said Samuel nonchalantly. He was a zone of mental composure: a self-imposed, self-controlled equanimity that came from his self belief in his own abilities.

'But you'll-'

'But I'll what?' interrupted Samuel finally, turning to look directly at John for the first time. The last thing he wanted was for someone to bring negative thoughts into his dressing tent before he was due to fight.

'But you'll not have the bulk to stand up to his punches at this weight,' said John.

'Maybe,' said Samuel, 'but that would be true anyway.'

'So why shed the weight?'

'Strategy, John.'

'Strategy! How is it strategy to fight at a weight that'll give you no punch resistance?'

'You of all people should understand, John Campbell-John. You're a soldier,' he paused for a moment and then added, 'and you're a cunning, conniving, scheming sod as well.' He said the words with a hint of venom that took John by surprise. 'What is always the best strategy?' he added, but John did not answer. The question was obviously rhetorical. 'Surprise, John, surprise. You know that very well.'

'But...' John paused for a moment unsure of his own thoughts. 'But if a general decides against a frontal assault and sends out a company of skirmishers instead...' He paused again as he thought it through. 'It doesn't matter that they may take the enemy by surprise, if they are unarmed. They still need to have their weaponry. Don't you see you'll be going into the ring unarmed?'

'We'll see,' said Samuel arrogantly, turning back to his preparations.

'But the big bugger is coming in at fifteen stones and four pounds. I've just been to his tent and it's true.'

'I'm sure it is,' said Samuel, 'and that's his mistake.'

'Mistake! It looks like sound tactics to me.'

Samuel stopped his preparations and sat down to face John finally giving him his full attention. 'Look,' he said irritably, 'Sweep always was my superior in strength and size. He didn't have to bulk up for that to be true.'

'But you've bulked down.'

'I've bulked down to accentuate my advantages.' Samuel tried to explain and John tried to understand. 'I am his equal in the knowledge of the science of pugilism and I am his superior in athleticism. He has now handed me another advantage.' John still did not understand and he looked blankly back at Samuel. 'He's thirty-two John - those old legs will now have to carry all that extra weight. He's given me the advantage of stamina.'

John recognised the truth in what Samuel was saying but still was unconvinced. 'But you're denying what makes Big Charlie Sweep so good. That's what he does. No matter what you throw at him he just keeps coming back. He's never beaten. Just when you think he is bested he comes back at you, and then he comes back again, and again, and again....'

If Samuel had not been so mentally tough all this negativity would have been damning, but he had, for months, analysed Sweep endlessly in his own mind. This man had put him on the seat of his pants in his own Academy. Samuel was neither a stupid nor a cowardly man and he had learned from that experience. 'Look; he's six feet one inch to my five foot eight. He is fifteen stones and four pounds to my eleven stones and twelve. Don't you think I know that? I know that I can't stand against him toe to toe. But that's been true in most of my fights. Sometimes it has taken a half hour or even three quarters of an hour for my opponents' strength to be sapped, but sap them I have.'

'But this is Big Charlie Sweep that you're fighting,' said John as if that simple statement counteracted all that Samuel had said.

'I know, I know,' said Samuel, 'but he's tampered with his natural fighting weight. He won't take his natural stamina into the ring with him. Don't you see that?'

'I see only a very big man who knows how to fight.'

'And I'm going to make him fight for an hour – for two hours or for three hours if necessary. I'm going to make those old legs carry that extra weight for round after round. And when he's spent I'm going to make him fight for another round and then another and then another. I can't deny his ability; if he is able to land clean then I must make sure that I am always moving back out of range so that the punch will knock me backwards and I won't absorb the full impact. I won't take the chance of walking *onto* his punches.' The words spat out of Samuel like bullets from a flintlock pistol motivated by his exasperation at John's lack of belief in him. After all these years and all these fights together, his closest friend still had no belief in him.

John came and sat next to Samuel and patted him on the back. It was a pat of respect for his friend, but then he leaned forward and rested his elbows on his knees and just stared at the floor. He could see the truth in everything Samuel had said, but deep own in his mind he still could not bring himself to believe it.

Samuel stood to continue his preparations. 'When will Toby fight?' he asked matter of factly. He was trying to get his mind back into that zone. Toby had been scheduled to fight before Samuel and Samuel was to be his second.

'He'll have to fight after the last race,' said John.

'Then he may be fighting in the dark,' said Samuel drily, 'for I believe this is going to be a very long day.'

Back in London, Rebecca was anxious. In her mind this fight symbolised a betrayal by her husband and yet, however much she despised him, deep down there was still love and affection. It had been locked away in some dark recess but now it surfaced and stung her like an escaping hornet. She feared for his safety. The man she had loved was not the extrovert - he was not the pugilist. The man she had loved was the other Samuel Medina; the man with a poet's soul; the Robin Hood figure who detested an injustice and who would stand up against it. But that man, of course, only partially existed. On the surface she accepted that he was a pugilist, but she had longed for the day when he would put such a profession behind him so that he could be the man she wanted him to be. It was a laudable aspiration but it denied that other side to Samuel's character: that showman that needed to perform was equally what made up the man that was Samuel Medina. She also denied him his youth. He was still only 24 years' old and she was denying him his right to be young. They had seemed to be kindred spirits when she had nursed him back to health and that had led to marriage, but it was a marriage taken too early. It had denied both of them the right to be young. For young women that was no great denial, for society offered little excitement. For the poor it offered endless drudgery. For the wealthy it offered only long, tiresome hours of needlecraft or poetry or romantic fiction, but little in the way of revelry. Perhaps a ball or two in the season to look forward to, which required planning and dressmaking to fill the long empty hours. But those kinds of events were not a part of Rebecca's youth since she was a Jewess. Young men, on the other hand, were expected to sow their wild oats and however inequitable this was it was on offer to the male of the species. As a Jew, Samuel would not have been eligible for this either under normal circumstances, but his fame in the ring had given him dispensation. It was a lure that he had at first ignored, instead taking himself a wife. But in the end it was a lure too tempting to ignore and he had taken the bait. Tragedy had been the catalyst. The death of a child is the most painful of all losses and it should have brought them together, but instead it had split them apart.

In the run up to this fight, however, their letters had been more personal and less businesslike than hitherto. Rebecca had continued to run Samuel's business affairs when John Campbell-John defaulted – which was now most of the time. She acted as a sort of longstop when John was out of town or just too drunk to complete his duties. Slowly, warmth had begun to evolve again between Rebecca and her husband. Samuel's 'road to Damascus moment' when he had been posing for Sir Joshua Lazenby had subsequently filtered through to his letters to his wife and begun to mend the relationship that had gone so badly wrong. So now Rebecca found she was anxious for him in a way that she had not been for many months. She did not know whether to feel glad or sorry.

She busied herself with the weekly accounts to take her mind off the fight. She was surprised at her own anxiety. She reluctantly had to admit to herself that she was worried about Samuel's safety. It affected her concentration and she was forced to add up the columns two and three times to make them tally. But then a realisation took her: many of the columns simply did *not* tally no matter how many times she totted them up. There was something wrong and her anxiety transferred itself from the fight to the business accounts. Figures had always been a friend to her. With some people mathematics is a wild animal that is never tamed, but for those who do not have that problem there is something comforting in figures that balance. Conversely, there is something disturbing when they do not. Rebecca expanded her checks, metaphorically rolled up her sleeves and set about a complete audit of the year's records. Her alarm grew by the hour. Something was wrong; something was very wrong.

John pulled back the flap to the tent. The noise of the crowd had already penetrated its flimsy walls and Samuel had witnessed its crescendo as the fight grew ever nearer and nearer. His mental preparations had enabled him to block most things out but the mounting noise had always been in the back of his mind. Now the tent flap released a shaft of bright light and it lunged like a swordsman into the subdued light within. Samuel took a deep breath. He was ready. He was wearing a pair of white breeches that came to just below his knees and a pair of light fighting slippers. Apart from that he was naked: he took with him on his gladiatorial journey only his fists and his wits. He held that breath for some moments and this accentuated his lithe and muscular physique. He looked magnificent. His oiled skin shone in that shaft of light; he was like a Greek god about to go into some mythical battle. But the battle was real enough. A pitched battle that would test his abilities to the extreme – that would define him in the echelons of his chosen profession. This would be the pinnacle of his career and he knew it. It would also define him in the eyes of the public. Not just the sporting public but the whole population, for this fight had transcended such constraints. If there was a destiny in the life of every man, then today was Samuel's.

These thoughts now entered his mind. He was walking towards his destiny - tall with his chest expanded to meet it head on and look it straight in the eye. This man of conflicting character - this complex man who could be kind and considerate and gentle – a man who could display a poet's soul, was about to engage in a fiercesome exhibition of brutality. This man who could be shyness personified in front of a women, but who relished the thought of the crowd's adoration. The showman would now suddenly replace the diffident. The introvert would defer to the extrovert. Through all his preparations he had been sustained by an unshakable belief in his own abilities and while his rational mind could see the size of the task he faced, he had an irrational belief in his own invincibility. Now, as he stood by the tent flap, suddenly he was in *the zone*. He was at that place that all sportsmen aspire to be. The hundred-year wave that happens when all the conflicting forces of nature suddenly line up and move in the same direction creating an unstoppable force. Nothing is at variance; there is no discrepancy, no inconsistency – only synchronization. He stepped through that tent flap and into the light. It was two o' clock and his fate awaited him.

A wall of spectators met him so that there was no obvious route to the ring but he was unfazed, safely cocooned in his zone of thought. A pathway seemed to miraculously open in front of him as if he was being sucked to the fighting ring by the will of the people. But all this happened outside his zone for he saw only the back of John Campbell-John who walked in front of him. There was going to be a monumental struggle for superiority but he was ready. He was ready to fight the fight of his life.

CHAPTER 28

As Samuel climbed into the ring he climbed out of the shadows into the sunlight; it was as if a great celestial spotlight had suddenly been switched on. The ringmaster bellowed his name but it hardly registered in his consciousness, but then a crescendo of sound followed the announcement and he knew he must respond to it. He jogged to the centre of the ring pirouetting and shadow boxing as he did so. Left jabs, round rights and upper cuts sliced the fresh May atmosphere and most of the crowd roared their approval. He was the only fighter to do this, to exhibit his skills in this way and the purists in the crowd disapproved. They were used to large, potent, lumbering men who traded merely on their close-quarter power and parrying skills. Many of the crowd were seeing Samuel Medina for the first time but had read of his showmanship and now they were experiencing his unique style for themselves. The cheers escaped easily from their mouths, set free by the communal excitement that had been growing for hours. This event was a spectacular unseen before in England and it brought Samuel briefly out of his zone. As he whirled and pirouetted, the ocean of faces entered into his consciousness. It was as though the whole landscape was made of faces: rolling hills of eyes and mouths, all moving in perfect unison, responding to his conducting like a colossal orchestra. He jogged back to his corner and John wiped the beads of sweat from his face. John spoke, but none of the words registered in Samuel's consciousness for he had put himself back in the zone. It was a zone of pure concentration; everything but the forthcoming fight fading from his mind.

For a brief moment of anticipation the crowd fell silent. An eerie hush of expectation as the multitude waited for their first view of Big Charlie. It was a name that Sweep detested, for in his mind it carried some hidden disrespect. He was Big *Charles* Sweep – a name that carried reverence. Nobody called him 'Charlie' to his face. His fears of disrespect were unfounded: whatever name he took into the ring there was no doubting that the sporting public had absolute respect for him. It was a respect that transcended class barriers. It was even more than that, for his reputation went much further than that of a fighter. He was seen as an embodiment of the Englishman's character: the *never say die* attitude that would count if England's enemies ever came to invade her shores.

In the minds of the public, Samuel and Charles were both perceived as symbolic of what it was to be *English*, but while Samuel was the spirit of the downtrodden man who would stand up against a more powerful foe for what he believed was right, Charles Sweep was the real British Bulldog, companion of John Bull himself – he was *the man;* he was the national hero.

For those spectators nearer the ring there was a preliminary view of Sweep. Unlike Samuel, he towered above the average height. As he walked to the ring his black hair could be seen above the multitude, it was as if God had bestowed a noble birth upon him. The cheers started early, much before the main crowd had their first sight of him, but as he reached the stage and started to climb the steps and that black head of hair rose into view, the preliminary cheer exploded into a percussive crescendo of noise. The ringmaster struggled to be heard, announcing the name *'Big Charles Sweep'*, barking as loud as he could. The people responded so loudly that ripple effects were being created: a cheer would start near the ring and then move backwards through the immensity of the crowd. In the end, the separate cheers all merged into one long and seemingly never ending cheer. The ringmaster announced the rules of engagement, but no one took any notice, the crowd being so wound up in expectation that they were just willing the fight to start. It was the ringmaster's job to wind up the crowd with words of anticipation - but today he was redundant. Sweep's only response was to puff out his chest and raise his fists, but that was enough for the cheers to swell again. Like Samuel, he wore nothing more than a pair of white breeches and fighting slippers, but there was no mistaking the two boxers. They both had black hair but unlike Samuel's, Sweep's contrasted with his milk-white skin. More than anything else, it was the disparity in size that distinguished them – but then, Samuel had been in such a position before.

And then the bell sounded, but the majority of the crowd did not hear it. Sweep lumbered forward to claim the centre of the ring, for that was to be his base of operations. Samuel conceded that from the outset and he circled to his right for a few moments, away from Sweep's powerful right hand. Surprisingly, Sweep did not follow him being content to maintain the centre. Samuel had expected that Sweep would come after him from the start and that he would need to use all his defensive skills and mobility, but now he found himself as the possible aggressor. If he wanted to land a punch he would have to go into the range of the big man's punches and he had not expected to be in a position to do that until at least half an hour into the fight. After half a minute neither fighter had thrown, never mind landed, a punch and the crowd were becoming restless. It was not unusual in bare-knuckle fights for two large, powerful men to stand toe to toe from the first bell and then one to have battered the other into defeat in a half minute. But here were these two idols of the ring still sizing each other up after such a period. It was as if this was a staring contest, but instead of the loser being the one to look away first, the loser would be the one who was first sucked into range.

The crowd's displeasure mounted and it was Samuel who moved first. He lined himself up on a diagonal, which was his modus of fighting, and moved into range on that diagonal throwing a combination of a straight left followed by a right cross. Sweep parried both punches for he was much more than just a powerful man. He was a pugilist; a master of the science. Samuel knew that Sweep would counter and that he must now get out of range before that happened. He moved backwards along that same diagonal, but Sweep launched his right hook whilst Samuel was still in range. Samuel saw it coming and lifted his right arm to his face to parry. He only just managed to get his fist to his face and Sweep's punch hit his own fist and then cannoned onto his chin. Samuel was moving backwards at impact and the punch sent him crashing to the canvas. The bell sounded to end the round and the crowd burst into voice. Samuel had been floored with the first punch that he had received and it would have been much worse had he not partially parried. His fist had taken the sting out of the punch and his senses were still intact.

He walked back to his corner unaided. 'How be it?' said John, alarm evident in his features. He had almost said *I told you so,* but refrained at the last minute.

'It be fine,' said Samuel, 'the punch merely knocked me backwards. I didn't take the full force of it.' John poured water over his head still unconvinced by the explanation.

Within the allowed half minute Samuel walked back to the scratch mark unaided. He was steady on his feet and his confidence was undiminished, but he was angry with himself. He again skipped around the ring tempting Sweep to come after him, but again Sweep held back. A realisation took him - he must not fight to the crowd. He must not let the crowd's impatience entice him into fighting the wrong fight. Sweep was trying to lure him into throwing away his advantages. Mobility and stamina were the keys, and if necessary he must win ugly and not entertain the crowd. There would be plenty of time to entertain, he hoped, when the stamina and potency had been drained from Sweep. But it was a difficult thing to achieve as the crowd bayed for blood. Samuel longed to respond. He longed to release all that natural silky talent; to throw hooks and uppercuts without restraint; to throw jabs and crosses, and overheads and bowlers. But he had had his wake-up call. He had been on the seat of his pants and he knew he must not put himself in that position again.

He went up onto the balls of his feet and danced around the ring moving always to his right so that he would not walk onto Sweep's powerful right. Intermittently he flicked out left jabs, but most of them fell short and the ones that landed did little damage – but then they were not intended to do. After half an hour the crowd had had little to cheer about. Samuel had danced around with the intention of drawing Sweep to him to sap his energy by throwing punches that swatted only fresh air, but Sweep had refused to be drawn. Neither man showed any sign of facial damage; the only redness was on Samuel's arms where he had parried some of Sweep's shots whilst moving away. Both men had that natural instinct to entertain and they desperately wanted to do just that, but both men kept their discipline and stuck to their game plans.

But then an opportunity presented itself to Samuel. He noticed that as he moved to his right Sweep's left jab would follow him. It flicked out like a snake's tongue. It was no more than a range finder but it was a harbinger of menace. If it landed, no matter how ineffectually, then that powerful right would hone in like a striking rattlesnake. There was danger here, but there was also an opening and Samuel went for it. Samuel moved to his right as normal and Sweep's left jab hissed after him, but it fell short and to the left of Samuel's head. Samuel now planted his feet so that he could get purchase and drove a low right hand under Sweep's left elbow, thudding venomously home to his side just under his rib cage. Samuel heard an audible hiss as air escaped over Sweep's teeth and he knew that the punch had done some damage. Over the next ten minutes he repeated the punch four more times and Sweep seemed to have no answer to it. Slowly the accumulation of these punches would have an effect and Samuel knew it.

An hour into the fight and the pattern was unchanged. Sweep had the centre of the ring but refused to be drawn into wasting his energies by chasing Samuel round the ring or punching thin air. Both men were waiting for the effects of fatigue to take their opponent so that they could then successfully deploy their artillery. Samuel's punches to the rib cage gave him the edge in this strategy, but Sweep knew that he only needed one clean, venomous punch and the fight would be over. Samuel began to sink those punches into his opponent's rib cage more and more and noticed that Sweep's left elbow was now almost permanently pinned against his side. This could have been a defensive strategy, but Samuel suspected that Sweep was hurt. Whatever the reason it was beginning to affect Sweep's equilibrium, as it was much more difficult to punch fluently with his left hand. Sweep attempted to flick out his left hand once more as Samuel moved out of range, but the punch was now easily evaded and it gave Samuel much more time to exploit it. The effects of his punches to Sweep's ribcage were now becoming evident and Samuel saw no reason to change this unexpected strategy. He planted his feet and dropped his right shoulder, transferring his power accordingly, and he launched the punches. Too late he registered that Sweep's eyes and left hand had sparked at the same instant.

And then oblivion.

Samuel came to in his corner; his seconds were holding him up and John was throwing water over him. He was shouting at him but the words did not register. His head swam in a daze, his eyes glazed. The roar of the crowd was now somehow distant and muted. John had one hand around the back of his head pulling it up by pulling down on his hair. They were forehead to forehead looking into each other's eyes, but only one man's brain registered any connection. John put smelling salts under Samuel's nose and for a heartbeat there was no reaction, but then the vapour stung through the mists of his mind and he pulled is head away violently. Then he began to perceive John's face through the dark haze. The ring post swirled at the edges of his vision. Some semblance of comprehension returned to Samuel's mind, and he mumbled a faint, 'What happened?'

'Sweep beat you to the punch with a left hook over your right,' said John but the explanation failed to register in Samuel's befuddled wits.

And then a sip of brandy was being forced between his lips and he was being dragged back to the mark. A final cascade of water was thrown at him - and he was left alone to face the power and might of Big Charles Sweep. The gathering numbered many thousands. The sound of the crowd cheering wildly for their hero's imminent victory blotted out all other sound but now, as the bell sounded, unheard, he was utterly alone and he was almost defenceless.

The big man instantly recognised that Samuel's senses had not returned and he smiled inwardly to himself. He moved purposefully forward to take his prize. Samuel's instincts partially kicked in and he raised his arms and took his fighting attitude but his legs betrayed him; that betrayal was to be his salvation. Sweep set himself for a big right hand but as it was travelling Samuel's legs gave way and he began to fall to the ground. As he fell the punch skimmed the top of his head instead of landing plumb. He had evaded the full force of the punch. He hit the canvas and the bell sounded to end the round in accordance with the Broughton rules of engagement.

Pandemonium broke out as Sweep's corner claimed that the fight was over, as Samuel had not properly answered the call to fight after the allowed half minute, but the referee adjudged that he had been felled by a punch and that the fight should continue. Ruddle now jumped into Sweep's corner to protest the referee's decision and for some moments confusion reigned. Ruddle was a caustic man and his words spat venom at the referee but more importantly he was a man of influence and the referee, knowing that, began to sway. He knew the clout that this man could exert and he was suddenly on the horns of a dilemma. He was being browbeaten to declare Sweep the victor, but he also knew that the immense crowd wanted to see the fight reach its natural conclusion. And all the time the clock was ticking.

The seconds ticked on; it was now nearly a minute since the bell had sounded for the second time to end the round. Samuel had had that initial thirty seconds to recover and by going to the canvas straight away he had gained another minute. The timekeeper looked at the feuding parties and he too was unsure what to do. *Was the fight over or not?* He looked at his pocket watch ticking away the seconds - tick – tick – tick - and he knew that they should be fighting if the fight was not over.

Meanwhile Samuel was the beneficiary of all this confusion. In his corner John Campbell-John was busy at work frantically trying to revive him. He threw more water at him and then slapped him around the face. He put smelling salts to his nose again and then repeatedly slapped him. After the allowed thirty seconds Samuel's senses were beginning to unscramble, but the effects of the punch were still in his legs. He needed longer to recover. He got it – the argument in the other corner with the referee was like manna from heaven. After a further half-minute, Samuel turned to John and said, 'Tell me *exactly* what happened – I need to know.'

Relief spread through John's veins as if he had entered a warm house in the depths of winter. That relieving warmth sped through him as he explained, for John knew that at this moment, Samuel's most effective weapon was his wits. 'He must have been feigning that injury to his ribs,' said John.

'No no,' said Samuel, 'he was hurt all right. He just fought through the pain. That's what he does. He saw that I was becoming predictable and he has punished me for it. I won't make the same mistake again.'

John smiled. It wasn't the logic of the words that comforted him - it was the lucidity. Samuel was back.

Another half-minute passed and that befuddlement also left his body and the strength returned to his legs. And then, after one minute and a half, the hesitant time-keeper finally came to a decision and sounded the bell.

Samuel walked unaided to the scratch mark. Confusion still reigned in Sweep's corner, but Sweep had had enough of the squabbling and he would now put and end to the wrangling. In his own mind it was pointless anyway for all he now had to do was to go out and finish the job with his hands. 'Enough,' he shouted and almost immediately his authority silenced the wrangling. 'It's time to fight,' and with that he turned and moved resolutely forward. He was a champion and champions don't quibble in corners.

Waiting for him in the centre of the ring was not the cowering, beaten man he had expected to find. The miserable pup he had floored only minutes before had undergone a miraculous transformation. Sweep blinked in surprise: the pup had somehow changed into a cunning snapping fox. That realisation was brought home to him when he threw his first punch. He powered himself by rotating his immense torso to his right and then uncoiling that power in the release of his fabled right cross. He expected it to end the contest. All he had to do was pummel a stationary target to the canvas and oblivion. His feet were planted firmly to add solidity to the blow, but it merely ripped through the afternoon air for Samuel had simply taken one backward step out of range. Psychologically, however, it was a thousand steps. It proclaimed that The Light of Israel was back in front of Sweep: a fighting man not a bested, beleaguered animal. There was none of the expected panic. Samuel Medina was not running scared of his mighty foe, Big Charles Sweep. He was once again the matador to Sweep's bull.

In the true character of the man, Sweep's resolve now redoubled itself. He went after Samuel to finish the job, but herein lay his problem: it represented a change in tactics. In his mind, Samuel had planned for a fight where Sweep would chase him like the proverbial bull, but Sweep had duped him by taking the centre of the ring, goading Samuel to come after him. Youth was Sweep's nemesis – he knew that, and he knew that it could destroy his age and experience. Stamina and endurance came with youth and he recognised that it came with this refreshed Samuel Medina. Sweep's former strategy had been to preserve his energy whilst luring his opponent into spending his advantages. But now Samuel found himself in an exactly opposite scenario. He had *got lucky* and he now had an opponent who had cast aside his reasoned strategy for one of outright aggression.

Unable to believe the evidence of his own eyes, Sweep believed that he was on the verge of victory, that he had only to take his prize. He roared after Samuel, scything great punches, but Samuel used his agility to evade these colossal arcing blows. Sweep had abandoned any attempt at finesse, abandoned all his scientific ability and was now trading purely on his strength. Raw power, fired by incredulous anger was now his only weapon, even if that weapon was a high calibre gun. Samuel skipped to his right, always away from that powerful right of Sweep's, but then peppered the big man's face with stinging long lefts. Fighting off his back foot, these punches spat out and aggravated the big man, whose response, as always, was to redouble his efforts. The punches carried no great venom but they began to cut up Sweep's face and for the first time in the fight one of the combatants was badly bloodied.

The crowd roared in anticipation. It had taken a long time for the fight to come to the boil but that anticipation now seemed to somehow heighten the spectacular sight that was unfolding before them. Like Sweep, the crowd to a man had expected to witness the end of the fight, and that end would be the slaughter of Samuel the Jew. But a collective realisation began to overtake them: the Jew was not finished after all; the Jew was fighting back.

For the next half hour Sweep hunted Samuel around the ring, trying to cut off his escape routes, trying to pin him in a corner, but each time, somehow, Samuel managed to use his agility to evade those huge swinging punches. But then the pace began to flag. They had been fighting now for the best part of two hours, but Sweep had expended more energy in the last half hour than he had done in the whole of the first hour and a half. Punching thin air drains the stamina and, of course, Sweep was carrying extra weight. But two hours of fighting had also drained Samuel's reserves of energy and both men were now at a crossroads. As the fight entered its third hour it was time for a change in the campaign.

Sweep returned to the centre of the ring. He was blowing heavily now and it forced him to take stock. Sweat trails mingled with blood ran down either side of his face and dripped copiously from his chin. His jaw hung open as he gasped for breath, forcing his rational mind to return to him and he knew he had to change his tactics again. He had been in this situation before, but previously his fatigue had been the result of throwing and receiving punches. In this fight he had not shipped a lot of punches, but the damage had been done to his legs and his lungs. An experienced pugilist, Sweep knew that when the legs are gone then the head will soon follow, and so he knew that he must conserve what reserves of energy that he had left. He must now gamble that he would outlast his opponent and the thought was a repellent one to him. He had not planned for the fight to turn out that way. He had expected to knock the Jew boy out cold.

Samuel, on the other hand, had planned exactly that strategy. If the early fight had not gone to plan it now seemed to be turning in his favour, apart from the fact that his own stamina was also spent. Both men hoped they would get a second wind that would blow them through to victory. With Sweep taking the centre of the ring and again refusing to come after him, Samuel reverted to his normal strategy, the strategy that had served him so well when he was faced with large powerful men, but had failed him earlier in the fight. He took up his position on the diagonal and moved forward along it into range. As he did so Sweep threw a left and right combination and Samuel parried both on his arms. He was reassured as he sensed that much of the power was no longer there. *I can now take these punches,* he thought to himself, but then remembered the catastrophe that had nearly lost him the fight earlier. He moved in again and parried without any attempt to throw a punch himself, and then moved out of range back along the imaginary diagonal. His uncertainties and doubts were being eroded and he resolved to take a chance. Again he moved in, but this time unloading a combination that beat Sweep to the punch. Sweep countered with a combination of his own, but Samuel parried both punches on his arms and then he leant in, dropping his right shoulder to plant an upper cut that came up through Sweep's guard. The man's black-haired head jerked backwards like a recoiling field gun. Sweat, blood and mucus flew into the air and landed on those gentlemen who had paid for the best seats. They cared little for they were engrossed in this fearsome fight. Some hurriedly wiped away the slimy cocktail but others were oblivious to it, their gaze riveted on the two antagonists. The crowd roared its approval at the violence of the fight. They almost all still expected Sweep to win, but they were thrilled that Samuel the Jew was putting up such a fine show.

The spinal jar from an upper cut is overwhelming and that punch was the most hurtful that Sweep had taken in the fight so far, but thus far there had been no accumulation of punches and his senses were in no way addled. Samuel briefly made the stupid mistake of admiring his work and was surprised when Sweep came back at him almost immediately. Adrenalin kicked in and Samuel attempted to move backwards, but Sweep's right cross landed squarely on his chin. Samuel took the punch full force unable to get his left arm up in time to parry the shot. It was another reminder to him, but with that reminder came reassurance: he had the punch resistance to take Sweep's waning power. The strength of this supremely powerful man was beginning to drain away, but Sweep was far from done. He had been on the verge of defeat before and somehow managed to find some reserves buried deep within him; he would do so again.

Samuel resolved to extinguish every last morsel of resilience. For the next half hour he pummelled away at Sweep's body, moving into range, planting his feet, and sinking murderous combination punches into Sweep's midriff, and then moving out of range again. Sickening thud after sickening thud sank into Sweep's midriff and bruises, in the shape of Samuel's knuckles, began to appear on his opponent's ever-reddening torso. But the danger of the man had not yet been extinguished. He was still throwing punches back with some success and Samuel's face began to redden also, running with blood from the sides of his eyes, but it was a risk that Samuel now determined to take. He was landing four punches to one and was gaining confidence that Sweep was fast running out of reserves.

The fight now entered its fourth hour and the appearance of both men paid testimony to the brutal trade they plied. Samuel's left eye was grotesquely swollen, a purple mound that made his head look misshapen, like a knobbly potato. His chest was splattered red with his own blood, which was matched by the once white breeches that were now streaked ruby-red. Sweep was less bloodied around the face but his body was bruised to a mottled montage of reds, scarlets, maroons, blues and blacks. But the fourth hour also marked a turning point in the response of the crowd. For the first time some of them realised that Sweep just might *not* win this fight. A small enclave in the crowd was from the Jewish community – they had previously been quiet but now found their voices and chanted, '*Samuel Medina, The Light of Israel, - Samuel Medina, The Light of Israel.*'

And then a relative quiet fell on the vast crowd. There was a collective intake of breath as disbelief suddenly overtook them. Samuel unleashed two more combination hooks to Sweep's body. He winced as the blows sunk in and his elbows were drawn instinctively down to his side to protect his solar plexus. But Samuel then followed it up with a ferocious uppercut that homed in on Sweep's chin. The spinal jar was devastating. The man's head flew back releasing another arc of mucus spiralling into the air, and then his legs shuddered and caved and he sank to his knees. The bell sounded to end the round and Sweep's seconds dragged their wounded giant back to his corner.

It was time for Sweep to live up to his reputation. He was the man who always came back, again and again. He was the man who had never been beaten. But even Sweep, in the whole of his fighting career had never been required to come back after more than three hours of fighting. This was a brave and proud man, however, and he lived up to his reputation, striding back to his mark unaided after the regulation one half minute. He threw punches, but Samuel had now worked out his end game. Sweep's punches were easily evaded and then, as time moved on, they began to diminish in number

Samuel picked his time to perfection. The same right-left combination to the body followed by that upper cut and Sweep fell to the canvas again. This pattern now repeated itself for another twenty minutes. Any normal man would have been bested long ago, but this proud warrior was no normal man. Samuel marvelled at the man's resilience. His own muscles screamed with pain, but still the man in front of him refused to yield. There was a screech from a distraught spectator in the crowd. '*Come on Big Charlie,*' he cried tears running down his face, '*do it for England.*' It represented the view of most of the crowd – not because Samuel was not a favourite, for he was, but because this fight represented something special. The winner was to be the unofficial champion of all England and in their minds that champion should be a pure Englishman, not a second-generation immigrant who was also a Jew.

It was at this point that Samuel realised Sweep's punches had stopped coming back and that only bravery was keeping this valiant man upright. Samuel knew then that he had bested Big Charles Sweep; he had effectively won the fight. There was no more danger. And then he did something of which he would in retrospect be ashamed. He went into his matador role. It was disrespectful: with his right hand raised, he walked up and down before this defenceless hulk of a hero and taunted the crowd to respond. Many did, but others saw the disrespect. Nevertheless a collective cry of '*Huzzah*,' rang out and Samuel responded by flicking out a left hand into the face of Sweep whilst keeping his right fist raised high into the sky. It wasn't what the crowd wanted – they wanted him to dispatch Sweep with the raised right fist. It was a collective bloodlust that could have come straight out of a gladiatorial fight in ancient Rome: they craved to see the clean kill - as when the Roman Emperor's thumb went down - the kill represented by a knockout. That crowd of mainly Sweep supporters now bayed for his demise, and they wanted it badly. But Samuel was not going to give them that just yet. In his exhausted mind, it was show time. It promoted a final adrenalin surge in his drained and weary body. '*Huzzah*,' again rang out from the crowd and Samuel looked skyward at his elevated fist. It was skinned and bloodied, a mixture of flesh, sinew and blood, but he did not see that: he saw a falcon waiting to swoop on its targeted prey. But once again Samuel flicked out another stinging left. The punch did not have full force but it opened another cut on Sweep's forehead and a new rivulet of blood flowed down and dripped off his eyebrow and into his eye to blur his vision even more.

To those at the back of the immense crowd a strange ritual appeared to be taking place on their skyline. A large and bloodied stationary figure was being mocked by two fistic birds of prey acting in unison. It would have been an uncomfortable sight to the uncommitted viewer – but there was no such person in the multitude that watched this cruel show. '*Huzzah*,' rang out again and again, but still one falcon flew high leaving the taunting to its partner, the other lower flying bird. And then Samuel did something outrageous; he walked all round the bloodied, swaying statue that was Sweep. It was the ultimate insult, the ultimate disrespect. Sweep was only semi-conscious and it was only his pride and his instinct that kept him on his feet. His corner pleaded for him to fight on but they were deluding themselves. The only thing he had left was his bravery and even that was now denied him for it had become detached from his conscious mind. And still Samuel did not unleash the high flying falcon. He turned a hundred and eighty degrees and walked all around

Sweep in the other direction. He was remembering all the insults that Sweep had made – all that goading that he had been forced to take, and he felt justified in belittling Sweep in this way.

'*Huzzah*', rang out once more and this time Samuel sensed that the time was right. He stood directly in front of his one-time hero and looked into his eyes. He saw nothing: Samuel, a compassionate man, now had no compassion within him. It had been left in his dressing tent for he knew that compassion was a weakness in the prize ring. At this moment he was totally immersed in the brutality of his profession. He transferred his weight onto the left leg and brought his flying right fist down hitting Sweep just above his left ear. The big man at first seemed to have absorbed the full force of the punch, but then a delayed reaction took place. He slowly sank to his knees and he fell forward onto his face, unconsciousness his only compassionate friend. The bell sounded.

The crowd let out a final unified '*Huzzah*' as they knew the fight was over. The collective brutality had assuaged its thirst for blood, but to some there was a feeling of great sadness. A hero had been found wanting. The distraught man, who had cried out for Sweep to, '*Do it for England,*' now shed a lonely tear. He was cocooned from the roars of the crowd and heard nothing but his own heart beating and his own thoughts of disbelief. '*Charlie you can't let him …,*' he called out but the words died away in his mouth and he did not finish the sentence - and no one was listening anyway, for the vast majority of the crowd was in a state of euphoria. A collective jubilation had overtaken them for they knew they had witnessed something remarkable. At this moment it did not seem to matter that many of them had also lost a great deal of money. Most had wanted and expected Charles Sweep to win, but any disappointment they felt was overtaken by the knowledge of the astonishing story that had unfolded before them. Sweep was dragged back to his corner, and his seconds frantically tried to revive him but deep down they knew what everybody else already knew. The seconds ticked agonisingly by. Water was poured copiously over the stricken giant, but they could have stood him in the glacial water of a cascading waterfall and it would have had no reviving effect. The smelling salts similarly failed to penetrate his unconsciousness and the seconds ticked on. The timekeeper looked frantically at his watch. His own adrenalin rush had kicked in and his heart beat twice as fast as the ponderous seconds before him. He counted out loud – 'twenty eight, twenty nine, thirty,' and then repeatedly rang his bell as loudly as he could to formally signify the end of the fight.

The ringmaster raised Samuel's arm high into the sky and the showman responded and then the crowd reciprocated. He was pronounced the winner by the ringmaster's words but the cheering crowd drowned them out. Pandemonium broke out. Jubilant fans invaded the ring and the seconds fought hard to protect Samuel from their enthusiasm. It seemed like a thousand hands patted his aching back.

One thought sustained him through this ordeal: The Light of Israel had bested Big Charles Sweep.

CHAPTER 29

'The K*ing* wants to see you,' said Rebecca, the note shaking in her hand as she read it. 'My God – the King! Do you hear me Samuel? It's from the King himself!'

Samuel looked at her in disbelief. 'The King himself!' he echoed, suddenly rendered inarticulate.

'Yes, the King,' said Rebecca, 'he's sending a carriage round for you tomorrow.'

'A carriage?' repeated Samuel, still overwhelmed by the information, but then the understanding kicked into his consciousness. 'Let me see.' He took the note and read it for himself.

'They're sending a carriage for me tomorrow.'

Rebecca just looked at him and gave him a knowing smile. 'I thought you said he didn't approve of fighting.'

'He doesn't – or at least he doesn't approve of gambling, or so they say. He's supposed to frown on the Prince of Wales's patronage of boxing.'

'So why does he want to see you?'

'He must have changed his mind and wants to offer his own congratulations. What else could it be?' said Samuel.

'I expect so,' said Rebecca. 'If he reads the newspapers he can't have avoided news of the fight. There's been little else to read for weeks.'

It's been *much* more that an ordinary fight, Rebecca thought to herself. For the first time she felt pride in her husband's abilities as a pugilist. The profession that she hated so much had brought a command from the King himself.

Samuel nodded to acknowledge the truth of the statement and stood up, groaning as he did so. It was Friday, five days after the fight, but his body still ached and the bruises still throbbed. The contusion on the side of his head had subsided and although his face was still stained blue and black his features had returned to something like their normal equilibrium. He looked human again, but it would be many days before his body would have time to recuperate fully. He had returned to London in triumph and it seemed that the whole city wanted to celebrate and revel in this most remarkable of fights. It had been the sole topic of conversation before it took place, but now it seemed to explode into new life. All the people wanted him – they wanted to be part of this great occasion – they wanted to be part of his achievement. It was as if the public's previous doubts about Samuel's 'Englishness' had evaporated: *he* was the Champion now. Songs had already been written and were being performed in the theatres and taverns that very night.

After the fight, Samuel had tried to accommodate his admirers, and for several hours had socialised - and at every turn there was a journalist wanting an interview. Everyone wanted a piece of him and the showman in him wanted to oblige, but he was utterly exhausted, his brain crying out for sleep - the sleep that would nourish his abused and painful body. Eventually giving in to it, he had called for a carriage, but instead of going to his rooms he had directed it to his home, anxious as to whether he would be welcome, but yearning for Rebecca's caring companionship that once he had enjoyed.

And so it was that in the early hours of the following morning a grotesquely battered man had knocked on his own front door and roused the household. Rebecca was called and stood before him in her nightgown. She held a candle to the misshapen face before her on the threshold and stifled a scream. She barely recognised him, and might not have done so were it not for his eyes. He did not speak; there was no need for his eyes spoke for him. They were the eyes of a small child returning home after trying to run away. They pleaded for acceptance but were fearful of rejection.

For a heartbeat Rebecca had hesitated, then had taken his arm and ushered him in. Still neither had spoken. A servant had helped her take him to her bed. She did it without thinking as though this was the place he belonged. He had collapsed a few feet short of the mattress and they struggled to get him on to it. She removed only his boots and his frockcoat for she knew that sleep was what he needed. Gently she bathed his sleeping, disfigured face; a face so hideous that it could not be loved – and yet it dawned on her that she did still love it; she still loved *him*.

Over three hours of fighting had left a terrible toll on his body. He slept for thirty-six hours and Rebecca feared for his life, but his body was merely recuperating; repairing damaged tissue and replenishing its reserves of energy. She had slept beside him for two nights and it had awakened her affection for him. She was transported back to those days when she had nursed him back to life after the first fight with the Gravedigger. Their love had grown from that ordeal and now she was again cast in the role of his nurse. She cuddled up to him in the dark hours and in the morning light she stroked his battered, ugly face and was not repelled by it. Life had run in a circle and it had conspired to heal their fractured relationship without any words being spoken.

He had awoken ravenously hungry, his body now demanding the sustenance of food to replace the sustenance of sleep. It showed that his body was weak but that it was healthy and that he would recover. Rebecca had seen that and was relieved – she knew that he would be well.

Now, three days later, Samuel paced the room, the King's message clutched in his scabbed fist. 'You must buy a new gown if you are to be presented to the King,' he said enthusiastically.

'But the invitation doesn't extend to me,' said Rebecca, 'Look, it only says *request the presence of Samuel Medina* – it doesn't mention me.'

'Nonsense,' said Samuel, turning towards her, 'you shall come with me. I want you to share in my good fortune.'

She reached up and kissed his cheek tenderly. Without thinking, he put his hand up to his cheek, his fingers touching the spot where her lips had lightly pressed. It was a small gesture but it had significance far beyond its size, and that significance was not lost on him. He realised suddenly how much he had missed her.

'I do share in your good fortune my love,' she said, 'I don't have to go with you to see the King for that to be true.'

Emotion suddenly seized his body. A lump took his throat and his eyes welled. Those simple words, *my love*, and wrenched his stomach and released his own feelings that had been locked away. The welling tears spilled over and flooded down his cheeks. With a harsh sob, he put his arms around her, fearful that she would once again be snatched away from him.

Rebecca put her hand to his wet, blue-black cheek and then kissed him tenderly on the lips. 'There-there *my love*,' she consoled him. Those two wonderful words again. *This* was the man she loved - the man with the poet's soul who could weep like a child. 'You shall go alone to see your King,' she said, 'and I will make sure that you look like a prince for him.

The coachman rapped at the front door and Samuel stood and took a deep breath, suddenly very nervous. Rebecca preened at his clothes one last time. She had sent for a tailor and the man had worked through the night to make up the suit. You look resplendent, she thought to herself, and was pleased with the tradesman's toils.

Samuel was regaled in a knee-length frock coat of black satin with a high stand-fall collar, with cutaway skirts at the front. She had got the idea for this from Big Charles Sweep himself who favoured this style. The sleeve opening was buttoned in such a way as to reveal the frill of his shirtsleeve. The coat was worn over black breeches with white stockings and shiny black, buckled shoes. 'You're fit now for your King,' said Rebecca, giving him one last possessive pat. She felt immense pride in him, and tried to conceal that she was carrying a terrible worry. She had been through the business accounts over and over again and she feared that vast sums were missing - but this wasn't the time unload this worry onto Samuel. 'We'll send for John when you come back,' she said, 'and celebrate,' she added quickly, to avoid arousing her husband's suspicions. Samuel smiled at her in gratitude, still not quite able to understand what had caused her change of heart, but immensely glad of it even so.

The royal carriage rattled regally through the streets. It was an open carriage and the wind caressed his hair and it bounced to the rhythm of the wheels on the rutted roads. He sat back in the seat to enjoy the luxury of the ride. Eyes turned at the sight of such a magnificent carriage recognising first the livery and the royal coat of arms and then they recognised its famous passenger. At Covent Garden the carriage was held up whilst a flock of geese, being herded through the streets, was moved hurriedly aside. The geese honked loudly, angry at being forced to get out of the way and the drover shouted and swore at them to cooperate. They were not inclined to do this, however, and one stood its ground flapping its wings aggressively and then stopped to shit as if in rebellion, much to the amusement of the passers by who laughed uncontrollably and then jeered the drover in support of the fowl. That short delay was enough for the crowd to gather round the vehicle. Samuel was instantly recognised. The crowd called his name and he nodded graciously to acknowledge them. The coachman called for the crowd to disperse but they were not about to let their hero go so easily. He turned to Samuel, 'Sir,' he said respectfully, 'you'd better stand and exhibit yourself or we'll never get away.

Samuel stood in the carriage and raised an arm in response to the crowd. He thought that would be enough to satisfy their acclaim, but they were not to be gratified so easily. A cheer went up to salute his celebrity and arms reached out to touch him. That cheer reverberated all around Covent Garden and more and more people came to see what the cheering was all about. Within five minutes the crowd had swelled to many hundreds and the area had become gridlocked with people. 'I was there,' shouted a sturdy fellow, 'but I wagered on Charlie Sweep.' The crowd laughed and Samuel joined them. '*I was there,*' shouted another man, 'I thought you were bested when you were put down the second time just after the bell had sounded.'

'So did I' hollered Samuel so that all could hear him. 'When you are hit by Big Charlie your senses are mashed like scrambled eggs.' The crowd laughed again. 'He's a big-un that Charlie Sweep,' shouted another man. 'Aye he is that, and he's a great fighter too – the best there is,' hollered Samuel, who was enjoying himself hugely; the crowd's recognition and acclaim were meat and drink to the showman in him.

'But not as good as you,' hollered another man, '*you* bested *him.*' A great 'H*uzzah!*' went up from the crowd and Samuel raised his hands to accept the accolade.

'Look my friends,' Samuel now hollered, 'I have a command to meet the King.' He took out the invitation and raised it into the air. His intention had been to ask the crowd to disperse so that the carriage could carry on, but the crowd only responded with another cheer. Question after question was shouted at him. Many had been at the fight, others had read about it in the newspapers. Those who could not read had pestered others to read the accounts to them; such was the interest in this fight. At this moment Samuel was the most famous man in England. The crowd wanted to know everything about the fight from the first bell to the last. How he had prepared for the fight, how he had overcome the weight and height difference, and how he had delivered the final blow. After half an hour Samuel was beginning to worry. Much as he was enjoying this he did not want to be late for his King, but the crowd's enthusiasm showed no signs of waning. The questions just kept on coming. He turned to the coachman and called for him to fetch a constable. The driver sent a small boy as a runner, but when eventually the runner returned, the constable saw no sense in turning a good-natured crowd into a discontented mob and contented himself with taking in the spectacle. Samuel realised that it was down to him. After an hour he became horribly aware that he had missed his appointment time and a panic rose within him. He raised his hand in an effort to silence the throng. He prided himself on his ability to play a crowd, but suddenly he had the problem in reverse. He knew how to fire them up but he had never been required to damp them down before. He knew, as all showmen do, that you should leave your crowd wanting more. But he had always had an exit before, a ring to climb out of, a stage wing to walk into, but here he was totally surrounded. He kept his hands raised for several minutes, but each time the crowd seemed to be responding another question would be fired at him and the crowd would again bay for an answer. He resolved to answer no more questions and just kept his arms raised and eventually there was some sort of lull. Then a man yelled out again, 'Tell us how you finished him, Samuel.' Another shouted, 'Show us your fist Samuel.'

'No no – no more,' said Samuel his hands still raised, he reached down with his hand to his pocket and again raised the King's command into the air but this only produced another cheer. 'My friends, my friends,' he shouted and the crowd quietened slightly to listen, 'I have my King's command here,' another cheer went up. He gestured with his hands for them to be quiet and they finally responded. 'The command is for *now* – I am commanded to go *now* and I'm already late.' The coachman took the cue and the carriage edged forward slightly. Samuel turned to look forward and he gestured with his arms for the crowd to part. Slowly they responded. The horses were agitated but the carriage continued to edge forward. He remained standing unsteadily as the carriage did so and another cheer went up. They cheered him on his way and he waved his paper command back at them.

Kew Palace was not as large as Samuel had expected. Nevertheless it was regal and it stood tall in its red-bricked splendour. The palace was set in gardens and had the appearance of a country residence, despite its proximity to the ever-encroaching capital. Samuel apologised nervously to the equerry for his lateness, but the man showed no sign of reciprocating his anxiety. 'His Majesty is still at luncheon with his children,' he said casually, 'if you'd care to wait, Sir,' he added, gesturing towards a chair.

Samuel realised that he was breathing heavily, partly from rushing and partly from apprehension. A bead of perspiration appeared on his forehead and then trickled down the side of his eye and then down his cheek. He took a kerchief from his pocket and mopped his brow and then straightened his cuffs and collar. He rehearsed in his mind over and over again how he would greet the King, but as the minutes ticked by his trepidation eased to apprehension and then to mere nervousness. After two tedious hours of waiting, boredom replaced anxiety as each minute by mind numbing minute crawled by. He looked about him, at the finery and opulence of this anti-room, but even that could not hold his attention for this span of time.

Suddenly, just as the first stirrings of anger were beginning to replace Samuel's boredom, two mammoth doors opened and the equerry reappeared. He bowed graciously to Samuel as if that were enough to apologise for the long delay. 'His Majesty will see you in the drawing room, Sir,' he said and then gestured in the direction that he should walk.

The equerry opened the door to the drawing room and entered in front of Samuel. He bowed and then announced, 'Mr Samuel Medina, your Majesty.' He backed away, closing the towering doors as he did so, taking great care not to turn his back on his Monarch. Samuel, his gaze fixed firmly on the ground, felt suddenly alone and isolated, as insignificant as a fly on the wall. Without looking up, he also bowed formally, 'Your Majesty,' he said, 'this is a great honour.' There was no response, however, and for a heartbeat he thought he had committed a terrible faux pas. The equerry had told him two things – firstly that he should not speak to the King unless the King had addressed him first and secondly that he should avoid eye contact. He realised that he had broken the first piece of advice so he resolutely endeavoured not to break the second. He determinedly looked downwards but his embarrassment grew by the second. It *was* only seconds but it felt like an eternity. He raised his eyes slightly motivated by his growing embarrassment but still fearful that he was breaking the royal rules. He saw a lady's feet. He tentatively raised his eyes further and saw that it was Queen Charlotte. She was busy at her embroidery but she sensed his embarrassment and she smiled back at him. He bowed to acknowledge her and she responded with an almost imperceptible movement of her head. But then she gestured with her head much more distinctly in the direction of a large table at the far end of the room. Samuel turned to look, but seated there was a mere boy of sixteen who he identified as Prince Adolphus Frederick, but the king was nowhere to be seen. He was now totally confused and his embarrassment continued to mount. He looked around the room trying to make sense of his bearings.

The drawing room was long and rectangular with large sash windows allowing light to flood in. The walls were panelled but painted pink. The long curtains were brilliant scarlet hanging almost from ceiling to floor, and this was reflected in the fabric on the furniture – the chairs and couches being likewise scarlet. The carpet was of a swirling Turkish design in the high fashion of the day, being a busy mix of vibrant reds, greens and blues. The sumptuousness was evident but it was not overstated in that stylish Georgian way.

Samuel's mind started to race as he tried frantically to decide what he should do, but he came to no conclusion and so he just stood there like a toy soldier without a playmate.

'That's enough children,' said the Queen matter of factly, 'you have teased Mr Medina long enough.' Giggles came from below the table, and Samuel looked down as two girls now crawled from beneath the elegant table – the thirteen-year-old Princess Sophia and the seven-year-old Princess Amelia. They were laughing and chatting, wildly pleased with their little wheeze. The two then reached back and each took a hand and pulled from within a man. 'Come, Papa,' said the Princess Amelia.

It was the King. He too had been hiding beneath the table. Crawling out from under it, dishevelled, his face flushed, his wig askew, he got to his feet clumsily with the help of his daughters and straightened himself, tugging down his satin waistcoat and then his frockcoat. Samuel was completely bemused. He had expected – well, he was not sure quite what he *had* expected. He had imagined he would see his King sat regally on his throne - however naïve that expectation might have been. But the last thing he had expected was to see his King playing hide and seek with his children like any normal family man. Samuel was dumbfounded. The King walked towards him boldly and held out his hand.

'My dear fellow,' he said, 'come and sit down. My children and I have so many questions for you.' Samuel instinctively shook his King's hand, nonplussed. In Samuel's eye it was somewhat gratifying that the King was also a family man and liked nothing more than to clown about with his children, but there was no acknowledgement from the King that his behaviour was in any way bizarre. Samuel had heard of the King's bouts of madness and now wondered if the rumours were true. Yet the man seemed perfectly normal in his eyes as he gestured Samuel to a chair. It faced a couch on which the King and his three children now seated themselves.

Samuel did as he was bid and looked at the King in anticipation. A plump man, the King's bulbous Hanoverian blue eyes were quite striking, sitting atop of a large nose, full, fat lips and a florid complexion. The Queen looked insignificant besides her husband; she was small, plain and thin, but dark-skinned: an inheritance from her Moorish ancestors. This oddly matched couple were nevertheless devoted.

'Can I see your fist, Mr Medina?' asked the young Prince Adolphus Frederick. Samuel raised his arm and made a fist. The

Prince stood regally, as he had been trained to do, and came forward, grasping Samuel's scarred fist in his adolescent hand, unable to circumnavigate it. 'Look Papa,' said the Prince, 'do you think it's bigger than that of our coachman?'

'Maybe,' said the King, 'but Henry is a big man too.

The King and his children snapped questions at Samuel for almost an hour. The young Prince in particular was so interested in knowing everything about the fight. And then the Queen raised her head from her embroidery.

'You are a Jew, Mr Medina, are you not?' she said in her heavy accent.

'Aye Ma'am,' answered Samuel not sure where this conversation was going. Was this an attack against his faith? His nervousness left him instantly, as it always did when he felt his faith was being threatened. A resolve took him. He prepared, if needs be, to defend that faith, for that is what he had always done, and not even his Queen would be immune from that - but then, it transpired that his unease was ill-founded.

'Then you have a rare honour, Mr Medina,' she continued, 'do you know that you are the first Jew to be formally presented to a reigning King of England?'

Samuel exhaled – the breath was elongated and with it he expelled his anxiety. 'No Ma'am,' he said, 'I didn't know that. I am indeed greatly honoured.' He bowed his head formally and the Queen reciprocated regally.

'My husband's advisers were against this meeting, you know.'

'Then I am doubly grateful to his Majesty for this honour,' said Samuel still picking his words very carefully, 'I am proud for myself and for my people. I value this honour far more than my victory over Charles Sweep.' He held his breath wondering whether he had chosen his words wisely.

'Well said Sir,' said the King, 'stout fellow, what! what!'

Samuel bowed again in acknowledgement. 'Your Majesty is too kind,' he said, relieved and reassured that he had been accepted.

'Papa,' said the young Prince enthusiastically if naively, 'can you ask Mr Medina to fight our coachman? I'm sure Henry could best him'

The King laughed at the suggestion. 'We can't ask him to do that,' he said, Mr Medina is our guest.'

With a wry smile Samuel addressed the Prince, 'And that would be most unfair to your coachman, your Highness. I am a master of the science of pugilism.' He turned to the King, 'Can I suggest to your Majesty that the Prince may be entertained if I exhibit my *skills* with your coachman, if he will oblige me in this endeavour?'

'But where?' said the King.

'Here in the drawing room will suffice, if your Majesty will permit.'

'No no,' said the Queen looking up from her embroidery, 'I must withdraw with the girls if you do this. You must consider our sensibilities.' Samuel bowed profusely to acknowledge her. 'Your Majesty,' said Samuel, 'I assure you that nothing will happen to upset your sensibilities. My wife has overseen my exhibitions so that they will in no way offend a lady's sensibility.'

'Oh Mama, can we stay?' said the young Princesses in unison.' The Queen looked at the two Princesses and then sighed as she looked back at Samuel. 'I am relying on you Mr Medina,' she said.

The coachman was indeed a big man. Henry stood at least as tall as Big Charles Sweep himself. He arrived feeling somewhat out of place, for he had never been summoned to the King's chambers before. He hid his unease well, however, and stood tall in his fine livery of purple with gold braid, complete with white gloves and a white wig. He was a former soldier and he now exhibited himself like a soldier on parade. His face had been handsome once but several scars and a broken nose now blemished it. One scar in particular ran from his forehead down to his eyebrow and then reappeared on his cheek and ran down the full length of his face to his chin. Samuel looked at the face and knew instantly that the job description of 'coachman' was a misnomer. He was in reality a bodyguard – his job was to protect the royal family. That scar must have been a terrible wound. A wound that could so nearly have taken his eye, but he had obviously been lucky for now two pale piercing blue eyes looked at Samuel with an analytical gaze. He agreed readily to spar with Samuel for in reality a refusal was never in his remit.

'Will this be cudgel, sabre or toe to toe, your Majesty,' he said in a deep bass voice, which resonated in the fine acoustics of the drawing room that was often used for musical recitals.

'Oh no, no, no,' said the Queen, 'Mr Medina if you please.' Samuel bowed again and took Henry by the arm and walked him to the far end of the room.

'I take it that you have fighting skills?' asked Samuel.

'Aye,' said Henry, 'I'm trained in the cudgel, sabre and pistol, Sir.' The sabre and the pistol were weapons of gentlemen and Henry had been taught these skills in the army. Samuel did not possess these skills, but was proficient in the cudgel. He had trained young gentlemen in his academy on its use; the cudgel was a formidable weapon for close combat fighting. A pistol gave only one shot before it needed reloading, and the sabre needed room to manoeuvre. The cudgel was a point of contact between them but it was a brutal weapon and not appropriate for this exhibition. Samuel explained that it would be a sparring session, an exhibition, but that his punches would be pulled and that no contact would be made and no blood would be spilled. On the other hand he was content for Henry to try to hit him, for he was confident that he could easily defend himself.

'But I also have skills in toe to toe fighting Sir,' said Henry. 'With respect, Sir, but you don't have my stature and I'm confident that I can hit you if I so wish.'

Samuel pondered. The coachman had effectively said that he was too big for him. He had no wish to offend his companion and he also acknowledged that the safety of the royal family would not be put into the hands of a less that competent man. In fact he reasoned that Henry was probably the best at what he did. He resolved to be cautious.

'Then we shall both pull our punches, Henry,' said Samuel, 'do you know how to do that.'

'Aye,' said Henry, 'I have to do it all the time when I train. If I didn't no one would train with me.'

'Splendid,' said Samuel realising rather late in the day that Henry would be a dangerous man in any real contest.

They both removed their gloves, frock coats and neckties. Henry removed his wig to display that his hair was beginning to grey at the sides. Samuel realised that Henry was probably in his forties with all the guile of well-tested man. He was proved right in that assessment. Samuel narrated his moves as he had done so many times and Henry reacted instinctively. He played his part beautifully as if he'd been trained to it. The royal children were thrilled, the young Prince in particular was an enthusiastic supporter of Henry, and it did not seem to matter to him that it was not really a genuine fight. '*Bravo!*' the King called at regular intervals.

The exhibition lasted a full half hour and Samuel was elated by the experience. He was a Jew and yet here he was in the presence of the King himself, and his Majesty was shouting his exultations for him, Samuel Medina, The Light of Israel. Life was sweet indeed at this point in his life. He was only twenty-four years old, and yet he had already achieved so much. He had wealth and fame and he had managed to invade the very highest levels of society. His own people loved him and he was even loved by the populace at large. He had managed to overcome the social stigma of Judaism to become a man that personified what it was to be English.

He was indeed rich in life's pleasures.

What Samuel could not have foretold was that these riches were to prove transitory. They were about to vanish from his life like sparks from a bonfire that ascend on the wind and evaporate into the night sky.

CHAPTER 30

Samuel was becoming frantic. The drizzle bathed his face as he tramped the streets in his search to find John Campbell-John. He had been searching for several hours and water dripped from the end of his nose and chin despite repeated swabbing movements of his hand. It was early June but the English weather was at its most capricious. He was sweating heavily beneath the weight of his greatcoat, which had become even heavier as it had absorbed the burden of hours of rain. The air was still and the atmosphere muggy, low cloud and drizzle capturing the smoke from a myriad of cooking fires, so that the city was encumbered by a haze that made it look drab and grey and this further blackened his mood. John had not been seen at his rooms for days, nor had he been seen at any of his usual places. After visiting Molly Jasper's it became apparent that Samuel was not the only person who was searching for him. A collective panic was abroad at the news of his disappearance and Samuel's attempts to find him only fuelled that alarm and that alarm fuelled Samuel's own anxiety. 'Been lookin' for 'im for days Mister,' said a tradesman, anxious about the money he was owed. People were now desperate to call in their debts, fearful that there would be nothing left for them. The vultures were gathering, but no corpse could be found to pick over. Samuel returned home disconsolate, his anxiety mounting by the hour.

'Did you find him?' asked Rebecca.

'I don't think he wants to be found,' said Samuel, 'it looks as if everybody wants him. They all want their money.'

'Who *are* all these people looking for him?' Deep down Rebecca knew the answer to that question.

Samuel grimaced. 'Who's *not* looking for him is a better question. He owes everybody.'

'But we knew he had debts.'

'Aye Rebecca, we did, but not to this extent. They're all looking for him, his jeweller, his lace maker, his bookmaker, his gun maker, his shoemaker.' He paused for a moment but then the list in his head continued to grow, 'his bookseller, his saddler, his coach maker, his tailor, his embroiderer, his hatter, his watchmaker, not to mention the debts for his household expenses – but even worse that those, my love; Molly Jasper is looking for him!'

'But how can that be? We've made him a rich man,' said Rebecca. 'We made him an equal partner.'

'Aye, but it seems he has just gambled it all away. What I don't understand is – why now? His share of the Sweep fight would have enabled him to pay off at least half of his debts – and on top of that he would have had his wagers.'

Looking at her husband, Rebecca realised why she loved him so. He was such a decent and honest man himself that he did not see the glaring truth that stood before him. 'Samuel, my love,' she said, 'isn't it obvious?'

'What?' he said shaking his head, unable to comprehend the point she was making.

'He didn't think that you could win.'

'Well he wasn't the only one who thought that,' Samuel grinned, 'most people thought I...' And then he gasped, '*No!*' as the realisation took him liked a thunderbolt. 'He bet on Sweep,' he murmured to himself. He turned to look at Rebecca, the pain of betrayal standing in his eyes. 'He bet on Sweep, didn't he?' he repeated.

'I fear so, my love,' she said, 'he saw a way out of his debt trouble and he took it. And now he's got his comeuppance for his blatant disloyalty.'

'But Sweep was odds on,' Samuel said. 'He would have needed a *huge* sum to make that bet. And with his debts the bookmakers would never have extended him that much credit.' Samuel looked at Rebecca as if he was a little child looking for reassurance, but he saw none in her face. A feeling of dread welled up inside him.

'You had better sit down, my love,' she said. He collapsed into his chair and she knelt before him and took his hand gently. 'I fear that he has taken us down with him.'

'What do you mean? But how? Why?' he stammered, his thoughts incoherent as he read Rebecca's expression.

'I was hoping against hope that you would find him so that he would come and explain it all away. But it's not to be.'

'What has he done?' he said, a cold fearful sweat suddenly covering his whole body. When fear took him in the ring adrenalin channelled it into action. But now he was presented with a fear that adrenalin could not ameliorate. He felt helpless.

'I've been through the accounts and they've been plundered. The investments have been cashed in and the proceeds are missing.'

'So there's no money for the investors in the Box Club,' said Samuel.

'None. Nor is there any money to back up the bank notes issued in your name,' she said.

'But that was the whole point of the venture,' he protested. 'My name was the guarantee – my *honourable* name.'

'Aye, my love,' she said, 'he has not only stolen your money, he has stolen your name.' The look of incredulity that had taken Samuel's face metamorphosed into a look of anger: a cold, menacing anger. It was an expression that Rebecca had not seen before and it disturbed her.

'How much?' he asked.

She paused for a heartbeat fearful of his reaction. '£2,000, or thereabouts,' she said finally.

'£2,000? God damn it!' he exclaimed, jumping to his feet. 'Then we are indeed ruined.' He held his head in his hands and pulled at his hair in despair. 'We face bankruptcy and the King's Bench...' he added, his voice fading away as he did so.

'Aye, it's bad Samuel,' said Rebecca, 'but I've had a few days to think about it.'

'You have known for days?' he asked incredulously.

'Suspected for days,' she amended, 'and it's given me time to work things out.'

The look of anger now changed into a look of anguish. 'I'm not sure that this is something we *can* work out,' he said.

Rebecca squeezed his hand to reassure him. 'Look, we are both young. If we lose everything we can still start again – together.' She reached up and cupped the side of his face with her hand. He took that hand in his own and kissed it tenderly. 'But what we mustn't lose is your good name – we must protect that at all costs. Do you understand that?'

'Aye,' said Samuel, bolstered by what she had said, 'my honourable name is what is important. I'll not have it said that Samuel Medina is a cheat – a swindler.'

'So the first thing we need is discretion.' Samuel looked at her nonplussed, not understanding what she meant. 'If the word gets out that John Campbell-John has stolen from us then there will be a *run* on the business,' she said, 'the Box investors will want to get their money out, and all the bank notes that we have issued will be presented for payment.'

'But given my honourable name - will they not give me time?'

'I'm afraid that will stand for nought if panic sets in,' she said. 'So we have to get that money put back to show that we are solvent.'

'But £2,000,' said Samuel, 'that's a King's ransom.'

''Tis my love – but I've done the arithmetic, and there's a lot we can raise. Think about it.'

'Aye, you're right. We have the receipts from the Sweep fight to start with.' He stopped as a realisation took him, 'but John was in charge of all that.'

'I know, and it seems that he has plundered about £200 of that as well.'

'The shit barn door!' exclaimed Samuel, frantically pacing the room. 'God damn the bastard for the son of a whore that he is.' He stopped in his tracks, looked at his wife apologetically realising he had broken a social taboo. One never swore in front of a lady, even if she was his wife. 'I'm sorry, my dear,' he said.

She shrugged it off with a tight smile. 'It seems that he was so eager to get away that he took only what he could quickly get his hands on before he fled. The vast majority of the takings are safe.'

'Thank God! Do we have any tallies yet?'

'I've sent out instructions that everything is to be brought to us here. I think we are looking at gross takings of about £1,900 of which John has taken £200, which will leave us about £1,700.'

'Our share of the Gravedigger fight was £400,' said Samuel, 'and the money I sent from the exhibitions. How much of that is left?'

'We have £190 with our bankers, and the house is worth about £80.'

'The house!' said Samuel forlornly, the depth of the problem suddenly deepening, 'can't we avoid that?'

'It's the house or your name Samuel,' she said, 'we have to decide which is the most important. How much of the exhibition fees that *you* kept can we add to that? Samuel looked at her sheepishly for he had been indulging in the high life with John Campbell-John.

'I'm afraid that I can only add about 50 sovereigns, my dear,' he said.

'Then we are very close,' she said passing over his profligacy.

'But we have the promotion expenses for the fight to pay: the tents, the enclosure, the ring and all the stewards. It must come to about £300.'

'I'm afraid that debt must wait, my love. Our first priority is to liquidise all the funds we can so that if any one of the investors seeks his money we pay it immediately and without hesitation. There must be no rumours – nobody must think their money is at risk.'

Samuel had no trouble in finding a buyer for his fashionable house and within four weeks had moved his family to rented accommodation. Their new rented rooms were modest and in the heart of the Jewish community. It was sparsely furnished and despite Rebecca's best efforts somehow it did not feel like a home. The house had been sold quickly and they had called in all the fight receipts. They had managed to reinvest £1,558 with the bank and that would almost cover their investors' debts. It was now a month since John's disappearance and the Medinas were beginning to feel better about their predicament. Their net worth was now below zero, carrying debts of about £300, but they believed that they had protected Samuel's good name. The black mood was beginning to lift until one morning there was a thunderous rapping at the front door. It was a few minutes past nine o'clock – much too early for social callers. Across the breakfast table, Samuel looked at Rebecca with a puzzled expression. She met his gaze not with puzzlement but with high apprehension, sensing that something was seriously wrong.

Samuel answered the door nervously - it was one of his collection agents. The man spat words at him, but at first they made little sense.

'Start again,' said Samuel, 'and slow down. Now what's the problem?' The man took a large gulp of air and started again as he had been bid.

'I can't get into the shop,' he said, 'They're queuing down the street – they all want their money, Mr Medina.'

'Queuing? They're queuing?' said Samuel.

'Well not really queuing,' said the agent, 'it's more like a mob. The ones at the back fear that they'll get nothing and are desperate to get to the front.' Rebecca came to join Samuel and she realised exactly what was happening. The agent looked from Samuel to her, 'What's going on, Mrs Medina?' he asked.

'It a *run*, Mr Isaac,' she said to the agent. 'They think we have pilfered their savings.' The agent looked at her for reassurance and she gestured that reassurance with no more than a nod, but it was enough to satisfy his concern. He exhaled heavily. 'So what do we do?' he asked.

'You pay them,' Mr. Isaac.

'Me!' exclaimed the agent, 'we'll be out of money in ten minutes. I've only the daily float to pay them with and what do I do when that's gone – they'll lynch me, Mrs Medina.'

'No, they won't,' said Rebecca. 'We are all prepared for this. You act as though nothing is wrong, and when you give them the money you say that you hope that they'll reinvest it with us as soon as possible. Remind them that the shop is open tomorrow, and to tell their friends that Samuel Medina guarantees their money is safe, the same as he always has done.'

'Me!' exclaimed the agent again.

'Don't worry,' said Rebecca, 'Samuel will come along to protect you.' She turned to Samuel. 'Go and open the shop. Be calm and insist on order and then start paying with a smile and all the assurance you can muster. I'll go straight to the bank and be with you as soon as I can.'

'Will you be safe bringing all that money?' Samuel's concern was etched onto his features.

'Don't worry, I'll get the bank to escort me back to St. Giles,' she said. 'Now go, we must stop these rumours in their tracks.'

By noon the crowds had dispersed. They had all been paid and the clamour and fervour had been released like steam escaping from a pressure valve. All those who had presented their notes or demanded their savings had received their money, and with each payment the anxiety diminished. As the apprehension eased it became easier to maintain order and by mid-morning the anxious mob had given way to a crowd of people waiting patiently for their money. The arrival of the bank messengers emphasised the propriety of the business, and some people at the end of the queue left without demanding payment.

It had been an awful day, but thanks to Rebecca's foresight, they had weathered it. They had wondered who might have started the rumour that had led to the run on Samuel's bank, but as they made their way home, tired and relieved at the end of that dreadful day, it no longer seemed to matter.

They were wrong.

At nine o'clock the following morning the whole episode repeated itself, as it did again the day after that and the day after that. All the funds at the bank were being depleted - they could just about meet their investor's demands, but they would be left with no working capital whatsoever.

'I've found out who's behind it all,' shouted Samuel whilst wiping his feet at the front door 'It's Ruddle - Sir Oliver Ruddle.'

Rebecca hurried towards him. 'What? Surely not!' she exclaimed, adding, 'But how?'

'He's been sending out runners each night to the taverns and the cock pits to spread the rumour that we've filched all the money.'

'I don't understand. Why would he do that?'

'Bad blood,' said Samuel. 'John crossed him - well several times really. He's just an antagonistic sort of a man. It's his way of taking his revenge.'

'Is he the one who was with Charlie Sweep when he caused the fight at the Academy?'

'That's him— he was probably behind the whole thing. John always believed that he was also behind the Magistrates closing the Academy.'

'But it all seems a little extreme doesn't it?' said Rebecca, 'sending out runners once maybe, but we've shown him that we can meet the demands. Why does he keep doing it?'

'Vengeance, retribution – he wants it. He wants it badly. He's the sort of man that must have it.'

'But have you wronged him so very much?'

'Only by winning when he bet against me. That's enough for Ruddle to bear a grudge.'

'But to go to these extremes seems perverse.'

'Aye, so it does,' said Samuel, 'but I think it's because *he* can't find John either.'

'So if he can't get John then he comes after you?' said Rebecca

'That's about the size of it my dear.'

'Well I suppose he's had his revenge of sorts now – but we've survived.' She thought intently for a moment, unsure of how to broach the next question. 'Did John ever tell you where his father lived?' she asked at last.

Samuel thought. 'No, not really – may have said Worcestershire; or was that his regiment - I'm not sure. Why?'

'Well I've been down to the Army Headquarters at Horse Guards to see if they can give me an address for him or his regiment,' said Rebecca

'Somewhere to start looking for him, I suppose.'

'Yes that's what I thought, but they were not very helpful. They made me sit in a cold waiting room for four hours. I suspect young women must turn up all the time trying to trace soldiers that have deceived them. And of course, being a Jewess didn't help. I think they thought I was a nuisance to them and if they just left me I would eventually give up and go home.'

'But knowing you, you didn't.' Samuel smiled fondly and teased a strand of hair from her brow.

'No, my love – I didn't give up. It was cold and it smelt of horse liniment and stale tobacco, but I saw it out.'

'Will it help if I go?' said Samuel.

'No need,' she said, 'they were less unhelpful when they realised that the name I had given didn't exist.'

'What! – that can't be right,' said Samuel, 'they were probably just trying to fob you off.'

'Possibly, but they say there is no record of a John Campbell-John in the army records.'

Samuel looked at her perplexed. 'What!' he said again, unable to come up with anything more coherent. He blew out his cheeks, said slowly, 'I had realised over the years that John was a rogue, but I never doubted that he was a real soldier.'

'It looks as if he's been deceiving us all, my dear,' she said.

'But he spoke like an officer and had the uniform as well,' said Samuel.

'That's true - he was certainly convincing. Whoever he is, he is a well-educated man,' she said.

Samuel looked at her again intently for several moments. The slow ticking of the clock rhythmically punctuated the silence, but its comfortable beat was like an old companion and it did not break into his consciousness. The clock then struck the quarter hour but even this went unnoticed whilst the significance of that phrase seeped little by little into his mind. '*Whoever* he is' he said, 'what do you mean *whoever he is*?'

'I think we have to face up to the possibility that the name John Campbell-John may be as fictitious as his army rank,' said Rebecca.

She was right and he now knew it. He had been just nineteen when he had first met John Campbell-John and he had naively taken him at face value, never questioning in his own mind the bona fides of the man who stood before him. But then, so had everybody else – he wasn't alone in that. He sighed, somehow saddened. 'It's a pretty state of affairs, my love,' he said.

'True enough, my dear; the authorities will try and find him, of course – one of the creditors will certainly file a complaint and the

Magistrate will issue a summons to appear before the King's Bench before long.'

'So it'll be debtor's prison, for John,' said Samuel.

'I fear so,' she said. She took his hand tenderly, but then sighed heavily, 'that is, of course if they can find him.'

CHAPTER 31

The summer of 1790 had been late in arriving. The greenness of spring had not deigned to arrive until May, leaving April with the redundant brownness of winter that should have been long gone by that normally inspirational month. But the shortened spring gave way to a blazing summer and the city baked in hot sunshine for weeks. It was a period of honest toil for Samuel and Rebecca as they took personal control of the business. It was never intended that the businesses would reap any great financial reward for them, but it was always accepted that it should be sound. The funds in the Box Club were to be invested and the interest would be split between the investors and the business. Their business plan was for the Club to cover its running costs out of its share of the interest and Samuel and Rebecca would keep the balance - the bank notes they issued paid no interest and so the interest on the investments came to them only after covering the running costs.

Both businesses had come close to being wiped out by the panicked runs caused by Sir Oliver Ruddle, but day after sweltering day Samuel and Rebecca had gone to their remaining shop, the other two having been closed down, and smiled and displayed respectability and paid out diligently whenever an investor presented for repayment. As September arrived, confidence was returning and they had built the business back up to approximately twenty-five per cent of what it had been before the run. But no capital, of course, meant no additional interest and they had little personal money coming in. It had been critical that the business be seen to re-establish its reputation; this had been their number one priority. Samuel offered to go into the ring again, but Rebecca would have none of it, and so it was decided that Samuel would re-open his Academy and start exhibiting again.

The Academy clients returned enthusiastically, drawn by his increased fame, although he spent most of his time during the first week doing little training: his young gentlemen wanted to know everything about the fight with Big Charlie Sweep and they threw questions at him at every opportunity. And when that subject temporarily waned then another question inevitably followed. 'Who will you fight next?' asked a particularly insistent young gentleman.

He was the son of a Duke and barely eighteen, but he paid handsomely for his tuition. A cry of *'Huzzah'* went up prompted by his youthful enthusiasm. Samuel raised his arms, the palms of his hands open to dispel their eagerness. They quieted as he had gestured for them to do, but held their breath awaiting his answer.

'I will not fight again,' said Samuel for what seemed like the hundredth time. 'You all know from the newspapers that I have given an assurance to my dear wife that I will fight no more pitched battles.'

There was a collective cry of *'No Sir!'* from his eager supporters. They were young and failed to appreciate the nature of the man they admired so much. They saw only a pugilist, not a man of morals and principles. From their lofted view of life, morality was usually paper-thin anyway and extended little beyond the rules of Georgian society – and even those applied only to their own kind - so they failed to comprehend. In their insular world a wife did as her husband bade her and they saw no problem.

'But you said *that* before the Sweep fight,' cried out another young gentleman.

'Aye that is true,' said Samuel. He paused and sighed heavily realising that they did not understand, but he tried to explain anyway. 'I am honour bound, gentlemen, to keep that promise and that is an end to it.'

They jeered him good-humouredly but then the questions returned to the Sweep fight and although this was tedious he was nevertheless relieved. It was September and the sweltering heat of the summer was still lingering, but he was somehow refreshed to be in his Academy again, aside from which it also meant much needed income.

Rebecca preened at his freshly laundered shirt. It was not new and that disappointed her for the gleaming whiteness that came with newness had faded. They were back stage at the Drury Lane Theatre and Samuel was preparing himself for his reappearance on stage to exhibit his skills. They had negotiated a fee of fifty guineas, and with that amount their spirits had risen and they could see an end to their money worries. They could see that riding the wave of Samuel's fame could pay off their debts. The more exhibitions that he could do the quicker his debts could be paid off. He was uncharacteristically nervous. For the first time in his life the prospect of failure had hit him. He had always had an unquenchable belief in his own abilities but he had never had the burden of debt before. In fact, fighting had always pledged the opposite – the promise of the wealth that came with victory. A promise that had tantalised him, spurred him on to take that victory as if it he were plucking the ripest fruit from the highest branch – the apple of victory. But now he was plainly aware that failure meant his burden of debt would remain. He was not even fighting a pitched battle – he was only going to spar; to exhibit his skills. He needed the crowd to continue their adoration of him. His forehead was furrowed in worry and Rebecca noticed.

'You seem troubled my love,' she said.

Samuel paused for a heartbeat. 'I wish John was here.'

'John!' exclaimed Rebecca, 'I'm sure *I* don't wish he was here. That odious, dishonourable man has beggared us.'

'Yes – of course my dear,' said Samuel, 'it's just that...' he paused, 'it's just that he was a wonderful presenter. He had a wonderful wit – he knew how to make an audience laugh.'

'But you have an eloquence of words that he never had,' said Rebecca. Samuel smiled inwardly at her loyalty. ''Tis true, my love,' she repeated, realising what he was thinking. 'You are the most eloquent of men.' She held his hand and kissed his cheek. 'The people love you,' she said, and anyway you have Solomon and Tobias to spar with, don't you?'

'Aye,' said Samuel with feigned confidence, 'that I have.'

Toby Tobias had been released temporarily from his duties by Lord Cowden; Solomon was Samuel's younger brother. Both had agreed to exhibit with Samuel on this first night. When Toby returned eventually to his duties, Solomon would take the major role. Both men had been schooled for some days by Samuel and knew what they had to do, but all the presentation was to be performed by Samuel himself, and he felt alone and exposed.

The curtain went up: Toby and Solomon were standing at the front on either side of the stage; Toby to the left and Solomon to the right. They each stood forcefully with their heads back and arms folded as if they were guarding the entrance to some emperor's palace. They wore only their white breeches and boxing slippers, their chests naked revealing their musculature. Toby in particular looked a magnificent spectacle. Samuel had insisted that he smear his arms and torso with oils, and his ebony skin now sparkled in the theatre lights. Behind them in the centre of the stage was a mock ring that in reality was no more than an incomplete set of ropes. They represented the elevation of the ring that was facing the audience, but the ropes of the far elevation were illusory, having been painted on a backdrop, and there were none to represent the sides - but from the audience's perspective the illusion was successful. Samuel waited in the wings and listened for the applause, but none came. His heart in his mouth he looked back at Rebecca for reassurance and she gestured that reassurance with a smile. He looked down to the stage boards and then took a deep breath and walked into the centre of the stage, his apprehension mounting with each step. It was the loneliest walk that he had ever taken.

And then a roar detonated like a skyrocket suddenly releasing its powder to explode in a cascade of multicoloured lights across the night-blackened heavens. *Bravo! Bravo!* shouted some, and others shouted, *Huzzah! Huzzah!* One by one people got to their feet and applauded vigorously. Samuel's fears were unfounded, brought on by months of anxiety. The reality was that while his reputation had initially been damaged by-rumours of impropriety, these past months of honest toil had dispelled them and he was again hailed as the people's hero.

With those cheers all his fears drained away and he was his old self - brash and self-confident. He considered gesturing for them to stop so that he could get on with his exhibition, but showman that he was, he strutted back and forth across the stage, raising his arms at intervals in acknowledgement of their acclaim. He remembered what Jeremiah Cotton had told him that he should always acknowledge applause. He broke into little sessions of sparring and the crowd went wild with delight. For twenty minutes he milked every last drop of acclamation. This privately self-effacing man had once again been transformed into the brash showman. Both these personalities were Samuel Medina – the two sides of this complex man.

Eventually he raised his arms and with the palms of his hands open gestured and quieted the crowd. They responded: he could almost taste their adoration for him. There was a strange paradox in that *he* was supposed to be the performer yet he was able to get an audience to perform to his own will. When they had quietened, he explained that the exhibition was to be in two parts. Firstly he would put on a demonstration of the science of pugilism, but in part two he would attempt to recreate scenes from his epic battle with that noble giant, Charles Sweep, with the help of Toby Tobias playing the part of Big Charles Sweep himself. This set the crowd off again and they cheered their appreciation of the delights he promised them.

The performance had been scheduled for two hours, but at every turn it was held up whilst the audience bayed their approval and delight. Samuel took no action to dispel that enthusiasm so that the crowd could enjoy the performance to the full. When questions were shouted he stopped the performance and explained and answered by way of demonstrations with Toby. He ad-libbed throughout, to the point where Toby and Solomon were confused, but none of it detracted from the performance. It was a showpiece, a master class of his profession. It extended to over four hours, by which time the inebriated in the audience - and there were many of those as there always were - had sobered up and were now intoxicated merely by the performance. When Samuel finally concluded the show, he was forced to come back for seven more encores and the performance entered its fifth hour, actually exceeding the length of the fight with Sweep. It had been a major triumph.

Samuel, Rebecca, Toby and Solomon reclined in Samuel's dressing room. The adrenalin was beginning to wear off to be replaced by fatigue. It was a wonderful fatigue however, like basking in the glow of the last rays of sunshine on a summer's evening. That circle of life that had brought him so many heartaches in the last few months was now moving back in his favour. Or so he thought.

There was suddenly a loud and persistent rapping at the dressing room door. With no sense of foreboding, Samuel opened the door. The sight that met his eyes hit him like a lightening bolt.

'Mr Samuel Medina?' said the first of two Bow Street Runners before him. Samuel paused, rendered speechless. 'Mr Samuel Medina?' the man repeated.

'Err – yes,' mumbled Samuel eventually. 'What can I do for you, Sirs?'

'I am acting on a warrant issued by the Magistrate at Bow Street, Sir,' said the constable handing him a piece of paper. Samuel read it but the words somehow did not seem to register in his consciousness. He was in mild shock and all he could think about was the months of hard work he had put in to avoid this very situation. He went back to the beginning of the paper and read it again, but still could not take in the words. Finally he became aware that he was to be taken into custody, and that was as far as his mind allowed him to comprehend; it blocked out the other words even as he was reading them.

'What is it?' cried Rebecca alarmed by Samuel's reaction.

'I am to be taken into custody,' he said quietly handing her the paper. She read it intently but at the same time the Bow Street Runners entered the room uninvited. Their shoes were thick with the muck of the city and they trailed it onto the clean floor of the dressing room. Toby, who habitually spent many hours of his day cleaning, made to reprimand them, but Solomon put a restraining hand on his arm and shook his head. He had realised the seriousness of the situation where Toby had not. Debtor's prison was not a concept of which the African was aware.

'But this is for a debt of only £348.15s 7d,' said Rebecca, aghast at the injustice of it.

'Only!' replied the constable derisively.

'Yes, I know it's a lot of money, Constable,' she said tartly, 'but my husband has earned fifty guineas this night alone. If you allow my husband to work, then the debt can be paid off within a few months.'

'Maybe so Mrs Medina,' said the constable, but you will have to take that up with the Magistrate.

'I certainly will, Constable,' said Rebecca forcefully, 'but in the meantime where will you take my husband?'

'To the Fleet, Mrs, pending a hearing before the Magistrate.'

Rebecca blenched. The Fleet prison on Farringdon Road was a debtor's prison. 'Surely that can be avoided,' she said, attempting to remain calm. 'Who is prosecuting this debt?'

'You will have to take that up with the Magistrate, Mrs,' the constable unhelpfully repeated.

'What if Samuel doesn't come with you voluntarily?' interrupted Solomon.

The two constables drew their batons in response and the atmosphere suddenly bristled with trepidation.

'Stop that talk Solomon,' snapped Rebecca. 'Samuel is an honourable, law-abiding citizen.'

'Nevertheless,' said Solomon, 'If the law is foolish enough to put Samuel in debtor's prison where he can't earn his living to satisfy his creditors, then what option does he have?'

The shock that had kept Samuel from speaking suddenly evaporated. The charged atmosphere had released adrenalin into his bloodstream and the fight or flight mechanism kicked into action. His speech returned and he took charge of the situation. 'Put away your batons, sirs,' he said, 'there are three professional pugilists in this room. We are all trained in the noble science of self-defence and that includes the cudgel. I am prepared to fight for what I believe is right and I promise you that you are simply not *able* to take me by force.'

'Samuel!' warned Rebecca. 'Fighting will not help you.'

'Maybe not, my dear, but I will fight for my principles,' said Samuel with his re-found assurance, 'the constables can be sure of that.'

'You may be right, Mr Medina,' said the first constable warily, 'but I have a duty at least to try. I am only doing my job, you understand.'

'I understand,' said Samuel, his tone still as combative, 'but it is in both our interests to avoid violence. I know I can win this struggle but it will go against me at my hearing.' The constable looked at him nonplussed. 'I'm offering you a way out,' prompted Samuel.

'How?' said the constable still not comprehending. Bow Street Runners were employed mainly for their brawn and not their intellect.

'You will go back to the Magistrate and tell him that you have served the order, and that I have agreed to appear at the hearing, whenever that date is set.'

'It's already set, Mr Medina, it's in the order.' Samuel looked and it was set for the 12th October, in three weeks' time.

'Very well,' said Samuel, 'tell the Magistrate that I was cooperative and have given an undertaking that I will appear and answer fully the charges of debt brought against me. You can tell him that he has my word on that.'

'I don't know about that, Sir,' said the constable. He turned and spoke with his colleague privately for some moments. They were clearly not sure what they should do, but they knew they would take a beating if they refused Samuel's offer. 'Very well, Sir,' said the constable reluctantly.

After the two men had shuffled away, they all sat pensively gazing anywhere but at each other, their earlier elation replaced by a feeling of despair. The muck left on the floor from the constables' boots gave off a pungent odour that penetrated their collective consciousness; the Bow Street Runners had left a reminder of their threatening presence.

'I don't understand why they are hounding you,' said Solomon at length. 'If you were a lord you could carry a debt for years before it came to this.'

'Aye, 'tis true enough, but I'm no lord,' said Samuel broodingly, 'and then again, what do I know about the ways of the gentry? There's neither rhyme nor reason to it as far as I can see.'

They all sat gloomily for what seemed like a time without end, their thoughts somehow stagnated by what had transpired - until Rebecca took charge.

'You will go to the North of England, Samuel,' she said positively. 'You will be out of the jurisdiction of the Bow Street Magistrate and you can earn money exhibiting there. You'd best go tonight, in case the Magistrate decides to send the constables back with reinforcements.' She was planning as she spoke for it was her way of coping. 'You will have to negotiate with the theatre owners as you go. Tell them that you have just filled the famous Drury Lane Theatre and they will probably be prepared to cancel their scheduled performances to fit you in.'

'Er – yes, my dear,' said Samuel, 'but it may not be as easy as that.'

'Maybe not,' she said, 'but I want you back here in three weeks, we need as much money as we can to reduce that debt. We need to show *good faith* – do you understand?'

'Aye,' said Samuel, 'but I'll need to take Solomon and Toby with me.'

'I have to go back to work, Sir,' interrupted Toby.

'Don't worry about that,' said Rebecca firmly. 'I'll go and see Lord Cowden, I'm sure he won't object,' she added, hoping against hope that she was right

'I'll need money for lodgings and food,' said Samuel.

'Aye, you will,' she said. 'Take what you need out of the fifty guineas, but you must go - and bring back with you as much money as you can. Do you understand? As much money as you possibly *can*.'

CHAPTER 32

'Goddamned bastard,' said Samuel.

'That won't get us anywhere,' said Rebecca reproachfully, looking round in embarrassment.

'Goddamned bastard,' Samuel repeated in disbelief. 'Are you *sure?*' He slumped down in a chair while he tried to take in what Rebecca was saying. They were in a waiting room at the King's Bench Assizes, Borough High Street, in Southwark. The room was wood-panelled and smelt of a combination of polish and stale sweat: the polish smell heavy in the air but still losing its battle against the stench of body odours. The room was three quarters full and there was a collective air of anxiety. Samuel and Rebecca spoke in undertones, trying in vain to talk privately in so public a place. Their dilemma was mirrored by everyone else in the room so that the collective hushed conversations merged and seemed to buzz like a swarm of honeybees in search of nectar. That hum was punctuated at intervals by the sounds of the Court business going on outside the room as the ushers called out the names of the plaintiffs, respondents or witnesses.

'I'm sure, my love,' Rebecca nodded. 'I've seen all the papers now. The debt is being prosecuted by none other than Sir Oliver Ruddle'

'Goddamned bastard,' Samuel hissed through gritted teeth. 'But I don't understand. I don't owe him a penny.'

'You do now,' Rebecca grimaced, 'he's bought up all your outstanding debts.'

'But that's just crazy,' said Samuel, burying his head in his hands.

'I'm not sure if it's that,' said Rebecca, 'but it's certainly vindictive in the extreme. I think we must assume that he's been unable to find John Campbell-John and so he's going to take his desire for vengeance out on you.'

'Goddamned bastard,' Samuel cursed again.

Rebecca had sent a note north to Samuel telling him to go straight to the Court, rather than come home, as she was fearful that he would be arrested. She was desperate that he presented himself to the Court of his own free will, with money to lodge against the debts. In consequence she now had only minutes in which to brief him before they went before the Court.

'I was sure that when I found out who was prosecuting the debt I would be able to go and see them and beg for time,' she said. 'I thought that if I could show them you had substantial earnings and lodge part payment with them, they would agree to withdraw their claim. But I never expected it to be Ruddle.'

'Goddamned bastard,' he said again. It was all he could think to say and it did not come close to how he felt about Ruddle at this moment.

'That's not helping, Samuel,' Rebecca reprimanded.

He apologised with a gesture of his head but remained silent.

'I tried to see him,' Rebecca continued, 'but I was told by his man to go and see his lawyer. That was a waste of time as well. It seems that Ruddle keeps his lawyer well employed with such work. He's such a vindictive man that he regularly resorts to the law to settle his disputes – that's what he does and his lawyers are thankful for it.'

'Godda…' Samuel started to say, but stopped himself as he caught sight of his wife's glowering gaze.

'How much money did you bring?' she asked.

'£112.15s,' Samuel said, bitterly aware of the disappointment in Rebecca's eyes. 'I know it's inadequate but I had to agree to perform for reduced fees to get the theatre owners to cancel their scheduled performances. I only managed to exhibit at three theatres. The crowds flocked in even so, and I've got another twelve bookings over the next eight weeks, so we should have cleared the debts in a couple of months.'

'So if they are prosecuting a debt of £348.15s.7d and we deposit £112.15s, the debt will be reduced to £236.0s.7d – that will just have to do for now. Did you bring proof of the forward bookings?'

Samuel nodded, 'Aye, my love.'

'Then you know what to say.

'Aye I do,' he said resignedly.

'The *Jew*, Samuel Medina,' said the barrister, emphasising the word 'Jew', 'owes my client a considerable amount of money, m'lord, and that debt is not disputed.' Samuel's heart sank. Ruddle had employed a barrister to prosecute his case, which put him at a considerable disadvantage. Not only that, but the barrister had quite openly referred to him as a Jew. It was made, of course, under the pretext that it was a statement of fact – but clearly it was intended as a derisory remark. He saw the Judge sneer at the comment and he recognised the danger he was in. It was a situation he had been in many times before but his solution previously had been to fight his way out of the problem. Clearly, this option was not now available to him. The very word *Jew* had undertones to it. In the eyes of the general public it meant money lending, extortion, or mistrust. It did not matter that historically so many professions had been barred to the Jew that by want of need they had been forced into certain businesses. Jews were perceived as merchants growing fat on other men's toils, or loan sharks, squeezing the last penny from an honest man in his time of trouble. Samuel though of Shakespeare's portrayal of Shylock in the *Merchant of Venice* and winced inwardly. The barrister had effectively charged him with being a Jew as well as being a debtor.

The Judge's bench was at the far end of the chamber and he had his own entrance. Below his elevated position sat the court officials who were also elevated and below them was the main floor of the chamber. The chamber was raised high above all those present, to emphasise the insignificance of those charged. Shafts of light cut into the chamber from windows built into the ceiling, and fell randomly on those assembled, one in particular falling on the Judge as though God himself had place him in the position of arbitrator.

Squinting as his eyes adjusted to the brightness, Samuel looked up at him and tried to gauge his reaction. The barrister who was bringing the petition sat at the front on the left-hand side of the chamber floor, and on his far right, standing in the prisoner's dock - which had been erected on the same level just in front of the side wall - was Samuel. The pews for the general public were beyond this plane, just in front of the main entrance. All courtrooms, of course, were designed to emphasize the power of the Judge and he was seated several feet higher that the defendant. From Samuel's vantage point the oak bench before the Judge obscured most of him so that Samuel could see only the top of his shoulders and his head. His long, powdered wig hung down on either side of his head and disappeared out of view behind the oak bench, so that he looked like a bloodhound trailing its ears from side to side with each movement of his head. Samuel eventually caught his eye and saw that sneer reappear, and deep down Samuel knew that justice would be hard to find this day. Nevertheless, the adrenalin began to flow in his veins. He was a natural fighter and if he could not use his fists then he vowed to himself he would use his wits and his eloquence.

He proceeded to explain, quite openly and forcefully, that he was a respected businessman who had a reputation for honest dealings.

While he was speaking, he inwardly cursed himself for not asking people to appear as character witnesses for him. He had thought it unnecessary, as surely no court would put him in prison for a debt that he could easily clear if left to follow his profession. Lord Cowden, in view of his standing in high society would have had great weight as a character witness, but then again, it was one thing to befriend a Jew and quite another to appear in open court to support him. Samuel explained that he had lodged £112. 15s. with the court, and produced the agreements to exhibit in eight provincial theatres. He proudly explained that he had recently exhibited his skills to the King and his family, and surely it must be accepted by the Court that he was a man of the highest character. His presentation was articulate and persuasive and on the face of it was surely enough to show up the nonsense of the case.

Ruddle's barrister, however, was skilled in his trade. He portrayed Samuel as a man of low birth and low character. A man who was well known to the Magistrates who had banned him from exhibiting at his Academy, a ban that he had flaunted; a man who had been similarly banned from engaging in a public pitched battle, but had nevertheless gone ahead and done so by way of trickery and deception. He was, affirmed Ruddle's barrister, a man by consequence who was devious and untrustworthy, who had no regard for the rule of law, and by inference, was a man who had no respect for judges. He was a man that ran a boxing academy where brawls took place, for so it had been heavily reported in the newspapers. Most damaging of all, he was a Jew, and of course everybody knew that Jews could not be trusted where money was concerned.

As Samuel listened to those words he watched the Judge's face and knew that he was doomed. The Judge, it seemed shared that common misconception – *Jew* triggered thoughts of deception, dishonesty and lies.

Sure enough, when the Judge started to speak it was clear which view of Samuel's character he had chosen to accept. 'Samuel Medina the Jew,' he paused, peering over the bench at the prisoner below him. 'It is not in dispute that you owe Sir Oliver Ruddle a considerable amount of money even after the lodgement with the Court of £112.15s. You claim that the remaining debt will be redeemed in a matter of months, but I am mindful of your past history of deceit and I remain unconvinced that you will honour such a claim.'

'Your Honour,' cried Samuel, unable to quell his anger. 'This is ridiculous. I am an honest man of business, not some common scoundrel engaged in roguery.'

'Silence!' shouted an usher, 'silence in the dock!' Two men at arms drew their truncheons and rushed to the dock to restrain the accused. Samuel held up his hands in a submissive gesture and they halted and lowered their weapons, but they then stood on either side of him, taking an arm apiece to reinforce the order of the Court. The Clerk to the Court spoke quietly to one of the ushers who slipped out of the courtroom, but returned seconds later with six other men at arms, all of whom carried swords and one a pistol.

'I will not tolerate such behaviour in my Court,' said the Judge, 'you show by your actions what a man of low character you are.'

'But your Honour, this is nonsense,' Samuel repeated. 'If you will let me go about my business the debt will be cleared in no time.' But even as he said it, he knew it would hold no sway; Sir Oliver Ruddle was not concerned about getting his money back; it was vengeance he was after. He must be rubbing his hands with glee, thought Samuel bitterly.

'Silence,' shouted the Judge. 'You have had your say and now it is my turn. I order this day that you be taken to the King's Bench Debtor's Prison and remain there until the debt of £236.0s.7d has been cleared.' He smacked his gavel down on the bench and in sonorous tones said, 'Take him down.'

Samuel's first sight of the prison sent a tremble down his spine. Ejected from the carriage that had conveyed him from the courtroom, he looked up at the imposing building and came to a halt; his legs simply stopped moving. As the full horror of his predicament took him like a chill wind over the sea, he shivered involuntarily. His mind was swimming and he tried to take a moment to calm himself, but the two constables who were delivering him pushed him forward. Each time he stopped he was jolted and shunted forward again. He was manacled, but the constables were well aware of his power and reputation and they were wary of him.

'Give me a moment if you please gentlemen,' he said quietly, looking intently at one of them.

The man looked at his colleague who gestured with his head compliantly. 'Just a moment then, Sir,' said the first constable.

The prison stood on a four-acre site enclosed by a wall thirty-five feet high and surmounted by iron spikes. The situation was incongruous for it lay but a mile from London Bridge in the Borough of Southwark and along its frontage ran a well-paved parade about twenty feet in width, beyond which were spacious racquet-grounds and a fives-court, and beyond that an open aspect. It had been sited in a fashionable part of the city and the area attracted the well-to-do to play games or merely to perambulate. And yet here also was a prison, and to a Londoner it seemed anything but incongruous; it was simply part of life. The main building had three stories and a basement, was three hundred feet long with a spur at either end projecting at right angles for about forty-five feet. It was daunting place at first sight, and must have terrified many a prisoner on the day of his incarceration, which in all probability had been the intention of the architect who designed it. Certainly it put the fear of God into Samuel.

The entrance to the prison was by a lobby in which there were two gates. Samuel was led by the constables through these gates, down into a yard and through to an inner lobby, which also had two gates and led into the prison proper. Samuel's short walk seemed to be accompanied by the clang of distant bolts being opened and shut at almost every step, and those clangs then seemed to echo around the huge structure; a constant reminder to the inhabitants of where they were. Over the inner lobby was a small building the constables referred to as the 'Strong Room'. It was a place for the solitary confinement of those who attempted to escape or who had broken the rules. In addition to the Strong Room, there were two much smaller cells; little more than pigsties to contain seriously delinquent prisoners. The Marshal of the prison had vested in him magisterial powers and had the power to confine men to these hellholes if they digressed. It was no accident that these rooms were visible to the new prisoner on his committal. They were occupied; Samuel heard the groans from within as he was thrust before the Marshal.

The Marshal had only recently been appointed having paid handsomely for the privilege - prisons were profit-making enterprises. They were privately run and the Marshal had in effect purchased for himself, via patent, the right to make himself vastly wealthy. Nothing in prison was free. Every debtor on his commitment or discharge had to pay gate fees. In addition to the Marshal's fee, they had to pay on commitment a shilling to the Cook of the Public Kitchen; a shilling to the Watchman and a shilling to the Clerk of the Chapel. Quite how a man imprisoned for debt was supposed to afford these monies was a mystery to Samuel. There were two public houses in the complex, the

'Tap' and the 'Brace', and they were rented from the Marshal, the publicans having to pay a fee for every butt of beer consumed. There was a small market attached to the prison, containing butchers, poulterers, fishmongers and greengrocers, each of whom paid a weekly rent. Each prisoner's apartment cost one shilling per week rental, and if he was unable to pay he took his chances in the back rooms where the common cells were situated. In these common cells there was overcrowding, no air, and no sanitation. Each man slept on the floor and waited to see which would get him first: the cold, the damp, disease - or the other inmates.

On top of all these fees, all visitors to the prison had also to pay a fee, and there were additional fees to the turnkeys, to the Deputy Marshal, and the Clerk to the Papers. It was ironical that a debtor's prison could make such financial demands on its inmates, but this was the culture of the privatised prison. If a debtor was unable to pay - or more probably his friend and relations could not stump up on his behalf - then his stay could be harsh; very harsh indeed. Those who were able to pay could purchase a much easier life for themselves. They could even lodge in nearby accommodation as long as they paid the Marshal for his loss of earnings. The prison pubs, coffee house, racquet court, were open to the public, but the prisoners had access to them if they had the means. Many spent their days in an inebriate state. All this Samuel learned to his dismay within a very short time of his committal.

'You have the gate fees?' asked the Marshal routinely, whilst reading the Magistrates Committal Order given to him by the constable.

Samuel had paid every last penny that he had into the court. 'I have no funds, Sir,' he said. 'I wasn't expecting committal – but my wife will return with the funds. I am sure of that.' The Marshal looked up at him having read the name *Samuel Medina* and realised the celebrity that was now before him.

'Well bless my soul,' he said. Like most Londoners, he had read endless columns in the newspapers about this man and his curiosity was aroused. He also sensed the opportunity to make money. 'I am surprised, Sir, to see you here. You must have been living extravagantly indeed to have squandered the vast sums that you were reported to have been earning.'

'No sir, I have not been profligate, I am the victim of circumstance,' said Samuel, the offence evident in his voice. 'Were I allowed to follow my profession, these debts would be cleared in a matter of weeks.'

'Yes, yes,' said the Marshal, clearly not believing him. He had heard it all before and he made no pretence of hiding his scepticism. But he added in a warmer tone, 'We must talk sir, I will be interested in hearing all about your fights.'

Samuel nodded obligingly. They were the first friendly words he had heard this day and they went a long way. 'I will look forward to that, Sir,' he said trustingly, unaware that the friendliness was illusory. 'But we must talk soon, for I don't expect to be here for very long.'

The Marshal smiled at him cynically. 'They all say that, Sir.'

'I have every confidence in my wife,' said Samuel, 'I'm certain that she will have raised the funds for my release within a short time.'

'I hope so,' said the Marshal disingenuously, 'but in the meantime, Sir, we have the immediate problem that you can't pay the gate fees and you can't pay for your room.'

'Will you not take my word that my wife will deposit these funds with you by the morning?'

'I'm afraid that the rules are quite clear, Sir,' lied the Marshal, for the rules were in fact all of his own making. 'If you can't pay the fees then you must go into the common cells at the back of the prison.' He wanted Samuel to experience the dreadfulness of these cells for he knew it would make him more compliant in the future. He neglected to inform Samuel that there was a way out of his immediate predicament: if Samuel were to swear an oath that he was not worth ten pounds and was unable to sustain himself, he would be entitled to receive three shillings and sixpence from the *County Money,* a paupers' fund that was intended to pay for the most basic accommodation and food.

'When your wife brings the money, Sir,' the Marshal smiled, 'then we can make better arrangements. There are eight rooms of superior size situated near my own apartments that can be purchased for five pounds. One is at present available to you, should your wife bring the necessary funds.'

Samuel bowed graciously at the offer. It was a bow of politeness only; he was beginning to realise the hopelessness of his case. The Marshal gestured with a flick of his hand and Samuel was led away to the common cell.

London could be a world of unpleasant smells. It was Samuel's city and he had grown up in it, but it had not prepared him for the stench that met him on entering the common cell. There were a dozen people there without sanitation, without bedding. They slept in any corner they could find, and straw was the best bedding they could hope for. It was at the back of the prison away from the ordinary inmates, who stayed away out of a mixture of fear and abhorrence of the stench. The common cell was a permanent reminder of their need to ensure that their friends and relatives kept providing for them.

Samuel made himself room on an unoccupied part of the wall on the left side of the cell, but was then accosted by an old hag of a woman. Old in this place was a relative term, but she had all the signs of agedness and more. She was skeletal thin with large eyes sunken into her emaciated skull. She seemed to blink in slow motion as her eyelids traversed what seemed like an endless ocean of eyeball, and the movement of the membrane pulsed like a measured rhythmic drum beat. Her hair was unkempt and matted and her mouth opened to reveal a toothless chasm.

'You can't sleep there,' she screeched, 'that's Jock's place.'

'Which one is Jock?' asked Samuel, his eyes watering from the indescribable stink of faeces, urine, vomit and foetid body odours, and his legs beginning to itch from the lice and fleas that had in no time at all found their way up his breeches to fasten hungrily onto new, fresh blood.

'Not here,' she squealed again, 'he's in the *Tap.*'

'The *Tap?*'

'Aye the *Tap* – the pub. Got any money deary - a couple of pence for a drop of Old Tom?'

What little money these people received, they spent on alcohol. Gin – 'Old Tom' as it was commonly called - and ale were their masters. It numbed their plight – it was their escape – it made the days bearable. It was better than paying a shilling a week for an unfurnished, shared room. The prisoners purchased their food - or something approximating food for the very poorest - from the market attached to the prison and had it cooked in the Public Kitchen, but this shell of a woman was evidence that those at the very bottom of the hierarchy of this sad community preferred to spend their money on alcohol rather that sustenance. The cell doors were not kept locked during the day and prisoners were allowed access to the pubs, coffee house or fives court, but at night when the gates of the prison were locked these wretched few returned to this festering sewer of human life.

'It's no good trying to fleece me woman,' said Samuel angrily his teeth bared as the words spat from his mouth. 'I have no funds to give you. Be gone with you!'

She scampered away still screeching her warning as she went. 'You can't sleep there – Jock'll get you if you do.'

Samuel's spirits sank like air rushing from a deflating balloon, and desperation took him like a vengeful master. For the first time in his adult life he was moved to tears. He felt them welling up inside him, but he fought hard to keep them from surfacing. He had always been a man brimming with confidence – a large and powerful man with a personality to match, who would be cowed by no man. He had never allowed himself to be intimidated or browbeaten and had stood up to the bully at every turn, but he was now rendered helpless and there seemed nobody to fight except his own inadequacies. He bowed his head to hide his shame; he was not hiding it from this rabble but from himself. The place was mostly silent, devoid of conversation, but interspersed with coughing and retching. Most of these people would only leave this place in a coffin. He tried to sleep, but the cold damp brick began to dig into his backbone and he squirmed, endlessly trying to find something that resembled comfort.

He dozed after a while, when what little light there was began to fail, but was abruptly wrenched back to consciousness by a belligerent wailing. He opened his eyes with a start. There before him, an inch from his own face was this other grotesque face. Its teeth were bared, yellowed and black, its breath foul, its language slurred but belligerent. Two great eyes protruded, showing acres of white that were traversed by a myriad of red-blooded rivulets, so that they resembled a scarlet spider's web. For a moment Samuel was disoriented. The words did not register in his mind. The accent was Scottish but the words were disguised more by the effects of alcohol that their foreignness. But then it became apparent to Samuel what the man was raving about, even if the words remained unintelligible. This was Jock, and he wanted his place by the wall. Samuel pushed him back by his shoulders with all his strength and the man was sent tumbling backwards across the floor of his cell. Samuel jumped to his feet and took his defensive stance, his left leg and left arm extended with his right fist protecting his chin. A look of incredulity took Jock's features. He was a large and powerful man, or at least he had been that once, and he was used to being the alpha male in this stinking cell. He climbed to his feet slowly and an anxious smile crossed his face. He was taller that Samuel but his strength in reality had been dissipated by his emaciated condition. He rushed at Samuel not with a punch, but took his lapels in both hands and then attempted to head-butt him. Before he could, Samuel sank his right fist hard into Jock's solar plexus. The fight was effectively over. The big man sank to his feet gasping for air. He was down, disabled like that for several minutes, until the old crone tried to help him back to the opposite corner, but she did not have the strength to do it. After several more minutes he crawled across the floor unaided like a wounded animal needing to lick its wounds.

Samuel sank back down to his uncomfortable but apparently sought-after position. The rush of adrenalin had worked wonders for his plummeting spirit. He consoled himself with the thought that Rebecca would come in the morning, and at the least he would be re-housed in a normal room and some form of sanity would return to his life. Clinging to this hope, he slept fitfully, disturbed by the coughing, moaning and wheezing of pitiful humanity and the rustle and squeak of the rats that preyed on it.

In the morning, however, Rebecca did not come, nor did she come that afternoon, nor the next morning, nor the morning after that. Samuel's despair worsened with every dreadful, hopeless, lingering hour that he was forced to endure.

CHAPTER 33

Samuel's spirits lifted at the sight of her face. He had spent three miserable, wretched days in the common cell, and Rebecca's face looked beautiful to him in its natural simplicity. She was dressed in a simple muslin dress, without an overcoat because the long summer was lingering on. The sun shone fiercely outside the prison gates, whilst inside the soaring temperature further soaked the inmates in a new layer of sweat to add to numerous other layers that had dried stale and sour on their skins. She held a handkerchief to her face and he assumed that she was sheltering herself from the rancid odours that swarmed about the prison, for this was where some of the detritus of society came to decay and fester like the putrefying mulch on the greenwood floor. And then, catching a glimpse of the anxiety stamped across her features, he realised that the handkerchief's function was actually to hide her emotions. Over the top of it, their eyes made contact as she approached him, and suddenly her resolve dissolved away like rainwater into the parched summer ground and the handkerchief fluttered from her fingers.

He caught it and returned it to her. 'Oh, my love,' he murmured. Without thinking he put his arms around her. She seemed to crumple in his arms, her own held tight to her body as if protecting herself from the horrors that confronted her. She buried her head in his chest and sobbed uncontrollably.

'What is it? Where have you been?' he asked but she needed time to collect herself, and he sensed that. He had so many questions, but he waited patiently, content for the moment just to have her in his arms. He had never seen her like this. She was a mentally strong woman, not given to displays of emotion. Even when their daughter had died she had kept the hurting inside her and done her weeping hidden away from the eyes of the world. He walked her through the imposing corridors through to the yard between the two entrance lobbies. There were other prisoners there, for any prisoner has access to any part of the prison before the gates were locked at night; they had some privacy as they walked.

After walking for a few minutes, Rebecca breathed in deeply and looking up at Samuel; saw the need in his eyes. Stealing herself, she suppressed her feelings and said in a remarkably calm voice, 'We need to talk, my love.' She blew her nose thoroughly, as if mentally expelling all that uncontrolled emotion and ridding herself of the putrid odours that had assaulted her nostrils, and then she hid her handkerchief away up her sleeve.

'Where have you been for three days?' Samuel injected concern into his voice, trying not to sound petulant.

'It's been awful, my love,' she said, clutching his arm.

'What has?'

'It's Sir Oliver Ruddle again.'

Samuel faltered in mid-stride. 'What's he done now?'

'He sent out runners again. He's broadcast to the world that you've been taken into the Kings Bench Prison as a common debtor. He's such a spiteful man.'

'I fear he's much more than that, he's a-' abruptly Samuel stopped speaking as he realised the implications of what Rebecca had said. In despair, he put a hand up to his face, muttered, 'Another run by our investors?'

'Yes, my love,' she said on a sob. Catching herself, she suppressed it. 'I knew you needed me to bring money, but the queues have been enormous. Everybody has wanted their money, but this time we've not been able to quell their demands.'

'How much have we lost?' he asked, a dread taking him as he spoke.

She saw the terror in his eyes and knew that she had to fulfil his worst fears. For a moment she did not answer, and then said softly, 'Everything; we have had to pay out everything we had in the bank. There is nothing left.'

'Everything!' he said the anguish evident in his tone.

'Everything, my love,' she repeated, 'we're penniless.' She tugged at his arm and they walked on in silence for some moments as the full horror took them. 'I wasn't sure what to do,' she said at length, her tone matching the solemnity of her expression. 'I started to pay all the demands to protect your good name. But after a while I began to wonder whether it was the right thing to do.'

'Oh, you did the right thing my love – I'm sure of it,' Samuel was quick to reassure her. 'My good name is the most important thing to me.'

'But *did* I? Are you *sure*? Whilst ever you are in here you have no good name. No one is interested in the injustice of it; they just want their money back.'

'Did you manage to meet all the demands?'

'Just. Your brother Solomon covered the final shortfall of fifteen pounds.'

Samuel shook his head in despair. 'He doesn't have that sort of money to lend.'

'I know,' said Rebecca, 'and he has also lent me the money to pay your entry fee. I've paid the Marshal, and there are still few shillings for you so that you can pay for a room – but I don't know where any more money will come from.'

'I'll be fine,' he said, but his tone was unconvincing. 'You've done more than you know. As long as I can get out of that stinking hole they've kept me in.' He turned to her, his eyes glassy with unshed tears, 'I cannot bear it a moment longer.'

She gazed up into his face and for the first time noticed the red blotches and suppurating sores where he had been bitten by fleas and lice, and she burst into tears. He could do no more that hold her tight because he could find no words to comfort her.

'I should have just closed the shop and made them wait for their money,' she sobbed. 'I should have used what little money we had to get you out of here.'

'You did what you thought was right,' he said, and she sobbed again. They held each other for several minutes without speaking further. It was no more than instinct; clinging together without any rational thought. At that moment they were just two helpless people with no one else to turn to. Two strong-willed and reliant people, but fate had conspired against them to drain away that will and reliance. Samuel had been in this position many times before in the ring, but he had always had his strength of mind to inspire his bruised and weary body. But now it was his mind that was bruised and weary. He was a lost sheep on the windswept hillside, unable to find his way home.

When Rebecca had gone, Samuel took the small amount of cash she had given him and went to see the head Turnkey.

'My name is Jack Norman, but you call me 'Turnkey' or 'Chum-Master,' the man said piercingly as if he was a sergeant-major taking a parade. 'There are six turnkeys but I'm the only one who acts as the Chum-Master. Do you understand that?'

'Err – yes,' said Samuel.

'My duty as Chum-Master is to arrange the accommodation of the prisoners. We operate a system of chummage.'

'Chummage?' asked Samuel but the Chum-Master ignored him and carried on.'

'We have 225 apartments here but we have, at present, over 800 inmates, so it is necessary to 'chum' you with other prisoners.' Do you understand?' he said again, adding without waiting for a response, 'The apartment will cost you a shilling a week and you will pay me.'

'I have a few shillings, Chum-Master,' said Samuel, 'but this is sure to run out quickly. What happens if I can't pay?'

'But ain't you Samuel Medina the fighter?' said the Chum-Master, 'surely you can find this small sum?'

'I'm not sure of anything at the moment, Chum-Master. I can't seem to get access to any funds.'

'Then you must '*swear*' yourself, Sir.'

'Swear myself, Sir?' Samuel repeated, nonplussed.

Surprised at Samuel's ignorance the Chum-Master launched into an explanation. 'You *swear* yourself not worth ten pounds and unable to subsist yourself, and then you are entitled to receive three shillings and sixpence from the County Money – didn't the Marshal tell you this? That would pay for your accommodation and some victuals, so long as you don't spend it all on ale and gin in the pub, like those in the common cells.'

'Then I fear I must *swear* myself, Chum-Master,' said Samuel, hiding his chagrin and inwardly cursing the Marshal whom he had so mistakenly thought was a friend.

'So be it,' said the Chum-Master pompously and from the voluminous pocket hanging from his belt produced the declaration for Samuel to sign. The pomposity in his features then suddenly dissolved and a mischievous smile appeared at the corner of his mouth. 'I now have to find you a chum, Mr Medina,' he said, 'and being that you are famous I think I know just the person.' He scribbled on a piece of paper and handed Samuel a ticket. It said simply:

Kings Bench Prison
Name: Mr Medina
*To go to room number:*8 in No10
With: Mr Scillari and Mr Burns and Mr Ackroyd.
Signed: J Norman. Chum Master.
Dated: 28 September 1791

'Number 8 in number 10?' Samuel looked down at the ticket, perplexed.

'Room no 8 on corridor 10,' said the Chum-Master returning to his pompous voice, but then that smirk returned to his face. 'I'll show you where you have to go.'

The Chum-Master accompanied Samuel to the door of No 8 in No.10, but then left, grinning as if he was the cat that got the cream. At the end of the corridor he lingered, eager to overhear what he knew was about to happen.

Samuel peered into a room that was a mere fifteen feet by ten, which according to the ticket, had to sleep four *chums*. There was only one bed, however, and in the far corner was a small desk next to a wardrobe. A man sat at the desk with his back to Samuel, engrossed in a pile of papers. He wore a powered wig that was now years out of fashion, but it was well maintained, as was the clean shirt that covered his ample shoulders. He sat awkwardly at the desk unable to get his long legs completely under its frontage but it seemed to Samuel that he was obviously a man of stature and breeding.

Samuel coughed to attract his attention. At first the gentleman seemed oblivious to his presence, but then turned and leered at him looking him up and down, but did not speak. Samuel held up his ticket to cover his embarrassment, cleared his throat to explain that he was a new *chum*, but before he could speak the man reacted; a reaction for which Samuel was totally unprepared.

The gentleman jumped to his feet, waving his arms and shouting. 'No-no; I no wanna any more chums,' he screeched in a heavy Italian accent. 'You go anda see the Chum-Master anda tell him that I, Scillari, say no. I say no – I no wanna another chum.' He kept repeating that phrase over and over again as his rage mounted. '*I no wanna another chum!*'

Samuel had never met such a man as this before. Physically he was exceedingly tall with a barrel chest, but his head seemed tiny in proportion to the rest of his body. His face was smooth with no sign of any facial hair. His hips and thighs were full, but were fatty rather than muscular, and clearly he had man-breasts. He looked freakish, but it was his voice that was most disconcerting. He just did not sound like a man. He was high-voiced, more like a child, but a child with feminine body language and gestures. His appearance was bizarre, to say the least.

Samuel realised after the first disconcerting moments, that this man must be a castrati. He remembered hearing about such men; it had been the subject of discussion over a protracted game of cards one night at one of Adele Fitzsymons's house parties. They had been discussing the qualities of her fine singing voice and the extraordinary practice of castrating young boys so that puberty would not take away their fine soprano voices. It had arisen principally in Italy, where the Catholic Church would not allow women to speak - let alone sing - in church. Samuel had shuddered as he had listened to the lurid details: he could not imagine anything more horrifying. At the age of seven - or even younger – the chosen boy soprano was placed in a bath of freezing water in an meagre attempt to deaden the pain; his jugular vein was squeezed until he became light headed and lost awareness of what was happening to him, and then a local surgeon-cum-butcher made an incision in his groin, pulled out the child's spermatic cord and testicles and simply cut them off. Remembering this now, Samuel's hand strayed protectively to his groin, a shiver raising gooseflesh on his arms at the thought of it. Many boys did not survive the crude operation, yet apparently this man had; this large, effeminate man who was spitting with high-voiced rage before him. The Catholic Church had a lot to answer for, thought Samuel with pity and compassion as he gazed at Scillari. And yet they dared to criticise Jews for the practice of circumcision!

Scillari continued to wave his arms wildly and shout in Samuel's face. When faced with such aggression Samuel's natural reaction was to stand up and fight toe to toe. And yet on this occasion his normal reflexes did not kick in. For a heartbeat he stared at the castrati, dumbfounded. His honour somehow stopped him from striking this man. In some strange way his mind told him that it would be like striking a woman.

'Calm yourself Sir,' he said, but Scillari was in no mood to be calmed. The ranting just got worse and his voice rose through the octaves like a lark ascending to the heavens. 'Calm yourself Sir,' Samuel said again, this time his voice deeper and more assertive. It had the opposite reaction to the one he had intended. The man was now frenzied, spitting out heavily accented words like a crazed animal - and then Samuel *did* strike him, but not in the way that he would hit a man by making a fist and punching him. He just slapped him across the face with his open palm, as if he was slapping a hysterical woman.

Surprisingly, in all his years of histrionic tantrums, Scillari had never been hit before. His ranting stopped and an expression of disbelief took his features, the whites of his eyes emerging like fallen fruit bobbing to the surface of a stream. His left hand came to the side of his stinging face and he was, for a moment rendered speechless.

'You strucka me,' he said, almost inaudibly, putting on a puppy-dog face. But then the volume returned, 'You're a brute,' he wailed and then flounced away to his desk. He sat down and pulled some papers to him and then picked up his quill, but he put it down almost immediately and stood up again to continue his tirade. 'Do you know who I am? I am the great *Scillari*. I've sung before kings. I no share with chums; I no share with *you*.'

'Then we have that in common, Sir,' said Samuel.

Scillari looked at him perplexed, momentarily quietened. 'Then you go and see the Chum Master anda say you don't want to share either,' he said at length, not understanding.

'No,' said Samuel, 'I meant that I have also had the honour of performing before King George.'

'*You*!' said Scillari, his brow furrowing. 'You are singer?'

'No, I'm not a singer,' smiled Samuel, 'I'm a pugilist.'

'What is pugilist?'

Samuel took up his stance to demonstrate. 'I'm a boxer, a fighter,' he said.

'And the King came to see you fight?' said Scillari, the disbelief evident in his voice.'

'Well no – not exactly,' said Samuel.

'Ah,' said Scillari scornfully. 'You not famous like me, eh?'

'I was summoned to the palace to exhibit my skills personally to the King and his family.'

'You did that?' Scillari was obviously impressed.

'Yes I did Sir,' said Samuel proudly, 'and what is more, the Prince of Wales came in person to see me fight, and then sent his personal physician to tend to me.'

'What is your name?' said Scillari inquisitively, his tone reflecting his changing attitude towards Samuel.

'My name, Sir, is Samuel Medina.'

'I no heard of you,' Scillari raised his head disdainfully to look down his nose at Samuel, but his curiosity was aroused and he could not maintain his indifference. 'I once appeared before one thousand two hundred people. How many people come to see you?'

'Why, only in May of this year,' Samuel smiled, 'I fought before a crowd of *two hundred thousand* people at Newmarket racecourse. They had to stop the races because the crowd was so big.'

The whites of Scillari's eyes bobbed into view again to register his incredulity. 'You lie,' he said, 'if so many people come to see you, then why you here, eh?'

Samuel told his story, and Scillari, for once in his life, listened intently. The Italian was totally self-centred, but in Samuel's story he saw echoes of his own predicament, notwithstanding that in reality his own incarceration was entirely of his own making. In his own mind he had been as much wronged as Samuel Medina. But as he listened he came to understand that Samuel was a performer just like himself. Here was a man with whom he had much in common. They both had the need to entertain, even if they expressed that need in very different ways. Scillari felt isolated in The King's Bench Prison – he was a lone figure, separated from his fellow inmates by his own arrogance, their inability to understand his creative needs and derided for his appearance.

The Italian was unusually quiet when Samuel had finished. 'But what's your story Mr Scillari?' Samuel prompted.

'I was a young boy who dreamed of being famous like Senesino and singing the lead in Handel's oratorios.'

'But didn't you know that would mean...' Samuel hesitated, unable to say the dreaded word, his face revealing his horror at the thought of it.

'Castration?' The big Italian shrugged, smiled a knowing smile. 'It has made me what I am. It has made me famous, so perhaps it is not so bad, eh?' But then his face fell and he acknowledged, 'I was the fourth of my brothers to undergo this surgery, and the first to survive it. I was the lucky one. Sandro, Georgio, and Giovanni - they all die when infection set in.'

'I'm sorry,' said Samuel, fearing the big man was about to burst into tears.

'It was long time ago,' Scillari waved away the comment with his hand, but his mood remained subdued. 'There wasn't even a guarantee that I would become a fine falsetto. They cannot tell at that age. But my parents were poor peasants from southern Italy with too many mouths to feed and a castrati in the family was a source of wealth to them.'

'How old were you?'

'Seven, but I don't remember the pain, though I remember then being sent away to Roma to study at the city's music academy. I missed my mama and papa.' He sighed heavily, but then his spirits were suddenly lifted. 'But I study hard and practise and practise. I was best student. I had pure angelic voice of the boy soprano but when I grow big and strong I could deliver it with the power of a man's set of lungs.'

'I bet you could,' said Samuel realising the pride Scillari obviously had in his voice.

'Tis true, I was the best. All the other students went on to sing in the Catholic churches all over Italy. The academy produced a never-ending supply of castrati voices for them.'

'But you didn't Mr. Scillari?

'No, no, I wanna sing on the musical stage, I wanna international fame. I was best.'

'So why London?'

'I have sung all over Europe: Milano, Vienna, Paris. But it's London that loves the castrati voice best. Tenducci, Caffarelli, Crescentini and Farinelli, they all make their names famous here. They are considered the greatest of all singers, their voices regarded as unsurpassed. The people here idolise them.' Scillari put his fingers to his lips and kissed them loudly to emphasise the greatness of his heroes.

'So you were in demand and earned a lot of money?' asked Samuel.

'I earn more than the famous composers – they all wanna me to perform their new works, I ensure its success; the public could not get enough of me. I earn five thousand pounds for one season and I live like a king. I use just one name – Scillari and everybody know it'

'So what went wrong?' Samuel was perplexed.

Scillari's enthusiasm left him like the air from a pricked balloon. 'I born too late, that what went wrong.'

'Too late?' Samuel repeated, confused. 'Too late for what?'

'The falsetto voice has taken the lead for over a hundred years,' Scillari explained, 'but now fashions change, yes? The theatre managers wanna operatic heroes with tenor voices now. They no wanna heroes with falsetto voices. Nobody wanna me anymore.' Sclliari was agitated as he spoke, his voice rising by octaves, his hands flapping in the air. It was a reflection of something that he dared not admit to himself. Scillari's mutilated hormonal system affected his temperament; his behaviour was grandiloquent and quarrelsome, and into this mix of temper tantrum had then been added fame and adulation. He could be the most difficult of men.

'Ah!' said Samuel, understanding at last. 'So the work just dried up.'

'Is true – no more work and then the money all gone,' explained Scillari, but this simple explanation hid a truth that he would not acknowledge to himself. As difficult as ever, he had never faced up to the fact that his fame had waned. He still behaved and spent like a luminary, his celebrity still manifest in his own mind. Unfortunately, it was manifesting nowhere else, and the histrionics that had been tolerated in an idol were no longer deemed acceptable. He became a pariah to society; a man who had walked with kings was now an embarrassment to the London scene. He had run up huge debts as he tried to swim against the tide that ran heartlessly against him. His sentence for debt was likely to be as permanent as any at the King's Bench prison. He owed massive amounts of money that paled Samuel's own debt into insignificance, and he had no way of paying them off.

The two men talked absorbedly and an unlikely bond grew between them. This was something else that Scillari would not have admitted it to himself; that he had found what he had most needed since the day of his incarceration. He had found a friend.

'You can stay,' he said suddenly, 'Scillari has decided, eh. And I will *show you the ropes.*'

'Your servant, Sir,' said Samuel nodding politely. He looked down at his ticket and read again the names. 'Where are Mr Burns and Mr Ackroyd?'

'As the original tenant of this room I am called the "master of the room", and so I have chummed them out. It was my prerogative, yes?'

Samuel raised his eyebrows, 'Chummed them out?' What does that mean?'

'I pay their one shilling to the Chum Master, and then I pay *them* two shillings each to go elsewhere.'

'They allow you to do that?'

'You can do almost whatever you like in here, so long as you can pay,' said Scillari. 'If you have enough money you can even get an *Out-Ticket.*'

'An Out-Ticket?'

'You can live outside the prison, so long as you remain nearby – and you can put up a bond as security. I wanna an out-ticket, but the bond is based on what your debt is and I owe too much for that.' Scillari shook his head sadly.

'Where do the chums go?'

Scillari shrugged, 'I no care,' then added, 'they sleep in the taprooms of the public house at night. The landlord lets them sleep there for nothing. They have a stow-hole for their bedding roll during the day, and then curl up on a seat or a table at night. They have their three shillings and six pence and two extra shillings from me. They are quite happy to be chummed out; it means they have more money for the ale.'

'But that must cost you...what?' Samuel tried and failed to tot up the amount in his head.

'Six shillings a week for Mr. Burns and Mr. Ackroyd and my own shilling. That's seven shillings a week.'

'But doesn't that leave you out of pocket? If you can afford that, surely you could afford an out-ticket?'

'No. I owe to much. But I can make a bit on the side. You are allowed to trade from your room. There are chandlers, tailors, and boot makers, barbers and-a more. I give music lessons. I teach the children of the Marshal. They are all tone-deaf, but he pays well. And-a every year a new tone-deaf child is born. There is always a supply of tone-deaf children to be taught,' Scillari gave a slow smile.

'So if we're to be chums, then I must pay one shilling to the chum master?'

Scillari nodded, 'And-a you must pay half of what it costs to chum out Mr Burns and Mr Ackroyd. That's another three shillings?'

'I fear that I may have to let you chum me out then, Sir,' said Samuel, 'for at the moment I don't seem to have access to any funds.'

Scillari looked at Samuel intently and what he said next surprised even him. 'Then I must stand your chummage until you can, Sir,' he said. 'I pay your weekly three shillings for the next month; I sure that you will be able to earn money even from inside this prison.'

Within an hour of their meeting all the hostility had drained away from Scillari. This man, who would not share a cell with anybody, was now actually offering to do just that and what is more, to pay Samuel's share as well. Their meeting had released a need within him - a need for companionship: a need he had denied, even to himself, for so very long.

'I can't let you do that,' said Samuel.

'No – it is-a decided,' said Scillari, 'we no more talk of it, you stay here. I, Scillari, say so.'

Samuel gave a polite bow, 'Thank you then, Mr Scillari, I am pleased to accept.'

'You are welcome,' said Scillari, 'and you must call me "Toto", as-a my friends do, yes?'

Outside the Chum Master listened intently to what was being said. *'Toto, call me Toto'*, he thought to himself. He was dumfounded.

All his perverse pleasure at putting these two ballistic characters together and watching the fireworks had been shattered. He slunk away back to his office, dragging his feet as he went, the smirk having been wiped from his face.

CHAPTER 34

There was a rap on the already open door. Both Scillari and Samuel looked around to see the Chum Master and with him two men carrying a bed. 'Yours, Mr Medina,' he said and directed the two men to put the bed against the wall opposite Scillari. They returned a few moments later with a small wardrobe and placed it next to the bed.

'You have a benefactor, Mr Medina,' said the Chum Master. Samuel looked at him nonplussed. The furniture screeched against the stone floor as the men manoeuvred it into position, taking Samuel's attention for a moment, but he then looked back at the Chum Master.

'A benefactor? Who is he?'

'*He* is a *she*,' said the Chum Master, 'and she is waiting to see you.'

'My wife?' asked Samuel.

'Oh no, this is a very fine lady,' said the Chum Master, 'not that Mrs Medina ain't a fine lady too,' he added hurriedly, realising his inadvertent insult. 'She's waiting for you in the yard between the entrance lobbies,' he said, changing the subject quickly. 'I thought she was too fine a lady to bring her here to your room.'

'Who is she?'

'She didn't offer her name, Mr Medina, and we know about discretion at the King's Bench. Important people who wouldn't want their identities known pay some of our prisoners' fees. I didn't press for a name, but she is a very fine lady.'

'And she brought this furniture with her?'

'Oh no, Mr Medina. She asked for my advice as to what you needed. I took the liberty of suggesting furniture and sending a runner to a local tradesman. There's many a business near the King's Bench whose sole trade is to supply what a prisoner needs. It seems that she wants to help you, but you must deal with that yourself.'

Samuel walked through the corridors of the prison his mind racing as he tried to guess the identity of his benefactor. The clanging sounds of the prison echoed around him, but they did not enter his consciousness, and then his thoughts settled on a name. It could only be she: Lady Theodora Fulworth, the Marchioness of Thame. Dora would understand his problems with debt, for she had had to live with it all her married life. His spirits rose as he entered the yard, but his eyes were overcome by the sudden bright sunlight and they took time to adjust from the dimness of the light-starved corridors. He put his hand above his eyes and as they regulated themselves the lady came into view. She was pacing the yard, and that pacing was taking her away from him, but even from her rear view he could see that he was wrong. Dora was tall and athletic; this lady was much more petite. Under her bonnet he could see that her hair was flaxen, not dark like Dora's. And then she turned and he could see her face. It was a delicate and pretty face but it was also a fashionable face. She had used *eau de citron* to blanch her skin. It was the height of fashion for a lady to appear ghostly white. Her dress was expensive, but tasteful and elegant, and she wore a cape around her shoulders. The neckline was also fashionably low but there was only a hint of cleavage, the skin on her breasts being equally blanched. She was a petite beauty, if somewhat out of her time – this was a time when flesh was more in demand - but she was a beauty nonetheless. Her anxious face lit up when she saw him and she walked towards him holding out her two gloved hands to greet him like a long and trusting friend. 'Samuel,' she said, 'how awful this must be for you.' She took his hands in her own and reaching up, kissed his cheek affectionately.

Samuel's expression was one of complete bewilderment; he had not a clue as to her identity. Her diction was very precise and she spoke as if she had been well educated. There was just a hint - an undertone of something that was familiar to him, but it was as illusive as a scurrying mouse.

'You have the better of me, Ma'am,' Samuel mumbled, thinking, *Who is she?*

'Have I changed so much?' she said precisely. She smiled up at him, adding in a West Country dialect, 'But I well remember *you*, deary.

Samuel looked at her intently – the face was familiar, as was the voice, but the synaptics would not combine to bring his thoughts in focus. He was utterly disoriented: he could see only a fine lady before him, and that was closing his mind to what should have been blindingly obvious to him.'

'It's Ginny,' she said, 'do you still not recognise me?'

'Ginny?' He was still puzzled, but then everything clicked into place. '*Ginny!*' he repeated.

Samuel's thoughts went back six years, to that night at the Cock and Hen Club when they had first met. He had been a naïve nineteen-year-old and John Campbell-John had set him up to lose his virginity with the seventeen-year-old Ginny. In his mind's eye he saw her as she had been then: a blue-green lustring dress lined with white; stays pushed up to emphasise her bosom - which was illusory as in truth she had little bosom to display - her eyebrows plucked and replaced higher up by black painted ones; her lips painted vivid red - and all to make her look older and like a tart. And every endeavour wasted because it had all detracted from what was her allure – her youthful beauty. He looked incredulously at this fine twenty-three year-old woman before him, for it seemed inconceivable that she could be the same person.

'Of course, Ginny Farmer – but you were only seventeen when we...,' his voice tailed away and he felt suddenly embarrassed for it did not seem right to refer to that first night in front of this fine lady, '...met,' he finished lamely.

'Yes, I was only seventeen and homeless and alone in London. I had only a life as a common prostitute to look forward to, but you were kind to me, Samuel Medina.'

'I didn't do so much,' he said.

'But you did, dear Samuel. You were my first customer and I was terrified, and you were so kind. You helped me get through that ordeal – in fact as it turned out, it wasn't an ordeal at all, as I recall.'

He smiled at that. 'If I remember I was terrified too.'

'Maybe you were a little,' she said pausing to order her thoughts. 'It made it easier, but you did so much more than be gentle with me: you bought a house for me. People just don't do that sort of thing. How could I ever forget *you*, Samuel Medina?'

'You seemed much too delicate to be a street Mabel,' he explained. 'I thought you would be safer and earn more money if you had a house to work from.'

'And you were right of course - if it weren't for you I'd still be doing tricks for pennies in the back streets; boozing to dull the pain of the awful days. I'd have been a gin-crazed hag by the time I was forty if it wasn't for you, dear Samuel.'

'Then I'm glad that I've helped you to improve yourself,' he said.

He was embarrassed. He was a genuinely decent man, and she saw that again in his manner. She smiled at him affectionately. 'When you started to earn money from fighting, you thought of me, Samuel. I have never forgotten your generosity.'

Samuel smiled down at her, 'And seeing that you have now left all that behind you, it seems that it was money well spent,' he teased.

'I know what I am, Samuel,' she said. 'I'm basically still a whore but you inspired me to be a better whore.'

'Me!'

'Yes. I saw the way you behaved and I've read all the newspaper articles about you. I've followed your career – your life - closely. You had ambition, but you were honourable. So in my own simple way I tried to be the same.'

'You must have quite a story to tell, Ginny.'

She reached out and touched his cheek warmly, stroking it with the back of her gloved hand. She then took his arm and they started to walk so that she could tell that story.

'For a while I was in demand with the toffs; innocence can be a powerful aphrodisiac and I played the part of the perpetual virgin. I got rid of all that terrible makeup I was told to wear - you were right about that too. I presented myself as a creature of virtue and purity. I know it doesn't really make sense, but I was much in demand and I earned a great deal of money. But I knew that I couldn't play the seventeen-year-old innocent forever, so I paid for elocution lessons. I paid to be taught to behave like a lady.'

'Is there more money in that?' he asked.

'Maybe,' she said, 'but I really wanted something else - I was setting out to catch a prize, you see.'

'I don't understand,' he said.

'I wanted to be a mistress, not a prostitute.'

'And have you succeeded?'

'Aye, I have – I have succeeded beyond my wildest dreams. I'm the mistress of a great gentleman. I have set up home for us and we are both very happy.'

'And his family?' asked Samuel.

'Ah – his family,' she shook her head. 'You ask the very difficult questions, dear Samuel. Yes you are right; I do have to share him. He has a wife and children at his country house in Oxfordshire. He tells me that she doesn't know about me. I imagine that she suspects – but if so, she doesn't ask questions.'

'So he does his duty by his family?' Samuel asked.

'Aye, he does, but when he is in London he stays with me. And Society even allows me to be on his arm on some occasions – or should I say that I am tolerated. And I make sure that I know how to behave and that I am genteel and don't let him down. He can be away for weeks and I spend my time well – I read so that I can join in the conversations. Not that there are many subjects available to women to converse in,' she added drily.

'Do you find it difficult?' he asked.

She laughed. 'Remarkably enough I find it very easy. When you have been brought up in a children's home a bit of play-acting is not so daunting – because basically that's what I do. I play a role – the role of the genteel lady.'

Samuel paused, turning to look her up and down appraisingly. 'And you play it very well, Ginny.'

'Yes – I do, don't I,' she said as they resumed their stroll. 'But you see, I have a great advantage, because I *look* the part. If I make a small mistake in my diction then – well, it seems that people don't seem to hear it. They just see this genteel lady before them.'

They walked and talked for some time. He already had some celebrity within the prison and was easily recognisable, but now even more envious glances were cast in his direction as they strolled around the yard. She was quite right in her assessment. People *did* look on her with preconceived eyes – they saw only a fine lady; a genteel woman to be respected and revered. They saw the image she projected and accepted it totally.

Samuel took her to his room and introduced her to Scillari, who went into raptures over her. He kissed her hand and offered her the only seat in the room. He fussed about her like an excited dog seeing his master return home from a long day at work. More - he was like a dog with two tails. Scillari had always got along with women far better than with men, and he was now transported back to a time when great ladies sought out his company. He gossiped with Ginny like an old lost friend and Samuel kept her secret from him, not wanting to spoil the illusion. After a while she suggested to Scillari that she needed to talk business with Samuel and he sat on his bed obediently and quietly - characteristics, which were totally alien to him. Scillari was a self-centred man and normally demanded to be the centre of attention, but now he meekly did as he was bid. They allowed him to stay and he was even grateful for that.

'How much do you owe, Samuel?' she asked.

Samuel grimaced, said, '£236.0s.7d.'

She paused for a moment to assess her response. 'A great deal of money – but to be honest I expected a lot more. I would have thought that you could raise that sum easily though. Having read all the newspapers, I know you're much in demand Samuel.'

'That's true of course – if they had allowed me to fight.'

'But why ever not?' she asked.

'Sir Oliver Ruddle, that's why not.' Samuel told her about Ruddle and his vindictiveness and she listened intently. When his tale was finished she smiled a reassuring smile at him and reaching forward put her hand comfortingly on his.

'You have been much wronged, Samuel, I can see that.'

'Aye, but I am young. I've fought all my life and I'll fight my way out of here.'

'Well said, Samuel,' she said, 'but in the meantime you need help. I have some wealth now, but I can't raise anything like £236.'

'I wouldn't accept it if you could,' said Samuel.

'Now stop that Sir,' she admonished him. 'You will swallow that pride and allow me to help.' To his surprise he submissively just nodded acquiescence, and she moved on serenely. 'I have sold the house that you bought for me. My cousin still works from there and she can now afford to buy it. It raised £28 but I will pay you £50 to help reduce your debts.'

'But-' said Samuel.

She interrupted him before he could finish. 'No buts Sir, this is simply the repayment of my debt to you, with interest of course.'

'You're most generous, Ma'am,' he nodded meekly. Like everyone else he now seemed to be a captive to her charm and will.

'And I will pay your weekly expenses.' Ginny turned to look enquiringly at the Italian, who was sitting on his bed listening avidly to the conversation, while pretending not to. 'Mr Scillari...' she said.

He sat up straight as if the teacher had just addressed him and he was intent on impressing her. '*Si*' he said attentively.

'Now, Mr Scillari, tell me honestly, how much does the Marshal demand of prisoners?'

'Mr Medina will need four shillings a week for the rent of this room,' said Scillari, 'and say another three shillings for food and laundry. But a private room would cost more, and you can even be *chummed out* to stay outside the prison, if you are prepared to pay.'

'How much?' she said, but Samuel now interrupted her. His wounded pride had resurfaced.

'I'm content to stay with Mr Scillari,' he blurted.

'Maybe you are,' she said serenely, 'but we have to decide what's best for you Sir.' Samuel again found himself, to his own amazement, nodding his agreement politely.

Scillari, however, having found in Samuel an unlikely friend did not want to lose him. 'But perhaps the money needed for the *chum out* would be better set against his debts, Ma'am?'

'Aye,' said Samuel eagerly. Somehow, however illogical it was, Scillari's suggestion seemed to ease his bruised pride.

'You are content with this suggestion, Samuel?' Ginny asked.

'Aye,' he said reluctantly. Somewhere deep in the prison a bolt was rapped into its holder. The clang rang out and echoed around the complex to remind him of his predicament. 'Aye...' he said again solemnly, his voice falling away as he spoke.

'Then I will give you ten shillings a week for your rent and upkeep, and I will provide another sovereign weekly to set against your debts.'

Samuel looked at her and she could see the deflation in his eyes. It was good news but somehow it lessened him. He shook his head, made to speak; changed his mind.

'You're a strange one Samuel Medina,' she smiled. 'You have done good by other people, especially me, so why should you turn away when those people want to do good by you?'

'Aye, I know I have too much pride for my own good,' he said.

'You can treat the weekly sovereign as a loan, if that helps your pride,' she said, 'but remember that it's not so much. On its own it would take you four years to pay off your debts. We want you out of here before then. What are your own plans to pay it off?'

'My plans have come to nought,' he shrugged dispiritedly. 'My businesses have folded. I will try to run my Academy from here but I doubt if many of my young gentlemen will want to come in here for their tuition.'

'I've spoken to the Marshal,' she said, 'and planted a thought in his mind.'

Curiosity brimmed in Samuel's eyes. 'A thought – what sort of a thought?'

'There is a fine fives court attached to this prison - is there not?' Samuel and Scillari nodded their confirmation. 'Then it seems to me that it can be a stage for your activities- your pugilism. What do you say to *that*?'

'Well – aye,' said Samuel, but Scillari was more enthusiastic. The word stage conjured in his mind thoughts of his illustrious past.

'It will be good-a place to entertain,' the Italian beamed, 'and-a I will sing you into the ring. They come-a miles to see us, eh?' Samuel and Ginny smiled at his eagerness.

'Aye, I could exhibit at the fives court, and charge entrance,' Samuel agreed. 'Yes, you're right, Ginny, that would be a way to bring in some funds.'

'I had in mind more than merely exhibiting, Samuel,' she said, 'what about fighting?'

'A pitched battle you mean?' said Samuel excitedly, all thoughts of his promise to Rebecca driven from his mind. 'Aye that would attract the crowds - but will the Marshal allow it?'

'I've planted the seed in his mind,' she said, 'let it grow for a couple of days – and then go and see him.'

Three days later, Samuel was sent for and duly made his way to the Marshal's apartments. As he approached he heard the sounds of young voices and thought how incongruous it was to see children playing in such grim surroundings. The Marshal and his family lived at the front of the prison, a reminder to all who forcibly resided there of his wealth - and the loss of their own. It rubbed salt into their wounds, but the sound of his children's laughter was delightful and a world away from the filth and depravity of the common cells. As Samuel waited outside the Marshal's rooms, he could hear singing from behind the closed door: Scillari was giving a singing lesson to yet another of the Marshal's children. A small, but far from melodic voice could be heard climbing and descending scales in various inaccurate keys, followed by Scillari's shrill voice growing in exasperation. Samuel smiled as he listened and he waited patiently. A high note was split and the sound of Scillari pierced the walls as he told the child to do it again and again and again, but then the high note continued to be split again and again and again. It was clearly a torture for Scillari, but one that he must endure if he was to have any comfort in his prison life as the sluggish years meandered on and on.

The Marshal's office was attached to his apartments, and now his clerk ushered Samuel in. He had wanted to see him, as Ginny had suggested three days ago. The thought of fighting again had added clarity to Samuel's thoughts and raised his spirits. Rebecca had been uneasy about the idea, but seeing the reality of the situation she had reluctantly agreed, recognising that getting her husband out of prison was more important than her dislike of his fighting. She had been attempting to raise loans in the Jewish community, but without success. Not that they were unsympathetic, but nobody, it seemed, was as wealthy and successful as Samuel had been. If loans were to be the answer then Samuel would have to fight again anyway, to be able to repay those loans. His impatience had grown as his spirits had risen, but he had fought the temptation to approach the Marshal too quickly, schooling himself to wait until the Marshal sent for him.

'Sit down, Sir,' said the Marshal, gesturing his clerk away with a flick of his hand. He wanted this conversation to be confidential.

Samuel sat facing him at the small desk and could see the Marshall was organizing his thoughts. He could still hear the sounds of the singing lessons, punctuated by Scillari's screeches, but he waited patiently. He thanked Ginny silently to himself, realising that the seed she had planted had taken root. And cleverly, as women will, she had planted it in such a way that the Marshal thought the idea was his own, which would give Samuel an edge in any negotiations. Samuel hid a smile; he was ready for him. He fixed a polite expression on his face and waited in silence.

'You are a famous man, Mr Medina,' the Marshal said eventually.

'Aye,' said Samuel, 'and I thank God for the talents he has given me.'

'Mmm,' pondered the Marshal, 'but God is testing you now, is he not?' It was Samuel's turn to ponder now.

'Aye,' he said eventually, 'there is truth in what you say Marshal.'

'What brings you to such a situation?' asked the Marshal.

'I'm the victim of another man's treachery, Sir,' said Samuel and briefly related his story.

'God is indeed testing you,' said the Marshal again, 'I take it that you have thought hard about raising funds to pay off your debts?'

'Aye,' said Samuel succinctly, playing his cards close to his chest, forcing the Marshal to raise the question himself.

The Marshal puffed out his cheeks, looked down at his desk and fiddled with some papers. Eventually, when Samuel remained silent, he looked up. 'Have you considered fighting again?'

'Aye, I have, Sir,' said Samuel, refusing to be drawn.

'But then you are on the horns of a dilemma are you not?' said the Marshal, 'you can raise funds by fighting, but you can't fight whilst you are in prison.'

'That's about the size of it, Sir,' said Samuel.

'Have you thought of any solution to your dilemma?'

'I think the solution is in your hands, Sir,' said Samuel, blankly. It occurred to him that they were both performing as if they were playing a hand of poker.

The Marshall nodded, 'You need my permission.'

'Aye,' said Samuel.

'So what do you propose?'

'I propose that you give me your permission,' said Samuel precisely.

'Permission for what exactly?'

It was Samuel who broke off the bluffing, like a gambler raising the stakes when it was the right time to do so. 'I'll need your permission to train; a place in which to train and, most importantly, your permission to be allowed out on the day of the fight.'

'Mmm,' said the Marshall leaning back in his chair contemplatively. 'I don't think I can give my permission for that.'

Samuel looked up, surprised. 'You don't have the powers to do that?'

'Oh yes,' said the Marshal, 'I have the powers, but *your* problem is that there is nothing in it for me.'

'I'm sure that we can negotiate a percentage of the gate,' said Samuel.

'Maybe,' said the Marshal, 'but I have another suggestion.'

'Another suggestion?' *Here it comes,* thought Samuel.

'I will promote a series of fights at the fives court, and I will pay you a fee for each fight.'

Samuel smiled inwardly to himself. The Marshal had finally arrived at the proposal he had been expecting, but he had successfully set up an alternative negotiating position. However, Samuel was confident that from here he could negotiate a good deal. 'So you will take the gate money?'

'Aye,' said the Marshal.

'You might want to reconsider that – I have the expertise in promotion and your return may be better if you were to take a percentage,' said Samuel.

'But you can't promote properly from inside the prison,' said the Marshal. 'No – I'll promote and I'll take the gate. How often can you fight, Sir?'

'Perhaps...' Samuel considered for a moment, 'perhaps every two months – it depends on how hard the fights are. If the opponent is skilled, then I'll need time to restore my body to its full vigour.'

Again, the Marshall nodded. 'So if we look at, say, six fights over the next year-'

'Y*ear*?' Samuel interrupted. 'I don't want to still be here in a year, Sir!'

'But your debts are considerable,' said the Marshal, 'I think you should resign yourself to a long stay.'

Samuel's heart sank at the thought. *The bastard wants to keep me in prison for as long as possible*, he thought to himself. 'So what fee are you proposing?'

'I thought ten pounds per fight would be a handsome offer,' said the Marshal.

Not a chance! Samuel thought. 'It's a most unhandsome offer, Sir. If I fight every two months then it scarcely represents much more than a sovereign a week. I would have reduced my debts by only sixty pounds in a year. You will grow rich on my toils, Sir,'

'I'll supply your food in addition,' said the Marshal, 'I take it that you must maintain your physique.'

It was a good concession, but stacked against the deal that was being offered it meant very little. Samuel realised that he was being condemned to four or five years of imprisonment. 'If you insist on promoting then I would want fifty pounds per fight or half the gate. I will consider nothing less.'

'I don't think you understand your situation here, Mr Medina. I thought it was clear; you can't fight without my permission.'

Samuel understood that all too well, but his sense of injustice was outraged and he fought hard to control himself. He wanted to challenge the Marshal to a set-to, for that's what he had always done when faced with an injustice. It was a time for hard negotiations not hard fighting, however, and he held himself in check, but the anger was evident in his eyes. 'And *you* should realise, Marshal, that I'm the goose that lays the golden egg.'

There was silence for several moments and each man looked intently at the other. They both had to reassess the situation. Somewhere in the street a dog barked incessantly. The Marshal realised that Samuel Medina may be a pugilist but that he was no knuckle-headed dupe. Samuel realised that the seed Ginny had planted was one of greed and that he should not be angered that the greed was now flowering. Inside, however, his confidence that he could negotiate a good deal was ebbing away.

In the end they both compromised, settling on twenty-five pounds per fight, with the Marshal picking up all of Samuel's training costs including his food, but he had the power of veto over potential opponents. It was not a bad deal, but it represented humiliation in Samuel's eyes. It condemned him to at least a year in prison; the maximum he could earn was a hundred and fifty pounds in the year and he could expect another fifty from Ginny by way of her sovereign a week. He was still short. He calculated these figures in his mind and depression took him. Those raised spirits that he had been feeling were suddenly gone, wrenched from him as though a vengeful child had stolen his favourite toy. The Marshal stood and offered his hand. It was not something he did with prisoners, but the deal needed to be formalized. They both spat on their hands and they gripped each other, and then vigorously shook, but just once. It did not represent an open greeting or even respect between the two men. It was just commerce.

Samuel was a man with abnormal levels of self-belief but he left with his head hung down. Scillari, who recognised immediately the pain in his face, met him. He towered over Samuel and threaded his elongated arm around his friend's shoulders, like some freakish cross between a father and a mother consoling a heartbroken child. 'We fight – yes?' he said.

'We fight,' said Samuel quietly, and then the word *fight* somehow registered in his mind. He looked up, stared Scillari directly in the eyes and drew a deep breath, and with that breath his shoulders straightened and his chest inflated. Fighting is what he did best. However much Rebecca disapproved and wanted Samuel to be that other person - that other person with the poet's soul - deep down he loved fighting. 'Oh yes, we fight,' he said. 'Damn the man's eyes – we fight Scillari, we fight.'

CHAPTER 35

It could have been carnival time, or an afternoon at the races, or a military display in a park. It was April, a sunny, Sunday afternoon in the year 1792. A church clock struck *one* in the distance, and Samuel took a deep breath that somehow expressed his pent up frustrations. He had been in the King's Bench prison since September 1791, and in that time he had managed to fight only once. He was desperate to earn money so that he could pay off his debts, but a fight scheduled for December was postponed twice because of thick fog and rescheduled to January, when it was again twice postponed this time by heavy falls of snow. The Marshal then decided that it would be unrealistic to expect large crowds to turn out to an outside venue in the depths of winter and so suspended the shows until the spring.

Today, however, the signs were looking good and the crowds were turning up in great numbers because after the first fight the word had gone round and they had a party on their minds. It had been a grey Sunday in November; the rain had held off and a decent crowd had turned up to see the set-to. Samuel's opponent had been a giant of a man called Walter Land. Land was well known to the magistrates of London as a street ruffian, a brawler, fence, sometime pimp, extortioner and drunkard. Land was facing transportation, and it was well known that it had taken six strapping constables to arrest him. The Marshal had thought it would be a good idea to match him against Samuel; they were both famous in their own way - or in the case of Land, infamous. When the two men climbed into the ring it had seemed that the matchmaking had produced a freak show. Samuel was used to being the smaller of the protagonists, but this set-to promised to be a Samuel and Goliath affair. Land was a towering figure of six feet and five inches, weighing upwards of twenty stones. To those at the rear of the venue Samuel had looked like a boy fighting a man, but as it turned out it was to be easy pickings for Samuel. Land had never received any training in the noble science and his strength was contained in a vast, overweight, bloated body. What is more, he was thirty-eight years old, with a girth extended by years of overindulgence. He had attempted to grapple with Samuel, but Samuel had far too much guile for that and his opponent was soon spent. Samuel made a show of it, however, extending the fight to just short of twenty minutes before dispatching the colossus like a lumberjack felling a tree.

But that November day had been much more than a set-to. It was a new sort of spectacular for the London masses. Alongside the fighters, the street vendors and entertainers, there was a musical show put on by Scillari. The castrati appointed himself as a sort of stage manager-cum-impresario. He had put together a string quartet from inside the prison walls, which although lacking skill made up for it with boundless enthusiasm. Within the prison he had mobilised others who were happy to offer their help, if for nothing more than to relieve their boredom. Carpenters constructed rudimentary scenery and others acted as scene setters. Scillari, after years in the profession, knew his audiences, and he knew what this particular audience wanted. The performance he put on for them was operatic but it was also bawdy and it was difficult to see who was having the better time, the enthusiastic audience or Scillari himself.

But that had been back in November. Now, on this sunny April afternoon, it was all coming together again. A stage-cum-boxing ring had been erected on the fives court by the inmates under Scillari's supervision. It was an unfenced platform with several rows of seating for the gentlemen, separated from the platform by a gap where the middling classes stood, their eyes on a level with the ring. More seating had been put in since the November fight and there had been little trouble selling the extra tickets. There was to be no free viewing and even the lower classes standing at the back were obliged to pay a shilling. It was overcrowded and claustrophobic and the noxious smells of the masses had to be tolerated by the finer gentlemen. But there were also sweeter smells being carried on the air. Great spits turned and roasting pigs hissed and crackled intermittently, the fats dripping and sizzling on red-hot coals. Vendors of hot pies and oysters vied for custom and puppet shows mocked the politicians of the day. The timing was perfect - it was as though London had awoken from long winter hibernation and it wanted to feast on whatever life had to offer.

Scillari had taken to the stage at midday. His quartet had started up but at first the crowd was too boisterous and showed little interest in the music. Scillari was barely able to hear the music over the hubbub and therefore had some difficulty intonating with it, but he cared little for that. His ego demanded that the quartet follow him rather than he follow them. What *was* clear was that when he started to sing, no crowd, no matter how rowdy, could drown him out. His voice soared high above the raucous babble and faces turned one by one, and then fell silent to listen to the strange gangling figure with the powdered face and wig and incongruously angelic voice. Scillari was performing again – it was not a famous opera house, but it was an expansive crowd and his self-image was somehow validated. He was a luminary in his own mind and nothing could take that away from him, and in Samuel he had found a vehicle that would once again drive him down fame's boulevards.

He sang arias from the comic operas that were now out of fashion, but he chose well and the audience laughed at the exaggerated gesticulations that passed for acting in the operatic world that he had inhabited. And when his performance was done he bowed and milked the applause as if he were taking endless encores at the end of the opera. But he was not done yet. He had persuaded Samuel that he needed an introduction and that he, Scillari, was just the man to give him one. Samuel's opponent entered the ring to nothing more than the jabber of the exited crowd and then nodded his head to the audience when his name *'Abraham the American'* was called out. But then Scillari hit his first note – a low C to the syllable *Saa* of Samuel - and then set out on a series of arpeggios rising in pitch as he sang out every syllable of the name *Sa-mu-el the Jew*. As each arpeggio reached its height the crowd whooped enthusiastically to acknowledge his musical dexterity and at the end Samuel climbed into the ring to thunderous applause. It was pure showmanship and Scillari was just the man to present it.

Samuel took up the baton and circled the ring, shadow boxing and then raising his fists in the air and the crowd roared their approval. They cared not that he was a debtor at this time; they had come to see a great fighter. The American was a known pugilist of no little skill and unusually not a tall man. He stood five-feet nine inches in height, only slightly taller than Samuel, and at around twelve stones weighing about the same. He was a boatswain on an American trading ship and part of the duties of his rank was to keep order when at sea. The boatswain had to be a tough man, for his was a harsh and dangerous environment attracting the hardest and roughest of men. As his Captain's enforcer, the boatswain – or bo'sun as he was more commonly called - was the man who imposed discipline a thousand miles from land. Abraham was just that sort of man and he supplemented his earnings by prize fighting when in port, at either side of the Atlantic.

Abraham had a hard, almost wicked face, blue-jowled and craggy. The salt air had weathered his skin so that his features looked to have been carved out of wood and made him look older than his thirty-four years. His eyes were sunken beneath high cheekbones and an overhanging forehead so that they looked vacant and impassive, giving his whole head a skull-like appearance. Samuel had seen him fight before and had been impressed. The man did not bring brute strength into the ring; he did not have the size for that, but he had craft and guile along with the ability to fight dirty at close quarters. Space was a luxury aboard ship and he had learned how to disable a man quickly with a powerful rabbit punch to the back of the neck, or his preferred punch, which was to the kidneys. He would grasp an opponent by the neck with his left hand making the opponent instinctively bring his two hands up to try to release that grip. The American would then move around to the side so that he could deliver repeated blows to the small of his opponent's back. This tactic was as effective in the prize-fighting ring as it was on the confined spaces below deck.

Samuel would not have chosen this man as an opponent for what he perceived was little more than an exhibition fight, but despite the Marshal's promise to give him a veto, he had had little say in the matter. He had got himself fighting fit, however, for he expected the fight to be difficult. He remembered the injuries he had suffered after the fight with Daniel the Gravedigger, the *Bristol Bonecrusher*, which had been caused by punches to his kidneys. He did not mean to suffer that again.

Just before the bell sounded a hush of expectancy fell on the crowd. The snarling of two dogs punctuated that silence as they had their own fight. They barked, bit and growled for a few frantic moments until one dog yelped away, head down in beaten submission. The crowd laughed seeing the irony in the situation and then quieted again, only to release a great roar when the bell sounded. Samuel took up his orthodox stance using a diagonal to move in an out of range. This style of fighting usually endeared him to the crowd; it represented a smaller man using his abilities to best the bigger opponent. After a few minutes, however, the crowd's allegiance began to change. He was not fighting a bigger man today, and what the crowd saw was the American trying to fight and they perceived that Samuel was running away from that fight. He suddenly appeared fearful in their eyes, and they started to *boo* him. After six minutes the pattern had been set. When they clinched, the American would drive his shoulder stiffly into Samuel's ribs. In his mind a shoulder was as good a punch. Samuel, however, made every effort to get back to long range rather than engage this man at close quarters.

It was an intelligent and shrewd strategy, but the crowd, ignorant of what Samuel was trying to achieve, did not like it. The sporting gentlemen amongst them appreciated skill, but they still wanted to see blood spilt. The crowd's unrest increased and the booing intensified and that unrest broke into Samuel's concentration, and bruised and hurt his pride. He now made the mistake of abandoning his strategy, which was sound, and began fighting to the crowd – to give them what they wanted.

He moved to the centre of the ring and planted his feet so that he could get purchase into his punches. Abraham rushed in with both arms raised and his fingers spread in an attempt the take a strangle hold on Samuel's throat. Samuel dropped his right shoulder and with immense strength sank a commanding blow under the American's left arm and just under his rib cage. He heard the breath rush from Abraham's lungs as the blow landed, and a cloud of spit and mucus rode on the gasping expelled breath and splattered against Samuel's chest like a sheet of torrential rain carried on a storm wind. But his momentum took him right to Samuel and he grabbed him by the throat as he had intended. The American was hurt and need time to recover and the throat hold gave him his best opportunity to do just that. He gulped in great gasps of air to try to recover and as he did so he instinctively tightened his grip on Samuel's throat. Samuel sank another blow to the man's rib cage and then another and another. In some ways he was lucky, for the American was in no state to go searching for his favoured kidney punches. But that luck was running out. Despite the American being badly disabled by those telling punches, he continued to throttle Samuel. The lack of a supply of blood to the brain began to have its effect. Samuel was forced to bring his hands up to try to release his opponent's grip. Try as he might he could not get free. He head-butted the American and blood spurted from an inch long gap above the man's right eye, but still that grip was held tight. The American now began to recover from those powerful body shots and he could see the distress in Samuel's eyes. He sensed a famous victory and he released his right hand from Samuel's throat, but still holding tight with his left. He then sidestepped to the right and sank a series of punches to the kidneys. Blow after blow found its mark and Samuel sank to his knees. The bell sounded. The crowd roared its appreciation.

Scillari and the Marshal were acting as Samuel's seconds and they dragged him back to his seat. They had a mere thirty seconds to get him back to the centre of the ring. The Marshal threw water over Samuel but Scillari produced smelling salts and thrust them under Samuel's nose. For a heartbeat they had no reaction but then Samuel pulled his head away violently as the pungent overpowering vapours assaulted his senses. 'You badly hurt, my friend,' said Scillari, 'I call off the fight – yes?'

'You'll do no such thing,' said the Marshal angrily, 'you will fight on, Sir – is that not right?' he added, turning to Samuel.

Samuel looked up at him. His senses were back in place, but his back still hurt as though it was being tightened in a vice. He stood and kicked away the stool in a combination of frustration and anger. The anger was directed at himself for allowing himself to be sucked into fighting for the crowd. He knew that he could give the crowd what they wanted when his opponent's potency had been negated. Why had he allowed himself to forget he was a pugilist and that boxing was a noble science? He went unaided back to the centre of the ring, but still instinctively holding his left elbow tight against his side in a forlorn attempt to ease the pain.

The bell sounded and the American rushed forward, again with his arms outstretched and his fingers spread. He expected to finish the fight quickly. He had turned the crowd over to himself and he was sure that he would now best the famous Samuel the Jew, The Light of Israel. Samuel, however, merely moved back along the diagonal leaving his opponent grasping thin air. Abraham looked ungainly and foolish as this was repeated several times, but the crowd started to boo again for they did not want a long-range fight – they wanted action, they wanted blows being landed, they wanted blood to be spilt. Samuel could feel the pain in his left side and knew that he must protect himself from further punishment, and so, despite his pride being hurt, he resisted the temptation to stand toe to toe with this skilled American. He tried to flick out his left jab to punish the onrushing foe. He knew the blows for what they were – they were too quick to be dangerous, but they had success with Abraham's face becoming bloodied very quickly. The pain from Samuel's bruised kidneys was aggravated by the effort. He knew that the perceived wisdom was that the jab opened up an opponent to a more powerful long-range shot; that was the orthodox thing to do. His senses told him to do just that, so, without thinking, he turned southpaw. He changed his stance and started to lead with his right. He was now effectively fighting one handed with only a right jab, afraid to launch his left from long range. But the tactic was sound enough and it brought him more success. The American's face was cutting up badly and his left eye began to close. Samuel saw that and started to hook with his right as well as jabbing with it. More importantly, however, Abraham started to blow heavily. Life aboard ship had modelled his fighting style. It had taught him how to fight at close quarters and how to dispatch a man quickly. What it could not prepare him for, however, was stamina. Samuel on the other hand had, with the Marshal's permission, run endless miles around the streets adjacent to the prison, so that those reserves of stamina were in his lungs and in his legs. This sailor had not had that luxury. When he was rating he had frequently been called upon to scale the rigging, but those days were long gone and the stamina was no longer in his legs. It was for this reason that part of his strategy was to despatch men quickly and he had come close to doing so - but in the end he had failed.

After twenty-five minutes he stopped pursuing his opponent around the ring and stood in the centre waiting for Samuel to come to him. Even then Samuel was cautious. He circled around him flicking stinging right hands and bloodying the man even more. Aware that the tide was turning, the fickle crowd cheered, their allegiance swinging back to Samuel. The American's left eye now closed which meant that he was open to more right hands simply because he could not see them coming, but even more alarming was that his mouth now fell open as he gasped for air. This was extremely dangerous and Samuel stepped in and punished him for it. He dropped his right shoulder this time, and planted a potent blow to the man's jaw. Samuel heard the jaw bone fracture, like eggshells being cracked against a baking bowl, and he saw the pain register in Abraham's one good eye. The American was still strong, but his legs would no longer carry him and were beginning to cramp. His vision was restricted, his movements now slow and cumbersome.

Knowing the fight was over Samuel now began to taunt the man. He planted his feet and started intuitively to move slowly to his right into the restricted field of his opponent's vision. Abraham sent punches back, but without vision in his left eye he was unable to find his range and these shots fell short. Samuel the showman now started to give the crowd what they wanted: he raised his right hand and they roared their approval – they were now firmly back with him. Many of them had seen the fight with Charlie Sweep and they wanted to see that demonstration of Samuel's destructive power again. The

American still had strength and Samuel was still taking a risk, but he brought the punch down against the side of Abraham's head. The sailor failed to see it coming and had not set himself to absorb its power. He went down heavily and the bell sounded; its chimes barely audible above the roaring of the crowd.

Samuel did not expect the beaten man to continue and he was proved right. Abraham's seconds doused him in water and slapped his face, but he was done. They hoisted him to his feet and walked him to the chalk mark, but when they let go his legs gave way and he fell face first in the centre of the ring. His body continued to function; his chest rising and falling as his lungs sucked in great gasps of air and then expelled it rapidly and repeatedly so that oxygen could be delivered to his bloodstream, but despite the automatic workings of his body, his senses had left him - he was unconscious. Samuel blew out his cheeks and his eyebrows rose, expressing the relief that he felt. It had been a close run thing. He wondered if his friend realised how close. He looked across at Scillari. The castrati was grinning from ear to ear like a mischievous schoolboy, opening and closing his mouth as though about to burst into song, but even Scillari would have been hard pressed to make himself heard above the crowd chanting Samuel's name. The referee tried to raise the victor's left arm, but Samuel winced and instead raised his own right arm in acknowledgement of victory. The American had been bested. But at what cost?

CHAPTER 36

Samuel ambled tentatively into his room. His gait was slow and ponderous because every step caused him pain. His posture was uneven as he was unable to straighten up and he walked like a crooked man, his spine bent to the left with his left arm tucked tight into his side. It probably was not good for him to walk in this way but his body had instinctively adopted this posture because it gave him a little relief from the soreness and tenderness of his throbbing back. His face was lined with pain, but also with worry and anxiety and his mood was black. He sat on the edge of his bed, making a pained grunting sound as he did so, and then swung his legs round so that he could lie across its length, but sat upright, his one pillow cushioning the small of his back. His frame of mind was a consequence of the dilemma that he faced. He needed to fight to earn money to pay off his debts and therefore to effect his discharge from the prison, but there was a realisation that was now stark and could not be avoided: he could not fight until his body had healed and he feared that this might take some time. It was clear that the fight with Abraham the American had aggravated his old injury and he feared that his convalescence may now take many weeks or even months; months in which he would be unable to train. It would have been better if he had incurred facial damage. That would have healed quickly and he could have trained whilst it did so. He could then have used his defensive skills in the ring to protect the scar tissue. But internal damage was much more serious, much more problematical. There was swelling and bruising to see on the outside, but it was the inside that was the problem. He tried to work out in his head a timescale of recovery but this only depressed him further. Rebecca had just been to see him and her visits normally had the effect of raising his spirits – but not today. She had avoided the fight, as she always did, but now her own anxiety at his condition had been plain for him to see and had fuelled Samuel's own depression even further.

Scillari was working at his desk, his huge legs overlapping its edges like an oversized eiderdown. He turned round and saw the melancholy on his friend's face. He put down his quill, thought for a moment about what to say and asked, 'And how is it with Mrs Medina today?'

'She is fine,' said Samuel automatically, without really thinking about the question. In reality he knew that she was a long way from being fine; he had read the concern etched into her features.

'Good – good,' said Scillari, making the same instinctive social response. He paused, not really knowing what to say but realising that it was his job to raise his friend's spirits. 'Have you been to the infirmary this morning?' he asked at length.

'Aye,' said Samuel without elaborating.

'And what-a did the surgeon say?'

'He prescribed bed rest again,' said Samuel. It was three days now since the fight and the surgeon had prescribed the same treatment each day.

'I go and see the Marshal,' said Scillari. 'The prison surgeon he know nothing. He smell of cognac all the time. If the Marshal wants you to fight again then he should pay for the best doctor, yes?'

'Thank you my friend,' said Samuel. 'The man is a drunk but I fear that he is right. My body just needs time to heal.'

Scillari stared at his friend and felt compassion. This was an emotion that he had never embraced before. The word *friend* was somehow very powerful to him. He had lived all his life in a totally self-centred way. He had always been a selfish and egotistical man, demanding of others things he failed to give back in return. He had been a *taker* and a *user*, and he realised that friendship had in fact been a very rare commodity in his life – and yet, now he had a friend and his friend now needed him. Like John Campbell-John before him, he had forged a friendship with Samuel Medina where he had failed to forge friendships elsewhere.

A sparrow landed on the windowsill and chirped in the spring sunshine that shone a shaft of light into the room like a sword. Scillari turned to look at the bird and smiled as he spoke, 'You resta, my friend, like the doctor says.' He stopped speaking for a heartbeat, the word *friend* giving him an unexpected feeling of pleasure. 'You enjoy doing nothing for a week or two, yes?'

'You can't *enjoy* prison, Toto,' said Samuel.

'Eh – prison is not so bad,' said Scillari. Samuel turned to him, a look of derision on his face, but he was too pained to conjure a witty riposte.

Gentle wit was also somewhat alien to Scillari, but he decided that it now fell on him to try. 'Is true,' he said, 'in prison you can play games, but you lose your job if you play games at work. Is true – yes?' Samuel did not acknowledge the comment but Scillari saw the faintest of smiles on his face and he took encouragement from the sign. 'In prison you get rewards for good behaviour. At work you just-a get more work for good behaviour. Is true – yes? In prison they allow your family and friends to visit. At work you can't even speak to your family and friends. Is true – yes?'

Samuel started to chuckle gently, but it hurt, so he stopped. 'Yes it's true,' he agreed, trying to adjust his position on the bed to ease his discomfort. 'It's true that prison is a wonderful place really - it's as true as I'm riding this donkey,' he added.

Scillari was now totally bewildered. 'Donkey! Where ees this-a donkey, eh? You not riding donkey!'

'No,' said Samuel a smile erupting across his face, Scillari's confusion causing him more amusement than the Italian's abysmal efforts at wit. He tried to sit up so that he could look directly at Scillari, but gave up and leaned back, looking instead at the ceiling as he spoke. 'I was being sarcastic,' he said.

'Ah sarcasm – I no understand the Engleesh sarcasm.'

'Evidently,' said Samuel dryly. 'Look,' he said after a pause, 'you want to get out of here, don't you?'

'Si, but I know I never will. My debts are too high. I will never be able to pay them off.'

'So what will you do?'

'I make my life as good as I can. You know that,' said Scillari. 'Everybody in prison knows that. Everybody gets through the days the best they can and those who can't, spend the days in a drunken stupor.'

Samuel closed his eyes for a moment and reflected on the wisdom of what his friend had said. He at least had hope, but Scillari had none and suddenly he felt ashamed of his own selfishness. 'You must let me pay you for singing at my set-tos,' he said.

'You pay me and-a it take you longer to get out,' said Scillari. 'No, you owe me nothing.'

'I owe you gratitude,' said Samuel, 'I'm sure many of the crowd came to hear you sing.'

'Put your gratitude on the donkey,' said Scillari with a grin.

This unexpected witticism made Samuel laugh until it hurt and he had to force himself to stop.

'I only get paid if I have contract. I know about contracts,' Scillari added.

'I don't need a contract with you my friend,' said Samuel.

'If I make contract, I sing and you pay – that is a contract,' said Scillari, 'I no make any contract with you. I sing free of charge for my friend. You no pay for that.'

'Thank you Toto,' said Samuel, 'then I will accept your generosity. And I hope to return it some day.'

'Pon my soul,' said Scillari mimicking an effete English gentleman, 'I am your servant, Sir.'

Samuel held his side again, trying not to laugh.

The prison surgeon arrived at Samuel's cell, with Scillari following immediately behind fussing like a broody hen. The surgeon made little attempt to hide his displeasure as he rarely attended prisoners in their own rooms, but Scillari had been hysterically insistent that he come to see Samuel. His shrill voice had echoed down the prison corridors, his wailing bringing smiles to the faces of all who heard him. It was now two months since the fight and in the last week Samuel had finally begun to feel better. The bruising at his side had disappeared and his constitution was returning to its previous robustness. He was considering starting to train again, his mind planning ahead to his next fight, and with it his spirits had begun to pick up, but two days ago a violent headache had manifested itself and his eyes had become sensitive to bright light. He had sat on his bed in the corner of the room, away from the shaft of sunlight that lunged into the room when the weather was fine. But now he was much worse. He had a fever and he was vomiting. He was shivering in his bed unable to get up, his mind confused as to what was happening to him. Scillari was alarmed and he was not the man to be calm in a crisis. In his repertoire there was only one option: panic – and that is exactly what he did.

The surgeon looked at Samuel with undisguised contempt as he did with all the inmates. He put his hand on his patient's forehead and felt the burning on his skin. 'Have you a rash, Sir?' he asked.

Samuel did not answer, his mind befuddled as the fever took over him. The surgeon leant over and now repeated the question with a shout, 'Have you a rash sir?' Again Samuel did not answer and the surgeon looked round and asked the same question of Scillari.

'I don't know, Sir,' he replied.

The surgeon pulled at Samuel's shirt until it came free of his breeches. A prominent red rash almost totally covered his torso. The surgeon quickly looked at Samuel's arms and then pulled away at his stockings so that he could see the lower part of his legs. The rash was also present on all his limbs. The only place that it was missing was his face, palms and the soles of his feet. 'Gaol fever,' said the surgeon to no one in particular. He turned and looked at Scillari, 'I'll have him transferred to the Infirmary,' he said matter-of-factly.

'Will he live?' Scillari's voice rose to an even higher pitch than usual, reflecting his apprehension.

'He has a chance,' the surgeon said, 'he is strong. Is this man the Jew boy fighter?' he added after a moment, awareness of Samuel's muscular physique taking him by surprise. He knew of the special fights that had been staged at the prison, but he had taken no particular interest in them. He had even treated Samuel after the fight, but had hardly looked him in the face and would not have recognised him again.

'Si,' said Scillari, 'this is Samuel Medina.'

'Well Sir,' said the surgeon, 'we shall have to see if God loves this Jew boy, for I fear he will need God's help.'

The infirmary was little more that a room with beds. It did have attached to it a crude theatre where operations could be performed – usually no more than boil lancing, wound stitching and tooth pulling – and it bore little relation to the more modern London hospitals. Gaol fever was rife in places where sanitary conditions were bad – principally among the poor, but anywhere where people were crowded together in rat-ridden, lice-infested hovels. Gaols met those criteria perfectly and hence typhus had come to be known as 'gaol fever'. Its victims rarely survived. Samuel was not the only victim of the disease in the infirmary. There was no effective treatment for it, nor was it known what caused it. All the physician could do was to hope and pray it would not develop into an epidemic – as so often happened. He prescribed a physic, but he knew the disease would run its course, which in most cases resulted in death. It was the one sure way that prisoners could escape their gaol sentence - and many did.

Rebecca came in daily to nurse her husband and the surgeon was happy for her to do so. Her instincts were good. She brought clean bedding to replace the filthy bedding of the infirmary. She kept him warm and hydrated and sat by his side day after day as the fever raged. Scillari nursed him through the night, taking his instructions from Rebecca and this relay continued for the best part of a week. Samuel's body shivered and sweated and delirium took his senses. Pain took his limbs and his head ached to the rhythm of his pounding heart. He drifted in and out of consciousness, but when conscious he seemed to have little awareness of his surroundings and his nurses. Anxiety was writ all over Rebecca and Scillari's faces and when they looked at each other they could see their own anxiety reflected back at them as in a mirror.

'You're a good friend to Samuel, Mr Scillari,' said Rebecca, as he came to take her place at Samuel's bedside one evening.

He said nothing, but he walked to her, put his long arms around her and held her in a comforting embrace. He towered over her like some giant alien life form, but she was comforted and allowed herself to weep the tears that she had been denying herself for days. They prayed together - a Jewess and a Catholic - but at this time their differences seemed not to matter. The only thing that mattered was that God should hear their prayers.

'It does not seem that the fever will ever break, Mr Scillari,' Rebecca said in despair, on the point of fetching a Rabbi to hear her husband's deathbed confession. 'I think I should summon Samuel's parents and brothers; they should be here before he dies.'

'No – no, It *will* break,' said Scillari alarmed by her words, 'and God will give him back to you,' he added, but his own apprehension was evident in his voice.

As Samuel lay fighting the biggest fight of his life Ginny Farmer stood in the reception room of the residence of Lady Theodora Fulworth, the Marchioness of Thame. She waited patiently, having called unannounced. She had donned her most elegant attire that was suitable for calling and looked every inch a fine lady. Ginny had heard of Samuel's illness - a runner had been sent to her from the Chum Master. She had gone to the prison, but learning that Rebecca was at Samuel's bedside, she had decided it would be improper for her to intrude on a wife's vigil, especially given the nature of her one-time relationship with Samuel. She had asked the Chum Master to keep her informed of Samuel's progress and he had been only too happy to oblige the fine lady. Ginny knew of the cancelled fights and that her plan to get her friend out of prison was well behind schedule. It was time for an alternative plan, and that was to personally seek donations from Samuel's friends. The debts now stood at £112.15*s* and this reduced sum she believed could be covered by donations or loans.

Lady Fulworth entered the room, but offered only a curt, 'Good day. And what can I do for you?'

'Lady Fulworth, it's so good of you to see me,' said Ginny with all the charm she could muster. 'I must apologise for calling unannounced,' she added.

Lady Fulworth, who had never considered herself a whore, though in point of fact was more of a tart than Ginny had ever been, knew exactly who Ginny was and, more importantly, what her background was. They had met socially on several occasions, but on those occasions Ginny had been on the arm of her fine gentleman and although the rules of respectability had been blurred, she had passed that unwritten rule by taking a reflected propriety from him. That dispensation, however, was no longer present. Lady Fulworth had toyed with the idea of saying that she was not at home. Curiosity had got the better of her, but nevertheless, she saw this visit as impertinent and made no effort to hide her displeasure. Ginny, aware that this might be the situation, was prepared for it.

'I can give you only the briefest of moments,' said Lady Fulworth, 'I have other engagements.' It was a lie and one designed to be seen as one. She looked at Ginny sternly to reinforce her status and her displeasure. She was polite, yet her disdain was obvious.

'You are most gracious, Lady Fulworth,' said Ginny with all the politeness required of a woman of her status. 'I am honoured that you have agreed to see me and I will not impose a moment longer than is necessary.'

'I think I will decide what is necessary,' snapped Lady Fulworth ungraciously.

'Of course, of course,' said Ginny, 'I am your obedient servant Ma'am.'

Lady Fulworth gave a barely perceptible nod, her dominance formally acknowledged, but she remained irritated. 'Oh get on with it Miss Farmer, what is it you want?'

'We have a mutual friend,' said Ginny.

Lady Fulworth's eyebrows shot up imperiously, 'I would be extremely surprised if we had.'

'Samuel Medina, Ma'am, I believe you are acquainted with him?'

This made Lady Fulworth uneasy. She was indeed a friend of Samuel's – and on occasion had been rather more than a friend - but he was a Jew. He may have tolerated by society because of his celebrity, but he was still a Jew.

'Yes, I have met Mr Medina, but I would hardly call him a friend,' she lied. 'I haven't seen him for the best part of a year.'

'I think Mr Medina is the most honourable of men,' said Ginny, 'I would say that he is the *most* honourable man that I have ever met.'

Lady Fulworth remained silent, unsure of what to say. She had only good memories of this man and recognised the truth in Ginny's statement.

Sensing that she had gained a small advantage, Ginny continued. 'His circumstances are much reduced.'

'Yes, I had heard that he was in the debtor's prison,' said Lady Fulworth, 'I was surprised – he did not seem to be a profligate man. But then you can never tell can you?'

'He is *not* a profligate man,' said Ginny, 'he has not squandered his money. He is in debtor's prison through circumstances and those circumstances are no fault of his own.'

'Pray tell,' said Lady Fulworth politely, feigning disinterest.

Ginny told her story and Lady Fulworth listened intently. When she was done there was an uncomfortable silence for some moments. 'It's a pretty sorry state of affairs,' Lady Fulworth said eventually. 'A most distressing tale and gaol fever is such a deadly disease.' Forgetting her earlier disdain, she added earnestly, 'Will he live?'

'I pray that he will,' said Ginny, 'but it is vital that we get him out of prison. He can then start to rebuild his life.'

'And how do you propose to do that?'

'By getting his friends to pay off his debts,' said Ginny.

'Ah! I see.' Lady Fulworth paused wondering how to proceed. It was common knowledge that her husband was the most reckless of gamblers and spendthrifts but she did not want to admit her own state of penury openly to this woman.

Ginny was nothing if not astute and had already prepared herself for this. 'Samuel would be too proud to accept a donation from you, Lady Fulworth, but I'm sure that I could get him to accept a loan. Lord Cowden has already pledged twenty guineas.'

'Lord Cowden is a wealthy man,' said Lady Fulworth disparagingly.

'Aye, that is true enough,' said Ginny, 'but it is generous of him nonetheless. And he knows Samuel to be an honourable man and that he will repay his debts as soon as he can.'

'Tis true,' said Lady Fulworth pensively, 'Samuel – err, from what I have heard of Mr Medina, he is indeed that sort of man.'

'A small loan of, say, ten guineas would be very generous, Lady Fulworth, and if we made it a preferential loan then you would be the first to be repaid. I'm sure that the capital would be returned to you in only a matter of months.'

Lady Fulworth stared intently at Ginny and then started to pace the room as she pondered. Life for her was already a financial nightmare and mentally she calculated how she could possibly juggle her finances to make such a loan. And yet she was distressed to learn of Samuel's plight and wanted to help. 'I can't be seen to be helping him you know,' she said, 'he *is* a Jew after all.'

'Of course,' said Ginny, 'this will be a purely private arrangement.'

'Good – good,' said Lady Fulworth, preoccupied with her calculations. 'Then that is settled,' she said forcefully snapping away from her deliberations. 'You shall have your ten guineas. I shall make the arrangements.'

Ginny nodded courteously. 'You are indeed most generous, Lady Fulworth.'

'I'll do more than that, Miss Farmer. I shall write you letters of introduction.'

Ginny's eyes widened; she had not dared to hope that Lady Fulworth would be so amenable, but it was as if her whole demeanour had changed and she seemed eager to help. 'Letters of introduction?' asked Ginny. 'To whom?'

'Lady Constance Forbes-Wingfield, do you know her.'

'I have met her, yes,' said Ginny, I didn't know she was a friend of Samuel's.'

'Well she is, and she is a very, very wealthy woman I might add. I'll ask her for fifty guineas on your behalf,' said Lady Fulworth. 'That'll make her morning cup of coffee stick in her throat,' she grinned. The transformation was infectious and Ginny found herself grinning back, but she nodded politely.

'And Sir Joshua Lazenby, do you know him?'

'The artist?' said Ginny, 'I'm afraid I don't.'

'No neither do I, but I do know that Samuel has posed for him, and they write to each other. A letter from the Marchioness of Thame, I am sure, will get you an audience with the eminent gentlemen.'

'You are indeed most kind,' said Ginny.

'Tush!' said Lady Fulworth, gesturing with a flick of her hand as if it were nothing. 'He may want to paint you mind.'

'That seems a small price to pay,' said Ginny.

'Yes, you are a striking little thing aren't you,' said Lady Fulworth surprisingly warmly, studying Ginny briefly as she spoke. She then stopped and thought for a moment, and in that moment she reverted to her position of dominance. 'I'll wish you good day now then, Miss Farmer. My footman will see you out,' she said abruptly and turning, strode for the door.

'And good day to you, Lady Fulworth,' said Ginny, nodding politely. And with that her ladyship was gone. Ginny stood for a moment and took a deep breath. She had successfully voyaged around those complex rules of society and had got what she came for – she had in fact got more than that. She allowed a broad, satisfied smile to cross her face. *I'm good, I'm really good,* she thought to herself.

It was only an hour after daybreak, but Rebecca had already arrived at the infirmary. She was wet through as the dawn had brought with it a heavy downpour of rain and she had tramped her way through the sodden streets, their grey grimness reflecting her despair. The sky was dark and threatening and it fuelled her depression. As she entered the infirmary the sight of Scillari lifted her gloom slightly and a small smile of recognition flitted inconsequentially across her face. He had maintained his vigil through the night and was now nodding in the chair beside the bed – a chair that looked like a child's chair beneath his elongated body. His left arm had fallen loose beside him, his hand swaying only inches from the floor. The rain lashed hard against the window, caught in a gust of wind. The sound of water cascading down the wall and gurgling in the gutters filled the room. She shook the excess water from her clothes at the door and then removed her bonnet and greatcoat before entering. Crossing the room and ignoring the grunts, coughs and groans of the sleeping inmates, she looked anxiously at her husband. He lay white-faced; his eyes were closed, sunken into black hollows, but he appeared to be still alive. Rebecca exhaled a sigh of relief and put her hand on Scillari's shoulder. 'Dear Toto,' she said quietly, kissing his cheek affectionately. Scillari roused himself slowly and stretched his gargantuan arms.

'How has he been?' Rebecca asked.

'He was-a very disturbed in the early hours and I was-a fearful, but he has slept peacefully for some hours now.'

She leaned across Samuel and saw that Scillari was right, that he was peaceful - so peaceful in fact that for a terrible moment she thought she had been mistaken and that he had died, but then saw his chest rising and falling slowly and deeply and she was encouraged by what she saw. His breathing had been so shallow for days and it had made her afraid. She leant across and kissed his forehead, and surprise took her suddenly. Her lips registered no fever. She put her hand to his forehead for confirmation and it was cool – the burning was gone. 'Toto – Toto!' she exclaimed.

'Scillari turned in alarm and saw the expression on her face. He misinterpreted shock for anguish and a feeling of icy dread enveloped him. 'Oh no! No. Did he die while I sleep?' he cried, believing himself to blame.

'No – no, Toto! Look, I think the fever has passed.'

Scillari also leaned over Samuel and put that great hand on his forehead and when he felt no fever he started to sob. He wailed like a woman, his feminine voice soaring uncontrollably. Those great shoulders rose and fell and his breathing was staccato and shallow as he fought to speak through his weeping. Ignoring the curses coming from the awakened occupants of the other beds, he snivelled and wiped his nose on the billowing sleeve of his linen shirt. His tears of joy triggered Rebecca and she too began to cry and they hugged each other robustly, her head resting on his chest and her tears wetting his shirt.

'He will live now,' wailed Scillari incoherently between sobs.

'Yes, Toto,' she said, wiping the tears away from his face with her handkerchief. 'God has answered our prayers, we must be thankful.'

The surgeon arrived to see what the commotion was all about. He was still in his nightshirt and hastily fastening his robe as he entered the infirmary, clearly angered that he had been roused so early. He was still hung over from an excess of brandy the previous evening. 'Is he dead?' he said brusquely. 'Some live, but most die,' he added thoughtlessly.

'No, no,' said Rebecca, 'I think the fever's past.' She gestured towards Samuel, who amazingly was still sleeping peacefully through the noise. The surgeon leant forward and examined him briefly and superficially, but it was enough for him to confirm the truth in what she had said.

'Well, well,' he said to himself, 'he is one of the lucky ones.' He turned to Rebecca and added with unbelievable insensitivity, 'His strong constitution has seen him through. It seems the *Jew* boy will live after all.'

'Eh!' shouted Scillari waving his great paw in the surgeon's face, 'it seems that God loves this *Jew* boy, eh?'

The surgeon stepped back in a combination of alarm and astonishment, but his resentful expression did not change. He could not comprehend Scillari's reaction; Samuel Medina was a Jew and that made him less than a person; to the surgeon's mind it was a given that Jews had no right to his respect. Looking at the two faces staring at him in open hostility, one a simple-faced, straight-laced Jewess, the other a huge, ill-proportioned, effeminate Italian, his instincts told him it was time to leave, 'I'm away back to my bed,' he said, 'the hour is too early.'

They watched him leave in silence, but when the door closed behind him they looked at each other and laughed uncontrollably; they were in no mood to be offended.

Outside the rain had stopped and the sky lightened in the course of only a few minutes. A sparrow landed on the windowsill and started to chirp. Rebecca realised that the birds must have continued to sing throughout her husband's illness; she had simply failed to hear them. This sparrow's chirping was not the sweet song of the nightingale, but it was the sweetest song she had ever heard. She walked to the window to see it, but the bird flew away. She watched it land on a roof opposite and with a smile lighting her face, she gave it a little wave – a little thank you - and in that moment she knew that whatever else might happen to them, she and Samuel were going to be alright, for if they could weather *this* storm, then they could weather anything.

CHAPTER 37

London, 1805

The fire had burned low. The last embers still glowed but they gave off little heat now and John Campbell-John suddenly shuddered. That shudder was as much to do with Samuel's story as the creeping cold and was overlaid with a tremble. Samuel leaned over and poked the fire with the poker and a sudden glow was released and was reflected in John's lined and craggy face. The first rays of dawn were beginning to pierce the black night sky, prompting the early birds to start the dawn chorus. John was cowed by the story he had been told. He stared at Samuel sheepishly and was overcome by shame; he could find no words to utter in his defence. Soft steps came down the stairs and both men turned their heads as a sleepy Rebecca, still dressed in her night attire enter the room.

'You didn't come to bed, my love,' she said sleepily, her hand covering a yawn. And then she saw the visitor. Startled, she stopped in her tracks, her hand moving to push back the hair that had escaped from her nightcap. Slowly, recognition dawned in her eyes and she stared at John in disbelief. Her stare magnified his shame and he had to look away, gazing unseeing at the floor. She continued to stare at him; and endless stare and John felt that stare burning into him, even though he could not bring himself to meet her eyes. She had held her breath subconsciously and now she released it in a long audible sigh - a sigh that said as much as a thousand words.

'You must offer Mr. Campbell-John some victuals Samuel,' she said, 'he is entitled to our proper Jewish hospitality. This is a good Jewish household.'

Both John and Samuel looked up at her in disbelief. John felt a sense of relief deep inside him, but that feeling was seriously misplaced. That feeling of disbelief was even more profound inside Rebecca - she had responded calmly and politely but she did not really know why, for the sight of John Campbell-John in her home had provoked quite different emotions to those she displayed.

Again she spoke calmly and politely, 'It is the Sabbath and I am not permitted to cook, but will you take some bread and cheese with us Mr Campbell-John?'

'Why – err yes, Mrs Medina,' he replied beginning to feel more at ease.

'Or should I call you something else?' She gazed at him, her eyebrow raised in query.

'Madam, I would be happy if you were to call me John again.' He spoke unwarily, not realising the verbal trap that was being set for him.

She stared icily into his eyes. 'But why would I do that?'

He was taken aback and for a heartbeat did not know how to respond. He suddenly felt the cold again and shivered perceptibly. 'Because it's my name Madam,' he said finally.

'But it's not, is it *Mr John Campbell-John!*' she said forcefully. '*Is it, Mr John Campbell-John?*' she repeated vehemently as he bowed his head like a schoolboy caught out in a lie by his headmaster.

'No Mrs Medina, Ma'am, it's not,' he mumbled feebly.

'No! The army have no record of a John Campbell-John have they?'

'No Ma'am,' he mumbled again.

Rebecca's stare grew even icier, her tone clipped, each word precisely enunciated. 'We already know *what* you are, Sir, but please do tell us *who* you are?'

He paused for a time as his mind sped like a sleigh careering down the ice. He had lived a lie all his adult life. The lies were now so ingrained into his psyche that they were more real than the truth. He had shared his deceit with no one and his pretence had been total – and now he had to decide whether to continue lying, to invent some new fabrication, to use his silver tongue to talk him out of this predicament - or to tell the truth. He had lied in this way so many times before – he was a master of the untruth. He could spin a tale at the drop of a hat and he was tempted to do so again, but for once he was overcome by shame, his own culpability plain to see in his mind's eye. His shame was so powerful that he could not bring himself to lie.

'My name is Edward John,' he said contritely.

'And is there a real John Campbell-John?' asked Rebecca.

'My father was called Campbell John, but...' he paused. He had been going to justify using the name but then decided against it. He told the story of his upbringing instead. A story that was received in total silence by Samuel and Rebecca who were both incredulous as the tale unfolded.

'And *I* thought you were a gentleman,' said Samuel when John had finished. 'And all the time you were no better than I.'

'I was never as *good* as you, Sammy boy.'

'No,' said Rebecca, 'and that is probably the only truthful thing that you have ever said to me.'

'Aye,' said John contritely, 'there is much in what you say Ma'am.'

In an uncomfortable silence, they ate bread and cheese and drank small beer together, but the icy chill remained.

'So, Sammy boy, what happened when you got out of prison?' asked John eventually, wanting to break the silence.

'Samuel had to go back to fighting,' Rebecca answered for her husband, accusing John with her eyes.

'And I took some beatings too,' said Samuel.

'I know,' said John, 'I read the reports in the papers. I couldn't understand why you were losing.'

'There's a rule of the ring,' said Samuel. 'The more punishment a man takes the less fight he has left in him. Every punch reduces his career.'

'But you didn't take punishment,' said John, 'you were unique. They couldn't land a punch on you.'

'But that was before the gaol fever,' said Samuel. 'I was never the same again. The reserves of stamina just weren't there any more.'

'But you had all that *skill*?'

'Perhaps if I'd been able to take a year off to recover... but I had to fight to pay off the debts. Ginny – you remember Ginny Farmer? – she collected enough funds to get me released from prison, but I still owed the money to my benefactors; I had no choice but to accept pitched battles. They would start well enough and then I'd just run out of strength. Some men traded on power but I traded on athleticism, and that required stamina – and it simply wasn't there any more.'

Rebecca cut across him, her fingers lacing and unlacing in agitation. 'He would come home with his face mangled and his ribs bruised black and blue. I had to bath his wounds with the tears running down my face as I did so. It was heartbreaking.' She stared piercingly at John as she spoke. All that anger she had kept within for so many years was now fighting for its freedom. 'Have you any comprehension of the wrong that you have done us Sir?' she added, her eyes, as always, speaking volumes.

'I do now Mrs Medina, Ma'am,' John said apologetically. He stared in abject misery at the table; his shame taking him over completely. There was a long and pregnant silence. John could not bring himself to raise his eyes to meet theirs. He had behaved dishonourably and now that dishonour had come back to bite him and he was consumed with humiliation and guilt.

Samuel was the first to speak. 'I had to take chances, you see. I could no longer wait for a man to spend his energy chasing me around the ring. I had to go in and deliver telling blows before *I* was spent.'

'And you took beatings.' John's voice was no more that a whisper.

'Not always, I still won more than I lost but I had to be prepared to take punches in order to land my own. If the man was still there when my own stamina failed then that is when the beatings came.'

'I'm so very sorry,' said John remorsefully and that uncomfortable silence fell on them once again. John picked at the cheese that had been presented to him, but it stuck in his throat and he was forced to wash it down with a gulp of small beer. The noise of the gulp was amplified by the silence, and both Samuel's and Rebecca's eyes darted to John at the sound of it. This man with the silver tongue was now unable to string two coherent words together in his own defence. His gaze still fixed on the table as he squirmed and longed for some relief. He stood eventually, still unable to meet their eyes; he coughed for no reason other than to hide his embarrassment. 'I must go,' he said hoarsely. 'I'm an unwelcome guest. I can only repeat that I am sorry and thank you for the generosity you have shown in allowing me to cross your threshold. Were I in your shoes I would not have done so.' Shoulders bowed, he started to move towards the door.

Rebecca pushed herself to her feet. 'Sit down Mr Campbell-John,' she said forcefully, 'we still owe you our hospitality.' He sat at once as if commanded and fixed his gaze to a point on the floor to avoid meeting her eyes.

Rebecca gave a long, drawn out sigh. Somehow her words had exorcised her pent up feelings. She glanced at Samuel and wondered if he felt the same as she did; she guessed so, for he had spent the night in his old friend's company and whatever had been said between them, he had seemed quite calm when she came downstairs. She felt that she could now sit and she did so, reaching out her fingers to rest them on her husband's hand. She had been focussed and in complete control, but now she trembled slightly and Samuel felt it. Their eyes met knowingly. No words were exchanged but they both knew what was meant. It meant – *there it's been said, after all these years.* Rebecca composed herself and took some bread and as she swallowed she became aware of her racing heartbeat; racing despite that out-of-place feeling of angered calmness that had enveloped and focussed her mind. Her breathing was shallow and she now consciously deepened it as her wrath drained away from her, but she still needed to drive her anger home. 'Because of your betrayal and the wrong you did him, Mr Campbell-John, Samuel nearly lost his life and suffered incalculable hardship and pain, but the debts were eventually paid off,' she said finally, 'and then I insisted that he stop fighting.'

John, his shame lodging in his throat as if he had swallowed a mouthful of sawdust, tried to speak and failed. He looked up at last to meet Rebecca's gaze, his eyes moist, his brow furrowed. 'I do not know what to say. I am ashamed, and so very sorry,' he said eventually, the words coming out as a hoarse whisper.

In an effort to lighten the atmosphere, Samuel glanced at his wife and gave a gentle smile. 'Rebecca is far more formidable than any I met in the ring,' he said, but the intended humour failed to resonate. There had been a chink in the dark mood that had pervaded the reunion, but it seemed that the comment had failed to prise that chink open. The uncomfortable atmosphere continued, the mood still heavy with suspicion and mistrust, but there was a lever now in that cavity and it just needed a few moments to gain a purchase.

Rebecca tilted her head to one side and the faintest of smiles lightened her pretty face. 'The debts were paid but I was pregnant and we had to earn a living,' she said.

'Aye, that was true enough,' said Samuel, 'I reopened the Academy and started exhibiting again.'

'And I see that you prospered,' said John wholeheartedly, sensing that this period represented a happier time for his friend. 'And your child is well?' he asked hesitantly.

'Yes Jacob is well and growing into a fine young man; he had his Bar mitzvah last year. And he now has two sisters and two brothers, Ruth and young Rebecca, Daniel and Saul.' The pride was evident in Samuel's voice. 'Toto is Daniel's mentor. He was born just after we eventually had enough money to pay of my friend's debts - they had been outstanding so long that his creditors were happy to accept a partial settlement. He was a good friend and we owed him that. He now gives my children singing lessons.'

'The days of riches and wealth were over for us,' said Rebecca, instantly dampening down that enthusiasm, 'but yes - we now live comfortably, that is true.'

'I am pleased to hear it,' said John thankful for even this morsel that Rebecca had thrown him.

'And of course I took to management and promotion,' said Samuel, 'Toby Tobias became a fine fighter. He listened and learned from me.'

'Tell me about those times,' said John eagerly.

'That is another story for another time,' interrupted Rebecca, 'but what of yourself, Mr Campbell-John - tell us instead what *you* have been doing?' She resisted the temptation to add, '*With our money!*' but John heard the words as though she had spoken them and bowed his head, the tips of his ears bright red.

'I ran from town to town,' he mumbled, 'but Molly Jasper's men were never far behind me wanting their money, or my hide. So I took a ship for the Americas, worked my passage.' He paused for a moment and lifting his head caught Samuel's eye and smiled hesitantly. 'I even managed to gamble my way into owning a fertile plantation.' Momentarily forgetting his guilt, suddenly and unexpectedly John laughed at the memory. 'You should have seen it, Sammy boy - the finest house for miles around... and the parties, why you cannot imagine-' Catching Rebecca's disapproving stare he flushed, coughed, murmured an apology and stuttered into silence.

Samuel hid a smile. 'So what happened then? Did you lose it the same way, on the turn of a card? Is that why you came back?'

John shrugged, the twinkle in his eye belying his nonchalance. 'Aye, you know me well Samuel, but I fear that that too is another story for another day.'

No Quarter Asked – No Quarter Given.

Bibliography

The memoirs of Daniel Mendoza. – By Daniel Mendoza
Observations on the Art of pugilism by Daniel Mendoza
Georgian London – by G E Mingay
Article – Daily Mail 31/12/05. – The Castrati by Glenys Roberts.
Article – Daily Mail 16/03/03. – A lusty piece of Wanton Fire by Olivia Stewart- Liberty
Article – Daily Mail 01/05/03. Lord of the Ring. – By Anne de Courcy
Article - The Sunday Express 28/12/03. The Original Party Queen by Catherine Barns based on the biography of Teresa Cornley : The Empress of Pleasure by Judith Summers
Channel 4 – The Regency House party.
TV programme 07/03 Georgian House No 57

Author's notes.

Characters

The narrative is based loosely on events in the life of a real fighter, Daniel Mendoza (1764 – 1836). Mendoza was a Jew in London at time when being Jewish was enough to be accosted in the street with little protection from the Law. In fact 'Jew Bating' verged on a national sport. Paradoxically the Jews came to England because they had more protection than they could get in their own countries. Mendoza fought under the name of *The Light of Israel*, which was the working title of the book.

Mendoza became one of the most famous men in England following his exploits in the ring and was even presented to King George III. His achievements had a considerable effect outside the ring, raising the respectability of boxing and the social status of Jews. He was a very accomplished and complex character and was an author as well as a fighter. Not only this, but when the Bank of England first issued paper bank notes Mendoza did indeed issue his own notes with his portrait on them, but in small denominations that the working classes could afford - Samuel's story in this respect is loosely based on fact.

Despite earning vast sums of money through his boxing and business ventures, Mendoza was in debt more than once during his lifetime because he enjoyed the accolades and lifestyle that fame brought him - he could be a rogue at times!

In developing the story, I have split Mendoza's character into two separate people, one the honourable pugilist Samuel Medina, and the other the roguish Captain John Campbell-John, who has the personality of a charming con artist. Campbell-John is a purely fictitious character, as are all the pugilists whom Samuel Medina fights, although they are amalgams of other bare-knuckle fighters about whom I have read. So, for example, Big Charles Sweep while totally fictitious has undertones of the great champion, James Figg (1686 – 1734) who was the first to be recognised, if unofficially, as the boxing champion of all England. Figg's fighting era, however, predates our story by about half a century.

The verbal contest between Medina and Sweep by way of correspondence in the press is based on fact. There was a published exchange of letters in 1788 between Mendoza and Richard

Humphries who fought each other three times. Similarly, the academy opened by Medina is also based on fact. The amounts of money earned by Medina are comparable with those earned by Mendoza and were huge by the standards of the time. The exception would be the fight with Sweep where Medina acted as his own promoter – this is fictitious. Mendoza however could command appearance fees of £50 because he could fill theatres and in fact broke all box office records.

If the reader is interested in learning more about Mendoza then I can recommend his autobiography – *The Memoirs of Daniel Mendoza*. He was a man of letters as well as fists.

In Georgian London there was a tradition of vast and elaborate parties for the cream of society. One of the most famous of the party throwers was Teresa Cornley who threw her lavish parties from Carlisle House. The parties thrown by Lady Constance Forbes-Wingfield are based loosely on Teresa Cornley's exploits, but other than that she is a totally fictitious character. I can recommend the biography of Teresa Cornley ;The Empress of Pleasure by Judith Summers

The cult of the castrati is based on fact and many of them achieved superstar status. Tenducci, Caffarelli, Crescentini and Farinelli were all megastars. Other than that the character of Toto Scillari is totally fictitious.

Currency

In pre-decimal currency – a sovereign was one pound, and a guinea was one pound and one shilling (one pound and five pence in new money). A crown was five shillings. There were twenty shillings in the pound, which equates to 100 pence today.

Pugilism

To our modern eyes these bare-knuckle fights were savage and bloodthirsty, but this was a time of cockfights, bear-bating and the stocks. Families enjoyed a holiday at public hangings, taking their children along to enjoy the spectacle; the condemned man's writhing as the rope slowly strangled him did not distress such a crowd. It was an age when it was common practice for ladies and gentlemen to visit insane asylums, not out of a sense of morality to improve conditions – that came later in Victorian times - but for its sheer entertainment value. It is difficult to our modern eyes to see how it was possible to offend the sensibilities of such ladies and yet it was considered essential that gentlemen of society respect those sensibilities; a coarse word at the wrong time would be unpardonable. Georgian society may seem strange to us, but so long as outward appearances were maintained (good manners were considered a must) then almost anything was acceptable.

There was clearly a bloodlust at these pugilistic encounters yet it was still considered a sport and the noblest of sports at that. Pugilists were men who embodied the virtues of what it was to be English: men who would stand up for what they believed was right and who followed a noble pastime. They reflected what their contemporaries believed was a sort of humanity: a man's right to stand and fight for what was his, or what he believed to be right.

The ring was not a place for faint hearts: pugilists could be maimed for life or even killed in the course of these pitched battles. They were known as 'pitched battles' for that was exactly what they represented. There was no concept of a points victory. A fight would continue for as long as it took, until one man was bested; beaten to the point where he could no longer go on.

Games.

Bouillotte was an early form of poker. Unlike whist there was betting on each hand and the hands could last only a few moments. The scope for large winnings was immense. Conversely the scope for large losses was equally savage.

For those who are interested, the rules are as follows: four players are each dealt a three-card hand from a twenty-card pack made up of only aces, kings, queens, nines and eights in four suits. A thirteenth card is dealt face up as a common card that all players could use to improve their hands. The players bet on their hands in a similar way to modern-day poker, the hands being ranked. The ranking is much simpler, however, being four of a kind, three of a kind or two of a kind. There is no ranking for runs or flushes as in modern-day poker, but where it differed mostly from its modern-day successor is the odds of pulling a good hand. With a pack of fifty-two cards the mathematical odds of pulling four cards of the same rank is a startling 4165 to 1. With only 20 cards there are, of course, only five opportunities to get four of a kind as against 13 in a fifty-two card pack but, conversely, there are only seven cards left sleeping after each deal. The odds of pulling a good hand are consequently much increased. On the basic principle that you lose the big money on a good hand to an even better hand, the game could be ruthless as good hands were being dealt at regular intervals. It has all the scope of the modern game for bluffing and raising, and to maximise the winnings by capitalising on a good hand, and all the dangers of being out-played. The game has an edge that is not present in whist. Whist was the favoured game of gentlemen. It had style and skill, and all the finesse that made it perfect for a house party, but Bouillotte was a game made for a gambling club.

Each player in each deal is dealt a three-card hand. In successive rounds of betting each player bets that he has a better hand than his opponents. A player may fold at any time but, of course, loses any stake that he has already bet in that deal. A deal finishes when all players but one fold, and that player takes the pot, or a *showdown* is reached. In the showdown the remaining players reveal their hands and the player with the best hand takes the pot.

Debtors Prisons.

The Kings Bench prison was indeed a real prison. There are a number of first hand accounts written by prisoners at the time and I have used these as a backdrop in telling the story. To that extent the conditions as betrayed should be accurate.

No Quarter Asked – No Quarter Given.